THE HISTORY DETECTIVE

THE *HISTORY* *DETECTIVE*

SOLVING PROBLEMS IN AMERICAN HISTORY

MICHAEL J. BAKALIS

Harbridge Press
Woodridge, Illinois

The History Detective: Soliving Problems in American History
Copyright © 2011 by Michael J. Bakalis
International Standard Book Number: 978-0-9830030-1-4
Library of Congress Control Number: 2010916504

PRINTED IN THE UNITED STATES OF AMERICA

SUSTAINABLE FORESTRY INITIATIVE

Certified Fiber Sourcing

www.sfiprogram.org

HARBRIDGE PRESS
WOODRIDGE, ILLINOIS

TABLE OF CONTENTS

FOR THE TEACHER

"A teacher who is attempting to teach without inspiring the pupil with a desire to learn is hammering on cold iron."

–HORACE MANN, AMERICAN EDUCATOR

"The art of teaching is the act of assisting discovery."

–MARK VAN DOREN, AMERICAN WRITER AND EDUCATOR

I. THE PURPOSE OF THIS BOOK

The History Detective has a very direct purpose: It is to encourage and enable students to think critically and to understand the process, puzzles, complexity, drama, and relevance of history. My hope is that students will begin to comprehend that historical inquiry should never be a boring endeavor but rather one that can be fun and important.

II. WHY TAKE THE PROBLEM-BASED APPROACH?

Multiple national surveys have demonstrated that students have little historical knowledge, are bored by studying history, and do not see its real relevance to the lives they live. The recent test mania has also had the effect of minimizing class time allotted to the study of history in order to make room for the additional time needed to have students reach targeted reading and mathematics competency levels. Another reality is that today's students have advanced technological skills but often shortened attention spans. They are comfortable with hands-on activity, rather than passive listening. The college professor model of lecturing won't work any longer if it is the dominant mode of instruction. Human beings are inherently curious problem solvers and risk takers. Thus, the focus of problem-based learning is on solving problems through critical thinking, making analyses, and connecting people and events that may, at first, seem unrelated. Making these connections between facts and evidence is what historical interpretation is all about. Historical facts are certainly important, for they form the basis of evidence, but there is no need to have students learn boring, irrelevant facts merely to regurgitate them on some multiple-choice test. The most effective teaching of history is a mixed formula of minimal lecturing, maximum Socratic dialogue, and teacher directed coaching of students who are searching for answers by themselves. Such an approach results in higher-order thinking rather than meaningless rote memorization. Combined, these three basic approaches are the foundation of the *Paideia* method of instruction.

III. How to use this book

Approaches used in problem-based history teaching can take many forms. The instructor is a crucial component, however, in constantly guiding the process so that certain common elements are present. Among these are:

1. Allowing the class to discover a large measure of information themselves rather than having excessive information given to them.
2. Coaching students about how and where to research for answers, how to analyze and evaluate evidence, and how to ask questions that begin to bring the evidence together for a tentative answer or interpretation of the problem under consideration.
3. Helping students see that the history of anything is almost always incomplete; evidence is always missing or conflicting. Drawing conclusions and discovering relationships is similar to putting together a jigsaw puzzle in which a third or a half of the pieces are missing. The final result of such an exercise is an incomplete picture but nevertheless a picture that allows students to mentally fill in the missing pieces. That is essentially what historians do when they offer interpretations of some historical event or person.
4. Enabling students to focus on the problem-based process and helping them write clearly and logically while using facts and evidence to offer their solutions to the problem. The goal is also to help them make oral arguments confidently and fluently as they state their case.

IV. SOME SELECTED CLASSROOM STRATEGIES

The History Detective can be used by the instructor in many ways. Perhaps the first thing for the instructor to do is to forget comprehensive coverage. Gaps of eras or events can be filled in by the teacher through direct instruction. Here is one of the places where didactic instruction or lecturing may be appropriate. For example, the book obviously does not present every conceivable problem in American history. There is no coverage, for instance, of the westward expansion or the closing of the American frontier. It is in places like this in which the teacher can fill in gaps and make transitions from one historic period to the next.

For the most part, however, the following type of approaches will work best in problem-based learning.

1. Students should work in teams to address individual historical problems. This will allow them to learn cooperation, how to resolve conflicting views, and how to assist one another in reaching consensus.

2. Students should be given ample in-class and out-of-class time to investigate the problem and to collect facts and evidence through Internet access and designated library time. Our young generation needs to see that while the Internet is a powerful research tool, real historians see libraries as their more reliable and powerful research vehicle.

3. After an exhaustive search for evidence, the teams should be given ample class time to sift through their findings; analyze, debate, and discuss them; and come to some consensus as to what form their answer to the problem will take. The teams can either present their answer in written essay form that can be duplicated for the entire class to critique, discuss, and evaluate, or they might make an oral PowerPoint presentation to the class, much as a lawyer might make his or her case to a jury, attempting through facts and evidence to prove the validity of their case. The class then can ask questions, criticize the evidence or lack of it, and offer a different answer to the problem as they see it. This sets the stage for a lively discussion or debate.

4. Throughout each step the teacher is not merely a passive observer, of course, but rather an active coach, moving about to work with each student team, giving direction, guiding the research, and asking probing questions the students might have overlooked. The instructor reviews drafts of written or oral presentations and gives guidance through constructive criticism.

5. A key function of the teacher is to continually make connections between the historical problem under consideration and the lives of students living in the 21st century. Every good and great teacher understands and consciously does this. Teachers must be prepared to answer the question seldom articulated but always on the mind of our young present-minded generation, and that is the So what? question. Clearly stated that means, "So what does this old stuff have to do with me and my life?" Thus, every problem in the book has a so-what series of questions entitled "Connection To Today," which should not be slighted in any class discussion. To not make the connection between the historical problem and its relevance for today is to not utilize the book correctly and to eliminate a crucial teaching and learning opportunity for the students.

Finally my hope is that after using this approach to problem-based learning, the student will have a deeper and more sophisticated appreciation of what history really is and will understand that historians really do operate as detectives attempting to solve problems with sometimes incomplete or total lack of evidence and that, as imprecise as that process might be, it is a quest that is important for all of us to undertake. History is ultimately our story, the drama of human existence that allows us to understand where we come from, who we are, why we hold certain values, and what we are prepared to live and die for. If students can be taught in that manner, and if this book can help in that journey we will, as teachers, be able to take pride in a task well done.

MICHAEL J. BAKALIS

PROBLEM-BASED LEARNING

Problem-based learning is an inclusive approach to education that involves a participatory community of learners in the process of solving academic and real world problems.

In today's K–12 educational environment its use is based on a number of research-based assumptions:

1. Human beings are problem-solving individuals. They are challenged and motivated when confronted with problems that need solutions.
2. The current generation of students is technologically sophisticated and has shorter attention spans and less tolerance for instruction that is primarily didactic.
3. The work world in which students will participate is increasingly one characterized by critical thinking, analysis of evidence and data, and a team approach to getting things done.
4. Along with basic content knowledge, the development of skills and competencies is a necessary requirement for success in academics and in the workforce.

Problem-based learning is both a curriculum and a process. As a curriculum, it can be appropriately used in virtually every academic area: math, science, language arts, and social studies. In any of these subjects students are presented with a problem that they must research and attempt to solve. They work in groups or teams, with the teacher acting not as a dispenser of information, but rather as a coach giving students guidance as to how to ultimately solve the problem. Students must do research, weigh evidence, and think critically and analytically about the problem they are examining. Thus students are not passively sitting and listening to a teacher presentation, but are involved in interesting, hands on, collaborative exercises in which they learn not only content but skills as well. The North Central Regional Educational Laboratory has identified certain skills that all students need to know to succeed in the 21st century world. All four broad categories listed below are integral parts of problem-based learning.

PROBLEM-BASED LEARNING

DIGITAL-AGE LITERACIES	INVENTIVE THINKING
• Basic Literacy • Scientific Literacy • Economic Literacy • Technological Literacy • Visual Literacy • Information Literacy • Multicultural Literacy • Global Awareness	• Adaptability/Managing Complexity • Self-direction • Curiosity • Creativity • Risk-taking • Higher-order Thinking and Reasoning
EFFECTIVE COMMUNICATION	HIGH PRODUCTIVITY
• Teaming and Collaboration • Interpersonal Skills • Personal Responsibility • Social and Civic Responsibility • Interactive Communication	• Prioritizing, Planning, and Managing for Results • Effective Use of Real-world Tools • Ability to Produce Relevant, High-quality Products

FOR THE STUDENT: WHY DO I NEED ALL THIS OLD HISTORY STUFF?

"To know nothing of what happened before you were born is to remain forever a child."

—Cicero, Ancient Roman Author and Orator

"Tell me and I forget. Show me and l remember. Involve me and l understand."

—Chinese Proverb

What would you think of young adults who reached teen-age years or beyond, but had never asked where they came from; why they think and act as they do; or why they seem different from individuals from other countries, races, age groups, religions, or even different states in America? My guess is that you might think these individuals were somewhat unusual, strange, or maybe not normal. This person would live life in some condition of personal amnesia.

In the same way, a person who knows nothing about his country's history is also operating in a kind of amnesia, and this kind is also harmful to a democratic nation such as ours. "If a nation expects to be ignorant and free," said Thomas Jefferson, "it expects what never was and never will be." In other words, our democracy cannot function or last if its citizens are ignorant or uninformed about what we are as a country and how we got that way. So being an informed citizen is a key use of, and reason to know, history. History allows us to understand today's problem and issues. How can anyone really understand discrimination in this country unless one knows something about the history of slavery and immigration? If history is taught and studied correctly, it allows us to understand and appreciate art, music, literature, poetry, and architecture as well. History broadens our awareness as a civilized and educated man or woman. Just think what a loss to an individual it would be if she happened to drive through Gettysburg, Pennsylvania, and think only that it looks like a nice town but have no idea what happened there during our Civil War or about the historic speech that President Abraham Lincoln delivered there. Could this person really be considered an informed American, fully capable of thinking and voting about issues in contemporary elections that could affect her life?

We Americans want most things to be really useful, such as "Can studying history get me a job?" The first thing studying history does is give a person the key skills every employer in our nation says are desperately needed and sadly lacking. And that is, people who have skills to read complex material, analyze data and information, research for answers, tie all this together, and solve problems. Employers are looking desperately for people who are critical thinkers and can attack problems in a systematic and logical way. And those skills are exactly the ones you learn with the correct study of history. The study of history is directly related as well to success in such professions as teaching, international business, policy analysis, politics, research, library work, law, and even medicine, architecture, and engineering.

But if history is so useful, why do so many students dislike it? The short answer is because it isn't always taught correctly; the way it is taught is captured by one word: boring! It's boring because too often the teaching approach is to lecture to students, assign them a chapter to read and answer some questions, and then give as much as they can back on a meaningless multiple-choice test that only assesses how much *stuff* each student can memorize, put in the test, and probably forget the next day. This is why survey after national survey reports history study as one of the most unpopular subjects in a school's curriculum. It doesn't have to be that way.

In the paragraphs above, I have stated a few times the phrase, "if history is taught and studied correctly." The word *correctly* is the key. The correct way to study history is not for the teacher to constantly stand before the class and give lectures, but rather for the students, individually and in teams, to think and operate as historians do. That is, to confront important historical problems, dig into them, interpret discoveries, and come up with answers that solve those problems. Then, and this is crucial, connect their answers about this "old stuff" to their lives today. History is more than laws, treaties, battles, and dates. It certainly is important to know that Lincoln was president before Reagan or Obama, but rote memorization of these dates, laws, and battles is really a waste of time. You can easily look up such facts if and when you might need the information. The key task in historical study is to achieve understanding, connections, meaning, and relevance to what is being studied. And history study that looks only at politics is totally incomplete history. Real historical study deals with art, literature, society, culture, and values. True historical study incorporates the insights of psychology, sociology, political science, economics, anthropology, and statistics.

It is this approach and method of studying history that is presented in this book. You will operate as a historical detective, confronting a problem, looking for clues and evidence that can lead you to solve that problem, sift through that evidence to separate the good from the bad, and finally tie everything together into your interpretation of the answer to the problem. You can do this individually, but it is really better to work in teams so that you can discuss things and bounce ideas off of one another as you try to answer the problem. You will find that this historical process is sometimes frustrating, and very often the evidence you want and need will be missing or incomplete or questionable. The history of any era, event, or person is always an incomplete one. The historian can never find every piece of evidence needed or know every single thing that happened in the past. But that's what interpreting history is all about. On the basis of the best evidence one can find, the pieces are put together and an answer is given. It's much like having a jigsaw puzzle of 1,000 pieces but finding that about 150 pieces are missing. You can put the puzzle together, but there will be holes or gaps that will still be there. Even with the missing pieces, though, you can still make a judgment as to what the puzzle is about and what the complete picture probably is. That's exactly what writing and studying history are all about.

My hope is that your use of this book will allow you to appreciate the work of the historian and the importance and relevance of history more than perhaps you have in the past. History is, after all, simply the story of us as human beings with all of our accomplishments, glorious moments, stupid decisions, and cruel and brutal behavior as well. The study of history can be an interesting, fun, and exciting journey if you simply think like a historical detective and put the scattered pieces together.

MICHAEL J. BAKALIS

INTRODUCTION

PROBLEM: THE HISTORIAN AS DETECTIVE: HOW DO WE REALLY KNOW THERE WAS A PERSON KNOWN AS GEORGE WASHINGTON?

Every American school child knows the name, George Washington. We are told he led the colonial army against the British in the War for Independence and that he later became the first President of the United States. But how do we know that all of that is true? Maybe someone made up all or part of that information. How do we even know that George Washington was ever a real person? And if he was real, do we know what he looked like? Or sounded like? We have seen artist's paintings of someone they claim is Washington, but was that really him? And how can we know what he looked like when different artists painted portraits or works that depicted a person who looked different in each painting?

If such a person as Washington existed, do we have any idea of what kind of person he was? What his beliefs were? How he governed as president? Certainly we have what we believe are letters he wrote and were written to him, but how do we know whether they are authentic? Other persons, such as Thomas Jefferson and Alexander Hamilton, in their letters, offer opinions about Washington, but why should we accept their views? Perhaps they were biased or didn't agree with him on some matter and chose to be negative.

These are the kinds of questions and issues that professional historians deal with in their daily work. Yet despite these challenges, they attempt to get as close to telling the actual true story about a person or event as they possibly can. This is why in many ways they operate as historical detectives. They are confronted with a historical question or problem such as Was George Washington a real person or what caused the Civil War? Like any detective they then set out to solve the mystery and make their case, and this involves finding *evidence* to prove what they are seeking to prove. The evidence for historians can be many things: letters, documents, artifacts such as pieces of clothing or the house the individual lived in. It can also be old newspapers, movies, video-tapes, or e-mails. Now as you think about the kinds of evidence historian-detectives look for, multiply all of these things a thousand times as you consider all the people, places, things involved in trying to answer the question, "What caused the Civil War?" Probably the only real conclusion one can reach when thinking about the work of historians is that we probably can never be 100 percent sure that what we know and what we say about historical figures or events is absolutely accurate and true. And that is where historical interpretation comes into the picture. The interpretation of history simply means that after an exhaustive search for evidence and knowing that we probably haven't found everything, we still need to offer some answer to the problem we are trying to solve. The answer we give is our interpretation of a given historical figure or event. Someone else, looking at the exact same evidence, might come up with a very different answer or interpretation of the problem.

So, now let's go back to our original question: How do we really know there was a person known as George Washington? Organize yourselves into teams and discuss how you will go about answering the question. Where will you start? What will you look for? How will you evaluate the evidence you find? What are the hard questions your team should ask about all the evidence you discover? What conclusion will you finally reach? Could there be other interpretations of your evidence? What might those interpretations be?

This is the thought process you should apply to resolving each of the problems of American history presented in this book. This is the way you will function as a history detective.

THINKING AND WORKING LIKE A HISTORIAN

The following is a letter found by a person who claimed he had discovered a document that was written by George Washington to his wife. Analyze the letter and determine whether you would use it if you were writing an essay on Washington.

3 FEBRUARY, 1791

My Dearest Martha,

I have completed my meeting with the Secretary of State, Mr. Jefferson. The meeting was very cordial and most informative. He seems to agree with me that a strong central government must take precedence over the rights of the individual states. Mr. Jefferson is a most imposing figure, his tall frame and dark brown hair make one focus attention on his every word.

Mr. Jefferson does have some serious disagreements with the Secretary of the Treasury, Mr. Hamilton, but I sincerely believe both men have the best interests of the country at heart and will sublimate those differences in the interest of national unity.

I miss the comforts of our home and am anxious to be in your company soon. I hope our son Lawrence is well. Please give him my feelings of fondest affection.

Your loving husband,
George

Explain your reasons for determining whether or not you would use this letter.

STARTING THE SEARCH FOR EVIDENCE

The following are some general Web sites dealing with the study of American history. These are only a very few of the many that exist, but you can start with these and they will lead you to many more that are both general and specific to the problem you're considering.

In addition, after each historical problem that is presented, you will find a section entitled, Starting the Search for Evidence, which includes some suggestions for your team to use to begin the search for facts, clues, and evidence that will allow you to analyze the problem and seek a solution to it. Here, there are not only suggested Web site categories to start with but also books that can be helpful and lead you to other book sources as well. Always remember, the Internet is an important and powerful research tool, but there is also evidence that can be found only in books on the subject. Finally, following the description of each problem are some questions for you to consider and some original historical documents for you to analyze. These documents are but a very small sample of what documents on the subject actually exist. You can look further for more because they are the real foundation of evidence needed to answer the problem.

Each problem then concludes with some questions to consider about how the presented problem has a connection and relevance to today and to your life. This is a most important part of the exercise because this will address part of the question, "Why do we have to study this old stuff?"

USEFUL AMERICAN HISTORY WEB SITES

GENERAL U. S. HISTORY
- Library of Congress
- Center for History and New Media
- Digital History
- PBS Online
- CNN.com Archives

COLONIAL PERIOD
- The Plymouth Colony Archive Web Site
- Achieving Early America
- Divining America: Religion and the National Culture—17th and 18th Century
- Library of Congress—Religion and the Founding of the American Republic
- The American Colonists Library
- Africans In America: The Terrible Transformation, 1450–1750
- Pilgrim Hall Museum
- Salem Witch Trials
- The Hall of Church History: The Puritans

AMERICAN REVOLUTION AND INDEPENDENCE
- (PBS) Liberty! The American Revolution
- The History Place: American Revolution
- George Washington as a Military Leader
- American Revolutionaries
- (Library of Congress) Documents from the Continental Congress and the Constitutional Convention
- (National Archives) The Charters of Freedom
- James Madison Center

- Constitutional Facts.com
- Alexander Hamilton on the Web
- Bill of Rights Institute

U.S. 1789–1877

- James Madison: His Legacy
- George Washington Resources
- The Thomas Jefferson Digital Archive
- History of the Cherokee
- Trail of Tears
- Documenting the American South
- Africans in America: Judgment Day 1831–1865 (PBS)
- The Underground Railroad
- The Civil War Homepage
- Civil War and Reconstruction
- Abraham Lincoln Online
- Lincoln/Net
- Lincoln's First Inaugural Address
- America's Reconstruction: People and Politics After the Civil War
- Civil War and Reconstruction, 1861–1877
- The Impeachment of Andrew Johnson

U.S. 1877–1900

- America in the 1890s
- Richest Man in the World: Andrew Carnegie
- Jim Crow Online
- U.S. Labor History
- The Industrial Revolution
- Child Labor in America

U.S. 1900–1918

- (Library of Congress) Feature Presentation Immigration in America
- TR, The Story of Theodore Roosevelt
- (PBS) Half the People, 1917–1996
- Life of Henry Ford
- The World War I
- The Great War (PBS)
- The Debate in the United States over the League of Nations
- The Great War: Evaluating the Treaty of Versailles

U.S. 1918–1945

- Breadline: 1929–1939
- Depression Papers of Herbert Hoover
- Franklin D. Roosevelt Presidential Library and Museum
- Examining the Causes of the 1929 Stock Market Crash
- Brother Can You Spare a Dime: The Effects of the New Deal and Great Depression
- Cold War International History Project
- The Road to Build the Atomic Bomb
- Harry S. Truman Presidential Library

U.S. 1945–1976

- John F. Kennedy Presidential Museum and Library
- Battlefield: Vietnam (PBS)
- The Cuban Missile Crisis
- Revisiting Watergate
- The Sixties
- The National Civil Rights Museum
- Martin Luther King, Jr., Papers Project
- Malcolm X

U.S. 1976–2008

- The Reagan Years
- The Ronald Reagan Presidential Library
- The Gulf War
- The American People: Reform and Rebellion During the Turbulent Sixties
- George W. Bush and the Iraq War
- The Election of 2008
- African Voices
- Race: Are We So Different?
- (Library of Congress) Immigration in America

PROBLEM 1:

WHY DID THE MASSACHUSETTS BAY COLONY, WHICH WAS FOUNDED ON THE PRINCIPLE OF RELIGIOUS TOLERATION, BECOME RELIGIOUSLY INTOLERANT?

LEFT: THE TRIAL OF ANNE HUTCHINSON

CENTER: ANNE HUTCHINSON

RIGHT: ROGER WILLIAMS

PROBLEM 1: WHY DID THE MASSACHUSETTS BAY COLONY, WHICH WAS FOUNDED ON THE PRINCIPLE OF RELIGIOUS TOLERATION, BECOME RELIGIOUSLY INTOLERANT?

During the 16th century, England's King Henry VIII split from the Roman Catholic Church and created the Church of England, also known as the Anglican Church. For many Englishmen, however, the new church seemed to resemble too closely the church they had left, and they sought an even more dramatic separation in belief, church ritual, church structure, and governance. This group of Englishmen, who were dissatisfied with the Anglican Church and wanted further changes and reforms, were called Puritans because of their calls to further purify the Church of England from what they perceived to be carryovers from Roman Catholicism. As their numbers increased and their demands grew more vocal, another English king, James I, refused to respond to their calls for change and began a persecution campaign against them. This persecution forced many of the Puritan reformers to leave England and settle in Holland, which was known for its policy of religious toleration. In their new home they were called Separatists. In Holland they enjoyed religious freedom but became increasingly concerned that their children were growing up more Dutch than English. This fact, along with the prospect of better economic opportunities, encouraged them to move to North America to establish homes where they could practice religion as they pleased, raise their children as English citizens, and hope to find economic opportunity. Thus, in 1620 they founded the second permanent settlement in North America and established the Massachusetts Bay Colony. From 1629 to 1642 between 14,000 and 20,000 people left England for the West Indies and New England, most of the settlers being Puritans.

One of the new settlers was the Reverend Roger Williams, who came to the Bay Colony in 1631. From his pulpit he preached that there was no right to take land from the Indians and declared that individuals should not be punished for religious differences. His position, that religious differences should be tolerated, was rejected by Massachusetts Bay Colony authorities, who threatened him unless he stopped preaching such doctrines. Williams, fearing what might happen to him, fled the colony and went to what later became Rhode Island and established a new colony based on complete freedom of religion.

Another Puritan, Anne Hutchinson, arrived in Boston in 1634. She was a follower of the Puritan minister, John Cotton, and believed the Massachusetts Bay Colony, which had been founded to give Puritans freedom to believe as they chose, would be a community open to a variety of ideas. Instead she found authorities to be close minded on issues in which she believed. Hutchinson started prayer meetings for women in her home and began discussing ideas such as that conforming to certain religious laws was no proof that a person was truly religious and that a preacher's sermons and even the Bible were not as important as whether a person truly, internally received the Holy Spirit. People, Hutchinson said, needed freedom to believe what they wanted to believe. Governor John Winthrop banned all private religious meetings in 1637, but Anne Hutchinson ignored that decree and continued to hold her meetings and discussions. She was officially accused of heresy, went to trial, and was excommunicated. In 1638 she and her family left Massachusetts for Rhode Island.

What had happened in Massachusetts? How could this colony, which had been founded by persons yearning for freedom to believe as they chose, now deny that freedom to others?

PROBLEM 1:
QUESTIONS FOR TEAM RESEARCH

1. What evidence do we have that the Puritans founded the Massachusetts Bay Colony primarily for religious freedom issues?

2. What degree of control did Puritan clergy have over the Massachusetts Bay Colony? Were the governors of the colony equally strong on religious doctrine?

3. Did Roger Williams and Anne Hutchinson present any real threat to the functioning of the colony? If so, what was it?

4. What was the possible fate of Roger Williams if he had not fled to Rhode Island?

5. Why was strict adherence to Puritan doctrine so important to the leaders of the colony?

6. Was Anne Hutchinson given a fair trial? Were there issues other than religion in her trial? If so, what were they and why were they important?

7. Were there any economic, social, or political considerations which contributed to the colony's religious intolerance? How did the colony officials justify their position on religious matters?

PROBLEM 1:
STARTING THE SEARCH FOR EVIDENCE

INTERNET: KEY WORDS AND PHRASES

Anne Hutchinson

Roger Williams

Puritans and religion

Religious intolerance in colonial New England

BOOKS

LaPlante, Eve, *American Jezebel: The Uncommon Life of Anne Hutchinson, The Woman Who Defied the Puritans*, NY, Harper Collins, 2004

Miller, Perry, *Roger Williams, A Contribution to the American Tradition*, Indianapolis and NY, Bobbs-Merrill Company, 1953

Morgan, Edmund S., *The Puritan Dilemma: The Story of John Winthrop*, NY, Longman/Addison Wesley, 1999

Stille, Darlene R., *Anne Hutchinson: Puritan Protestor*, Minneapolis, Compass Point Book, 2006

Winslow, Ola Elizabeth, *Master Roger Williams, A Biography*, NY, Macmillan Company, 1957–OLA

TRIAL AND INTERROGATION OF ANNE HUTCHINSON, 1637

[See Edmund Morgan, *The Puritan Dilemma*, Chapter 10, for background on Anne Hutchinson and her trial and banishment from the Massachusetts Bay Colony.]

The Examination of Mrs. Ann Hutchinson at the Court at Newtown

Mr. Winthrop, governor. Mrs. Hutchinson, you are called here as one of those that have troubled the peace of the commonwealth and the churches here; you are known to be a woman that hath had a great share in the promoting and divulging of those opinions that are causes of this trouble, and…you have spoken divers things as we have been informed very prejudicial to the honour of the churches and ministers thereof, and you have maintained a meeting and an assembly in your house that hath been condemned by the general assembly as a thing not tolerable nor comely in the sight of God nor fitting for your sex, and notwithstanding that was cried down you have continued the same, therefore we have thought good to send for you to understand how things are, that if you be in an erroneous way we may reduce you that so you may become a profitable member here among us, otherwise if you be obstinate in your course that then the court may take such course that you may trouble us no further, therefore I would intreat you to express whether you do not hold and assent in practice to those opinions and factions that have been handled in court already, that is to say, whether you do not justify Mr. Wheelwright's sermon and the petition.

Mrs. Hutchinson. I am called here to answer before you but I hear no things laid to my charge.

Gov. I have told you some already and more I can tell you. *(Mrs. H.)* Name one Sir.

Gov. Have I not named some already?

Mrs. H. What have I said or done?

Gov. Why for your doings, this you did harbour and countenance those that are parties in this faction that you have heard of. *(Mrs H.)* That's matter of conscience, Sir.

Gov. Your conscience you must keep or it must be kept for you.

Mrs. H. Must not I then entertain the saints because I must keep my conscience.

Gov. Say that one brother should commit felony or treason and come to his other brother's house, if he knows him guilty and conceals him he is guilty of the same. It is his conscience to entertain him, but if his conscience comes into act in giving countenance and entertainment to him that hath broken the law he is guilty too. So if you do countenance those that are transgressors of the law you are in the same fact.

Mrs. H. What law do they transgress?

Gov. The law of God and of the state.

Mrs. H. In what particular?

Gov. Why in this among the rest, whereas the Lord doth say honour thy father and thy mother.

Mrs. H. Ey Sir in the Lord. (*Gov.*) This honour you have broke in giving countenance to them.

Mrs. H. In entertaining those did I entertain them against any act (for there is the thing) or what God hath appointed?

Gov. You knew that Mr. Wheelwright did preach this sermon and those that countenance him in this do break a law.

Mrs. H. What law have I broken?

Gov. Why the fifth commandment.

Mrs. H. I deny that for he saith in the Lord....

Gov. You have councelled them. (*Mrs. H.)* Wherein?

Gov. Why in entertaining them.

Mrs. H. What breach of law is that Sir?

Gov. Why dishonouring of parents.

Mrs. H. But put the case Sir that I do fear the Lord and my parents, may not I entertain them that fear the Lord because my parents will not give me I leave?

Gov. If they be the fathers of the commonwealth, and they of another religion, if you entertain them then you dishonour your parents and are justly punishable.

Mrs. H. If I entertain them, as they have dishonoured their parents I do.

Gov. No but you by countenancing them above others put honor upon them.

Mrs. H. I may put honor upon them as the children of God and as they do honor the Lord.

Gov. We do not mean to discourse with those of your sex but only this; you do adhere unto them and do endeavour to set forward this faction and so you do dishonour us.

Mrs. H. I do acknowledge no such thing neither do I think that I ever put any dishonour upon you.

Gov. Why do you keep such a meeting at your house as you do every week upon a set day?

Mrs. H. It is lawful for me so to do, as it is all your practices and can you find a warrant for yourself and condemn me for the same thing? The ground of my taking it up was, when I first came to this land because I did not go to such meetings as those were, it was presently reported that I did not allow of such meetings but held them unlawful and therefore in that regard they said I was proud and did despise all ordinances, upon that a friend came unto me and told me of it and I to prevent such aspersions took it up, but it was in practice before I came therefore I was not the first.

Gov. For this, that you appeal to our practice you need no confutation. If your meeting had answered to the former it had not been offensive, but I will say that there was no meeting of women alone, but your meeting is of another sort for there are sometimes men among you.

Mrs. H. There was never any man with us.

Gov. Well, admit there was no man at your meeting and that you was sorry for it, there is no warrant for your doings, and by what warrant do you continue such a course?

Mrs. H. I conceive there lies a clear rule in Titus, that the elder women should instruct the younger [*Titus* 2:3-5] and then I must have a time wherein I must do it....

Gov. But suppose that a hundred men come unto you to be instructed will you forbear to instruct them?

Mrs. H. As far as I conceive I cross a rule in it.

Gov. Very well and do you not so here?

Mrs. H. No Sir for my ground is they are men.

Gov. Men and women all is one for that, but suppose that a man should come and say Mrs. Hutchinson I hear that you are a woman that God hath given his grace unto and you have knowledge in the word of God I pray instruct me a little, ought you not to instruct this man?

Mrs. H. I think I may. Do you think it not lawful for me to teach women and why do you call me to teach the court?

Gov. We do not call you to teach the court but to lay open yourself….

Gov. Your course is not to be suffered for, besides that we find such a course as this to be greatly prejudicial to the state, besides the occasion that it is to seduce many honest persons that are called to those meetings and your opinions being known to be different from the word of God may seduce many simple souls that resort unto you, besides that the occasion which hath come of late hath come from none but such as have frequented your meetings, so that now they are flown off from magistrates and ministers and this since they have come to you, and besides that it will not well stand with the commonwealth that families should be neglected for so many neighbours and dames and so much time spent, we see no rule of God for this, we see not that any should have authority to set up any other exercises besides what authority hath already set up and so what hurt comes of this you will be guilty of and we for suffering you.

Mrs. H. Sir I do not believe that to be so.

Gov. Well, we see how it is we must therefore put it away from you, or restrain you from maintaining this course.

Mrs. H. If you have a rule for it from God's word you may.

Gov. We are your judges, and not you ours and we must compel you to it.

Mrs. H. If it please you by authority to put it down I will freely let you for I am subject to your authority….

Mr. Dudley, Dep. Gov. Here hath been much spoken concerning Mrs. Hutchinson's meetings and among other answers she saith that men come not there, I would ask you this one question then, whether never any man was at your meeting?

Gov. There are two meetings kept at their house.

Dep. Gov. How; is there two meetings?

Mrs. H. Ey Sir, I shall I not equivocate, there is a meeting of men and women and there is a meeting only for women.

Dep. Gov. Are they both constant?

Mrs. H. No, but upon occasions they are deferred.

Mr. Endicot. Who teaches in the men's meetings none but men, do not women sometimes?

Mrs. H. Never as I heard, not one.

Dep. Gov. I would go a little higher with Mrs. Hutchinson. About three years ago we were all in peace. Mrs. Hutchinson from that time she came hath made a disturbance, and some that came over with her in the ship did inform me what she was as soon as she was landed. I being then in place dealt with the pastor and teacher of Boston and desired them to enquire of her, and then I was satisfied that she held nothing different from us, but within half a year after, she had vented divers of her strange opinions and had made parties in the country, and at length it comes that Mr. Cotton and Mr. Vane were of her judgment, but Mr. Cotton cleared himself that he was not of that mind, but now it appears by this woman's meeting that Mrs. Hutchinson hath so forestalled the minds of many by their resort to her meeting that now she hath a potent party in the country. Now if all these things have endangered us as from that foundation and if she in particular hath disparaged all our ministers in the land that they have preached a covenant of works, and only Mr. Cotton a covenant of grace, why this is not to be suffered, and therefore being driven to the foundation and it being found that Mrs. Hutchinson is she that hath depraved all the ministers and hath been the cause of what is fallen out, why we must take away the foundation and the building will fall.

Mrs. H. I pray Sir prove it that I said they preached nothing but a covenant of works.

Dep. Gov. Nothing but a covenant of works, why a Jesuit may preach truth sometimes.

Mrs. H. Did I ever say they preached a covenant of works

then?

Dep. Gov. If they do not preach a covenant of grace clearly,

then they preach a covenant of works.

Mrs. H. No Sir, one may preach a covenant of grace more clearly than another, so I said....

D. Gov. I will make it plain that you did say that the ministers did preach a covenant of works.

Mrs. H. I deny that....

D. Gov. What do I do charging of you if you deny what is so fully proved.

Gov. Here are six undeniable ministers who say it is true and yet you deny that you did say that they did preach a covenant of works and that they were not able ministers of the gospel, and it appears plainly that you have spoken it, and whereas you say that it was drawn from you in a way of friendship, you did profess then that it was out of conscience that you spake and said The fear of man is a snare wherefore should I be afraid, I will speak plainly and freely.

Mrs. H. That I absolutely deny, for the first question was thus answered by me to them. They thought that I did conceive there was a difference between them and Mr. Cotton. At the first I was somewhat reserved, then said Mr. Peters I pray answer the question directly as fully and as plainly as you desire we should tell you our minds. Mrs. Hutchinson we come for plain dealing and telling you our hearts. Then I said I would deal as plainly as I could, and whereas they say I said they were under a covenant of works and in the state of the apostles why these two speeches cross one another. I might say they might preach a covenant of works as did the apostles, but to preach a covenant of works and to be under a covenant of works is another business.

Dep. Gov. There have been six witnesses to prove this and yet you deny it.

Mrs. H. I deny that these were the first words that were spoken.

Gov. You make the case worse, for you clearly shew that the ground of your opening your mind was not to satisfy them but to satisfy your own conscience....

Mrs. H. I acknowledge using the words of the apostle to the Corinthians unto him, that they that were ministers of the letter and not the spirit did preach a covenant of works....

Gov. Let us state the case and then we may know what to do. That which is laid to Mrs. Hutchinson's charge is this, that she hath traduced the magistrates and ministers of this jurisdiction, that she hath said the ministers preached a covenant of works and Mr. Cotton a covenant of grace, and that they were not able ministers of the gospel, and she excuses it that she made it a private conference and with a promise of secrecy, & now this is charged upon her, and they therefore sent for her seeing she made it her table talk, and then she said the fear of man was a snare and therefore she would not be affeared of them....

Mrs. H. If you please to give me leave I shall give you the ground of what I know to be true. Being much troubled to see the falseness of the constitution of the church of England, I had like to have turned separatist; whereupon I kept a day of solemn humiliation and pondering of the thing; this scripture was brought unto me—he that denies Jesus Christ to be come in the flesh is antichrist—This I considered of and in considering found that the papists did not deny him to be come in the flesh nor we did not deny him—who then was antichrist?…The Lord knows that I could not open scripture; he must by his prophetical office open it unto me…. I bless the Lord, he hath let me see which was the clear ministry and which the wrong. Since that time I confess I have been more choice and he hath let me to distinguish between the voice of my beloved and the voice of Moses, the voice of John Baptist and the voice of antichrist, for all those voices are spoken of in scripture. Now if you do condemn me for speaking what in my conscience I know to be truth I must commit myself unto the Lord.

Mr. Nowell. How do you know that that was the spirit?

Mrs. H. How did Abraham know that it was God that bid him offer his son, being a breach of the sixth commandment?

Dep. Gov. By an immediate voice.

Mrs. H. So to me by an immediate revelation.

Dep. Gov. How! an immediate revelation.

Mrs. H. By the voice of his own spirit to my soul. I will give you another scripture, *Jer.* 46. 27, 28—out of which the Lord shewed me what he would do for me and the rest of his servants. But after he was pleased to reveal himself to me…Ever since that time I have been confident of what he hath revealed unto me…Therefore I desire you to look to it, for you see this scripture fulfilled this day and therefore I desire you that as you tender the Lord and the church and commonwealth to consider and look what you do. You have power over my body but the Lord Jesus hath power over my body and soul, and assure yourselves thus much, you do as much as in you lies to put the Lord Jesus Christ from you, and if you go on in this course you begin you will I bring a curse upon you and your posterity, and the mouth of the Lord hath spoken it….

Gov. The court hath already declared themselves satisfied concerning the things you hear, and concerning the troublesomeness of her spirit and the danger of her course amongst us, which is not to be suffered. Therefore if it be the mind of the court that Mrs. Hutchinson for these things that appear before us is unfit for our society, and if it be the mind of the court that she shall be banished out of our liberties and imprisoned till she be sent away, let them hold up their hands….Mrs. Hutchinson, the sentence of the court you hear is that you are banished from out of our jurisdiction as being a woman not fit for our society, and are to be imprisoned till the court shall send you away.

Mrs. H. I desire to know wherefore I am banished?

Gov. Say no more, the court knows wherefore and is satisfied.

Source: Thomas Hutchinson, *History of the Colony and Province of Massachusetts* (Boston, 1767). Some spelling has been modernized.

PROBLEM 1:
CONNECTION TO TODAY

1. If the Massachusetts Bay Colony was a "theocracy," what lessons can we learn about how theocracies operate anywhere in the world?

2. Are there examples of "theocracies" in the world today? If so, where are they and how do they operate, and do they exhibit religious intolerance?

3. Explain why countries or societies founded on certain ideas and principles sometimes lose sight of those founding ideas? Has this happened anywhere in the world? Has it happened in our country?

4. What does the problem of the Puritans and the Massachusetts Bay Colony tell us about the relationship between church and state? What is that relationship in our country today? Should it be any different?

PROBLEM 2: SINCE IN THE 17TH CENTURY BOTH NATIVE AMERICANS AND AFRICANS WERE ENSLAVED BY THE WHITE AMERICAN COLONISTS, WHY DID AMERICAN SLAVERY ULTIMATELY BECOME A VIRTUALLY ALL BLACK INSTITUTION?

LEFT: INSPECTION AND SALE OF A NEGRO

RIGHT: TRADING WITH THE INDIANS

PROBLEM 2: SINCE IN THE 17TH CENTURY BOTH NATIVE AMERICANS AND AFRICANS WERE ENSLAVED BY THE WHITE AMERICAN COLONISTS, WHY DID AMERICAN SLAVERY ULTIMATELY BECOME A VIRTUALLY ALL BLACK INSTITUTION?

At the beginning of the European colonization of North America in the early 17th century, the origins and nature of slavery as an institution were not always clear. We have historical evidence that many Native American tribes practiced some form of slavery even prior to the coming of the Europeans. Most often such slavery occurred as the result of conflict between tribes, with the winning side capturing some people from the losing side and making them slaves. But this form of slavery did not include the aspect of buying and selling individuals; instead such individuals were used primarily for small-scale labor. It would be inaccurate to say that something resembling slavery as an institution was in place in Native American society.

The introduction of Africans to the North American continent presents the historian with some conflicting information. Many Africans brought to North America in the early 17th century immediately assumed the position of being slaves, but other Africans seemed to have a much less clear status. Some African imports seemed rather to have a status that more clearly resembled that of white indentured servants who could essentially use their labor to purchase their freedom after a given length of time.

What is clear from the historical evidence is that the white European colonists had negative attitudes and opinions of both Native Americans and African Negroes. To many colonists Native Americans were uncivilized, brutal savages, and Africans were increasingly viewed as inferior, uncivilized savages who just happened to come from another continent. Such attitudes, when added to the more advanced firearm technology possessed by the Europeans, constituted a formula for oppressing and enslaving both the strangers the colonists found in the New World as well as strangers they imported to it.

Thus, throughout the 17th century and beyond, both Native Americans and African Negroes were enslaved by white European settlers. Although we lack absolutely precise information as to how many Native Americans were enslaved, it is believed they numbered in the tens of thousands. It is estimated that between 1670 and 1715 Carolina merchants handled from 30,000 to 50,000 Indians in the slave trade. While we have no evidence that blacks owned Indian slaves, the reverse was true, and many Indians not only owned black slaves but engaged in selling Negroes to whites. In the early 19th century it is estimated that the Cherokee nation owned almost 1,300 black slaves; the Chicasaw Indians held more than 5,000 Negroes as slaves at the beginning of the American Civil War.

Yet, while these cases of Europeans using American Indians as slaves are evident, as are the isolated cases of Indians owning black slaves, the fact is that by the beginning of the 19th century slavery in America had become institutionalized, and that institution was made up overwhelmingly of men, women, and children of African descent.

Why did this happen? Clearly there were advantages to enslaving more Native Americans because they did not incur the cost of transporting them from a distant continent thousands of miles away. Why then, in America, did slavery evolve from an institution utilizing the forced labor of both Native Americans and African Negroes to one that became Negro slavery?

PROBLEM 2:
QUESTIONS FOR TEAM RESEARCH

1. What evidence do we have regarding any different attitudes the English colonists had between blacks and Indians?

2. Why did white southern colonists focus on selling Indian slaves to the West Indies?

3. What were some of the elements of both African and Native American cultures which made them more or less likely to function well as slaves?

4. Were there geographic and/or environmental elements which impacted whether blacks or Indians would work better as slaves?

5. Why was the experience of both blacks and Indians better in South America than in the North American colonies?

PROBLEM 2:
STARTING THE SEARCH FOR EVIDENCE

INTERNET: KEY WORDS AND PHRASES

Colonial attitudes toward Negroes in 17th Century America

Colonial attitudes toward Native Americans in 17th Century America

American slavery

Slavery in Caribbean and South America

BOOKS

Drescher, Seymour and Engerman, Stanley L., eds, *A Historical Guide to World Slavery*, Oxford, Oxford University Press, 1998

Gallay, Alan, *The Indian Slave Trade: The Rise of the English Empire in the American South, 1670–1717*, New Haven, Yale University Press, 2002

Jordan, Winthrop P., *White Over Black: American Attitudes Toward the Negro 1550–1812*, NY, Norton, 1977

Kolchin, Peter, American *Slavery: 1619–1877*, NY, Hill and Wang, 2003

Wood, Betty, *The Origins of American Slavery: Freedom and Bondage in the Colonies*, NY, Hill and Wang, 1998

COLONIAL AMERICANS OPINIONS
OF AFRICAN NEGROES AND NATIVE AMERICANS

Rev. Cotton Mather, 1696
Mather was a prominent Puritan clergyman in Boston, Massachusetts.

> Give Ear, ye pitied *Blacks*, Give Ear! It is allowed in the *Scriptures*, to the *Gentiles*, That they *May keep Slaves*; although the Law of *Charity* requires your Owners to Use you as those that have *Reasonable Souls* within you. Yes, 'twould be against the Conscience of any Good man to keep you for *Slaves* if he find himself unable to use you according to that Law of *Charity*. But the most of you have so little cause to desire your being any other than *Slaves* as you are, & where you are, that it would soon make you miserable to be otherwise. You are better *Fed* & better *Clothed* & better *Managed* by far than you would be if you were your *Own men*. All that now remains for you is to become first the *Good Servants of the Lord Jesus Christ*, & then of those that have purchased you….

William Moraley, early 1730s
Moraley was a white English indentured servant in the middle colonies.

> I have often heard them say they did not think God made them Slaves, any more than other Men, and wondered that Christians, especially *Englishmen*, should use them so barbarously. But there is a necessity of using them hardly, being of an obdurate, stubborn Disposition; and when they have it in their power to rebel, are extremely cruel.

William Byrd, 1736
Byrd was an influential Virginia planter and slaveholder.

> They import so many Negros hither that I fear this Colony will some time or other be confirmed by the Name of New Guinea. I am sensible of many bad consequences of multiplying these Ethiopians amongst us. They blow up the pride, & ruin the Industry of our White People who, seeing a Rank of poor

Creatures below them, detest work for fear it should make them look like Slaves....

Another unhappy Effect of Many Negros is the necessity of being severe. Numbers make them insolent, and then foul Means must do what fair will not. We have however nothing like the Inhumanity here that is practiced in the [Caribbean] Islands, & God forbid we ever should....

Gov. James Glen, 1751
In a report to the British Board of Trade, the governor of South Carolina asserts that the American-born slaves are content and have "no notion of liberty."

I have said there are 40,000 Negroes in the province, these if valued as new Negroes from Africa are now sold, may be reckoned at £20 sterling per head, but this valuation does not satisfy me for when it is considered that many of these are natives of Carolina, who have no notion of liberty, nor no longing after any other country, that they have been brought up among white people, and by white people have been made, at least many of them, useful mechanics, as coopers, carpenters, masons, smiths, wheelwrights, and other trades, and that the rest can all speak our language, for we imported none during the war. I say when it is considered that these are pleased with their masters, contented with their condition, reconciled to servitude, seasoned to the country, and expert at the different kinds of labour in which they are employed, it must appear difficult if not impracticable to ascertain their intrinsic value. I know a gentleman who refused five hundred guineas for three of his slaves, and there-fore there is no guessing at the value of the strong seasoned handy slaves, by the prices of weak, raw, new Negroes.

Francis Daniel Pastorius, Pennsylvania, 1700

Pastorius was the founder of German Town, the first German settlement in Pennsylvania.

The natives, the so-called savages…they are, in general, strong, agile, and supple people, with blackish bodies. They went about naked at first and wore only a cloth about the loins. Now they are beginning to wear shirts. They have, usually, coal-black hair, shave the head, smear the same with grease, and allow a long lock to grow on the right side. They also besmear the children with grease and let them creep about in the heat of the sun, so that they become the color of a nut, although they were at first white enough by Nature.

They strive after a sincere honesty, hold strictly to their promises, cheat and injure no one. They willingly give shelter to others and are both useful and loyal to their guests.…

I once saw four of them take a meal together in hearty contentment, and eat a pumpkin cooked in clear water, without butter and spice. Their table and bench was the bare earth, their spoons were mussel-shells with which they dipped up the warm water, their plates were the leaves of the nearest tree, which they do not need to wash with painstaking after the meal, nor to keep with care of future use. I thought to myself, these savages have never in their lives heard the teaching of Jesus concerning temperance and contentment, yet they far excel the Christians in carrying it out.

They are, furthermore, serious and of few words, and are amazed when they perceive so much unnecessary chatter, as well as other foolish behavior, on the part of the Christians.

Each man has his own wife, and they detest harlotry, kissing, and lying. They know of no idols, but they worship a single all-powerful and merciful God, who limits the power of the Devil. They also believe in the immortality of the soul, which, after the course of life is finished, has a suitable recompense from the all-powerful hand of God awaiting it.

John Lawson, North Carolina, 1709

A British naturalist and explorer, Lawson visited many Indian settlements in the Carolinas and later settled in North Carolina. Just before the outbreak of the Tuscorara War, he was captured and killed by Tuscarora Indians.

They are really better to us than we are to them. They always give us Victuals at their Quarters, and take care we are arm'd against Hunger and Thirst. We do not so by them (generally speaking) but let them walk by our Doors Hungry, and do not often relieve them. We look upon them with Scorn and Disdain, and think them little better than Beasts in Human Shape; though, if well examined, we shall find that for all our Religion and Education we possess more Moral Deformities and Evils than these Savages do, or are acquainted withal.

We reckon them Slaves in Comparison to us, and Intruders, as oft as they enter our Houses, or hunt near our Dwellings. But if we will admit Reason to be our Guide, she will inform us that these *Indians* are the freest People in the World, and so far from being Intruders upon us, that we have abandon'd our own Native Soil to drive them out and possess theirs. Neither have we any true Balance in Judging of these poor Heathens, because we neither give Allowance for their Natural Disposition, nor the Sylvian Education and strange Customs (uncouth to us) they lie under and have ever been train'd up to…We trade with them, it's true, but to what End? Not to show them the Steps of Virtue and the Golden Rule, to do as we would be done by. No, we have furnished them with the Vice of Drunkenness, which is the open Road to all others, and daily cheat them in everything we sell, and esteem it a Gift of Christianity not to sell to them so cheap as we do to the Christians, as we call ourselves. Pray let me know where is there to be found one Sacred Command or Precept of our Master that counsels us to such Behaviour? Besides, I believe it will not appear, but that all the Wars which we have had with the Savages were occasion'd by the unjust Dealings of the Christians towards them.

Francis Cample, Pennsylvania, 1740

An Irish immigrant, Cample settled in the new town of Shippensburg in the Cumberland Valley.

Oct. 10th, 1740. The building of our little fort, and the digging of the well within its enclosure, has been a good work. Had it not been for the recent killing of young Alex[ande]r Askew, near to where Robert McInnis was shot seven years ago, the friendship of the Indians might not have been suspected, and this very necessary work might have been postponed until a more serious calamity would have overtaken us. I have no confidence in the friendship of these savages, and have always felt that we have been warming a viper which will some day show us its fangs. Our only safety, in my opinion, depends wholly upon our vigilance and the preparation we make in our defense....

March 10th, 1742. A quarrel occurred last night out at the Spring amongst a party of drunken Indians, during which four of their cabins were set on fire and burned to the ground. One of the Indians, named Bright Star, a desperate man, was seriously injured in the fight, and will likely die of his wounds. I saw him not an hour ago, and considered him then in a dying condition. These savages will give us trouble yet.

Shikellamy, New York, 1745

An Oneida leader, Shikellamy expressed his opinion of Christians' attempts to convert the Indians, as recounted by a Moravian missionary.

We were told that two ministers and an Indian had been lately here—probably it was the Presbyterian [David] Brainerd and his interpreter Tatami. He had assembled the Delawares in Shikellamy's house, and (as Shikellamy's people told us) informed that that on Sundays they should assemble as the whites do and pray as they do. Hence he would build a house for that purpose, and stay with them two years...To this Shikellamy said: "We are Indians, and don't wish to be transformed into white men. The English are our Brethren, but we never promised to become what they are. As little as we desire the preacher to become

Indian, so little ought he to desire the Indians to become preachers. He should not build a house here, they don't want one." They departed for Philadelphia the next day.

Minavavana, French Canada, 1761

Minavavana, a Chippewa leader in French Canada, declared the Indians' position after the British conquest of French Canada.

Englishman, it is to you that I speak, and I demand your attention!

Englishman, you know that the French king is our father…it is you that have made war with this, our father. You are his enemy, and how then could you have the boldness to venture among us, his children? You know that his enemies are ours….

Englishman, although you have conquered the French, you have not yet conquered us! We are not your slaves. These lakes, these woods and mountains were left to us by our ancestors. They are our inheritance, and we will part with them to none. Your nation supposes that we, like the white people, cannot live without bread—and pork—and beef! But you ought to know that He, the Great Spirit and master of Life, has provided food for us in these spacious lakes and on these woody mountains.

PROBLEM 2:
CONNECTION TO TODAY

1. To what extent was white racism the justification for slavery and has racism remained in terms of international relations today?

2. Does actual slavery as an institution exist anywhere in the world today? If so, where does it exist and are there any efforts to end it?

3. What has been the result today of the different paths that blacks and American Indians took in our history?

4. From the perspective of America today whose lives are "better-off," African-Americans or Native Americans?

PROBLEM 3: IF THE MAJORITY OF AMERICAN COLONISTS WERE EITHER SUPPORTIVE OF THE KING AND PARLIAMENT OR NEUTRAL IN THE CONFLICT WITH ENGLAND IN 1775, HOW COULD A MINORITY GROUP HAVE DECLARED A REVOLUTION BY 1776?

ABOVE: THE BATTLE OF LEXINGTON

ABOVE: THOMAS PAINE

RIGHT: THE SIGNING OF THE DECLARATION OF INDEPENDENCE

PROBLEM 3: IF THE MAJORITY OF AMERICAN COLONISTS WERE EITHER SUPPORTIVE OF THE KING AND PARLIAMENT OR NEUTRAL IN THE CONFLICT WITH ENGLAND IN 1775, HOW COULD A MINORITY GROUP HAVE DECLARED A REVOLUTION BY 1776?

*I*t is important to keep in perspective the time frame from the founding of Jamestown in 1607 to the Declaration of Independence from Great Britain in 1776. During that span of 160 to 170 years, Americans had thought of themselves and behaved as Englishmen who were loyal to the king and the English Parliament. Such a long history identifying with England did not die quickly or easily. Even in the years after 1763, as differences of opinion between the colonies and the mother country grew, virtually no one talked of separating from England. As late as 1775 the majority of American leaders were opposed to independence. Violence and armed conflict between the colonists and the British broke out, and still individuals were seeking a peaceful reconciliation. Both in England and in America, plans of compromise were put forth to settle all differences, restore peace, and return to a normal colonial-mother country relationship. As late as January 1776, only five months before the Declaration of Independence was proclaimed, George Washington's officers were offering toasts to the health of the English king as they sat in their military quarters in Boston.

The American colonists were generally divided into three identifiable groups. One group was labeled Loyalists, or Tories, because of their continued allegiance to the king. They did not always agree with the acts of Parliament but still preferred to have the colonies under the control of England rather than run by those they considered the "mobs" of America. Their numbers were fewest in New England and Virginia but constituted a majority in Georgia and South Carolina. They were also very strong in North Carolina and may have been a majority in New York. A second group was those classified as moderates, or neutrals. These individuals would have preferred that the relationship between England and the colonies not be changed, but they were reluctant to openly declare their views because they feared retaliation from those who wanted independence. A third group, who wanted a complete break from England and total independence, were the radicals, known also as the Whigs. While specific numbers are impossible to know, estimates are that each of these groups represented approximately one-third of colonial America.

Whatever the exact numbers, what is clear is that the radicals represented a colonial minority, yet they succeeded in starting a revolution and declaring independence. How could this minority of persons have moved the thirteen colonies from loyalty to the crown to defiance of the king and from adherence to the laws of Parliament to denial of any authority of Parliament? How could this minority have pulled off a political revolution?

PROBLEM 3:
QUESTIONS FOR TEAM RESEARCH

1. What strategies or tactics did the minority who favored revolution use to succeed in achieving their goal?

2. What events occurred between 1775 and 1776 that made it increasingly difficult for the colonies to reach some peaceful compromise or accommodation with England?

3. Who were the key people who pushed for independence, and why did they do so?

4. Why did the majority of colonists who either opposed independence or were neutral about it not stop the minority who wanted a break from England?

5. Why did Canada not declare independence from England and subsequently remain part of the British Commonwealth? What conditions were different there?

PROBLEM 3:
STARTING THE SEARCH FOR EVIDENCE

INTERNET: KEY WORDS AND PHRASES

The Loyalists during the American Revolution

Samuel Adams

Tom Paine's *Common Sense*

The Declaration of Independence

BOOKS

Axelrod, Alan, *The Real History of the American Revolution: A New Look at the Past*, NY, Sterling, 2007

Becker, Carl, *The Declaration of Independence: A Study in the History of Political Ideas*, NY, Vintage Books, 1958

Miller, John Chester, *Sam Adams: Pioneer in Propaganda*, Palo Alto, Stanford University Press, 1960

O'Reilly-Fleming, Thomas, *Liberty, the American Revolution*, NY, Viking, 1997

Van Tyme, Claude Halstead, *The Loyalists in the American Revolution*, NY, P. Smith, 1929

DECLARATION OF INDEPENDENCE

Here is the complete text of the Declaration of Independence. The original spelling and capitalization have been retained.

(Adopted by Congress on July 4, 1776)

THE UNANIMOUS DECLARATION OF THE THIRTEEN UNITED STATES OF AMERICA

When, in the course of human events, it becomes necessary for one people to dissolve the political bands which have connected them with another, and to assume among the powers of the earth, the separate and equal station to which the laws of nature and of nature's God entitle them, a decent respect to the opinions of mankind requires that they should declare the causes which impel them to the separation.

We hold these truths to be self-evident, that all men are created equal, that they are endowed by their Creator with certain unalienable rights, that among these are life, liberty and the pursuit of happiness. That to secure these rights, governments are instituted among men, deriving their just powers from the consent of the governed. That whenever any form of government becomes destructive to these ends, it is the right of the people to alter or to abolish it, and to institute new government, laying its foundation on such principles and organizing its powers in such form, as to them shall seem most likely to effect their safety and happiness. Prudence, indeed, will dictate that governments long established should not be changed for light and transient causes; and accordingly all experience hath shown that mankind are more disposed to suffer, while evils are sufferable, than to right themselves by abolishing the forms to which they are accustomed. But when a long train of abuses and usurpations, pursuing invariably the same object evinces a design to reduce them under absolute despotism, it is their right, it is their duty, to throw off such government, and to provide new guards for their future security—Such has been the patient sufferance of these colonies;

and such is now the necessity which constrains them to alter their former systems of government. The history of the present King of Great Britain is a history of repeated injuries and usurpations, all having in direct object the establishment of an absolute tyranny over these states. To prove this, let facts be submitted to a candid world.

He has refused his assent to laws, the most wholesome and necessary for the public good.

He has forbidden his governors to pass laws of immediate and pressing importance, unless suspended in their operation till his assent should be obtained; and when so suspended, he has utterly neglected to attend to them.

He has refused to pass other laws for the accommodation of large districts of people, unless those people would relinquish the right of representation in the legislature, a right inestimable to them and formidable to tyrants only.

He has called together legislative bodies at places unusual, uncomfortable, and distant from the depository of their public records, for the sole purpose of fatiguing them into compliance with his measures.

He has dissolved representative houses repeatedly, for opposing with manly firmness his invasions on the rights of the people.

He has refused for a long time, after such dissolutions, to cause others to be elected; whereby the legislative powers, incapable of annihilation, have returned to the people at large for their exercise; the state remaining in the meantime exposed to all the dangers of invasion from without, and convulsions within.

He has endeavored to prevent the population of these states; for that purpose obstructing the laws for naturalization of foreigners; refusing to pass others to encourage their migration hither, and raising the conditions of new appropriations of lands.

He has obstructed the administration of justice, by refusing his assent to laws for establishing judiciary powers.

He has made judges dependent on his will alone, for the tenure of their offices, and the amount and payment of their salaries.

He has erected a multitude of new offices, and sent hither swarms of officers to harass our people and eat out their substance.

He has kept among us, in times of peace, standing armies without the consent of our legislatures.

He has affected to render the military independent of, and superior to, civil power.

He has combined with others to subject us to a jurisdiction foreign to our constitution, and unacknowledged by our laws; giving his assent to their acts of pretended legislation;

For quartering large bodies of armed troops among us;

For protecting them, by mock trial, from punishment for any murders which they should commit on the inhabitants of these states;

For cutting off our trade with all parts of the world;

For imposing taxes on us without our consent;

For depriving us in many cases, of the benefits of trial by jury;

For transporting us beyond seas to be tried for pretended offenses;

For abolishing the free system of English laws in a neighboring province, establishing therein an arbitrary government, and enlarging its boundaries so as to render it at once an example and fit instrument for introducing the same absolute rule in these colonies;

For taking away our charters, abolishing our most valuable laws, and altering fundamentally the forms of our governments;

For suspending our own legislatures, and declaring themselves invested with power to legislate for us in all cases whatsoever.

He has abdicated government here, by declaring us out of his protection and waging war against us.

He has plundered our seas, ravaged our coasts, burned our towns, and destroyed the lives of our people.

He is at this time transporting large armies of foreign mercenaries to complete the works of death, desolation and tyranny, already begun with circumstances of cruelty and perfidy scarcely paralleled in the most barbarous ages, and totally unworthy the head of a civilized nation.

He has constrained our fellow citizens taken captive on the high seas to bear arms against their country, to become the executioners of their friends and brethren, or to fall themselves by their hands.

He has excited domestic insurrections amongst us, and has endeavored to bring on the inhabitants of our frontiers, the merciless Indian savages, whose known rule of warfare, is undistinguished destruction of all ages, sexes and conditions.

In every stage of these oppressions we have petitioned for redress in the most humble terms: our repeated petitions have been answered only by repeated injury. A prince, whose character is thus marked by every act which may define a tyrant, is unfit to be the ruler of a free people.

Nor have we been wanting in attention to our British brethren. We have warned them from time to time of attempts by their legislature to extend an unwarrantable jurisdiction over us. We have reminded them of the circumstances of our emigration and settlement here. We have appealed to their native justice and magnanimity, and we have conjured them by the ties of our common kindred to disavow these usurpations, which, would inevitably interrupt our connections and correspondence. They too have been deaf to the voice of justice and of consanguinity. We must, therefore, acquiesce in the necessity, which denounces our separation, and hold them, as we hold the rest of mankind, enemies in war, in peace friends.

We, therefore, the representatives of the United States of America, in General Congress, assembled, appealing to the Supreme Judge of the world for the rectitude of our intentions, do, in the name, and by the authority of the good people of these colonies, solemnly publish and declare, that these united colonies are, and of right ought to be free and independent states; that they are absolved from all allegiance to the British Crown, and that all political connection between them and the state of Great Britain, is and ought to be totally dissolved; and that as free and independent states, they have full power to levy war, conclude peace, contract alliances, establish commerce, and to do all other acts and things which independent states may of right do. And for the support of this declaration, with a firm reliance on the protection of Divine Providence, we mutually pledge to each other our lives, our fortunes and our sacred honor.

NEW HAMPSHIRE: Josiah Bartlett, William Whipple, Matthew Thornton

MASSACHUSETTS: John Hancock, Samual Adams, John Adams, Robert Treat Paine, Elbridge Gerry

RHODE ISLAND: Stephen Hopkins, William Ellery

CONNECTICUT: Roger Sherman, Samuel Huntington, William Williams, Oliver Wolcott

NEW YORK: William Floyd, Philip Livingston, Francis Lewis, Lewis Morris

New Jersey: Richard Stockton, John Witherspoon, Francis Hopkinson, John Hart, Abraham Clark

Pennsylvania: Robert Morris, Benjamin Rush, Benjamin Franklin, John Morton, George Clymer, James Smith, George Taylor, James Wilson, George Ross

Delaware: Caesar Rodney, George Read, Thomas McKean

Maryland: Samuel Chase, William Paca, Thomas Stone, Charles Carroll of Carrollton

Virginia: George Wythe, Richard Henry Lee, Thomas Jefferson, Benjamin Harrison, Thomas Nelson, Jr., Francis Lightfoot Lee, Carter Braxton

North Carolina: William Hooper, Joseph Hewes, John Penn

South Carolina: Edward Rutledge, Thomas Heyward, Jr., Thomas Lynch, Jr., Arthur Middleton

Georgia: Button Gwinnett, Lyman Hall, George Walton

NOTE. Mr. Ferdinand Jefferson, Keeper of the Rolls in the Department of State, at Washington, says: "The names of the signers are spelt above as in the facsimile of the original, but the punctuation of them is not always the same; neither do the names of the States appear in the facsimile of the original. The names of the signers of each State are grouped together in the facsimile of the original, except the name of Matthew Thornton, which follows that of Oliver Wolcott."

—Revised Statutes of the United States, 2d edition, 1878

PROBLEM 3:
CONNECTION TO TODAY

1. Why can minorities sometimes overcome their lack of numbers and succeed in their plans even though there are greater numbers who opposed them?

2. Can you think of other situations in other countries where a dedicated minority has achieved its objectives?

3. Why do majorities often refuse to act to defend what they want?

4. How legitimate were the arguments put forth in the Declaration of Independence of 1776? Are some of the reasons offered to justify independence simply propaganda? How many of the arguments are verifiable by the historical facts? What was the purpose in writing a Declaration of Independence?

PROBLEM 4:

HOW COULD THIRTEEN DISORGANIZED AMERICAN COLONIES WIN A WAR AND REVOLUTION AGAINST ENGLAND, THE GREATEST ECONOMIC AND MILITARY POWER OF THE 18TH CENTURY WORLD?

RIGHT: GENERAL GEORGE WASHINGTON

BELOW: GENERAL BURGOYNE'S SURRENDER OF THE BRITISH ARMY

PROBLEM 4: HOW COULD THIRTEEN DISORGANIZED AMERICAN COLONIES WIN A WAR AND REVOLUTION AGAINST ENGLAND, THE GREATEST ECONOMIC AND MILITARY POWER OF THE 18TH CENTURY WORLD?

*T*hink about the following situation for a minute. Suppose Hawaii, which is part of the United States of America, decided that it no longer benefited from being a part of the nation and that it would be better off being a separate country, and so it decided to declare its independence. And suppose the government of the United States refused to allow or recognize Hawaiian independence or its existence as a separate country and sent federal troops to Hawaii to stop the move for independence. Who do you think would ultimately win in this situation? Remember Hawaii is just one state, thousands of miles away from the mainland United States, and the United States is the richest and most militarily powerful nation in the world. The United States of America has the best trained, best equipped army, navy, and air force of any nation on earth. Hawaii has only a part-time army in the state national guard. How could Hawaii win in this battle? Is there any conceivable way they could beat the United States armed forces? Probably most of us would say, "It's impossible for Hawaii to gain its independence. In any war with the whole U.S. military, the state would be totally crushed."

Now consider this somewhat similar situation in our history in the 18th century. England was the most powerful economic and military power in the world. It had colonies in many parts of the world, and everyone who lived in those colonies was part of the British Empire and recognized and gave allegiance to the English king, the English Parliament, and all English laws. In North America the thirteen colonies were all part of that governmental structure, even though they were, like Hawaii, physically thousands of miles away from the English capital in London. The colonies had no central government, only separate colonial governments. They had no central army, only a poorly trained and badly equipped part-time militia. They had no president or legal Congress to raise money or make decisions, yet they went ahead and declared their independence from England and claimed to establish a new nation; today we are all Americans who live in this country called the United States of America.

How could this have happened? How could a group of thirteen colonies, with virtually no military capability defeat the greatest economic and military nation of the time? How can you analyze and explain this extraordinary event?

PROBLEM 4:
QUESTIONS FOR TEAM RESEARCH

1. What role did distance and means of transportation have in this situation? How long did it take to get from London to Boston? Or from Virginia to Massachusetts? What difference did this make for either side?

2. How did armies move from one place to another? Where and how did the British get their means of transportation?

3. Who had better and more modern fighting equipment and did it make a difference in this war?

4. What was the standard way armies fought in 18th century Europe? Did the British use that method in the colonies? Did the colonial rebels use that same approach? What difference did it make?

5. What uniforms did the two sides have and did it make any difference in the actual fighting?

6. What experience did the colonial rebels actually have in fighting a war? Did that make any difference? What experience did George Washington have in military strategy or in leading any army into battle?

7. What did the politics between nations in Europe have to do with the success or failure of what happened in the battles of the American Revolution?

8. Did all the colonial population support breaking away from England? What was the attitude of the population in England about the war?

9. How long did the war last and how did this time frame impact the final outcome?

10. How did the colonies survive economically when trade with England was cut off because of the rebellion and war?

11. What role, if any, did the existence of slavery in the colonies have in determining the outcome of the war?

12. What were the estimated casualties for each side and did this affect the war's outcome?

13. Why didn't the British just capture rebel leaders like Samuel and John Adams, Jefferson, Madison, and all those who had signed the document of rebellion, The Declaration of Independence, and just stop the rebellion?

PROBLEM 4:
STARTING THE SEARCH FOR EVIDENCE

INTERNET: KEY WORDS AND PHRASES

Military strategy of George Washington during the American Revolution

British attitudes about the American War for Independence

European support for the American Revolution

The British army during the American Revolution

BOOKS

Cunliffe, Marcus, *George Washington: Man and Monument*, NY, New American Library, 1987

Dann, John C., ed, *The Revolution Remembered: Eyewitness Accounts of the War for Independence*, Chicago, University of Chicago Press, 1980

Freeman, Douglas Southhall, *George Washington: A Biography*, NY, Scribner, 1948–57

Marrin, Albert, *The War for Independence. The Story of the American Revolution*, NY, Athenean, 1988

Peckham, Howard Henry, *The War for Independence: A Military History*, Chicago, University of Chicago Press, 1950

Correspondence of General George Washington Regarding the War of Independence from England

To General Cornwallis, October 17, 1781

My Lord: I have had the Honor of receiving Your Lordship's Letter of this Date.

An Ardent Desire to spare the further Effusion of Blood, will readily incline me to listen to such Terms for the Surrender of your Posts and Garrisons at York and Gloucester, as are admissible.

I wish previous to the Meeting of Commissioners, that your Lordship's proposals in writing, may be sent to the American Lines: for which Purpose, a Suspension of Hostilities during two Hours from the Delivery of this Letter will be granted.

• • •

To Thomas McKean, Head Quarters near York, October 19, 1781

Sir: I have the Honor to inform Congress, that a Reduction of the British Army under the Command of Lord Cornwallis, is most happily effected. The unremitting Ardor which actuated every Officer and Soldier in the combined Army on this Occasion, has principally led to this Important Event, at an earlier period than my most sanguine Hopes had induced me to expect.

The singular Spirit of Emulation, which animated the whole Army from the first Commencement of our Operations, has filled my Mind with the highest pleasure and Satisfaction, and had given me the happiest presages of Success.

On the 17th instant, a Letter was received from Lord Cornwallis, proposing a Meeting of Commissioners, to consult on Terms for the Surrender of the Posts of York and Gloucester. This Letter (the first which had passed between us) opened a Correspondence, a Copy of which I do myself the Honor to inclose; that Correspondence was followed by the Definitive Capitulation, which was agreed to, and Signed on the 18th. Copy of which is also herewith transmitted, and which I hope, will meet the Approbation of Congress.

I should be wanting in the feelings of Gratitude, did I not mention on this Occasion, with the warmest Sense of Acknowledgements, the very chearfull and able Assistance, which I have received in the Course of our Operations, from his Excellency the Count de Rochambeau, and all his Officers of every Rank, in their respective Capacities. Nothing could equal this Zeal of our Allies, but the emulating Spirit of the American Officers, whose Ardor would not suffer their Exertions to be exceeded.

The very uncommon Degree of Duty and Fatigue which the Nature of the Service required from the Officers of Engineers and Artillery of both Armies, obliges me particularly to mention the Obligations I am under to the Commanding and other Officers of those Corps.

I wish it was in my Power to express to Congress, how much I feel myself indebted to The Count de Grasse and the Officers of the Fleet under his Command for the distinguished Aid and Support which have been afforded by them; between whom, and the Army, the most happy Concurrence of Sentiments and Views have subsisted, and from whom, every possible Cooperation has been experienced, which the most harmonious Intercourse could afford.

Returns of the Prisoners, Military Stores, Ordnance Shipping and other Matters, I shall do myself the Honor to transmit to Congress as soon as they can be collected by the Heads of Departments, to which they belong.

Colo. Laurens and the Viscount de Noiailles, on the Part of the combined Army, were the Gentlemen who acted as Commissioners for forming and setting the Terms of Capitulation and Surrender herewith transmitted, to whom I am particularly obliged for their Readiness and Attention exhibited on the Occasion.

Colo Tilghman, one of my Aids de Camp, will have the Honor to deliver these Dispatches to your Excellency; he will be able to inform you of every minute Circumstance which is not particularly mentioned in my Letter; his Merits, which are too well known to need my observations at this time, have gained my particular Attention, and could wish that they may be honored with the Notice of your Excellency and Congress.

Your Excellency and Congress will be pleased to accept my Congratulations on this happy Event, and believe me to be With the highest Respect etc.

P. S. Tho' I am not possessed of the Particular Returns, yet I have reason to suppose that the Number of Prisoners will be between five and Six thousand, exclusive of Seamen and others.

PROBLEM 4:
CONNECTION TO TODAY

1. Does the historically recent U.S. involvement in Viet Nam and Iraq and Afghanistan have any connection to the English problem with the American colonies?

2. In the problem of the American Revolution under consideration here what role did public opinion both in England and in the colonies have on the course and direction of the conflict? Are there any lessons we can learn and apply to situations in our own time?

3. Recently when certain areas of Russia sought to break away and declare their independence, the U.S. protested the Russian attempt to suppress the independence movement. Was this action a contradiction to what had happened in our own country or were there circumstances which made this different?

4. Political scientists sometimes speak of a nation's "usable" power. What do you think is meant by this term? Are there some aspects of a nation's power that are *not* usable? Did this concept apply to the British in 1776? Does it apply to the U.S. today?

PROBLEM 5:
A GOVERNMENT TOO STRONG OR TOO WEAK? THE DILEMMA OF 1787

RIGHT:
THE BILL OF RIGHTS

BELOW:
JAMES MADISON

BOTTOM RIGHT:
THE CONSTITUTIONAL CONVENTION OF 1787

PROBLEM 5: A GOVERNMENT TOO STRONG OR TOO WEAK? THE DILEMMA OF 1787

The thirteen American colonies had somehow overcome enormous odds and had won independence from England and created a new nation. But it was clear right away that declaring the creation of a new nation and actually thinking and acting like one united people were two very different things. For many, their identity and loyalty were to their state rather than to the new nation. They thought and identified themselves as Virginians or Massachusetts men rather than as Americans. There were differences, too, in the various states' basic needs and interests. Pennsylvania was a very different place from Georgia or Rhode Island. The economic interests and demographics of the regions were dramatically different.

What they did agree on immediately after gaining independence was that they would not gain independence from one too powerful and too intrusive government in England only to replace it with a new overly powerful intrusive central government in the newly created United States of America. Thus at first the new nation was governed by the Articles of Confederation, a structure that created a weak central government and left much autonomy and authority to the states. But it soon became clear that this new government structure was much too weak and ineffective, and something different was needed. But what could that be? A new, too powerful central government was something none could accept, yet to keep the current weak Articles of Confederation threatened the very existence of the new nation. Too much freedom and liberty for the states would lead to chaos if every state was doing whatever it chose to do. On the other hand, too much central authority could lead to an authoritarian government and restrict newly won freedoms.

This is the problem the men who met in Philadelphia during the hot summer of 1787 faced. How did they resolve these conflicting needs and issues? From the perspective of our lives today, did they succeed?

PROBLEM 5:
QUESTIONS FOR TEAM RESEARCH

1. What was really wrong with the Articles on Confederation? Where did that government structure fail? Could its shortcomings have been fixed?

2. Who was complaining about the Articles of Confederation? Is there evidence of widespread public concern and dissatisfaction?

3. What persons or groups were at the forefront of pushing for a new governmental structure?

4. Were the issues of liberty and authority resolved? If so, how? If not, why not?

5. How were the conflicting needs of big and small states resolved? In other words, should small states such as Delaware and Rhode Island have the same decision-making voice and authority as large states such as New York and Pennsylvania?

6. How democratic was the new constitution? Who was given full participation? Who was not?

7. Did the men who wrote the new constitution follow or turn their backs on the principles of the Declaration of Independence and the American Revolution?

8. Was the final version of the Constitution a unique original document or did the writers have other models to replicate?

9. Did all the states agree to accept the new constitution? What were some of the objections to it and how were they resolved?

10. What groups of people benefited most from the new constitution? Which groups, if any, benefited least?

11. If there were some who did not benefit from the original constitution, have we done anything since then to correct the situation?

PROBLEM 5:
STARTING THE SEARCH FOR EVIDENCE

INTERNET: KEY WORDS AND PHRASES

James Madison and the U.S. Constitution

The Constitutional Convention of 1787

Alexander Hamilton and the U.S. Constitution

Compromises at the Constitutional Convention of 1787

BOOKS

Burns, Edward Menall, *James Madison, Philosopher of the Constitution*, New Brunswick, Rutgers University Press, 1961

Collier, Christopher; Collier, James Lincoln, *Decision in Philadelphia: the Constitutional Convention of 1787,* NY, Random House, 1986

Morton, Joseph C., *Shapers of the Great Debate at the Constitutional Convention of 1787*, Westport, Greenwood Press, 2006

Solbery, Winton U., *The Constitutional Convention and the Formation of the Union*, Urbana, University of Illinois Press,1990

Stewart, David O., *The Summer of 1787: The Men Who Invented the Constitution*, NY, Simon and Schuster, 2007

FEDERALIST NO. 48

These Departments Should Not Be So Far Separated as to Have No Constitutional Control Over Each Other

To the People of the State of New York:

IT WAS shown in the last paper that the political apothegm there examined does not require that the legislative, executive, and judiciary departments should be wholly unconnected with each other. I shall undertake, in the next place, to show that unless these departments be so far connected and blended as to give to each a constitutional control over the others, the degree of separation which the maxim requires, as essential to a free government, can never in practice be duly maintained.

It is agreed on all sides, that the powers properly belonging to one of the departments ought not to be directly and completely administered by either of the other departments. It is equally evident, that none of them ought to possess, directly or indirectly, an overruling influence over the others, in the administration of their respective powers. It will not be denied, that power is of an encroaching nature, and that it ought to be effectually restrained from passing the limits assigned to it. After discriminating, therefore, in theory, the several classes of power, as they may in their nature be legislative, executive, or judiciary, the next and most difficult task is to provide some practical security for each, against the invasion of the others. What this security ought to be, is the great problem to be solved.

Will it be sufficient to mark, with precision, the boundaries of these departments, in the constitution of the government, and to trust to these parchment barriers against the encroaching spirit of power? This is the security which appears to have been principally relied on by the compilers of most of the American constitutions. But experience assures us, that the efficacy of the provision has been greatly overrated; and that some more adequate defense is indispensably necessary for the more feeble, against the more powerful, members of the government. The legislative department is everywhere extending the sphere of its activity, and drawing all power into its impetuous vortex.

The founders of our republics have so much merit for the wisdom which they have displayed, that no task can be less pleasing than that of pointing out the errors into which they have fallen. A respect for truth, however, obliges us to remark, that they seem never for a moment to have turned their eyes from the danger to liberty from the overgrown and all-grasping prerogative of an hereditary magistrate, supported and fortified by an hereditary branch of the legislative authority. They seem never to have recollected the danger from legislative usurpations, which, by assembling all power in the same hands, must lead to the same tyranny as is threatened by executive usurpations.

In a government where numerous and extensive prerogatives are placed in the hands of an hereditary monarch, the executive department is very justly regarded as the source of danger, and watched with all the jealousy which a zeal for liberty ought to inspire. In a democracy, where a multitude of people exercise in person the legislative functions, and are continually exposed, by their incapacity for regular deliberation and concerted measures, to the ambitious intrigues of their executive magistrates, tyranny may well be apprehended, on some favorable emergency, to start up in the same quarter. But in a representative republic, where the executive magistracy is carefully limited; both in the extent and the duration of its power; and where the legislative power is exercised by an assembly, which is inspired, by a supposed influence over the people, with an intrepid confidence in its own strength; which is sufficiently numerous to feel all the passions which actuate a multitude, yet not so numerous as to be incapable of pursuing the objects of its passions, by means which reason prescribes; it is against the enterprising ambition of this department that the people ought to indulge all their jealousy and exhaust all their precautions.

The legislative department derives a superiority in our governments from other circumstances. Its constitutional powers being at once more extensive, and less susceptible of precise limits, it can, with the greater facility, mask, under complicated and indirect measures, the encroachments which it makes on the co-ordinate departments. It is not unfrequently a question of real nicety in legislative bodies, whether the operation of a particular measure will, or will not, extend beyond the legislative sphere. On the other side, the executive power being restrained within a narrower compass, and being more simple in its nature, and the judiciary being described by landmarks still less uncertain, projects of usurpation by either of these departments would immediately betray and defeat themselves. Nor is this all: as the legislative department alone has access to the pockets of the people, and has in some constitutions full discretion, and in all a prevailing influence, over the pecuniary rewards of those who fill the other departments, a dependence is thus created in the latter, which gives still greater facility to encroachments of the former.

I have appealed to our own experience for the truth of what I advance on this subject. Were it necessary to verify this experience by particular proofs, they might be multiplied without end. I might find a witness in every citizen who has shared in, or been attentive to, the course of public administrations. I might collect vouchers in abundance from the records and archives of every State in the Union. But as a more concise, and at the same time equally satisfactory, evidence, I will refer to the example of two States, attested by two unexceptionable authorities.

The first example is that of Virginia, a State which, as we have seen, has expressly declared in its constitution, that the three great departments ought not to be intermixed. The authority in support of it is Mr. Jefferson, who, besides his other advantages for remarking the operation of the government, was himself the chief magistrate of it. In order to convey fully the ideas with which his experience had impressed him on this subject, it will be necessary to quote a passage of some length from his very interesting "Notes on the State of Virginia," p. 195. "All the powers of government, legislative, executive, and judiciary, result to the legislative body. The concentrating these in the same hands, is precisely the definition of despotic government. It will be no alleviation, that these powers will be exercised by a plurality of hands, and not by a single one. One hundred and seventy-three despots would surely be as oppressive as one. Let those who doubt it, turn their eyes on the republic of Venice. As little will it avail us, that they are chosen by ourselves. An *elective despotism* was not the government we fought for; but one which should not only be founded on free principles, but in which the powers of government should be so divided and balanced among several bodies of magistracy, as that no one could transcend their legal limits, without being effectually checked and restrained by the others. For this reason, that convention which passed the ordinance of government, laid its foundation on this basis, that the legislative, executive, and judiciary departments should be separate and distinct, so that no person should exercise the powers of more than one of them at the same time. *but no barrier was provided between these several powers.* The judiciary and the executive members were left dependent on the legislative for their subsistence in office, and some of them for their continuance in it. If, therefore, the legislature assumes executive and judiciary powers, no opposition is likely to be made; nor, if made, can be effectual; because in that case they may put their proceedings into the form of acts of Assembly, which will render them obligatory on the other branches. They have accordingly, *in many* instances, *decided rights* which should have been left to *judiciary controversy*, and *the direction of the executive, during the whole time of their session, is becoming habitual and familiar.*"

The other State which I shall take for an example is Pennsylvania; and the other authority, the Council of Censors, which assembled in the years 1783 and 1784. A part of the duty of this body, as marked out by the constitution, was "to inquire whether the constitution had been preserved inviolate in every part; and whether the legislative and executive branches of government had performed their duty as guardians of the people, or assumed to themselves, or exercised, other or greater powers than they are entitled to by the constitution." In the execution of this trust, the council were necessarily led to a comparison of both the legislative and executive proceedings, with the constitutional powers of these departments; and from the facts enumerated, and to the truth of most of which both sides in the council subscribed, it appears that the constitution had been flagrantly violated by the legislature in a variety of important instances.

A great number of laws had been passed, violating, without any apparent necessity, the rule requiring that all bills of a public nature shall be previously printed for the consideration of the people; although this is one of the precautions chiefly relied on by the constitution against improper acts of legislature.

The constitutional trial by jury had been violated, and powers assumed which had not been delegated by the constitution.

Executive powers had been usurped.

The salaries of the judges, which the constitution expressly requires to be fixed, had been occasionally varied; and cases belonging to the judiciary department frequently drawn within legislative cognizance and determination.

Those who wish to see the several particulars falling under each of these heads, may consult the journals of the council, which are in print. Some of them, it will be found, may be imputable to peculiar circumstances connected with the war; but the greater part of them may be considered as the spontaneous shoots of an ill-constituted government.

It appears, also, that the executive department had not been innocent of frequent breaches of the constitution. There are three observations, however, which ought to be made on this head: *first*, a great proportion of the instances were either immediately produced by the necessities of the war, or recommended by Congress or the commander-in-chief; *secondly*, in most of the other instances, they conformed either to the declared or the known sentiments of the legislative department; *thirdly*, the executive department of Pennsylvania is distinguished from that of the other States by the number of members composing it. In this respect, it has as much affinity to a legislative assembly as to an executive council. And being at once exempt from the restraint of an individual responsibility for the acts of the body, and deriving confidence from mutual example and joint influence, unauthorized measures would, of course, be more freely hazarded, than where the executive department is administered by a single hand, or by a few hands.

The conclusion which I am warranted in drawing from these observations is, that a mere demarcation on parchment of the constitutional limits of the several departments, is not a sufficient guard against those encroachments which lead to a tyrannical concentration of all the powers of government in the same hands.

[SIGNED] PUBLIUS (JAMES MADISON)
FROM THE NEW YORK PACKET, FEBRUARY 1, 1788

PROBLEM 5:
CONNECTION TO TODAY

1. What is the relationship of you as an individual citizen to the Constitution of 1787?

2. Identify some issues faced by 21st century America that are directly connected to the Constitution of 1787?

3. Are there parts of the Constitution that are now outdated and should be changed? What are those things and how would you change them?

4. The countries of Europe have created a European Union which is still a loose confederation of individual sovereign nations. Many hope that someday this will turn into one united European country, perhaps called "The United States of Europe." What lessons could the Europeans learn from the American experience if they hope to realize such a dream?

PROBLEM 6:
WHERE SHOULD WE PUT THE NATION'S CAPITAL?

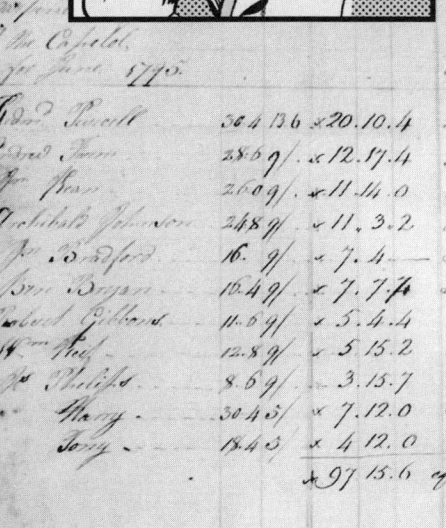

ABOVE:
DOCUMENT RELATING TO THE BUILDING OF "FEDERAL CITY"

LEFT: PROPOSED WHITE HOUSE PLAN FOR THE NEW CAPITAL

PROBLEM 6:
WHERE SHOULD WE PUT THE NATION'S CAPITAL?

One of the issues facing the start of a new nation was where to locate and what to name the new capital. During the time of the Revolutionary War and during the writing of the Constitution of 1787, the places where meetings were held and decisions made were Philadelphia and New York. But it soon became clear that the question of where to locate the nation's capital would not be an easy one to answer.

Some key political questions needed to be considered. Where should the capital be located, in the North or in the South? If one region was chosen, would that alienate the other region? What state should be the seat of the nation's government? If a particular state was chosen, would that, too, alienate other states and give that chosen state some special status or political advantage? And who would decide what the name of the capital would be? Was there some way to please all, or at least the majority of Americans, on this key decision?

How and why did this issue finally get resolved?

PROBLEM 6:
QUESTIONS FOR TEAM RESEARCH

1. What evidence do we have that the issue of the nation's capital was one of serious disagreement between the states?

2. Who were the key political leaders in the discussion and resolution of this issue?

3. What were the internal conditions in the country that impacted the discussion and resolution of this issue?

4. Did the final agreement satisfy all the contending parties?

5. What would have been the consequences of leaving the capital in Philadelphia or New York?

PROBLEM 6:
STARTING THE SEARCH FOR EVIDENCE

INTERNET: KEY WORDS AND PHRASES

History of the U.S. capital

History of Washington D.C.

Hamilton, Madison, and the national debt

Hamilton, Madison, and Jefferson and the decision to locate the U.S. capital

BOOKS

Aikman, Lonnelle, *We the People: The Story of the United States Capital*, Washington D.C., U.S. Capital Historical Society, 1981

Allen, William C., *History of the United States Capitol*, Washington D.C., Superintendant of Documents, 2001

Ellis, Joseph J., *Founding Brothers: The Revolutionary Generation*, NY, Alfred A. Knopf, 2000

Hoig, Stan, *A Capitol for the Nation*, NY, Cobblehill Books, 1990

The Story of Washington D.C. (video), Chicago, Questar Video, 1992

George Washington's Message to Congress Concerning the Seat of Government

United States, January 24, 1791

Gentlemen of the Senate and House of Representatives: In execution of the powers with which Congress were pleased to invest me by their Act intitled "An Act for establishing the temporary and permanent seat of the Government of the United States" and on mature consideration of the advantages and disadvantages of the several positions, within the limits prescribed by the said Act, I have, by Proclamation, bearing date this day, a copy of which is herewith transmitted, directed Commissioners, appointed in pursuance of the Act, to survey and limit a part of the territory of ten miles square, on both sides the river Potomack, so as to comprehend George Town in Maryland, and to extend to the Eastern branch. I have not by this first Act given to the said territory the whole extent of which it is susceptible in the direction of the River; because I thought it important that Congress should have an opportunity of considering whether by an amendatory law, they would authorize the location of the residue at the lower end of the present, so as to comprehend the Eastern branch itself, and some of the Country on its lower side in the State of Maryland, and the town of Alexandria in Virginia. If, however, they are of opinion that the federal territory should be bounded by the water edge of the Eastern-branch, the location of the residue will be to be made at the upper end of what is now directed. I have thought best to await a survey of the territory before it is decided on what particular spot on the North Eastern side of the River the public buildings shall be erected.

• • •

Thomas Jefferson's Memorandum on the Compromise of 1790

The assumption of the state debts in 1790 was a supplementary measure in Hamilton's fiscal system. When attempted in the House of Representatives it failed. This threw Hamilton himself and a number of members into deep dismay. Going to the

President's one day I met Hamilton as I approached the door. His look was sombre, haggard, and dejected beyond description. Even his dress uncouth and neglected. He asked to speak with me. We stood in the street near the door. He opened the subject of the assumption of the state debts, the necessity of it in the general fiscal arrangement and its indispensible necessity towards a preservation of the Union: and particularly of the New England states, who had made great expenditures during the war, on expeditions which tho' of their own undertaking were for the common cause: that they considered the assumption of these by the Union so just, and its denial so palpably injurious, that they would make it a sine qua non of a continuance of the Union. That as to his own part, if he had not credit enough to carry such a measure as that, he could be of no use, and was determined to resign. He observed at the same time, that tho' our particular business laid in separate departments, yet the administration and its success was a common concern, and that we should make common cause in supporting one another. He added his wish that I would interest my friends from the South, who were those most opposed to it. I answered that I had been so long absent from my country that I had lost a familiarity with its affairs, and being but lately returned had not yet got into the train of them, that the fiscal system being out of my department, I had not yet undertaken to consider and understand it, that the assumption had struck me in an unfavorable light, but still not having considered it sufficiently I had not concerned in it, but that I would revolve what he had urged in my mind. It was a real fact that the Eastern and Southern members (S. Carolina, however, was with the former) had got into the most extreme ill humor with one another. This broke out on every question with the most alarming heat, the bitterest animosities seemed to be engendered, and tho' they met every day, little or nothing could be done from mutual distrust and antipathy. On considering the situation of things I thought the first step towards some conciliation of views would be to bring Mr. Madison and Colo. Hamilton to a friendly discussion of the subject. I immediately wrote to each to come and dine with me the next day, mentioning that we should be alone, that the object was to find some temperament for the present fever, and that I was persuaded that men of sound heads and honest views needed nothing more than explanation and mutual understanding to enable them to unite in some measures which might enable us to get along. They came. I opened the subject to them, acknowledged that my situation had not permitted me to understand it sufficiently, but encouraged them to consider the thing together. They did so. It ended in Mr. Madison's acquiescence in a proposition that the question should be again brought before the House by way of amendment from the Senate, that tho' he would not vote for it, nor entirely withdraw his opposition, yet he should not be strenuous, but leave it to its fate. It was observed, I forget by which of them, that as the pill would be a bitter one to the Southern states, something should be done to soothe them; that the removal of the seat of government to the Potomac was a just measure, and would probably be a popular one with them, and would be a proper one to follow the assumption. It was agreed to speak to Mr. White and Mr. Lee, whose districts lay on the Potomac and to refer to them to consider how far the interests of their particular districts might be a sufficient inducement to them to yield to the assumption. This was done. Lee came into it without hesitation. Mr. White had some qualms, but finally agreed. The measure came down by way of amendment from the Senate and was finally carried by the change of White's and Lee's votes. But the removal to Potomac could not be carried unless Pennsylvania could be engaged in it. This Hamilton took on himself, and chiefly, as I understood, through the agency of Robert Morris, obtained the vote of that state, on agreeing to an intermediate residence at Philadelphia. This is the real history of the assumption, about which many erroneous conjectures have been published. It was unjust, in itself oppressive to the states, and was acquiesced in merely from a fear of disunion, while our government was still in its most infant state. It enabled Hamilton so to strengthen himself by corrupt services to many that he could afterwards carry his bank scheme and every measure he proposed in defiance of all opposition; in fact it was a principal ground whereon was reared up that Speculating phalanx, in and out of Congress which has since been able to give laws and to change the political complexion of the government of the U.S.

PROBLEM 6:
CONNECTION TO TODAY

1. If the political leaders of our past could find a workable solution to as big a problem as where to locate the nation's capital, what has changed today which makes political compromise difficult and often impossible?

2. Was there anything wrong from a moral or ethical standpoint in the final agreement or in the way in which it was reached?

3. If the European Union ever does become "The United States of Europe," where should the capital of that new nation be located? What problems would be encountered in choosing any location? Does the American example give them a model to copy? Explain.

4. The city of Jerusalem today is considered by Christians, Jews, and Muslims to have a special connection to each group's history and heritage. In which country Jerusalem should be located has been the subject of much conflict. Is there anything that the American experience with our capital could offer them in terms of how they could resolve that long-standing dispute?

PROBLEM 7:

SINCE WE HAD NEVER HAD A PRESIDENT OF THE UNITED STATES BEFORE, HOW DID GEORGE WASHINGTON DEFINE WHAT PRESIDENTS SHOULD DO?

PRESIDENT GEORGE WASHINGTON AT INAUGURAL RECEPTION

PROBLEM 7: SINCE WE HAD NEVER HAD A PRESIDENT OF THE UNITED STATES BEFORE, HOW DID GEORGE WASHINGTON DEFINE WHAT PRESIDENTS SHOULD DO?

Watching how U.S. presidents operate in our own time, we take for granted what that important position is all about. Presidents campaign for office, establish a cabinet, initiate a legislative agenda, meet with foreign leaders to establish foreign policy, give regular speeches to the people, hold press conferences, and speak to the Congress and the country at the annual State of the Union address. What is important to keep in mind is that none of the above tasks and functions were understood at the beginning of the creation of the United States as a new nation. Article II of the U.S. Constitution gives a very general description of the executive branch of the U.S. government.

In 1789 there was no doubt in the minds of Americans as to who the first president of the new nation would or should be. George Washington was the most famous, respected, and admired man in the country, and he was the overwhelming choice of the people to become the president. Washington himself, exhausted from leading the country through war and revolutions, had no desire for the position. He said, "I have no wish beyond that of living and dying an honest man on my own farm," but ultimately he could not refuse the call of the nation at this critical juncture and was unanimously selected by the Electoral College to be the first President of the United States. But what did it really mean to be president?

Washington's every step and action would be watched by the entire nation and would set the standard for all those who followed him. Question after question, none of which had ever been asked or answered before confronted the new nation. What title should the executive have? President? General? Your Excellency? Would the President receive a salary? Expenses? Should there be an inaugural ceremony? Would the President be expected to speak at such a ceremony? Who would be advisers, and what departments of government should there be since there was no mention of a President's cabinet in the Constitution. And what was the President supposed to do all day long? Should he have an "open door" policy and meet with average citizens? In foreign and domestic affairs, should he initiate policy or merely execute what the Congress enacted? What did it mean to be commander-in-chief? When could he call out troops, and when could he not? Did he need the approval of Congress? Since the Constitution made no reference to political parties, what role should he play as they began to take shape? The Constitution said the President should from time to time "give to the Congress information on the state of the union," but what did "from time to time" mean, and should the president appear in person to the Congress or merely send a written document? And even though Washington most likely could have served as President for life, how long should presidents remain in office?

These and many more were the unanswered questions faced by Washington when he assumed the office of president, and no one was more sensitive to the role he played than Washington himself. Few, he said, "can realize the difficult and delicate part which a man in my situation has to act…my station is new, and if I may use the expression, I walk on untrodden ground. There is scarcely an action, the motive of which may not be subject to a double interpretation. There is scarcely any part of my conduct which may not hereafter be drawn into precedent."

Given all of these uncertainties and unanswered questions, what did Washington do to define the American presidency and what precedents did he set for future presidents?

PROBLEM 7:
QUESTIONS FOR TEAM RESEARCH

1. Were there any models anywhere in the world in 1789 where Washington and his fellow founding fathers could look to see how the president of a democratic republic should act? If so, where and what lessons could they have learned?

2. Why were the writers of the U.S. Constitution so general and so vague about the office of president? Would it have been better if they had been very specific about the office?

3. How did Washington deal with the unforeseen development of political parties during his presidency?

4. What were some key, concrete things Washington did or didn't do which set precedents for the future and defined what the job of president was all about?

5. Where was Washington tested to determine what it meant to be "Commander-in-Chief"? What did he do, and what, if any, precedents did he establish?

PROBLEM 7:
STARTING THE SEARCH FOR EVIDENCE

INTERNET: KEY WORDS AND PHRASES

The Constitutional Convention

John Adams and the Office of President

George Washington and the Office of President

Washington's Farewell Address

BOOKS

Adams, John, *My dearest friend: Letters of Abigail and John Adams*, Cambridge, Belknap Press, 2007

Bowman, John Stewart, *The History of the American Presidency*, Edison, Chartwell Books, 1998

Cunliffe, Marcus, *The American Heritage History of the Presidency*, NY, Simon and Schuster, 1968

Cunliffe, Marcus, *George Washington, Man and Monument*, NY, New American Library, 1982

Freeman, Douglas Southhall, *Washington*, NY, Scribner, 1968

Federalist No. 69, First published in the Friday, March 14, 1788 issue of the New York Packet

The Real Character of the Executive

To the People of the State of New York:

I proceed now to trace the real characters of the proposed Executive, as they are marked out in the plan of the convention. This will serve to place in a strong light the unfairness of the representations which have been made in regard to it.

The first thing which strikes our attention is, that the executive authority, with few exceptions, is to be vested in a single magistrate. This will scarcely, however, be considered as a point upon which any comparison can be grounded; for if, in this particular, there be a resemblance to the king of Great Britain, there is not less a resemblance to the Grand Seignior, to the khan of Tartary, to the Man of the Seven Mountains, or to the governor of New York.

That magistrate is to be elected for four years; and is to be re-eligible as often as the people of the United States shall think him worthy of their confidence. In these circumstances there is a total dissimilitude between *him* and a king of Great Britain, who is an *hereditary* monarch, possessing the crown as a patrimony descendible to his heirs forever; but there is a close analogy between *him* and a governor of New York, who is elected for *three* years, and is re-eligible without limitation or intermission. If we consider how much less time would be requisite for establishing a dangerous influence in a single State, than for establishing a like influence throughout the United States, we must conclude that a duration of *four* years for the Chief Magistrate of the Union is a degree of permanency far less to be dreaded in that office, than a duration of *three* years for a corresponding office in a single State.

The President of the United States would be liable to be impeached, tried, and, upon conviction of treason, bribery, or other high crimes or misdemeanors, removed from office; and would afterwards be liable to prosecution and punishment in the ordinary course of law. The person of the king of Great Britain is sacred and inviolable; there is no constitutional tribunal to which he is amenable; no punishment to which he can be subjected without involving the crisis of a national revolution. In this delicate and important circumstance of personal responsibility, the President of Confederated America would stand upon no better ground than a governor of New York, and upon worse ground than the governors of Maryland and Delaware.

The President of the United States is to have power to return a bill, which shall have passed the two branches of the legislature, for reconsideration; and the bill so returned is to become a law, if, upon that reconsideration, it be approved by two thirds of both houses. The king of Great Britain, on his part, has an absolute negative upon the acts of the two houses of Parliament. The disuse of that power for a considerable time past does not affect the reality of its existence; and is to be ascribed wholly to the crown's having found the means of substituting influence to authority, or the art of gaining a majority in one or the other of the two houses, to the necessity of exerting a prerogative which could seldom be exerted without hazarding some degree of national agitation. The qualified negative of the President differs widely from this absolute negative of the British sovereign; and tallies exactly with the revisionary authority of the council of revision of this State, of which the governor is a constituent part. In this respect the power of the President would exceed that of the governor of New York, because the former would possess, singly, what the latter shares with the chancellor and judges; but it would be precisely the same with that of the governor of Massachusetts, whose constitution, as to this article, seems to have been the original from which the convention have copied.

The President is to be the commander-in-chief of the army and navy of the United States, and of the militia of the several States, when called into the actual service of the United States. He is to have power to grant reprieves and pardons for offenses against the United States, *except in cases of impeachment*; to recommend to the consideration of Congress such measures as he shall judge necessary and expedient; to convene, on extraordinary occasions, both houses of the legislature, or either of them, and, in case of disagreement between them *with respect to the time of adjournment*, to adjourn them to such time as he shall think proper; to take care that the laws be faithfully executed; and to commission all officers of the United States. In most of these particulars, the power of the President will resemble equally that of the king of Great Britain and of the governor of New York. The most material points of difference are these: First. The President will have only the occasional command of such part of the militia of the nation as by legislative provision may be called into the actual service of the Union. The king of Great Britain and the governor of New York have at all times the entire command of all the militia within their several jurisdictions. In this article, therefore, the power of the President would be inferior to that of either the monarch or the governor. Secondly. The President is to be commander-in-chief of the army and navy of the United States. In this respect his authority would be nominally the same with that of the king of Great Britain, but in substance much inferior to it. It would amount to nothing more than the supreme command and direction of the military and naval forces, as first General and admiral of the Confederacy; while that of the British king extends to the *declaring* of war and to the *raising* and *regulating* of fleets and armies, all which, by the Constitution under consideration, would appertain to the legislature.[1] The governor of New York, on the other hand, is by the constitution of the State vested only with the command of its militia and navy. But the constitutions of several of the States expressly declare their governors to be commanders-in-chief, as well of the army as navy; and it may well be a question, whether those of New Hampshire and Massachusetts, in particular, do not, in this instance, confer larger powers upon their respective governors, than could be claimed by a President of the United States. Thirdly. The power of the President, in respect to pardons, would extend to all cases, *except those of impeachment.* The governor of New York may pardon in all cases, even in those of impeachment, except for treason and murder. Is not the power of the governor, in this article, on a calculation of political consequences, greater than that of the President? All conspiracies and plots against the government, which have not been matured into actual treason, may be screened from punishment of every kind, by the interposition of the prerogative of pardoning. If a governor of New York, therefore, should be at the head of any such conspiracy, until the design had been ripened into actual hostility he could insure his accomplices and adherents an entire impunity. A President of the Union, on the other hand, though he may even pardon treason, when prosecuted in the ordinary course of law, could shelter no offender, in any degree, from the effects of impeachment and conviction. Would not the prospect of a total indemnity for all the preliminary steps be a greater temptation to undertake and persevere in an enterprise against the public liberty, than the mere prospect of an exemption from death and confiscation, if the final execution of the design, upon an actual appeal to arms, should miscarry? Would this last expectation have any influence at all, when the probability was computed, that the person who was to afford that exemption might himself be involved in the consequences of the measure, and might be incapacitated by his agency in it from affording the desired impunity? The better to judge of this matter, it will be necessary to recollect, that, by the proposed Constitution, the offense of treason is limited to levying war upon the United States, and adhering to their enemies, giving them aid and comfort; and that by the laws of New York it is confined within similar bounds. Fourthly. The President can only adjourn the national legislature in the single case of disagreement about the time of adjournment. The British monarch may prorogue or even dissolve the Parliament. The governor of New York may also prorogue the legislature of this State for a limited time; a power which, in certain situations, may be employed to very important purposes.

The President is to have power, with the advice and consent of the Senate, to make treaties, provided two thirds of the senators present concur. The king of Great Britain is the sole and absolute representative of the nation in all foreign transactions. He can of his own accord make treaties of peace, commerce, alliance, and of every other description. It has been insinuated, that his authority in this respect is not conclusive, and that his conventions with foreign powers are subject to the revision, and stand in need of the ratification, of Parliament. But I believe this doctrine was never heard of, until it was broached upon the present occasion. Every jurist[2] of that kingdom, and every other man acquainted with its Constitution, knows, as an established fact, that the prerogative of making treaties exists in the crown in its utmost plentitude; and that the compacts entered into by the royal authority have the most complete legal validity and perfection, independent of any other sanction. The Parliament, it is true, is sometimes seen employing itself in altering the existing laws to conform them to the stipulations in a new treaty; and this may have possibly given birth to the imagination, that its co-operation was necessary to the obligatory efficacy of the treaty. But this parliamentary interposition proceeds from a different cause: from the necessity of adjusting a most artificial and intricate system of revenue and commercial laws, to the changes made in them by the operation of the treaty; and of adapting new provisions and precautions to the new state of things, to keep the machine from running into disorder. In this respect, therefore, there is no comparison between the intended power of the President and the actual power of the British sovereign. The one can perform alone what the other can do only with the concurrence of a branch of the legislature. It must be admitted, that, in this instance, the power of the federal Executive would exceed that of any State Executive. But this arises naturally from the sovereign power which relates to treaties. If the Confederacy were to be dissolved, it would become a question, whether the Executives of the several States were not solely invested with that delicate and important prerogative.

The President is also to be authorized to receive ambassadors and other public ministers. This, though it has been a rich theme of declamation, is more a matter of dignity than of authority. It is a circumstance which will be without consequence in the administration of the government; and it was far more convenient that it should be arranged in this manner, than that there should be a necessity of convening the legislature, or one of its branches, upon every arrival of a foreign minister, though it were merely to take the place of a departed predecessor.

The President is to nominate, and, *with the advice and consent of the senate*, to appoint ambassadors and other public ministers, judges of the Supreme Court, and in general all officers of the United States established by law, and whose appointments are not otherwise provided for by the Constitution. The king of Great Britain is emphatically and truly styled the fountain of honor. He not only appoints to all offices, but can create offices. He can confer titles of nobility at pleasure; and has the disposal of an immense number of church preferments. There is evidently a great inferiority in the power of the President, in this particular, to that of the British king; nor is it equal to that of the governor of New York, if we are to interpret the meaning of the constitution of the State by the practice which has obtained under it. The power of appointment is with us lodged in a council, composed of the governor and four members of the Senate, chosen by the Assembly. The governor *claims*, and has frequently *exercised*, the right of nomination, and is *entitled* to a casting vote in the appointment. If he really has the right of nominating, his authority is in this respect equal to that of the President, and exceeds it in the article of the casting vote. In the national government, if the Senate should be divided, no appointment could be made; in the government of New York, if the council should be divided, the governor can turn the scale, and confirm his own nomination.[3] If we compare the publicity which must necessarily attend the mode of appointment by the President and an entire branch of the national legislature, with the privacy in the mode of appointment by the governor of New York, closeted in a secret apartment with at most four, and frequently with only two persons; and if we at the same time consider how much more easy it must be to influence the small number of which a council of appointment consists, than the considerable number of which the national Senate would consist, we cannot hesitate to pronounce that the power of the chief magistrate of this State, in the disposition of offices, must, in practice, be greatly superior to that of the Chief Magistrate of the Union.

Hence it appears that, except as to the concurrent authority of the President in the article of treaties, it would be difficult to determine whether that magistrate would, in the aggregate, possess more or less power than the Governor of New York. And it appears yet more unequivocally, that there is no pretense for the parallel which has been attempted between him and the king of Great Britain. But to render the contrast in this respect still more striking, it may be of use to throw the principal circumstances of dissimilitude into a closer group.

The President of the United States would be an officer elected by the people for *four* years; the king of Great Britain is a perpetual and *hereditary* prince. The one would be amenable to personal punishment and disgrace; the person of the other is sacred and inviolable. The one would have a *qualified* negative upon the acts of the legislative body; the other has an *absolute* negative. The one would have a right to command the military and naval forces of the nation; the other, in addition to this right, possesses that of *declaring* war, and of *raising* and *regulating* fleets and armies by his own authority. The one would have a concurrent power with a branch of the legislature in the formation of treaties; the other is the *sole possessor* of the power of making treaties. The one would have a like concurrent authority in appointing to offices; the other is the sole author of all appointments. The one can confer no privileges whatever; the other can make denizens of aliens, noblemen of commoners; can erect corporations with all the rights incident to corporate bodies. The one can prescribe no rules concerning the commerce or currency of the nation; the other is in several respects the arbiter of commerce, and in this capacity can establish markets and fairs, can regulate weights and measures, can lay embargoes for a limited time, can coin money, can authorize or prohibit the circulation of foreign coin. The one has no particle of spiritual jurisdiction; the other is the supreme head and governor of the national church! What answer shall we give to those who would persuade us that things so unlike resemble each other? The same that ought to be given to those who tell us that a government, the whole power of which would be in the hands of the elective and periodical servants of the people, is an aristocracy, a monarchy, and a despotism.

[SIGNED] PUBLIUS. (ALEXANDER HAMILTON)

1. A writer in a Pennsylvania paper, under the signature of *Tamony*, has asserted that the king of Great Britain owes his prerogative as commander-in-chief to an annual mutiny bill. The truth is, on the contrary, that his prerogative, in this respect, is immemorial, and was only disputed, contrary to all reason and precedent, as Blackstone vol. i., page 262, expresses it, by the Long Parliament of Charles I. but by the statute the 13th of Charles II., chap. 6, it was declared to be in the king alone, for that the sole supreme government and command of the militia within his Majesty's realms and dominions, and of all forces by sea and land, and of all forts and places of strength, *ever was and is* the undoubted right of his Majesty and his royal predecessors, kings and queens of England, and that both or either house of Parliament cannot nor ought to pretend to the same.

2. Vide Blackstone's "Commentaries," vol i., p. 257.

3. Candor, however, demands an acknowledgment that I do not think the claim of the governor to a right of nomination well founded. Yet it is always justifiable to reason from the practice of a government, till its propriety has been constitutionally questioned. And independent of this claim, when we take into view the other considerations, and pursue them through all their consequences, we shall be inclined to draw much the same conclusion.

PROBLEM 7:
CONNECTION TO TODAY

1. How would our history be different if Washington had decided to stay in for a third term or remain as president for life?

2. How have the development of political parties changed the definition and job of being president of the United States?

3. What are some things that presidents in our time do that Washington didn't do or couldn't do?

4. Was Washington's decision to be president for only two terms a good or bad thing for his time? What about for our time?

5. Are modern U.S. presidents too powerful? Explain.

6. Have presidents in our time ever gone beyond the U.S. Constitution in terms of what powers they have exercised? Explain.

PROBLEM 8:
JEFFERSON, HAMILTON, AND THE GREAT AMERICAN QUESTION: WHAT SHOULD GOVERNMENT DO?

LEFT:
THOMAS JEFFERSON

RIGHT:
ALEXANDER HAMILTON

PROBLEM 8: JEFFERSON, HAMILTON, AND THE GREAT AMERICAN QUESTION: WHAT SHOULD GOVERNMENT DO?

*T*oday our two major political parties, the Democrats and Republicans, portray themselves as entities that embrace two fundamentally conflicting philosophies regarding the role of government. Both parties believe their approach ultimately benefits the entire country, but those benefits are derived in dramatically different ways. Today's Democrats believe government has an important active role to play. For them government must act as a society equalizer and do things that people cannot do for themselves. They seek to eliminate barriers, such as discrimination, and check what they believe are the inevitable abuses of unregulated and uncontrolled capitalism. The Republicans argue that too much government involvement stifles individualism and creativity; they believe that a minimally regulated free market provides maximum opportunities for all individuals to achieve in a free democratic society.

The philosophical positions of our political parties today have not always remained constant and have changed as conditions in the country have changed. Political parties have been created and have disappeared even though our Constitution did not anticipate or make any provisions for them. But where and why did parties begin this divergence regarding the proper role of government? As President, George Washington sought to have men of different views at his side to provide advice and counsel; his two key advisers were Thomas Jefferson, who served as secretary of state, and Alexander Hamilton, who served as secretary of the treasury. Thomas Jefferson, the aristocrat, and Alexander Hamilton, a man born of humble origins, represented two very different views of what the role of this new government should be. Their views and disputes would set a tone for political debate that remains with us today. The following statements by each of these men can put the problem in context.

Alexander Hamilton: "All communities divide themselves into the few and the many. The first are the rich and wellborn, the other the mass of the people…The people are turbulent and changing, they seldom judge or determine right. Give therefore to the first class a distinct permanent share in the government. They will check the unsteadiness of the second, and as they cannot receive any advantage by change, they therefore will ever maintain good government."

Thomas Jefferson: "A wise and frugal government which shall restrain men from injuring one another, which shall leave them otherwise free to regulate their own pursuits of industry and improvement, and shall not take from the mouth of labor the bread it has earned—this is the sum of good government…Sometimes it is said that man can not be trusted with the government of himself. Can he, then, be trusted with the government of others?"

How were these two different approaches resolved at the beginning of our nation's history? And what has been the evolution and legacy of this debate in our subsequent history?

PROBLEM 8:
QUESTIONS FOR TEAM RESEARCH

1. Did the origins and social class of Jefferson and Hamilton in any way shape their philosophy of government?

2. How did President Washington attempt to handle these two cabinet members with very different political views? Did he succeed?

3. What were the political consequences of this philosophical split?

4. What government philosophy best characterizes the administrations of George Washington and John Adams?

5. Which approach, Jefferson's or Hamilton's, was more acceptable for the time? What evidence do we have to support your position?

6. The two positions depict a differing view of human nature. What influenced both men in their lives and in the environment in which they lived to come to such fundamentally different conclusions?

PROBLEM 8:
STARTING THE SEARCH FOR EVIDENCE

INTERNET: KEY WORDS AND PHRASES

Alexander Hamilton and the Constitution

Thomas Jefferson and the Constitution

The origin of American political parties

The Federalists and the Democratic Republicans

BOOKS

Bishop, Arthur, ed, *Thomas Jefferson, 1743–1826: Chronological Documents–Bibliographical Aids*, Dobbs Ferry, Oceana Publications, 1971

Brookhiser, Richard, *Alexander Hamilton, American*, NY, Free Press, 1999

Hamilton, Alexander, *Writings*, NY, Library of America, 2001

Jefferson, Thomas, *The Life and Selected Writings of Thomas Jefferson*, NY, Modern Library, 1944

Koch, Adrienne, *The Philosophy of Thomas Jefferson*, NY, Columbia University Press, 1943

Alexander Hamilton: Discussion of the New Jersey and Virginia Plans, June 18, 1787

Mr. Hamilton. To deliver my sentiments on so important a subject, when the first characters in the union have gone before me, inspires me with the greatest diffidence, especially when my own ideas are so materially dissimilar to the plans now before the committee. My situation is disagreeable, but it would be criminal not to come forward on a question of such magnitude. I have well considered the subject, and am convinced that no amendment of the confederation can answer the purpose of a good government, so long as state sovereignties do, in any shape, exist; and I have great doubts whether a national government on the Virginia plan can be made effectual....

Let us take a review of the variety of important objects, which must necessarily engage the attention of a national government. You have to protect your rights against Canada on the north, Spain on the south, and your western frontier against the savages. You have to adopt necessary plan for the settlement of your frontiers, and to institute the mode in which settlements and good government are to be made.

How is the expense of supporting and regulating these important matters to be defrayed? By requisition on the states, according to the Jersey plan? Will this do it? We have already found it ineffectual. Let one state prove delinquent, and it will encourage others to follow the example; and thus the whole will fail. And what is the standard to quota among the states their respective proportions? Can lands be the standard? How would that apply between Russia and Holland? Compare Pennsylvania with North-Carolina, or Connecticut with New-York. Does not commerce or industry in the one or other make a great disparity between these different countries, and may not the comparative value of the states from these circumstances, make an unequal disproportion when the data is numbers? I therefore conclude that either system would ultimately destroy the confederation, or any other government which is established on such fallacious principles. Perhaps imposts, taxes on specific articles, would produce a more equal system of drawing a revenue.

Another objection against the Jersey plan is, the unequal representation. Can the great States consent to this? If they did it would eventually work its own destruction.

How are forces to be raised by the Jersey plan? By quotas? Will the states comply with the requisition? As much as they will with the taxes.

Examine the present confederation, and it is evident they can raise no troops nor equip vessels before war is actually declared. They cannot therefore take any preparatory measure before an enemy is at your door. How unwise and inadequate their powers! and this must ever be the case when you attempt to define powers. Something will always be wanting. Congress, by being annually elected, and subject to recall, will ever come with the prejudices of their states rather than the good of the union. Add therefore additional powers to a body thus organized, and you establish a *sovereignty* of the worst kind, consisting of a single body. Where are the checks? None. They must either prevail over the state governments, or the prevalence of the state governments must end in their dissolution. This is a conclusive objection to the Jersey plan.

Such are the insuperable objections to both plans: and what is to be done on this occasion? I confess I am at a loss. I foresee the difficulty on a consolidated plan of drawing a representation from so extensive a continent to one place. What can be the inducements for gentlemen to come 600 miles to a national legislature? The expense would at least amount to £100,000. This however can be no conclusive objection if it eventuates in an extinction of state governments. The burthen of the latter would be saved, and the expense then would not be great. State distinctions would be found unnecessary, and yet I confess, to carry government to the extremities, the state governments reduced to corporations, and with very limited powers, might be necessary, and the expense of the national government become less burthensome.

Yet, I confess, I see great difficulty of drawing forth a good representation. What, for example, will be the inducements for gentlemen of fortune and abilities to leave their houses and business to attend annually and long? It cannot be the wages; for these, I presume, must be small. Will not the power, therefore, be thrown into the hands of the demagogue or middling politician, who, for the sake of a small stipend and the hopes of advancement, will offer himself as a candidate, and the real men of weight and influence, by remaining at home, add strength to the state governments? I am at a loss to know what must be done; I despair that a republican form of government can remove the difficulties. Whatever may be my opinion, I would hold it however unwise to change that form of government. I believe the British government forms the best model the world ever produced, and such has been its progress in the minds of the many, that this truth gradually gains ground. This government has for its object *public strength* and *individual security.* It is said with us to be unattainable. If it was once formed it would maintain itself. All communities divide themselves into the few and the many. The first are the rich and well born, the other the mass of the people. The voice of the people has been said to be the voice of God; and however generally this maxim has been quoted and believed, it is not true in fact. The people are turbulent and changing; they seldom judge or determine right. Give therefore to the first class a distinct, permanent share in the government. They will check the unsteadiness of the second, and as they cannot receive any advantage by a change, they therefore will ever maintain good government. Can a democratic assembly, who annually revolve in the mass of the people, be supposed steadily to pursue the public good? Nothing but a permanent body can check the imprudence of democracy. Their turbulent and un-controuling disposition requires checks. The senate of New-York, although chosen for four years, we have found to be inefficient. Will, on the Virginia plan, a continuance of seven years do it? It is admitted, that you cannot have a good executive upon a democratic plan. See the excellency of the British executive. He is placed above temptation. He can have no distinct interests from the public welfare. Nothing short of such an executive can be efficient. The weak side of a republican government is the danger of foreign influence. This is unavoidable, unless it is so constructed as to bring forward its first characters in its support. I am therefore for a general government, yet would wish to go the full length of republican principles.

Let one body of the legislature be constituted during good behaviour or life.

Let one executive be appointed who dares execute his powers.

It may be asked is this a republican system? It is strictly so, as long as they remain elective.

And let me observe, that an executive is less dangerous to the liberties of the people when in office during life, than for seven years....

• • •

Thomas Jefferson's Correspondence with Elbridge Gerry on the Proper Role of Government, January 26, 1799 (Selections)

...I do then, with sincere zeal, wish an inviolable preservation of our present federal constitution, according to the true sense in which it was adopted by the States, that in which it was advocated by it's friends, & not that which it's enemies apprehended, who therefore became it's enemies; and I am opposed to the monarchising it's features by the forms of it's administration, with a view to conciliate a first transition to a President & Senate for life, & from that to a hereditary tenure of these offices, & thus to worm out the elective principle. I am for preserving to the States the powers not yielded by them to the Union, & to the legislature of the Union it's constitutional share in the division of powers; and I am not for transferring all the powers of the States to the general government. & all those of that government to the Executive branch. I am for a government rigorously frugal & simple, applying all the possible savings of the public revenue to the discharge of the national debt; and not for a multiplication of officers & salaries merely to make partisans, & for increasing, by every device, the public debt, on the principle of it's being a public blessing. I am for relying, for internal defence, on our militia solely, till actual invasion, and for such a naval force only as may protect our coasts and harbors from such depredations as we have experienced; and not for a standing army in time of peace, which may overawe the public sentiment; nor for a navy, which, by it's own expenses and the eternal wars in which it will implicate us, will grind us with public burthens, & sink us under them. I am for free commerce with all nations; political connection with none; & little or no diplomatic establishment. And I am not for linking ourselves by new treaties with the quarrels of Europe; entering that field of slaughter to preserve their balance, or joining in the confederacy of kings to war against the principles of liberty. I am for freedom of religion, & against all maneuvres to bring about a legal ascendancy of one sect over another: for freedom of the press, & against all violations of the constitution to silence by force & not by reason the complaints or criticisms, just or unjust, of our citizens against the conduct of their agents. And I am for encouraging the progress of science in all it's branches; and not for raising a hue and cry against the sacred name of philosophy; for awing the human mind by stories of raw-head & bloody bones to a distrust of its own vision, & to repose implicitly on that of others; to go backwards instead of forwards to look for improvement; to believe that government, religion, morality, & every other science were in the highest perfection in ages of the darkest ignorance, and that nothing can ever be devised more perfect than what was established by our forefathers. To these I will add, that I was a sincere well-wisher to the success of the French revolution, and still wish it may end in the establishment of a free & well-ordered republic; but I have not been insensible under the atrocious depredations they have committed on our commerce. The first object of my heart is my own country. In that is embarked my family, my fortune, & my own existence. I have not one farthing of interest, nor one fibre of attachment out of it, nor a single motive of preference of any one nation to another, but in proportion as they are more or less friendly to us. But though deeply feeling the injuries of France, I did not think war the surest means of redressing them. I did believe, that a mission sincerely disposed to preserve peace, would obtain for us a peaceable & honorable settlement & retribution; and I appeal to you to say, whether this might not have been obtained, if either of your colleagues had been of the same sentiment with yourself.

These, my friend, are my principles; they are unquestionably the principles of the great body of our fellow citizens....

PROBLEM 8:
CONNECTION TO TODAY

1. Thomas Jefferson is today considered the founder of the present day Democratic Party. Are his views consistent with those of present day Democrats? If so, how? If not, why not?

2. Hamilton's Federalist Party ultimately disappeared from the American political scene. How and why did this happen? What party became its successor? Is today's Republican Party the heir of Hamilton? Is so, how? If not, why not?

3. Why have parties died in our country?

4. What has been the role, impact, and life of third parties or minor political parties in our history?

5. Why do we in America not have five, ten, or more political parties as do other countries in the world?

6. Which position regarding government, Jefferson's or Hamilton's, do you mostly agree with? What are the arguments regarding today's politics you could use to defend your position?

PROBLEM 9:

WHY DID THE ELECTION OF 1800 TURN OUT NOT TO BE WHAT JEFFERSON BELIEVED WAS "THE REVOLUTION OF 1800"?

LEFT: JOHN ADAMS

RIGHT:
AN ANTI-JEFFERSON CARTOON IN 1800, SHOWING THE AMERICAN EAGLE ATTEMPTING TO STOP JEFFERSON FROM VIOLATING THE CONSTITUTION.

THE PROVIDENTIAL DETECTION

Courtesy of the Ridgway Library, Philadelphia

Anonymous cartoon, showing the American Eagle, symbolizing patriotism, preventing Jefferson from sacrificing the "Constitution & Independence" of America on the "Altar of Gallic Despotism." The "Eye of God" and the letter to Mazzei, which drops from Jefferson's hand, indicate that his un-American principles have been finally unmasked, while the writings that feed the fire on the altar—Rousseau's, Paine's, Godwin's, Volney's, Helvetius'—show his principles to be French and atheistic. The print appeared *c.* 1800.

PROBLEM 9: WHY DID THE ELECTION OF 1800 TURN OUT NOT TO BE WHAT JEFFERSON BELIEVED WAS "THE REVOLUTION OF 1800"?

As the nation approached the presidential election of 1800, political parties, which the Constitution had not anticipated, had taken full shape. The Federalists staked out their position as the party that favored a strong, active central government; believed in a broad interpretation of the U.S. Constitution; and generally was pro-English in its view of foreign relations. The opposition party, the Democratic-Republicans, believed in a limited federal government, took a narrow view of how the Constitution should be read, and was pro-French in its foreign relations position. Alexander Hamilton and John Adams were leading figures for the Federalists, while Thomas Jefferson and James Madison led the Democratic-Republicans. The election of 1800 became a battle between the two parties and two very different philosophies of government. After a spirited and vicious campaign, the election was thrown into the House of Representatives, and Thomas Jefferson was finally elected the third president of the United States. This election marked the first time in our history that one political party had deposed the rule of a different party, and the Federalists never fully recovered from the loss. Eventually they disappeared from the American political landscape.

Jefferson himself believed his election constituted a bloodless political revolution in which a new philosophy and new ideas would govern America. He said, "The revolution of 1800 was as real a revolution in principles of government as that of 1776 was in its form."

Was Jefferson right to believe he had initiated a political revolution? How can we judge what he said against what he did as president? Some historians believe that the America Jefferson left when his two terms as president ended was not much different from the America he lived in during the election of 1800. Why did Jefferson's election turn out not to be the "Revolution of 1800?"

PROBLEM 9:
QUESTIONS FOR TEAM RESEARCH

1. How important were the philosophical differences about the role of government as issues in the election of 1800?

2. What impact did the personalities and character of the candidates have in the election?

3. Did the way Jefferson achieved the presidency have any impact on his ability to govern? If so, why and how?

4. As president, what did Jefferson find regarding the conflict between political beliefs and practical governing?

5. In what ways was Jefferson correct in believing his election set a new and different national direction?

PROBLEM 9:
STARTING THE SEARCH FOR EVIDENCE

INTERNET: KEY WORDS AND PHRASES

The election of 1800

The revolution of 1800

Thomas Jefferson's Inaugural Address

The presidency of Thomas Jefferson

BOOKS

Dunn, Susan, *Jefferson's Second Revolution: The Election of 1800 and the Triumph of Republicanism*, Boston, Houghton Mifflin, 2004

Ferling, John, *Adams vs. Jefferson: The Tumultuous Election of 1800*, NY, Oxford University Press, 2004

Larsen, Edward, *A Magnificent Catastrophe: The Tumultuous Election of 1800: America's First Presidential Campaign*, NY, Free Press, 2007

Pierce, Neal, *The People's President: The Electoral College in American History and the Direct Vote Alternative*, NY, Simon and Schuster, 1968

Weisberger, Bernard, *America Afire: Jefferson, Adams, and the Revolutionary Election of 1800*, NY, William Morrow, 2000

President Thomas Jefferson's First Inaugural Address, March 4, 1801 (Full Text)

Friends and Fellow-Citizens:

Called upon to undertake the duties of the first executive office of our country, I avail myself of the presence of that portion of my fellow-citizens which is here assembled to express my grateful thanks for the favor with which they have been pleased to look toward me, to declare a sincere consciousness that the task is above my talents, and that I approach it with those anxious and awful presentiments which the greatness of the charge and the weakness of my powers so justly inspire. A rising nation, spread over a wide and fruitful land, traversing all the seas with the rich productions of their industry, engaged in commerce with nations who feel power and forget right, advancing rapidly to destinies beyond the reach of mortal eye—when I contemplate these transcendent objects, and see the honor, the happiness, and the hopes of this beloved country committed to the issue, and the auspices of this day, I shrink from the contemplation, and humble myself before the magnitude of the undertaking. Utterly, indeed, should I despair did not the presence of many whom I here see remind me that in the other high authorities provided by our Constitution I shall find resources of wisdom, of virtue, and of zeal on which to rely under all difficulties. To you, then, gentlemen, who are charged with the sovereign functions of legislation, and to those associated with you, I look with encouragement for that guidance and support which may enable us to steer with safety the vessel in which we are all embarked amidst the conflicting elements of a troubled world.

During the contest of opinion through which we have passed the animation of discussions and of exertions has sometimes worn an aspect which might impose on strangers unused to think freely and to speak and to write what they think; but this being now decided by the voice of the nation, announced according to the rules of the Constitution, all will, of course, arrange themselves under the will of the law, and unite in common efforts for the common good. All, too, will bear in mind this sacred principle, that though the will of the majority is in all cases to prevail, that will to be rightful must be reasonable; that the minority possess their equal rights, which equal law must protect, and to violate would be oppression. Let us, then, fellow-citizens, unite with one heart and one mind. Let us restore to social intercourse that harmony and affection without which liberty and even life itself are but dreary things. And let us reflect that, having banished from our land that religious intolerance under which mankind so long bled and suffered, we have yet gained little if we countenance a political intolerance as despotic, as wicked, and capable of as bitter and bloody persecutions. During the throes and convulsions of the ancient world, during the agonizing spasms of infuriated man, seeking through blood and slaughter his long-lost liberty, it was not wonderful that the agitation of the billows should reach even this distant and peaceful shore; that this should be more felt and feared by some and less by others, and should divide opinions as to measures of safety. But every difference of opinion is not a difference of principle. We have called by different names brethren of the same principle. We are all Republicans, we are all Federalists. If there be any among us who would wish to dissolve this Union or to change its republican form, let them stand undisturbed as monuments of the safety with which error of opinion may be tolerated where reason is left free to combat it. I know, indeed, that some honest men fear that a republican government can not be strong, that this Government is not strong enough; but would the honest patriot, in the full tide of successful experiment, abandon a government which has so far kept us free and firm on the theoretic and visionary fear that this Government, the world's best hope, may by possibility want energy to preserve itself? I trust not. I believe this, on the contrary, the strongest Government on earth. I believe it the only one where every man, at the call of the law, would fly to the standard of the law, and would meet invasions of the public order as his own personal concern. Sometimes it is said that man can not be trusted with the government of himself. Can he, then, be trusted with the government of others? Or have we found angels in the forms of kings to govern him? Let history answer this question.

Let us, then, with courage and confidence pursue our own Federal and Republican principles, our attachment to union and representative government. Kindly separated by nature and a wide ocean from the exterminating havoc of one quarter of the globe; too high-minded to endure the degradations of the others; possessing a chosen country, with room enough for our descendants to the thousandth and thousandth generation; entertaining a due sense of our equal right to the use of our own faculties, to the acquisitions of our own industry, to honor and confidence from our fellow-citizens, resulting not from birth, but from our actions and their sense of them; enlightened by a benign religion, professed, indeed, and practiced in various forms, yet all of them inculcating honesty, truth, temperance, gratitude, and the love of man; acknowledging and adoring an overruling Providence, which by all its dispensations proves that it delights in the happiness of man here and his greater happiness hereafter—with all these blessings, what more is necessary to make us a happy and a prosperous people? Still one thing more, fellow-citizens—a wise and frugal Government, which shall restrain men from injuring one another, shall leave them otherwise free to regulate their own pursuits of industry and improvement, and shall not take from the mouth of labor the bread it has earned. This is the sum of good government, and this is necessary to close the circle of our felicities.

About to enter, fellow-citizens, on the exercise of duties which comprehend everything dear and valuable to you, it is proper you should understand what I deem the essential principles of our Government, and consequently those which ought to shape its Administration. I will compress them within the narrowest compass they will bear, stating the general principle, but not all its limitations. Equal and exact justice to all men, of whatever state or persuasion, religious or political; peace, commerce, and honest friendship with all nations, entangling alliances with none; the support of the State governments in all their rights, as the most competent administrations for our domestic concerns and the surest bulwarks against antirepublican tendencies; the preservation of the General Government in its whole constitutional vigor, as the sheet anchor of our peace at home and safety abroad; a jealous care of the right of election by the people—a mild and safe corrective of abuses which are lopped by the sword of revolution where peaceable remedies are unprovided; absolute acquiescence in the decisions of the majority, the vital principle of republics, from which is no appeal but to force, the vital principle and immediate parent of despotism; a well disciplined militia, our best reliance in peace and for the first moments of war, till regulars may relieve them; the supremacy of the civil over the military authority; economy in the public expense, that labor may be lightly burthened; the honest payment of our debts and sacred preservation of the public faith; encouragement of agriculture, and of commerce as its handmaid; the diffusion of information and arraignment of all abuses at the bar of the public reason; freedom of religion; freedom of the press, and freedom of person under the protection of the habeas corpus, and trial by juries impartially selected. These principles form the bright constellation which has gone before us and guided our steps through an age of revolution and reformation. The wisdom of our sages and blood of our heroes have been devoted to their attainment. They should be the creed of our political faith, the text of civic instruction, the touchstone by which to try the services of those we trust; and should we wander from them in moments of error or of alarm, let us hasten to retrace our steps and to regain the road which alone leads to peace, liberty, and safety.

I repair, then, fellow-citizens, to the post you have assigned me. With experience enough in subordinate offices to have seen the difficulties of this the greatest of all, I have learnt to expect that it will rarely fall to the lot of imperfect man to retire from this station with the reputation and the favor which bring him into it. Without pretensions to that high confidence you reposed in our first and greatest revolutionary character, whose preeminent services had entitled him to the first place in his country's love and destined for him the fairest page in the volume of faithful history, I ask so much confidence only as may give firmness and effect to the legal administration of your affairs. I shall often go wrong through defect of judgment. When right, I shall often be thought wrong by those whose positions will not command a view of the whole ground. I ask your indulgence for my own errors, which will never be intentional, and your support against the errors of others, who may condemn what they would not if seen in all its parts. The approbation implied by your suffrage is a great consolation to me for the past, and my future solicitude will be to retain the good opinion of those who have bestowed it in advance, to conciliate that of others by doing them all the good in my power, and to be instrumental to the happiness and freedom of all.

Relying, then, on the patronage of your good will, I advance with obedience to the work, ready to retire from it whenever you become sensible how much better choice it is in your power to make. And may that Infinite Power which rules the destinies of the universe lead our councils to what is best, and give them a favorable issue for your peace and prosperity.

PROBLEM 9:
CONNECTION TO TODAY

1. Did the campaign tactics of the two parties in 1800 set the tone for what American campaigns are today?

2. How really different are our two political parties today? Does it matter in any way?

3. What role did the candidates themselves have on the outcome of the election of 1800? What role does the candidate have today? Is the particular candidate more or less important than positions or political party?

4. Why do presidents sometimes find that they have to do things when they become president that they were against as a candidate for president? Are there any recent examples?

5. Does compromise on issues by a president mean that he has violated his word or campaign promises? What are the alternatives?

PROBLEM 10:
WHAT SHOULD BE DONE WITH THE INDIANS?

NATIVE AMERICANS BEING REMOVED FROM THEIR LAND

PROBLEM 10: WHAT SHOULD BE DONE WITH THE INDIANS?

Our history books talk about the discovery of America, but, of course, what is really meant is the discovery of a continent by white Europeans. North and South America had been there and been inhabited by people long before Europeans found out about those lands.

The immediate result of the contact between Europeans and Native Americans, who became known as Indians, was cultural clash. Because of race, history, tradition, language, ways of life, spirituality, and technological advancement, there was little that these two groups had in common. Contact often resulted in conflict in the earlier years of European settlement. And if the Indian tribes were not negatively impacted by war, they were often defeated by the spread of new European diseases, for which they had developed no natural immunity.

As the European population grew and expanded geographically, the country increasingly spoke about the Indian Problem. Simply put, the Europeans' problem with the Indians arose because the tribes had large tracts of land, and the white settlers wanted that land. In the view of most Americans, after the creation of the new nation, the Indian nations were standing in the way of what they defined as progress. The most forceful advocate of this view was Andrew Jackson from the western state of Tennessee.

As a military man Jackson had led troops to fight and defeat the Indians and, through war and negotiation as well, acquire millions of acres of Indian land to make available to white settlers. After becoming president, Jackson then supported legislation, called the Indian Removal Act of 1830, that gave the President the power to negotiate treaties to remove Indians east of the Mississippi River from their lands. By the terms of these treaties, the tribes would give up their lands east of the Mississippi in exchange for lands west of that river. Such a law, it was believed, would open up vast new areas for American settlers, be fair to Indians, avoid open conflict, and not impact American migration because few believed Americans would ever settle west of the Mississippi River. The results of the law were mixed. Some Indians moved peacefully while others resisted. For many Indians the results were devastating, the most famous example being the Trail of Tears, in which 4,000 Cherokee people died from exposure to cold temperatures, starvation, and disease as they were forcibly removed from their lands in the east to western destinations.

Was such a policy inevitable? Why did things turn out this way for American Indians? Were there some possible alternative policies that might have been pursued? When one thinks of the possible options in addressing the question of what to do with the Indians, at least six possibilities come to mind. For example:

1. Annihilate them—Through war and disease continue the reduction of their numbers until they ceased to exist or were too small in numbers to pose any threat or resistance.
2. Remove them—This is what was attempted, but how far could this eventually go—to the Pacific Ocean?
3. Assimilate them—Teach them European ways, intermarry with them, and build communities in which they were an integral part? This approach was much more widespread in Central and South America.
4. Enslave them—After all, this is what had been done to African Americans, and it would have eliminated the issue of who owned what property.
5. Negotiate with them—This might have entailed paying a fair price for their land or paying for only a part of the land and allowing the Indians to retain the rest, thus eliminating the cause for removal.
6. Leave them alone—This would have meant, if not mixing, at least living side by side as two separate nations in a given area, much as European countries do.

Which of these approaches could have and should have been taken? What were the workable options in answering the question what should we do about the Indians?

PROBLEM 10:
QUESTIONS FOR TEAM RESEARCH

1. What was the predominant attitude of the English settlers regarding the Native Americans?

2. What was Andrew Jackson's view of the Indians?

3. Was the Indian Removal Act of 1830 a viable piece of legislation? How long did it last? Was it replaced by anything regarding U.S. policy toward Indians?

4. Why was the experience in Central and South America with the Indians so much different than what happened in North America?

5. What are the positive and negative aspects in each of the possible options presented in regard to how we could have addressed the Indian issue?

PROBLEM 10:
STARTING THE SEARCH FOR EVIDENCE

INTERNET: KEY WORDS AND PHRASES

Andrew Jackson and Indian Removal

Indian Removal Act: Primary Documents of American History

Andrew Jackson and the Supreme Court

Native American "Trail of Tears"

Cherokee Indians

BOOKS

Green, Michael, *Voices from the Trail of Tears*, Winston-Salem, North Carolina, John F. Blair Publisher, 2006

Brands, H. W., *Andrew Jackson: His Life and Times*, NY, Anchor Book, 2006

Meacham, John, *American Lion: Andrew Jackson in the White House*, NY, NY Times Notable Books, 2009

Remini, Robert, *Andrew Jackson*, NY, Palgrave MacMillan, 2008

Rozema, Vicki, ed., *Voices from the Trail of Tears*, Winston-Salem, North Carolina, John F. Blair Publisher, 2006

President Andrew Jackson's Message on Indian Removal, 1830 (Full Text)

It gives me pleasure to announce to Congress that the benevolent policy of the Government, steadily pursued for nearly thirty years, in relation to the removal of the Indians beyond the white settlements is approaching to a happy consummation. Two important tribes have accepted the provision made for their removal at the last session of Congress, and it is believed that their example will induce the remaining tribes also to seek the same obvious advantages.

The consequences of a speedy removal will be important to the United States, to individual States, and to the Indians themselves. The pecuniary advantages which it promises to the Government are the least of its recommendations. It puts an end to all possible danger of collision between the authorities of the General and State Governments on account of the Indians. It will place a dense and civilized population in large tracts of country now occupied by a few savage hunters. By opening the whole territory between Tennessee on the north and Louisiana on the south to the settlement of the whites it will incalculably strengthen the southwestern frontier and render the adjacent States strong enough to repel future invasions without remote aid. It will relieve the whole State of Mississippi and the western part of Alabama of Indian occupancy, and enable those States to advance rapidly in population, wealth, and power. It will separate the Indians from immediate contact with settlements of whites; free them from the power of the States; enable them to pursue happiness in their own way and under their own rude institutions; will retard the progress of decay, which is lessening their numbers, and perhaps cause them gradually, under the protection of the Government and through the influence of good counsels, to cast off their savage habits and become an interesting, civilized, and Christian community.

What good man would prefer a country covered with forests and ranged by a few thousand savages to our extensive Republic, studded with cities, towns, and prosperous farms embellished with all the improvements which art can devise or industry execute, occupied by more than 12,000,000 happy people, and filled with all the blessings of liberty, civilization and religion?

The present policy of the Government is but a continuation of the same progressive change by a milder process. The tribes which occupied the countries now constituting the Eastern States were annihilated or have melted away to make room for the whites. The waves of population and civilization are rolling to the westward, and we now propose to acquire the countries occupied by the red men of the South and West by a fair exchange, and, at the expense of the United States, to send them to land where their existence may be prolonged and perhaps made perpetual. Doubtless it will be painful to leave the graves of their fathers; but what do they more than our ancestors did or than our children are now doing? To better their condition in an unknown land our forefathers left all that was dear in earthly objects. Our children by thousands yearly leave the land of their birth to seek new homes in distant regions. Does Humanity weep at these painful separations from everything, animate and inanimate, with which the young heart has become entwined? Far from it. It is rather a source of joy that our country affords scope where our young population may range unconstrained in body or in mind, developing the power and facilities of man in their highest perfection. These remove hundreds and almost thousands of miles at their own expense, purchase the lands they occupy, and support themselves at their new homes from the moment of their arrival. Can it be cruel in this Government when, by events which it can not control, the Indian is made discontented in his ancient home to purchase his lands, to give him a new and extensive territory, to pay the expense of his removal, and support him a year in his new abode? How many thousands of our own people would gladly embrace the opportunity of removing to the West on such conditions! If the offers made to the Indians were extended to them, they would be hailed with gratitude and joy.

And is it supposed that the wandering savage has a stronger attachment to his home than the settled, civilized Christian? Is it more afflicting to him to leave the graves of his fathers than it is to our brothers and children? Rightly considered, the policy of the General Government toward the red man is not only liberal, but generous. He is unwilling to submit to the laws of the States and mingle with their population. To save him from this alternative, or perhaps utter annihilation, the General Government kindly offers him a new home, and proposes to pay the whole expense of his removal and settlement.

PROBLEM 10:
CONNECTION TO TODAY

1. What does this problem tell us about 19th century American views regarding race? Are those attitudes present today? Against blacks? Asians? Native Americans?

2. What are the numbers and socio-economic conditions of American Indians today? Where do they live? Are their numbers increasing or decreasing? Are the conditions today a legacy of past policies?

3. What is the origin of the Indian Reservation system? What is U.S. policy toward Indian nations today? Is this policy a continuation of the historical past?

4. Is the granting of casino licenses to certain Indian tribes a form of "reparations" to them because of past U.S. policy?

5. Should U.S. policy today keep the reservations, disband them, or move to totally assimilate American Indians?

PROBLEM 11: WHY WAS THERE NO SUSTAINED, LARGE-SCALE BLACK REVOLUTION AGAINST THEIR MORE THAN TWO HUNDRED YEARS STATUS AS AMERICAN SLAVES?

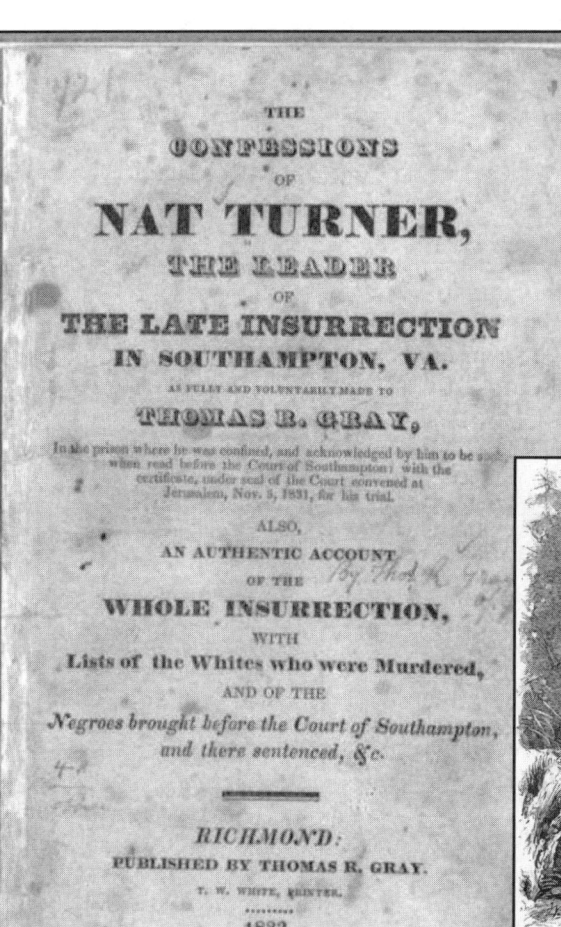

THE
CONFESSIONS
OF
NAT TURNER,
THE LEADER
OF
THE LATE INSURRECTION
IN SOUTHAMPTON, VA.

AS FULLY AND VOLUNTARILY MADE TO
THOMAS R. GRAY,

In the prison where he was confined, and acknowledged by him to be
when read before the Court of Southampton; with the
certificate, under seal of the Court convened at
Jerusalem, Nov. 5, 1831, for his trial.

ALSO,
AN AUTHENTIC ACCOUNT
OF THE
WHOLE INSURRECTION,
WITH
Lists of the Whites who were Murdered,
AND OF THE
Negroes brought before the Court of Southampton,
and there sentenced, &c.

RICHMOND:
PUBLISHED BY THOMAS R. GRAY.
T. W. WHITE, PRINTER.
1832.

LEFT:
NAT TURNER'S ACCOUNT OF THE REVOLT HE LED

BELOW:
CAPTURE OF A RUNAWAY SLAVE

Discovery of Nat Turner.

PROBLEM 11: WHY WAS THERE NO SUSTAINED, LARGE-SCALE BLACK REVOLUTION AGAINST THEIR MORE THAN TWO HUNDRED YEARS STATUS AS AMERICAN SLAVES?

On his numerous lecture tours in the North, the famous escaped slave, Frederick Douglass, was always asked by his white audiences why the slaves did not rebel and seek their freedom because, his audience remarked, they personally would have if they were held in captivity. Douglass attempted to provide a response, but the question is not easily answered. If we define a revolt as a concerted action by a group of slaves with the purpose of seeking freedom by destroying the lives and property of white slave holders, historians have identified only about nine such actions between 1691 and 1865. That is an incredibly small number for an institution that had been present for more than two hundred years prior to the American Civil War. Certain slave revolts, such as those of Nat Turner, Denemark Vesey, and Gabriel, have become famous, but only because they stand out as the exception and not the rule in the history of American slavery.

Out of 1.6 million white families in the South, about 384,000 collectively owned approximately 4 million black slaves. Thus, the majority of white southerners owned no slaves at all, while 20 percent of slave holders owned only one slave, and two-thirds of slave holders owned fewer than 20 slaves. Thus, it would seem that over that long period of time, there must have been many opportunities for slaves to revolt or escape because the odds against such action, while large, do not seem insurmountable. Estimates are that at most an average of 2,000 slaves escaped each year between 1830 and 1860. This still represents a small number compared to the 4 million blacks held in captivity. Even in a place like South Carolina, which in 1765 had 40,000 whites and 90,000 blacks, there was no major uprising. The South also had 250,000 free Negroes in 1860, yet this group of individuals seemed to play no role in assisting their fellow black men and women in planning or plotting to secure their freedom. Even during the years of the Civil War, when southern men had to leave their homes and go to battle and when the South was increasingly in turmoil and being devastated, there were no major slave revolts at a time one would think they would have a greater chance for success.

How can we account for this most unusual situation? Are there logical explanations as to why there was an absence of sustained revolt, rebellion, and escape? What conclusion can we draw about the status of the slave and the institution of slavery itself as it operated for more than 200 years in this country?

PROBLEM 11:
QUESTIONS FOR TEAM RESEARCH

1. What were the conditions that might have prevented or discouraged slave revolts in the American South?

2. What role did the number of blacks, the size of the location in which they worked, and the legal system have in encouraging or discouraging rebellion?

3. Why did the free Negroes in the South not play a major role in helping those who were enslaved?

4. Is it possible that the majority of the slave population was "content" with their status?

5. Can we discover any other evidence of slave dissatisfaction with their status besides outright revolt or rebellion?

PROBLEM 11:
STARTING THE SEARCH FOR EVIDENCE

INTERNET: KEY WORDS AND PHRASES

Slave rebellions in the United States

Nat Turner's Rebellion

Negro resistance to American slavery

U.S. policy toward runaway slaves

BOOKS

Aptheker, Herbert, *American Negro Slave Revolts*, NY, International Publisher, 1983

Bracey, John; Meier, August; Rudwich, Elliot, eds, *American Slavery: The Question of Resistance*, Belmont, CA, Wadsworth Publishing, 1971

Davis, David Brion, *Inhuman Bondage: The Rise and Fall of Slavery in the New World*, NY, Oxford University Press, 2006

Genovese, Eugene D., From *Rebellion to Revolution: Afro-American Slave Revolts in the Making of the Modern World*, Baton Rouge, State University Press, 1979

Glasrud, Bruce; Smith, Alan M., *Race Relations in British North America 1607–1783*, Chicago, Nelson-Hall, 1982

THE CONFESSION STATEMENT OF NAT TURNER (FULL TEXT)

I was thirty-one years of age the second of October last, and born the property of Benjamin Turner, of this county. In my childhood a circumstance occurred which made an indelible impression on my mind, and laid the groundwork of that enthusiasm which has terminated so fatally to many, both white and black, and for which I am about to atone at the gallows. It is here necessary to relate this circumstance. Trifling as it may seem, it was the commencement of that belief which has grown with time; and even now, sir, in his dungeon, helpless and forsaken as I am, I cannot divest myself of. Being at play with other children, when three or four years old, I was telling them something, which my mother, overhearing, said it had happened before I was born. I stuck to my story, however, and related some things which went, in her opinion, to confirm it. Others being called on, were greatly astonished, knowing that these things had happened, and caused them to say, in my hearing, I surely would be a prophet, as the Lord had shown me things that had happened before my birth. And my mother and grandmother strengthened me in this my first impression, saying, in my presence, I was intended for some great purpose, which they had always thought from certain marks on my head and breast....

My grandmother, who was very religious, and to whom I was much attached, my master, who belonged to the church, and other religious persons who visited the house, and whom I often saw at prayers, noticing the singularity of my manners, I suppose, and my uncommon intelligence for a child, remarked I had too much sense to be raised, and, if I was, I would never be of any service to any one as a slave. To a mind like mine, restless, inquisitive, and observant of everything that was passing, it is easy to suppose that religion was the subject to which it would be directed; and, although this subject principally occupied my thoughts, there was nothing that I saw or heard of to which my attention was not directed. The manner in which I learned to read and write, not only had great influence on my own mind, as I acquired it with the most perfect ease, so much so, that I have no recollection whatever of learning the alphabet; but, to the astonishment of the family, one day, when a book was shown me, to keep me from crying, I began spelling the names of different objects. This was a source of wonder to all in the neighborhood, particularly the blacks—and this learning was constantly improved at all opportunities. When I got large enough to go to work, while employed I was reflecting on many things that would present themselves to my imagination; and whenever an opportunity occurred of looking at a book, when the school-children were getting their lessons, I would find many things that the fertility of my own imagination had depicted to me before. All my time, not devoted to my master's service, was spent either in prayer, or in making experiments in casting different things in moulds made of earth, in attempting to make paper, gunpowder, and many other experiments, that, although I could not perfect, yet convinced me of its practicability if I had the means.

I was not addicted to stealing in my youth, nor have ever been; yet such was the confidence of the Negroes in the neighborhood, even at this early period of my life, in my superior judgment, that they would often carry me with them when they were going on any roguery, to plan for them. Growing up among them with this confidence in my superior judgment, and when this, in their opinions, was perfected by Divine inspiration, from the circumstances already alluded to in my infancy, and which belief was ever afterwards zealously inculcated by the austerity of my life and manners, which became the subject of remark by white and black; having soon discovered to be great, I must appear so, and therefore studiously avoided mixing in society, and wrapped myself in mystery, devoting my time to fasting and prayer.

By this time, having arrived to man's estate, and hearing the Scriptures commented on at meetings, I was struck with that particular passage which says, "Seek ye the king-dom of heaven, and all things shall be added unto you." I reflected much on this pas-sage, and prayed daily for light on this subject. As I was praying one day at my plough, the Spirit spoke to me, saying, "Seek ye the kingdom of heaven, and all things shall be added unto you." Question. "What do you mean by the Spirit?" Answer. "The Spirit that spoke to the prophets in former days," and I was greatly astonished, and for two years prayed continually, whenever my duty would permit; and then again I had the same revelation, which fully confirmed me in the impression that I was ordained for some great purpose in the hands of the Almighty. Several years rolled round, in which many events occurred to strengthen me in this my belief. At this time I reverted in my mind to the remarks made of me in my childhood, and the things that had been shown me; and as it had been said of me in my childhood, by those by whom I had been taught to pray, both white and black, and in whom I had the greatest confidence, that I had too much sense to be raised, and if I was I would never be of any use to any one as a slave; now, finding I had arrived to man's estate, and was a slave, and these revelations being made known to me, I began to direct my attention to this great object, to fulfil the purpose for which, by this time, I felt assured I was intended. Knowing the influence I had obtained over the minds of my fellow-servants (not by the means of conjuring and such like tricks—for to them I always spoke of such things with contempt), but by the communion of the Spirit, whose revelations I often communicated to them, and they believed and said my wisdom came from God,—I now began to prepare them for my purpose, by telling them something was about to happen that would terminate in fulfilling the great promise that had been made to me.

About this time I was placed under an overseer, from whom I ran away, and after remaining in the woods thirty days, I returned, to the astonishment of the Negroes on the plantation, who thought I had made my escape to some other part of the country, as my father had done before. But the reason of my return was, that the Spirit appeared to me and said I had my wishes directed to the things of this world, and not to the kingdom of heaven, and that I should return to the service of my earthly master—"For he who knoweth his Master's will, and doeth it not, shall be beaten with many stripes, and thus have I chastened you." And the Negroes found fault, and murmured against me, saying that if they had my sense they would not serve any master in the world. And about this time I had a vision—and I saw white spirits and black spirits engaged in battle, and the sun was darkened—the thunder rolled in the heavens, and blood flowed in streams—and I heard a voice saying, "Such is your luck, such you are called to see; and let it come rough or smooth, you must surely bear it."

I now withdrew myself as much as my situation would permit from the intercourse of my fellow-servants, for the avowed purpose of serving the Spirit more fully; and it appeared to me, and reminded me of the things it had already shown me, and that it would then reveal to me the knowledge of the elements, the revolution of the planets, the operation of tides, and changes of the seasons. After this revelation in the year

1825, and the knowledge of the elements being made known to me, I sought more than ever to obtain true holiness before the great day of judgment should appear, and then I began to receive the true knowledge of faith. And from the first steps of righteousness until the last, was I made perfect; and the Holy Ghost was with me, and said, "Behold me as I stand in the heavens." And I looked and saw the forms of men in different attitudes; and there were lights in the sky, to which the children of darkness gave other names what they really were; for they were the lights of the Saviour's hands, stretched forth from east to west, even as they were extended on the cross on Calvary for the redemption of sinners. And I wondered greatly at these miracles, and prayed to be informed of a certainty of the meaning thereof; and shortly afterwards, while laboring in the field, I discovered drops of blood on the corn, as though it were dew from heaven; and I communicated it to many, both white and black, in the neighborhood-and I then found on the leaves in the woods hieroglyphic characters and numbers, with the forces of men in different attitudes, portrayed in blood, and representing the figures I had seen before in the heavens. And now the Holy Ghost had revealed itself to me, and made plain the miracles it had shown me; for as the blood of Christ had been shed on this earth, and had ascended to heaven for the salvation of sinners, and was now returning to earth again in the form of dew,—and as the leaves on the trees bore the impression of the figures I had seen in the heavens,—it was plain to me that the Saviour was about to lay down the yoke he had borne for the sins of men, and the great day of judgment was at hand.

About this time I told these things to a white man (Etheldred T. Brantley), on whom it had a wonderful effect; and he ceased from his wickedness, and was attacked immediately with a cutaneous eruption, and blood oozed from the pores of his skin, and after praying and fasting nine days he was healed. And the Spirit appeared to me again, and said, as the Saviour had been baptized, so should we be also; and when the white people would not let us be baptized by the church, we went down into the water together, in the sight of many who reviled us, and were baptized by the Spirit. After this I rejoiced greatly, and gave thanks to God. And on the 12th of May, 1828, I heard a loud noise in the heavens, and the Spirit instantly appeared to me and said the Serpent was loosened, and Christ had laid down the yoke he had borne for the sins of men, and that I should take it on and fight against the Serpent, for the time was fast approaching when the first should be last and the last should be first. Ques. "Do you not find yourself mistaken now?" Ans. "Was not Christ crucified?" And by signs in the heavens that it would make known to me when I should commence the great work, and until the first sign appeared I should conceal it from the knowledge of men; and on the appearance of the sign (the eclipse of the sun, last February), I should arise and prepare myself, and slay my enemies with their own weapons. And immediately on the sign appearing in the heavens, the sea was removed from my lips, and I communicated the great work laid out for me to do, to four in whom I had the greatest confidence (Henry, Hark, Nelson, and Sam). It was intended by us to have begun the work of death on the 4th of July last. Many were the plans formed and rejected by us, and it affected my mind to such a degree that I fell sick, and the time passed without our coming to any determination how to commence—still forming new schemes and rejecting them, when the sign appeared again, which determined me not to wait longer.

Since the commencement of 1830 I had been living with Mr. Joseph Travis, who was to me a kind master, and placed the greatest confidence in me; in fact, I had no cause to complain of his treatment to me. On Saturday evening, the 20th of August, it was agreed between Henry, Hark, and myself, to prepare a dinner the next day for the men we expected, and then to concert a plan, as we had not yet determined on any. Hark, on the following morning, brought a pig, and Henry brandy; and being joined by Sam, Nelson, Will, and Jack, they prepared in the woods a dinner, where, about three o'clock, I joined them.

Q. Why were you so backward in joining them?

A. The same reason that had caused me not to mix with them years before, I saluted them on coming up, and asked Will how came he there. He answered, his life was worth no more than others, and his liberty as dear to him. I asked him if he thought to obtain it. He said he would, or lose his life. This was enough to put him in full confidence. Jack, I knew, was only a tool in the hands of Hark. It was quickly agreed we should commence at home (Mr. J. Travis) on that night; and until we had armed and equipped ourselves, and gathered sufficient force, neither age nor sex was to be spared—which was invariably adhered to. We remained at the feast until about two hours in the night, when we went to the house and found Austin....

I took my station in the rear, and, as it was my object to carry terror and devastation wherever we went, I placed fifteen or twenty of the best armed and most to be relied on in front, who generally approached the houses as fast as their horses could run. This was for two purposes—to prevent their escape, and strike terror to the inhabitants; on this account I never got to the houses, after leaving Mrs. Whitehead's, until the murders were committed, except in one case. I sometimes got in sight in time to see the work of death completed; viewed the mangled bodies as they lay, in silent satisfaction, and immediately started in quest of other victims. Having murdered Mrs. Waller and ten children, we started for Mr. Wm. Williams,—having killed him and two little boys that were there; while engaged in this, Mrs. Williams fled and got some distance from the house, but she was pursued, overtaken, and compelled to get up behind one of the company, who brought her back, and, after showing her the mangled body of her lifeless husband, she was told to get down and lay by his side, where she was shot dead.

The white men pursued and fired on us several times. Hark had his horse shot under him, and I caught another for him as it was running by me; five or six of my men were wounded, but none left on the field. Finding myself defeated here, I instantly determined to go through a private way, and cross the Nottoway River at the Cypress Bridge, three miles below Jerusalem, and attack that place in the rear, as I expected they would look for me on the other road, and I had a great desire to get there to procure arms and ammunition. After going a short distance in this private way, accompanied by about twenty men, I overtook two or three, who told me the others were dispersed in every direction. On this, I gave up all hope for the present; and on Thursday night, after having supplied myself with provisions from Mr. Travis, I scratched a hole under a pile of fence-rails in a field, where I concealed myself for six weeks, never leaving my hiding-place but for a few minutes in the dead of the night to get water, which was very near. Thinking by this time I could venture out, I began to go about in the night, and eavesdrop the houses in the neighborhood—pursuing this course for about a fortnight, and gathering little or no intelligence, afraid of speaking to any human being, and returning every morning to my cave before the dawn of day. I know not how long I might have led this life, if accident had not betrayed me. A dog in the neighborhood passing by my hiding-place one night while I was out, was attracted by some meat I had in my cave, and crawled in and stole it, and was coming out just as I returned. A few nights after, two Negroes having started to go hunting with the same dog, and passed that way, the dog came again to the place, and having just gone out to walk about, discovered me and barked; on which, thinking myself discovered, I spoke to them to beg concealment. On making myself known, they fled from me. Knowing then they would betray me, I immediately left my hiding-place, and was pursued almost incessantly, until I was taken, a fortnight afterwards, by Mr. Benjamin Phipps, in a little hole I bad dug out with my sword, for the purpose of concealment, under the top of a fallen tree.

During the time I was pursued, I had many hair-breadth escapes, which your time will not permit you to relate. I am here loaded with chains, and willing to suffer the fate that awaits me.

PROBLEM 11:
CONNECTION TO TODAY

1. Does the history of American slavery have any connection or relevance to the status of the black "underclass" that today exists in many American cities?

2. In our time the country of South Africa was one with a black population four or five times the number of whites in the country, yet the whites were able to maintain a separated society in which they controlled the wealth and political power. How can we explain this?

3. Today's African-Americans often complain that the blacks who are successful in American society do not return in great numbers to assist those who remain in poverty. Are there any parables to this in the 19th century America?

4. Why do you think there is no mass movement of poor African-Americans who are stuck in urban ghettos to change their condition and status?

PROBLEM 12:

AFTER MORE THAN 200 YEARS OF A NON-SYSTEM OF PRIMARILY PRIVATE EDUCATION AVAILABLE TO THE FEW, HOW WAS AMERICAN EDUCATION TRANSFORMED INTO A PUBLICLY-SUPPORTED, COMPULSORY SYSTEM FOR THE MANY?

RIGHT:
HORACE MANN

BELOW:
19TH CENTURY
AMERICAN
COUNTRY
SCHOOLHOUSE

PROBLEM 12: AFTER MORE THAN 200 YEARS OF A NON-SYSTEM OF PRIMARILY PRIVATE EDUCATION AVAILABLE TO THE FEW, HOW WAS AMERICAN EDUCATION TRANSFORMED INTO A PUBLICLY-SUPPORTED, COMPULSORY SYSTEM FOR THE MANY?

We speak today of an American educational system that is identified with certain common elements throughout the entire nation. Our schools are public, which means that everyone can attend and that schools are financially supported by tax dollars that everyone pays, whether or not their children attend those schools. We also decree that education up to a certain age is compulsory, which simply means that parents and children have no choice in this matter; the law says they must attend school. We also give control of education not to the federal government but to the states, which, in turn, delegate authority to governing entities we call local school boards. And we authorize those local boards to be controlled not by educators but by lay people who are average citizens and who may or may not have any special training or expertise in education.

It is important to note that for more than half of our nation's history, the system outlined above did not exist. From 1607 until the mid-1800s, colonial and American education was a hodgepodge of uncoordinated schooling models and options that were noncompulsory, not universally taxed, and primarily privately or religiously controlled. For that very long period of time, there was no public educational system in America. But from the 1830s to the end of the 19th century, this changed. The essential parts of the American public education system were firmly in place. How in the space of 60 to 70 years could this have happened when it hadn't happened for the previous 200 years? In order to grasp the magnitude of this change, consider the following hypothetical situation.

What do you think would happen in the United States if a law were passed that made it compulsory for everyone to go to college and required that everyone pay taxes so that all public higher education would be free? As extreme and unlikely as this example seems, Americans in the 19th century were presented with a set of public policy ideas regarding elementary and secondary education that seemed to them as extreme and unprecedented as our hypothetical public college scenario. Yet by 1900, what had seemed extreme, unlikely, unprecedented, and unduly intrusive into the private lives of families and the concept of parental freedom and control had happened.

How can we explain this dramatic and fundamental change in American society?

PROBLEM 12:
QUESTIONS FOR TEAM RESEARCH

1. What were the regional differences in schooling between New England, the middle states, and the South?

2. Which region had taken the most early steps toward public education? What factors allowed that region to take the lead?

3. How did the stated purposes of education change from the 17th to the 19th century in America.

4. What conditions of 19th century America favored the creation of an American educational "system"?

5. What strategies did educational leaders employ to overcome resistance to tax-supported, compulsory, public education?

PROBLEM 12:
STARTING THE SEARCH FOR EVIDENCE

INTERNET: KEY WORDS AND PHRASES

Horace Mann and American education

Henry Barnard and school reform

The American Common School Movement

Opposition to the Common School Movement

BOOKS

Cremin, Lawrence A., *The American Common School, A Historic Conception*, NY, Bureau of Publications, Teacher College, Columbia University, 1951

Cremin, Lawrence A., *Traditions of American Education*, NY, Basic Books, 1977

Mann, Horace, *Lectures on Education*, NY, Arno Press, 1969

Messerli, Jonathan, *Horace Mann: Biography*, NY, Knopf, 1972

Williams, E.I.F., *Horace Mann, Educational Statesman*, NY, Macmillan, 1937

JAMES G. CARTER'S ASSESSMENT OF MASSACHUSETTS SCHOOLS

Before we attempt, however, to take a single step towards reform let us see what we have to amend. Unless faults can be shown to exist in the organization of our system of popular education, and great ones; it will do but little good to recommend improvements. For it is with communities as with individuals; and "no one," says Fisher Ames, "is less likely to improve, than the coxcomb, who fancies he has already learned out." The pride, which we of New England have been accustomed to feel and, perhaps, to manifest, in our free schools, as the best in the country, and in the world, has not improved their condition. But, on the contrary, the great complacency with which we contemplate this institution is a most effectual bar to all improvements in it. The time has come, when we owe it to our country and ourselves to speak the whole truth in this matter, even though it disturb our self-satisfaction a little.

It will be convenient to point out the faults of the public provisions for popular education under the two following heads; first, the "Summer Free Schools," which are, generally, taught in the country towns for a few months in the warm season of the year by females; and second, the "Winter Free Schools," which are taught by men, commonly, for a shorter period, during the cold season. Children of both sexes of from four to ten or twelve years, usually attend these primary summer schools, and females often to a much later age. This is a very interesting period of human life. No one, who has reflected much upon the subject of early discipline; no one, I trust, who has even followed me through the preceding essays, can doubt, that it is one of the most important parts, if not the very most important part of our lives, as it regards the influence of education in its widest sense. It is important as it regards the development of the powers of the body, or physical education. Because the parts of the body, the limbs, the muscles, the organs, or whatever are the technical names for them, now assume a firmness and consistency in discharging their proper functions, or they become distorted and enfeebled; and these habits, thus early contracted, became a part of ourselves and are as abiding as our lives. Yet what has been done in this branch of education? Nothing at all, absolutely nothing at all, even in our best schools. This period is vitally important as it regards the cultivation of the heart and its affections. What has been done here? Chance and ill-directed efforts make up all the education, which we have received or are giving to our children in the schools in this department. Finally, it is important to us, as it regards the discipline of the head, the developement of the understanding and its faculties. What have we done in this department? We have done something, indeed, and think that we have done much. We have done, and we continue to do, *more* than we do *well*. We resort to many expedients and apply many means, without distinctly understanding, either what we wish to attain, whether it be possible to attain it, or if so, the adaptation of our means to its attainment. Success here, therefore, if the best possible results have ever been gained in any instance, has been more the result of chance than of skill.

To whom do we assign the business of governing and instructing our children from four to twelve years of age? Who take upon themselves the trust of forming those principles and habits, which are to be strengthened and confirmed in manhood, and make our innocent little ones through life, happy or miserable in themselves, and the blessings or the curses of society? To analyze, in detail, the habits, which are formed and confirmed in these first schools, to trace the abiding influence of good ones, or to describe the inveteracy of had ones, would lead me from my present purpose. But are these interesting years of life and these important branches of education committed to those, who understand their importance or their influence upon the future character? Are they committed to those, who would know: what to do, to discharge their high trust successfully if they did, indeed, understand their importance? I think not. And I am persuaded, that all, who have reflected but for a moment upon the age, the acquirements, and the experience of those who assume to conduct this branch of education, must have come to the same conclusion.

The teachers of the primary summer schools have rarely had any education beyond what they have acquired in the very schools where they begin to teach. Their attainments, therefore, to say the least, are usually *very moderate*. But this is not the worst of it. They are often very young, they are constantly changing their employment, and consequently can have but little experience; and what is worse than all, they never have had any direct preparation for their profession. This is the only service, in which we venture to employ young, and often, ignorant persons, without some previous instruction in their appropriate duties. We require experience in all those, whom we employ to perform the slightest mechanical labour for us. We would not buy a coat or a hat of one, who should undertake to make them without a previous apprenticeship. Nor would any one have the hardihood to offer to us the result of his first essay in manufacturing either of these articles. We do not even send an old shoe to be mended, except it be to a workman of whose skill we have had ample proof. Yet we commit our children to be educated to those, who know nothing, absolutely nothing, of the complicated and difficult duties assigned to them. Shall we trust the developement of the delicate bodies, the susceptible hearts, and the tender minds of our little children to those who have no knowledge of their nature? Can they, can these rude hands finish the workmanship of the Almighty? No language can express the astonishment, which a moments reflection on this subject excites in me.

But I must return to the examination of the qualifications of the female teachers of the primary summer schools, from which purpose I have unconsciously a little departed to indulge in a general remark. They are a Class of teachers unknown in our laws regulating the schools unless it be by some latitude of construction. No standard of attainments is fixed, at which they must arrive before they assume the business of instruction. So that any one *keeps school,* which is a very different thing from *teaching school* who wishes to do it, and can persuade, by herself, or her friends, a small district to employ her. And this is not a very difficult matter, especially when the remuneration for the employment is so very trifling. The farce of an examination and a certificate from the minister of the town, for it is a perfect farce, amounts to no efficient check upon the obtrusions of ignorance and inexperience. As no standard is fixed by law, each minister makes a standard for himself, and alters it as often as the peculiar circumstances of the case require. And there will always be enough of peculiar circumstances to render a refusal inexpedient.

Let those, who are conversant with the manner in which these schools are managed, say, whether this description of them undervalues their character and efficacy. Let those, who conduct them, pause and consider whether all is well, and whether there are not abuses and perversions in them, which call loudly for attention and reformation. Compare the acquirements, the experience, the knowledge of teaching possessed by these instructers, not one with another, for the standard is much too low; but with what they might be, under more favourable circumstances and with proper preparation. Compare the improvement made in these little nurseries of piety and religion, of knowledge and rational liberty, not one with another, for the progress in all of them is much too slow; but with what the infant mind and heart are capable of, at this early age, under the most favourable auspices. And there can be no doubt, that all will arrive at the same conclusions; a dissatisfaction with the condition of these schools; and an astonishment, that the public have been so long contented with so small results from means, which all will acknowledge capable of doing so much,

The young man, who lays down his axe and aspires to take up the "rod" and rule in a village school, has, usually, in common with other young men, a degree of dignity and self-complacency, which it is dangerous to the extent of his power to disturb. And when he comes to his minister, sustained by his own influence in the parish, and that of a respectable father and perhaps a large family of friends, and asks of him the legal approbation for a teacher, it is a pretty delicate matter to refuse it. A firm and conscientious refusal of approbation to a school-master, has led, in more instances than one, to a firm and conscientious refusal to hear the minister preach. And, by the parish difficulties growing out of so small an affair, he has found himself at last "unsettled" and thrown with his family, perhaps in his old age, upon the world to seek and gain his subsistence as he may. This is truly martyrdom. And martyrs in ordinary times are rare. Even good men can make peace with their consciences on better terms. So much for the literary qualifications of instructers.

It is the intention of the school-law to secure good, moral characters in the public instructers by requiring the approbation, as to this qualification, of the selectmen of the town, where the school is to be taught. No doubt selectmen are as good judges of morality as any body of men, which could readily be appealed to. But either we are a very moral people, or they are not very discriminating; for instances are rare, indeed, of refusal of their approbation on this ground. If a young man be moral enough to keep out of the State-Prison, he will find no difficulty in getting approbation for a school-master. These things ought not to be so. Both the moral and the intellectual character of the rising generation are influenced more by their instructers, during the period of from four to twelve years of age, than by any cause so entirely within our control. It becomes then of momentous concern to the community, in a moral and religious, as well as in political point of view, that this influence should be the greatest and the best possible. That it is not now so, every one, I trust, who has followed me through my preceding essays, is convinced. And if something be not done, and that speedily, to improve the condition of the free schools, and especially the primary *summer schools,* they will not only fail of their happiest influence, but in a short time of all influence which will be worth estimating.

If the policy of the legislature, in regard to free schools, for the last twenty years be not changed, the institution, which has been the glory of New England will, in twenty years more, be extinct. If the State continue to relieve themselves of the trouble of providing for the instruction of the whole people, and to shift the responsibility upon the towns, and the towns upon the districts, and the districts upon individuals, each will take care of himself and his own family as he is able, and as he appreciates the blessing of a good education. The rich will, as a class, have much better instruction than they now have, while the poor will have much worse or none at all. The academies and private schools will be carried to much greater perfection than they have been, while the public free schools will become stationary or retrograde; till at length, they will be thrown for support upon the gratuitous, and of course capricious and uncertain efforts of individuals; and then, like the lower schools of the crowded cities of Europe, they will soon degenerate into mere mechanical establishments, such as the famous *seminaries* of London, Birmingham, and Manchester of which we hear so much lately, not for rational moral and intellectual instruction of human beings, but for training young animals to march, sing, and draw figures in sand,—establishments, in which the power of one man is so prodigiously multiplied, that he can overlook, direct and control the intellectual exercises of a thousand! And this wretched mockery of education, they must be right glad to accept as a charity, instead of inheriting as their birthright as good instruction as the country affords.

• • •

CONSERVATIVE OPPOSITION TO FREE PUBLIC EDUCATION: EDITORIAL IN THE PHILADELPHIA NATIONAL GAZETTE, 1830

"Education and general information—these must indeed constitute our only true National Bulwark. May the day soon come when in point of literary acquirements the poorest peasant shall stand on a level with his more wealthy neighbours."

It is our strong inclination and our obvious interest that literary acquirements should be universal; but we should be guilty of imposture, if we professed to believe in the possibility of that consummation. Literature cannot he acquired without leisure, and wealth gives leisure. Universal opulence, or even competency, is a chimera, as man and society are constituted. There will ever be distinctions of condition, of capacity, of knowledge and ignorance, in spite of all the fond conceits which may he indulged, or the wild projects which may be tried, to the contrary. The "peasant" must labor during those hours of the day, which his wealthy neighbor can give to the abstract culture of his mind; otherwise, the earth would not yield enough for the subsistence of all: the mechanic cannot abandon the operations of his trade, for general studies; if he should, most of the conveniences of life and objects of exchange would be wanting; languor, decay, poverty, discontent would soon be visible among all classes. No government, no statesman, no philanthropist, can furnish what is incompatible with the very organization and being of civil society. *Education, the most comprehensive, should be, and is, open to the whole community; but it must cost to every one, time and money; and those are means which every one cannot possess simultaneously.* Doubtless, more of education and of information is attainable for all in this republic, than can be had any where else by the poor or the operatives, so called.

We can readily pardon the editor of the United States *Gazette* for not perceiving that the scheme of Universal Equal Education at the expense of the State, is virtually "Agrarianism." It would be a compulsory application of the means of the richer, for the direct use of the poorer classes; and so far an arbitrary division of property among them. The declared object is, to procure the opportunity of instruction for the child or children of every citizen; to elevate the standard of the education of the working classes, or equalize the standard for all classes; which would, doubtless, be to lower or narrow that which the rich may now compass. But the most sensible and reflecting possessors of property sufficient to enable them to educate their children in the most liberal and efficacious way, and upon the broadest scale, would prefer to share their means for any other purpose, or in any other mode, than such as would injuriously affect or circumscribe the proficiency of their offspring. A public meeting of "the Mechanics and other Working Men of the City and County of New York," was held in the city, on the 17 inst., and among the principles for which they have "resolved" to contend, we find the following:

> "In Education—The adoption of a general system of instruction, at the expense of the State, which shall afford to children, however rich or poor, equal means to obtain useful learning. To effect this, it is believed that a system of direct taxation will not be necessary, as the surplus revenue of the State and United States Governments will, in a very few years, afford ample means—but even if it were necessary to resort to direct taxation to accomplish this all-important object, and the amount paid by the wealthy should he far greater than that paid by our less eligibly situated fellow-citizens, an equivalent to them would be found in the increased ability and usefulness of the educated citizen to serve and to promote the best interests of the State; in the increased permanency of our institutions—and in the superior protection of liberty, person and property."

Thus, a direct tax for "the equal means of obtaining useful learning" is not deemed improbable, and it is admitted that the amount which would he paid by the wealthy would be "far greater" than that paid by their "less eligibly situated fellow citizens." Here, we contend, would be the action, if not the name, of the Agrarian system. Authority—that is, the State—is to force the more eligibly situated citizens to contribute a part (which might he very considerable) of their means, for the accommodation of the rest; and this is equivalent to the idea of an actual, compulsory partition of their substance. The more thriving members of the "mechanical and other working classes" would themselves feel the evil of the direct taxation; they would find that they had toiled for the benefit of other families than their own. One of the chief excitements to industry, among those classes, is the hope of earning the means of educating their children respectably or liberally: that incentive would he removed, and the scheme of

State and equal education be thus a premium for comparative idleness, to be taken out of the pockets of the laborious and conscientious.

We have no confidence in any compulsory equalizations; it has been well observed that they pull down what is above, but never much raise what is below, and often "depress high and low together beneath the level of what was originally the lowest." By no possibility could a perfect equality he procured. A scheme of universal equal education, attempted in reality, would he an unexampled bed of Procrustes, for the understandings of our youth, and in fact, could not be used with any degree of equality of profit, unless the dispositions and circumstances of parents and children were nearly the same; to accomplish which phenomenon, a nation of many million, engaged in a great variety of pursuits, could be beyond human power....

PROBLEM 12:
CONNECTION TO TODAY

1. Is compulsory education still a good idea in 21st century America? If so, why? If not, why not?

2. Does the concept of local control of schools by lay people still make sense? What might be some alternatives?

3. Today the U.S. federal government plays a much larger role in American education than at any previous time in our history. Is this a positive or negative thing?

4. Some people today say the public education system created in 19th century America is breaking up. Do you agree?

5. What can today's school reform advocates learn from the strategies used by the 19th century school reformers?

PROBLEM 13: HOW COULD A LITTLE-KNOWN PRIVATE CITIZEN WITH VIRTUALLY NO NATIONAL EXPERIENCE BECOME PRESIDENT OF THE UNITED STATES DURING A CRISIS IN WHICH THE NATION MOVED TO THE BRINK OF CIVIL WAR?

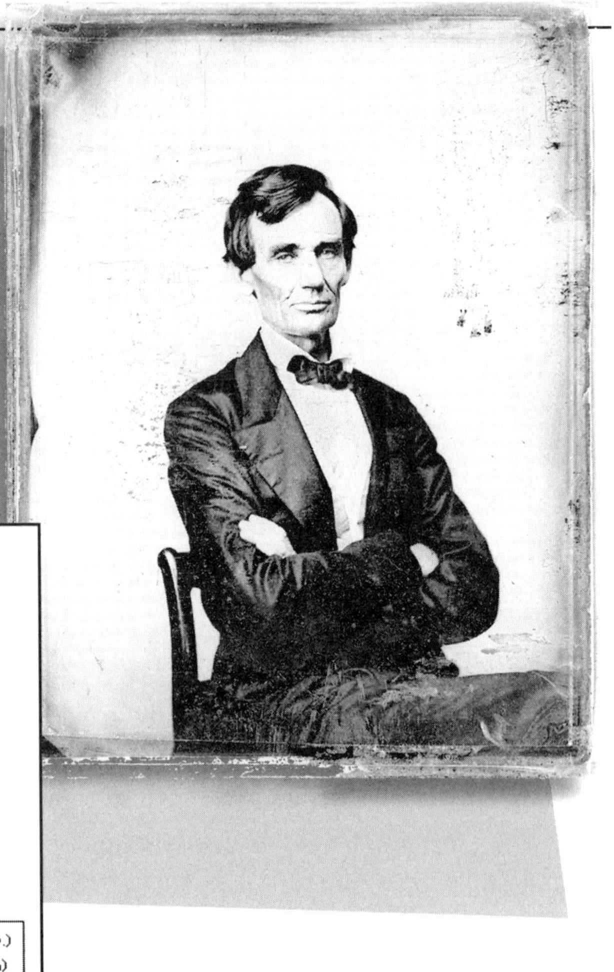

RIGHT: ABRAHAM LINCOLN IN 1860

BELOW: PIE CHART OF THE 1860 ELECTION RESULTS

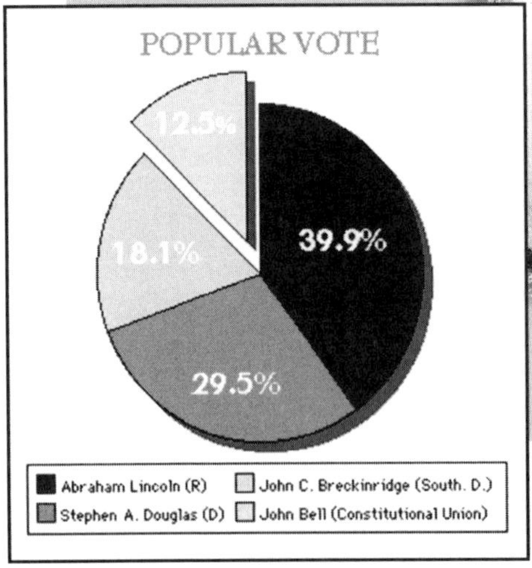

POPULAR VOTE

12.5%

18.1%

39.9%

29.5%

■ Abraham Lincoln (R) □ John C. Breckinridge (South. D.)
■ Stephen A. Douglas (D) □ John Bell (Constitutional Union)

PROBLEM 13: HOW COULD A LITTLE-KNOWN PRIVATE CITIZEN WITH VIRTUALLY NO NATIONAL EXPERIENCE BECOME PRESIDENT OF THE UNITED STATES DURING A CRISIS IN WHICH THE NATION MOVED TO THE BRINK OF CIVIL WAR?

As the presidential election of 1860 approached, the country was in crisis. The issue of what to do about the institution of slavery was tearing the nation apart. In the previous 40 years the country seemed to be able to avoid a break-up through a number of political compromises between the free states of the North and the slave-holding states of the South. But now efforts at compromise seemed not to be possible, and there was increasingly serious talk of the slave states breaking away from the rest of the country and forming a new slave-holding nation. What had been heated arguments were now turning increasingly into threats and violence.

Yet in the middle of such a perilous time, the person elected President of the United States was a little known private citizen from a frontier state who had virtually no national experience. Abraham Lincoln of Illinois had only served in the state legislature and in one uneventful and undistinguished term in the U.S. Congress. Just two years before his election as president, in a bid to become a United States senator, he had he had lost to Stephen A. Douglas. Lincoln's competition for the nomination for president by the newly formed Republican party were men with extensive experience in major state and national offices who had widely known names and reputations. Lincoln had done some traveling and speaking outside of Illinois, but the overwhelming majority of Americans knew virtually nothing about him. In fact, in this time before radio, television, telephones, movies, and computers, most Americans had no idea what he looked like or could recognize the sound of his voice.

Yet despite these circumstances, this private citizen, Abraham Lincoln, won the Republican nomination for president and went on to win the general election and become the sixteenth President of the United States. How could this have happened? How did Lincoln overcome these obstacles and win the presidency?

PROBLEM 13:
QUESTIONS FOR TEAM RESEARCH

1. How did Republicans nominate a presidential candidate in 1860? Did it give Lincoln any advantage over other competitors?

2. How really well-known was Lincoln? Did he do or say anything that put him ahead of other candidates for the nomination? How important were issues in the nomination process? Did Lincoln himself play a major role in securing the nomination or did his political supporters get it for him?

3. How were presidential campaigns run in 1860, when they had none of the media we have today and transportation across the country was slow?

4. Who did Lincoln run against in the general election and what were the issues? Where did Lincoln stand on the issues? What about the opposition's positions?

5. What kind of political organization did Lincoln have across the country? What were the newspapers saying about his candidacy?

6. What were the final vote totals? What were the circumstances that allowed him to win?

7. Even though Lincoln won, what did the election signal was happening in the country?

PROBLEM 13:
STARTING THE SEARCH FOR EVIDENCE

INTERNET: KEY WORDS AND PHRASES

The election of 1860

Republican Convention of 1860

Newspapers and the election of 1860

Stephen A. Douglas and the election of 1860

BOOKS

Chadwick, Bruce, *1858: Abraham Lincoln, Jefferson Davis, Robert E. Lee, Ulysses S. Grant, and the War They Failed to See*, Naperville, IL, Source Books, Inc., 2008

Chadwick, Bruce, *Lincoln for President, an Unlikely Candidate, an Audacious Strategy, and Victory No One Saw Coming*, Naperville IL, Source Books, Inc., 2009

Crenshaw, Ollinger, *The Slave States in the Presidential Election of 1860*, Baltimore, Johns Hopkins Press, 1945

Fite, Emerson David, *The Presidential Campaign of 1860*, NY, Macmillan, 1911

Luebke, Frederick, *Ethnic Voters and the Election of Lincoln*, Lincoln, University of Nebraska Press, 1971

1860 REPUBLICAN PARTY PLATFORM, ADOPTED AT CHICAGO, 1860 (FULL TEXT)

Resolved, That we, the delegated representatives of the Republican electors of the United States, in Convention assembled, in discharge of the duty we owe to our constituents and our country, unite in the following declarations:

1. That the history of the nation, during the last four years, has fully established the propriety and necessity of the organization and perpetuation of the Republican party, and that the causes which called it into existence are permanent in their nature, and now, more than ever before, demand its peaceful and constitutional triumph.

2. That the maintenance of the principles promulgated in the Declaration of Independence and embodied in the Federal Constitution, "That all men are created equal; that they are endowed by their Creator with certain inalienable rights; that among these are life, liberty, and the pursuit of happiness; that to secure these rights, governments are instituted among men, deriving their just powers from the consent of the governed," is essential to the preservation of our Republican institutions; and that the Federal Constitution, the Rights of the States, and the Union of the States, must and shall be preserved.

3. That to the Union of the States this nation owes its unprecedented increase in population, its surprising development of material resources, its rapid augmentation of wealth, its happiness at home and its honor abroad; and we hold in abhorrence all schemes for Disunion, come from whatever source they may: And we congratulate the country that no Republican member of Congress has uttered or countenanced the threats of Disunion so often made by Democratic members without rebuke and with applause from their political associates; and we denounce those threats of Disunion, in case of a popular overthrow of their ascendency, as denying the vital principles of a free government, and as an avowal of contemplated treason, which it is the imperative duty of an indignant People sternly to rebuke and forever silence.

4. That the maintenance inviolate of the rights of the States, and especially the right of each State to order and control its own domestic institutions according to its

own judgment exclusively, is essential to that balance of powers on which the perfection and endurance of our political fabric depends; and we denounce the lawless invasion by armed force of the soil of any State or Territory, no matter under what pretext, as among the gravest of crimes.

5. That the present Democratic Administration has far exceeded our worst apprehensions, in its measureless subserviency to the exactions of a sectional interest, as especially evinced in its desperate exertions to force the infamous Lecompton Constitution upon the protesting people of Kansas; in construing the personal relation between master and servant to involve an unqualified property in persons; in its attempted enforcement, everywhere, on land and sea, through the intervention of Congress and of the Federal Courts of the extreme pretensions of a purely local interest; and in its general and unvarying abuse of the power intrusted to it by a confiding people.

6. That the people justly view with alarm the reckless extravagance which pervades every department of the Federal Government; that a return to rigid economy and accountability is indispensible to arrest the systematic plunder of the public treasury by favored partisans, while the recent startling developments of frauds and corruptions at the Federal metropolis, show that an entire change of administration is imperatively demanded.

7. That the new dogma, that the Constitution, of its own force, carries Slavery into any or all of the Territories of the United States, is a dangerous political heresy, at variance with the explicit provisions of that instrument itself, with contemporaneous exposition, and with legislative and judicial precedent; is revolutionary in its tendency, and subversive of the peace and harmony of the country.

8. That the normal condition of all the territory of the United States is that of freedom; That as our Republican fathers, when they had abolished Slavery in all our national territory, ordained that "no person should be deprived of life, liberty, or property, without due process of law," it becomes our duty, by legislation, whenever such legislation is necessary, to maintain this provision of the Constitution against all attempts to violate it; and we deny the authority of Congress, of a ter-

ritorial legislature, or of any individuals, to give legal existence to Slavery in any Territory of the United States.

9. That we brand the recent re-opening of the African slave-trade, under the cover of our national flag, aided by perversions of judicial power, as a crime against humanity and a burning shame to our country and age; and we call upon Congress to take prompt and efficient measures for the total and final suppression of that execrable traffic.

10. That in the recent vetoes, by their Federal Governors, of the acts of the Legislatures of Kansas and Nebraska, prohibiting Slavery in those Territories, we find a practical illustration of the boasted Democratic principle of Non-Intervention and Popular Sovereignty, embodied in the Kansas-Nebraska bill, and a demonstration of the deception and fraud involved therein.

11. That Kansas should, of right, be immediately admitted as a State under the Constitution recently formed and adopted by her people, and accepted by the House of Representatives.

12. That, while providing revenue for the support of the General Government by duties upon imports, sound policy requires such an adjustment of these imposts as to encourage the development of the industrial interest of the whole country; and we commend that policy of national exchanges which secures to the working men liberal wages, to agriculture renumerative prices, to mechanics and manufactures an adequate reward for their skill, labor, and enterprise, and to the nation commercial prosperity and independence.

13. That we protest against any sale or alienation to others of the Public Lands held by actual settlers, and against any view of he Homestead policy which regards the settlers as paupers or suppliants for public bounty; and we demand the passage by Congress of the complete and satisfactory Homestead measure which has already passed the House.

14. That the Republican party is opposed to any change in our Naturalization Laws or any State legislation by which the rights of citizenship hitherto accorded to im-

migrants from foreign lands shall be abridged or impaired; and in favor of giving a full and efficient protection to the rights of all classes of citizens, whether native or naturalized, both at home and abroad.

15. That appropriations by Congress for River and Harbor improvements of a National character, required for the accommodation and security of an existing commerce, are authorized by the Constitution, and justified by the obligations of Government to protect the lives and property of its citizens.

16. That a Railroad to the Pacific Ocean is imperatively demanded by the interest of the whole country; that the Federal Government ought to render immediate and efficient aid in its construction; and that, as preliminary thereto, a daily Overland Mail should be promply established.

17. Finally, having thus set forth our distinctive principles and views, we invite the coöperation of all citizens, however differing on other questions, who substantially agree with us in their affirmance and support.

PROBLEM 13:
CONNECTION TO TODAY

1. Could someone with Lincoln's background in 1860 be elected president today? Explain why or why not?

2. What has been the presidential record of individuals who had little or no national political experience?

3. Compare the way campaigns were run in 1860 with how they are run today? What are the positive and negative aspects of both eras?

4. If Lincoln was a minority vote president, what impact did that have on his ability to govern effectively? What presidents in the past 50 years have also been minority vote presidents? How did that impact their effectiveness?

5. Is there some way we could ensure that we do not elect presidents who do not receive a majority of the popular vote? How could we do that?

PROBLEM 14:
AFTER MORE THAN EIGHTY YEARS OF COMPROMISE BETWEEN THE NORTH AND SOUTH OVER THE ISSUE OF SLAVERY, WHY WAS COMPROMISE NOT POSSIBLE IN 1860–61 WHEN THE NATION ERUPTED IN CIVIL WAR?

HENRY CLAY

PROBLEM 14: AFTER MORE THAN EIGHTY YEARS OF COMPROMISE BETWEEN THE NORTH AND SOUTH OVER THE ISSUE OF SLAVERY, WHY WAS COMPROMISE NOT POSSIBLE IN 1860–61 WHEN THE NATION ERUPTED IN CIVIL WAR?

The institution of slavery had been part of the American scene for more than 150 years before it became a major political issue of contention. The deliberations surrounding the writing of the Constitution of the United States in 1787 brought the issue to the forefront as it became clear that major philosophical and economic differences divided the delegates from the northern and southern states at the Constitutional Convention. The southern states wanted Negroes counted as persons for the purpose of determining how many representatives they would have in the federal House of Representatives. The northern states, not having slaves, objected. A somewhat strange compromise was reached as it was agreed by both sides that Negro slaves would be counted as three-fifths of a person. A second issue at the Convention pertained to the slave trade itself. The northern states wanted to stop it, while the southern states desired that the trade be allowed to continue. Once again a compromise was reached at the Convention that allowed the trade to continue from 1787 until 1807, at which time it would be stopped.

The Louisiana Purchase by the United States added enormous areas of new land in which new states of the union could be created. The issue now became whether these new states would be slave states or free states. This was an important question because each new state would send representatives to the federal House and Senate and thus have influence over national policy. An early test for the issue came in 1817 when Missouri sought to become a state. The North and South each wanted the new area for its side. Conflict was avoided when another compromise was made. It was decided that Missouri would be admitted as a slave state but that slavery would not be allowed anywhere north of Missouri's southern border. This became known as the Missouri Compromise of 1820. But almost 30 years later the issue surfaced once again.

Zachary Taylor won the presidency in 1848 but voiced no position regarding whether or not slavery should be allowed in the newer territories. California then sought admission as a state in 1849. Once again controversy arose between pro- and anti-slavery forces, and once again a compromise was forged. California was admitted as a free state, and no restrictions were placed on New Mexico and Utah. The final boundaries to Texas were established, and the state was given monetary compensation for the area that became New Mexico. The slave trade, but not slavery itself, was abolished in the nation's capital to satisfy those who opposed slavery, but the pro-slavery forces received the Fugitive Slave Act, which gave slave holders the ability to get federal help to recapture escaped slaves. Again, conflict was averted through the Compromise of 1850.

The issue of slavery in the territories refused to disappear and surfaced again in 1854 with the possibility of two new states, Kansas and Nebraska, seeking to enter the Union. Here yet another compromise was fashioned. The Missouri Compromise was repealed to satisfy the South, and the North received the potential for something northern Democrats felt was a democratic solution, the idea known as popular sovereignty. Simply put, this meant that the people in the territories would vote on whether they chose to be a slave or free state.

Yet seven years later southern states were seceding from the Union, President Lincoln called up troops to stop a rebellion, and the American Civil War had begun. What had happened to this long history of seeking compromises? Why was compromise not possible in 1860-61 even though it had been done before?

PROBLEM 14:
QUESTIONS FOR TEAM RESEARCH

1. What social, economic, and demographic changes had occurred in the U.S. between 1787 and 1860? Did these have any impact on the possibilities of compromise?

2. What did the quality of political leadership between 1820 and 1860 have to do with the possibility of compromise?

3. What role did the election of 1860 have on the ability or inability of the North and South to compromise?

4. Were all the compromises from 1787 to 1854 just tactics for "buying time" for something else to happen that would permanently solve the slavery controversy? What would each side be "buying time" for?

5. What role did the issue of the "morality" of slavery have to do with the possibility of compromise?

PROBLEM 14:
STARTING THE SEARCH FOR EVIDENCE

INTERNET: KEY WORDS AND PHRASES

The Compromise of 1820

The Compromise of 1850

John Brown

Southern newspapers and the election of 1860

BOOKS

Hamilton, Holman, *Prologue to Conflict, The Crisis and Compromise of 1850*, Lexington, University of Kentucky Press, 1964

Johansson, Robert Walter, *Douglas, Stephen A.*, Urbana, University of Illinois Press, 1997

Kutler, Stanley I., *The Dred Scott Decision: Law or Politics?*, Boston, Houghton Mifflin, 1967

Reynolds, David S., *John Brown, Abolitionist*, NY, Knopf, 2005

Rozwenc, Edwin C., *The Compromise of 1850*, Boston, Heath, 1957

THE DRED SCOTT DECISION

Report of the decision of the Supreme Court of the United States, and the opinions of the judges thereof, in the case of Dred Scott versus John F. A. Sandford. December term, 1856

Mr. Chief Justice Taney delivered the opinion of the Court…. In the opinion of the Court the legislation and histories of the times, and the language used in the Declaration of Independence, show that neither the class of persons who had been imported as slaves nor their descendants, whether they had become free or not, were then acknowledged as a part of the people nor intended to be included in the general words used in that memorable instrument…. They had for more than a century before been regarded as beings of an inferior order and altogether unfit to associate with the white race, either in social or political relations; and so far inferior that they had no rights which the white man was bound to respect; and that the Negro might justly and lawfully be reduced to slavery for his benefit. He was bought and sold and treated as an ordinary article of merchandise and traffic whenever a profit could be made by it. This opinion was at that time fixed and universal in the civilized portion of the white race…. No one, we presume, supposes that any change in public opinion or feeling, in relation to this unfortunate race, in the civilized nations of Europe or in this country should induce the Court to give to the words of the Constitution a more liberal construction in their favor than they were intended to bear when the instrument was framed and adopted…. And upon a full and careful consideration of the subject, the Court is of opinion that, upon the facts stated in the plea in abatement, Dred Scott was not a citizen of Missouri within the meaning of the Constitution of the United States and not entitled as such to sue in its courts…. We proceed…to inquire whether the facts relied on by the plaintiff entitle him to his freedom…. The act of Congress, upon which the plaintiff relies, declares that slavery and involuntary servitude, except as a punishment for crime, shall be forever prohibited in all that part of the territory ceded by France, under the name of Louisiana, which lies north of thirty-six degrees thirty minutes north latitude and not included within the limits of Missouri. And the difficulty which meets us…is whether Congress was authorized to pass this law under any of the powers granted to it by the Constitution…. As there is no express regulation in the Constitution defining the power which the general government may exercise over the person or property of a citizen in a territory thus acquired, the Court must necessarily look to the provisions and principles of the Constitution, and its distribution of powers, for the rules and principles by which its decisions must be governed. Taking this rule to guide us, it may be safely assumed that citizens of the United States who migrate to a territory…cannot be ruled as mere colonists, dependent upon the will of the general government, and to be governed by any laws it may think proper to impose…. For example, no one, we presume, will contend that Congress can make any law in a territory respecting the establishment of religion…or abridging the freedom of speech or of the press…. These powers, and others…are…denied to the general government; and the rights of private property have been guarded with equal care…. An act of Congress which deprives a citizen of the United States of his liberty or property, without due process of law, merely because he came himself or brought his property into a particular territory of the United States…could hardly be dignified with the name of due process of law. The powers over person and property of which we speak are not only not granted to Congress but are in express terms denied and they are forbidden to exercise them…. And if Congress itself cannot due this…it could not authorize a territorial government to exercise them…. It seems, however, to be supposed that there is a difference between property in a slave and other property…. Now…the right of property in a slave is distinctly and expressly affirmed in the Constitution. The right to traffic in it, like an ordinary article of merchandise and property, was guaranteed to the citizens of the United States, in every state that might desire it, for twenty years. And the government in express terms is pledged to protect it in all future time if the slave escapes from his owner. This is done in plain words—too plain to be misunderstood. And no word can be found in the Constitution which gives Congress a greater power over slave property or which entitles property of that kind to less protection than property of any other description…. Upon these considerations it is the opinion of the Court that the act of Congress which prohibited a citizen from holding and owning property of this kind in the territory of the United States north of the line therein mentioned is not warranted by the Constitution and is therefore void; and that neither

Dred Scott himself, nor any of his family, were made free by being carried into this territory; even if they had been carried there by the owner with the intention of becoming a permanent resident.

—Annotated by Rep. Benjamin Chew Howard (1791-1872),
recorder of United States Supreme Court decisions, 1857

PROBLEM 14:
CONNECTION TO TODAY

1. Are there times when compromise of any kind is just not possible? What would characterize such a time?

2. Slavery is considered a moral issue. Is it possible to compromise on moral issues? Explain.

3. Is it fair to say that the issue of abortion in our time resembles the issue of slavery in that the advocates of both sides of the abortion issue basically say there is nothing to compromise about?

4. When political compromises fail, does that mean the political system itself has failed? What are some contemporary examples of political compromises that have succeed and failed?

5. Can you imagine what kind of compromise might have been fashioned in 1860? What would it have been, and why might it have averted war?

6. Does the nature of our political parties today make compromise easier or more difficult? Explain.

PROBLEM 15: IF THE ORIGINAL THIRTEEN COLONIES AND SUBSEQUENT STATES ENTERED AN ENTITY CALLED THE UNITED STATES OF AMERICA ON A VOLUNTARY BASIS, WHY COULD THE SOUTH NOT LEAVE THE UNION IN 1860 IN THE SAME VOLUNTARY WAY IF THEY CHOSE TO DO SO?

JOHN C. CALHOUN

PROBLEM 15: IF THE ORIGINAL THIRTEEN COLONIES AND SUBSEQUENT STATES ENTERED AN ENTITY CALLED THE UNITED STATES OF AMERICA ON A VOLUNTARY BASIS, WHY COULD THE SOUTH NOT LEAVE THE UNION IN 1860 IN THE SAME VOLUNTARY WAY IF THEY CHOSE TO DO SO?

The issue regarding the permanence of the union of states that comprise the United States of America is a complex one. In our pledge of allegiance to the flag of the United States we all recite the phrase, "one nation, under God, indivisible, with liberty and justice for all," which clearly states that the United States cannot be divided. President Lincoln clearly believed that the secession of southern states was an illegal act of domestic rebellion that had to be suppressed. But on what authority did Lincoln act? The U.S. Constitution says nothing about secession, and the Tenth Amendment to that document reserves powers not delegated to the United States to the individual states. One could interpret this to mean that the states could act to secede because the Constitution does not specifically prohibit it.

The issue is further complicated by the ideals and values that we as a nation hold to be fundamental. Our Declaration of Independence states clearly that, "governments are instituted among men, deriving these just powers from the consent of the governed; that whenever any form of government becomes destructive of these ends, it is the right of the people to alter and abolish it, and to institute new government...." Given these words, the history of our own rebellion against Great Britain as well as the lack of specificity regarding the permanence of the Union in our Constitution, what was Lincoln's rationale for forbidding states from seceding? By what authority did he say or believe he acted? Was Lincoln on solid legal, historical, and moral ground?

PROBLEM 15:
QUESTIONS FOR TEAM RESEARCH

1. Historically what have been the arguments for and against secession? Are these arguments based on any legal foundation?

2. What kinds of social, political, and economic pressures did Lincoln face as he confronted the issue of secession? What impact did these factors have on his decision to stop the secessionist movement?

3. What arguments would you make for the right of a state to leave the union? What arguments would you make against such a right?

4. Was Lincoln's position one that was influenced not by legal or constitutional concerns but rather by what impact secession would have on the states that remained in the Union?

5. If the United States of America had been permanently divided into two separate nations, what direction would each have taken?

6. If slavery had not been abolished during the Civil War, would it have survived into the 20th century? Explain.

PROBLEM 15:
STARTING THE SEARCH FOR EVIDENCE

INTERNET: KEY WORDS AND PHRASES

The Hartford Convention

The Virginia and Kentucky Resolutions

John C. Calhoun and the Nullification Crisis

Abraham Lincoln and the Union

BOOKS

Banner, James M., *The Hartford Convention: The Federalists and the Origins of Party Politics in Massachusetts 1789–1815*, NY, Knopf, 1970

Ellis, Richard E., *The Union at Risk: Jacksonian Democracy, States Rights and the Nullification Crisis*, NY, Oxford University Press, 1987

Niven, John, *John C. Calhoun and the Price of Union: A Biography*, Baton Rouge, Louisiana University Press, 1988

Phillips, Ulrich Bonnell, *The Course of the South to Secession, An Interpretation*, NY, Hill and Wang, 1964

Watkins, William J., Jr., *Reclaiming the American Revolution: the Kentucky and Virginia Resolutions and Their Legacy*, NY, Palgrave Macmillan, 2004

South Carolina Nullification Ordinance, November 24, 1832

An ordinance to nullify certain acts of the Congress of the United States, purporting to be laws laying duties and imposts on the importation of foreign commodities.

Whereas the Congress of the United States by various acts, purporting to be acts laying duties and imposts on foreign imports, but in reality intended for the protection of domestic manufactures and the giving of bounties to classes and individuals engaged in particular employments, at the expense and to the injury and oppression of other classes and individuals, and by wholly exempting from taxation certain foreign commodities, such as are not produced or manufactured in the United States, to afford a pretext for imposing higher and excessive duties on articles similar to those intended to be protected, hath exceeded its just powers under the constitution, which confers on it no authority to afford such protection, and hath violated the true meaning and intent of the constitution, which provides for equality in imposing the burdens of taxation upon the several States and portions of the confederacy: And whereas the said Congress, exceeding its just power to impose taxes and collect revenue for the purpose of effecting and accomplishing the specific objects and purposes which the constitution of the United States authorizes it to effect and accomplish, hath raised and collected unnecessary revenue for objects unauthorized by the constitution.

We, therefore, the people of the State of South Carolina, in convention assembled, do declare and ordain and it is hereby declared and ordained, that the several acts and parts of acts of the Congress of the United States, purporting to be laws for the imposing of duties and imposts on the importation of foreign commodities, and now having actual operation and effect within the United States, and, more especially, an act entitled "An act in alteration of the several acts imposing duties on imports," approved on the nineteenth day of May, one thousand eight hundred and twenty-eight and also an act entitled "An act to alter and amend the several acts imposing duties on imports," approved on the fourteenth day of July, one thousand eight hundred and thirty-two, are unauthorized by the constitution of the United States, and violate the true meaning and intent thereof and are null, void, and no law, nor binding upon this State, its officers or citizens; and all promises, contracts, and obligations, made or entered into, or to be made or entered into, with purpose to secure the duties imposed by said acts, and all judicial proceedings which shall be hereafter had in affirmance thereof, are and shall be held utterly null and void.

And it is further ordained, that it shall not be lawful for any of the constituted authorities, whether of this State or of the United States, to enforce the payment of duties imposed by the said acts within the limits of this State; but it shall be the duty of the legislature to adopt such measures and pass such acts as may be necessary to give full effect to this ordinance, and to prevent the enforcement and arrest the operation of the said acts and parts of acts of the Congress of the United States within the limits of this State, from and after the first day of February next, and the duties of all other constituted authorities, and of all persons residing or being within the limits of this State, and they are hereby required and enjoined to obey and give effect to this ordinance, and such acts and measures of the legislature as may be passed or adopted in obedience thereto.

And it is further ordained, that in no case of law or equity, decided in the courts of this State, wherein shall be drawn in question the authority of this ordinance, or the validity of such act or acts of the legislature as may be passed for the purpose of giving effect thereto, or the validity of the aforesaid acts of Congress, imposing duties, shall any appeal be taken or allowed to the Supreme Court of the United States, nor shall any copy of the record be permitted or allowed for that purpose; and if any such appeal shall be attempted to be taken, the courts of this State shall proceed to execute and enforce their judgments according to the laws and usages of the State, without reference to such attempted appeal, and the person or persons attempting to take such appeal may be dealt with as for a contempt of the court.

And it is further ordained, that all persons now holding any office of honor, profit, or trust, civil or military, under this State (members of the legislature excepted), shall, within such time, and in such manner as the legislature shall prescribe, take an oath well and truly to obey, execute, and enforce this ordinance, and such act or acts of the legislature as may be passed in pursuance thereof, according to the true intent and meaning of the same, and on the neglect or omission of any such person or persons so to do, his or their office or offices shall be forthwith vacated, and shall be filled up as if such person or persons were dead or had resigned; and no person hereafter elected to any office of honor, profit, or trust, civil or military (members of the legislature excepted), shall, until the legislature shall otherwise provide and direct, enter on the execution of his office, or be he any respect competent to discharge the duties thereof until he shall, in like manner, have taken a similar oath; and no juror shall be impaneled in any of the courts of this State, in any cause in which shall be in question this ordinance, or any act of the legislature passed in pursuance thereof, unless he shall first, in addition to the usual oath, have taken an oath that he will well and truly obey, execute, and enforce this ordinance, and such act or acts of the legislature as may be passed to carry the same into operation and effect, according to the true intent and meaning thereof.

And we, the people of South Carolina, to the end that it may be fully understood by the government of the United States, and the people of the co-States, that we are determined to maintain this our ordinance and declaration, at every hazard, do further declare that we will not submit to the application of force on the part of the federal government, to reduce this State to obedience, but that we will consider the passage, by Congress, of any act authorizing the employment of a military or naval force against the State of South Carolina, her constitutional authorities or citizens; or any act abolishing or closing the ports of this State, or any of them, or otherwise obstructing the free ingress and egress of vessels to and from the said ports, or any other act on the part of the federal government, to coerce the State, shut up her ports, destroy or harass her commerce or to enforce the acts hereby declared to be null and void, otherwise than through the civil tribunals of the country, as inconsistent with the longer continuance of South Carolina in the Union; and that the people of this State will henceforth hold themselves absolved from all further obligation to maintain or preserve their political connection with the people of the other States; and will forthwith proceed to organize a separate government, and do all other acts and things which sovereign and independent States may of right do.

Done in convention at Columbia, the twenty-fourth day of November, in the year of our Lord one thousand eight hundred and thirty-two, and in the fifty-seventh year of the Declaration of the Independence of the United States of America.

PROBLEM 15:
CONNECTION TO TODAY

1. The issue of secession is not one that died with the Civil War. Texas, Vermont, and other states have recently discussed the possibility of secession. On what grounds have these states made their case?

2. What could happen today if a state declared that they wanted independence from the United States? Would there be lawsuits? Would the President, like Lincoln, send in federal troops to prevent the movement?

3. Is it hypocrisy for the United States to oppose foreign governments that seek to suppress independence or break-away areas from their country? On what grounds could we object?

4. How has Canada dealt with movements of provinces such as Quebec that seek independence from the country?

PROBLEM 16:
DOES ABRAHAM LINCOLN DESERVE THE TITLE, "THE GREAT EMANCIPATOR"?

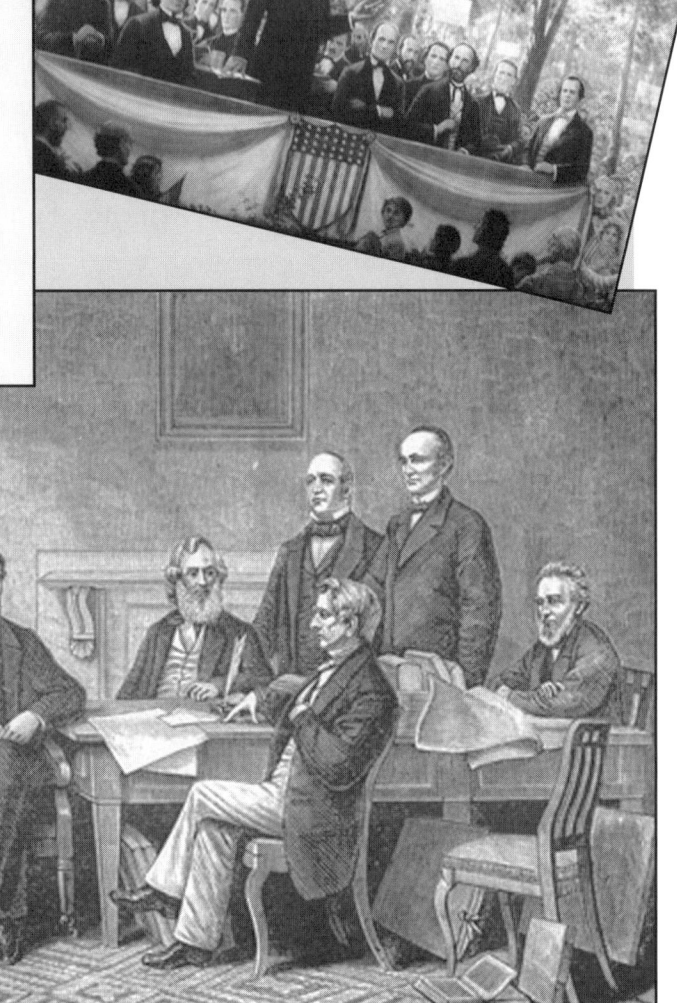

RIGHT: U.S. SENATE CANDIDATE ABRAHAM LINCOLN DEBATING STEPHEN A. DOUGLAS IN 1858

BELOW: PRESIDENT ABRAHAM LINCOLN AND HIS CABINET AT THE SIGNING OF THE EMANCIPATION PROCLAMATION IN 1863

PROBLEM 16: DOES ABRAHAM LINCOLN DESERVE THE TITLE, "THE GREAT EMANCIPATOR"?

On virtually all surveys regarding the standing of American presidents, Abraham Lincoln is ranked as the greatest of the nation's chief executives. The story of his rise from humble origins to the presidency represents the essence of the American dream. The challenge he faced in the Civil War was the greatest domestic crisis ever confronted by an American president, and his assassination as he brought the conflict to an end placed him in the hallowed category of national martyr and legend. When Americans are asked why he is held in such high regard, the most frequent response is that he freed the slaves and that he was the Great Emancipator. But do the historical facts justify those responses by average Americans?

A search of the historical record reveals an often confusing picture of Lincoln's attitude toward Negroes. As a lawyer Lincoln defended the right of a slave owner to regain his slaves when they had been captured after attempting to escape. He often spoke as though Negroes were not the equal of whites and that he certainly would not have a Negro woman as a wife. His answer to the problem of slavery was to deport the Negroes back to Africa because he did not believe free blacks and whites could live together in the United States. In his campaign for the presidency he promised not to interfere with slavery where it already existed, because he said the Constitution gave him no authority to do so. And his public statements regarding the reason for the Civil War were focused on stopping an illegal rebellion and keeping the union from falling apart, not on ending slavery.

Yet Lincoln also took very strong public positions regarding the end of slavery. He said he believed Negroes were human beings, and no human beings should be kept in positions in which they lived as slaves. He strongly opposed the extension of slavery into areas in which it had not previously existed. As President he acted against the advice of many in his cabinet and issued the Emancipation Proclamation in 1863, which stated to the nation and to the world that at the end of the Civil War the union not only would remain intact but also that slavery would end as an institution forever in the United States. How can we explain what Lincoln really believed about Negroes? About slavery? What final judgment can we make as to whether or not Abraham Lincoln deserved his title as the Great Emancipator?

PROBLEM 16:
QUESTIONS FOR TEAM RESEARCH

1. Should historians judge people by contemporary standards and values or by those of the time in which an individual lived? Why? What difference does this make in writing history?

2. What were the political considerations in Lincoln's mind in the years prior to his winning the presidency and after he became president?

3. Were there circumstances or events that made Lincoln's thinking about the issue of slavery evolve or change? What were they?

4. Did the Emancipation Proclamation actually free any slaves? If so when and where? If not, why not?

PROBLEM 16:
STARTING THE SEARCH FOR EVIDENCE

INTERNET: KEY WORDS AND PHRASES

Lincoln's views on slavery

Lincoln's views on Negroes

Lincoln-Douglas Debates

Lincoln's First Inaugural Address

The Emancipation Proclamation

BOOKS

Burchard, Peter, *Lincoln and Slavery*, NY, Atheneum Books, 1999

Johanssen, Robert Walter, *Lincoln, the South, and Slavery*, Baton Rouge, Louisiana State University, 1993

Roberts, Russell, *Lincoln and the Abolition of Slavery*, San Diego, Lucent Books, 2000

Striner, Richard, *Father Abraham: Lincoln's Relentless Struggle to End Slavery*, NY, Oxford University Press, 2006

Zarefsky, David, *Lincoln, Douglas, and Slavery: In the Crucible of Public Debate*, Chicago, University of Chicago Press, 1990

President Abraham, First Inaugural Address, March 4, 1861

Fellow citizens of the United States:

In compliance with a custom as old as the government itself, I appear before you to address you briefly, and to take, in your presence, the oath prescribed by the Constitution of the United States, to be taken by the President "before he enters on the execution of his office."

I do not consider it necessary, at present, for me to discuss those matters of administration about which there is no special anxiety, or excitement.

Apprehension seems to exist among the people of the Southern States, that by the accession of a Republican Administration, their property, and their peace, and personal security, are to be endangered. There has never been any reasonable cause for such apprehension. Indeed, the most ample evidence to the contrary has all the while existed, and been open to their inspection. It is found in nearly all the published speeches of him who now addresses you. I do but quote from one of those speeches when I declare that "I have no purpose, directly or indirectly, to interfere with the institution of slavery in the States where it exists. I believe I have no lawful right to do so, and I have no inclination to do so." Those who nominated and elected me did so with full knowledge that I had made this, and many similar declarations, and had never recanted them. And more than this, they placed in the platform, for my acceptance, and as a law to themselves, and to me, the clear and emphatic resolution which I now read:

"Resolved, That the maintenance inviolate of the rights of the States, and especially the right of each State to order and control its own domestic institutions according to its own judgment exclusively, is essential to that balance of power on which the perfection and endurance of our political fabric depend; and we denounce the lawless invasion by armed force of the soil of any State or Territory, no matter under what pretext, as among the gravest of crimes."

I now reiterate these sentiments: and in doing so, I only press upon the public attention the most conclusive evidence of which the case is susceptible, that the property, peace and security of no section are to be in anywise endangered by the now incoming

Administration. I add too, that all the protection which, consistently with the Constitution and the laws, can be given, will be cheerfully given to all the States when lawfully demanded, for whatever cause—as cheerfully to one section, as to another.

There is much controversy about the delivering up of fugitives from service or labor. The clause I now read is as plainly written in the Constitution as any other of its provisions:

> "No person held to service or labor in one State under the laws thereof, escaping into another, shall, in consequence of any law or regulation therein, be discharged from such service or labor, but shall be delivered up on claim of the party to whom such service or labor may be due."

It is scarcely questioned that this provision was intended by those who made it, for the reclaiming of what we call fugitive slaves; and the intention of the law-giver is the law. All members of Congress swear their support to the whole constitution—to this provision as much as to any other. To the proposition then, that slaves whose cases come within the terms of this clause, "shall be delivered up," their oaths are unanimous. Now, if they would make the effort in good temper, could they not, with nearly equal unanimity, frame and pass a law, by means of which to keep good that unanimous oath?

There is some difference of opinion whether this clause should be enforced by national or by state authority; but surely that difference is not a very material one. If the slave is to be surrendered, it can be of but little consequence to him, or to others, by which authority it is done. And should any one, in any case, be content that his oath shall go unkept, on a merely unsubstantial controversy as to how it shall be kept?

Again, in any law upon this subject, ought not all the safeguards of liberty known in civilized and humane jurisprudence to be introduced, so that a free man be not, in any case, surrendered as a slave? And might it not be well, at the same time, to provide by law for the enforcement of that clause in the Constitution which guaranties that "The citizens of each State shall be entitled to all privileges and immunities of citizens in the several States?"

I take the official oath today, with no mental reservations, and with no purpose to construe the Constitution or laws, by any hypercritical rules. And while I do not choose now to specify particular acts of Congress as proper to be enforced, I do suggest, that it will be much safer for all, both in official and private stations, to conform to, and abide by, all those acts which stand unrepealed, than to violate any of them, trusting to find impunity in having them held to be unconstitutional.

It is seventy-two years since the first inauguration of a President under our national Constitution. During that period fifteen different and greatly distinguished citizens, have, in succession, administered the executive branch of the government. They have conducted it through many perils; and, generally, with great success. Yet, with all this scope for precedent, I now enter upon the same task for the brief constitutional term of four years, under great and peculiar difficulty. A disruption of the Federal Union heretofore only menaced, is now formidably attempted.

I hold, that in contemplation of universal law, and of the Constitution, the Union of these States is perpetual. Perpetuity is implied, if not expressed, in the fundamental law of all national governments. It is safe to assert that no government proper, ever had a provision in its organic law for its own termination. Continue to execute all the express provisions of our national Constitution, and the Union will endure forever—it being impossible to destroy it, except by some action not provided for in the instrument itself.

Again, if the United States be not a government proper, but an association of States in the nature of contract merely, can it, as a contract, be peaceably unmade, by less than all the parties who made it? One party to a contract may violate it—break it, so to speak; but does it not require all to lawfully rescind it?

Descending from these general principles, we find the proposition that, in legal contemplation, the Union is perpetual, confirmed by the history of the Union itself. The Union is much older than the Constitution. It was formed in fact, by the Articles of Association in 1774. It was matured and continued by the Declaration of Independence in 1776. It was further matured and the faith of all the then thirteen States expressly plighted and engaged that it should be perpetual, by the Articles of Confederation in 1778. And finally, in 1787, one of the declared objects for ordaining and establishing the Constitution, was "to form a more perfect union."

But if destruction of the Union, by one, or by a part only, of the States, be lawfully possible, the Union is less perfect than before the Constitution, having lost the vital element of perpetuity.

It follows from these views that no State, upon its own mere motion, can lawfully get out of the Union,—that resolves and ordinances to that effect are legally void; and that acts of violence, within any State or States, against the authority of the United States, are insurrectionary or revolutionary, according to circumstances.

I therefore consider that, in view of the Constitution and the laws, the Union is unbroken; and, to the extent of my ability, I shall take care, as the Constitution itself expressly enjoins upon me, that the laws of the Union be faithfully executed in all the States. Doing this I deem to be only a simple duty on my part; and I shall perform it, so far as practicable, unless my rightful masters, the American people, shall withhold the requisite means, or, in some authoritative manner, direct the contrary. I trust this will not be regarded as a menace, but only as the declared purpose of the Union that it will constitutionally defend, and maintain itself.

In doing this there needs to be no bloodshed or violence; and there shall be none, unless it be forced upon the national authority. The power confided to me, will be used to hold, occupy, and possess the property, and places belonging to the government, and to collect the duties and imposts; but beyond what may be necessary for these objects, there will be no invasion—no using of force against, or among the people anywhere. Where hostility to the United States, in any interior locality, shall be so great and so universal, as to prevent competent resident citizens from holding the Federal offices, there will be no attempt to force obnoxious strangers among the people for that object. While the strict legal right may exist in the government to enforce the exercise of these offices, the attempt to do so would be so irritating, and so nearly impracticable with all, that I deem it better to forego, for the time, the uses of such offices.

The mails, unless repelled, will continue to be furnished in all parts of the Union. So far as possible, the people everywhere shall have that sense of perfect security which is most favorable to calm thought and reflection. The course here indicated will be followed, unless current events, and experience, shall show a modification, or change, to be proper; and in every case and exigency, my best discretion will be exercised, according to circumstances actually existing, and with a view and a hope of a peaceful solution of the national troubles, and the restoration of fraternal sympathies and affections.

That there are persons in one section, or another who seek to destroy the Union at all events, and are glad of any pretext to do it, I will neither affirm or deny; but if there be such, I need address no word to them. To those, however, who really love the Union, may I not speak?

Before entering upon so grave a matter as the destruction of our national fabric, with all its benefits, its memories, and its hopes, would it not be wise to ascertain precisely why we do it? Will you hazard so desperate a step, while there is any possibility that any portion of the ills you fly from, have no real existence? Will you, while the certain ills you fly to, are greater than all the real ones you fly from? Will you risk the commission of so fearful a mistake?

All profess to be content in the Union, if all constitutional rights can be maintained. Is it true, then, that any right, plainly written in the Constitution, has been denied? I think not. Happily the human mind is so constituted, that no party can reach to the audacity of doing this. Think, if you can, of a single instance in which a plainly written provision of the Constitution has ever been denied. If, by the mere force of numbers, a majority should deprive a minority of any clearly written constitutional right, it might, in a moral point of view, justify revolution—certainly would, if such right were a vital one. But such is not our case. All the vital rights of minorities, and of individuals, are so plainly assured to them, by affirmations and negations guaranties and prohibitions in the Constitution, that controversies never arise concerning them. But no organic law can ever be framed with a provision specifically applicable to every question which may occur in practical administration. No foresight can anticipate, nor any document of reasonable length contain express provisions for all possible questions. Shall fugitives from labor be surrendered by national or by State authority? The Constitution does not expressly say. May Congress prohibit slavery in the territories? The Constitution does not expressly say. Must Congress protect slavery in the territories? The Constitution does not expressly say.

From questions of this class spring all our constitutional controversies, and we divide upon them into majorities and minorities. If the minority will not acquiesce, the majority must, or the government must cease. There is no other alternative; for continuing the government, is acquiescence on one side or the other. If a minority, in such case, will secede rather than acquiesce, they make a precedent which, in turn, will divide and ruin them; for a minority of their own will secede from them, whenever a majority refuses to be controlled by such minority. For instance, why may not any portion of a new confederacy, a year or two hence, arbitrarily secede again, precisely as portions of the present Union now claim to secede from it. All who cherish disunion sentiments, are now being educated to the exact temper of doing this. Is there such perfect identity of interests among the States to compose a new Union, as to produce harmony only, and prevent renewed secession?

Plainly, the central idea of secession, is the essence of anarchy. A majority, held in restraint by constitutional checks, and limitations, and always changing easily, with deliberate changes of popular opinions and sentiments, is the only true sovereign of a free people. Whoever rejects it, does of necessity, fly to anarchy or to despotism. Unanimity is impossible; the rule of a minority as a permanent arrangement, is wholly inadmissible; so that rejecting the majority principle, anarchy, or despotism in some form, is all that is left.

I do not forget the position assumed by some, that constitutional questions are to be decided by the Supreme Court; nor do I deny that such decisions must be binding in any case upon the parties to a suit, as to the object of that suit, while they are also entitled to very high respect and consideration, in all parallel cases, by all other departments of the government. And while it is obviously possible that such decision may be erroneous in any given case, still the evil effect following it, being limited to that particular case, with the chance that it may be over-ruled, and never become a precedent for other cases, can better be borne than could the evils of a different practice. At the same time the candid citizen must confess that if the policy of the government, upon vital questions, affecting the whole people, is to be irrevocably fixed by decisions of the Supreme Court, the instant they are made, in ordinary litigation between parties, in personal actions, the people will have ceased, to be their own rulers, having, to that extent, practically resigned their government, into the hands of that eminent tribunal. Nor is there, in this view, any assault upon the court, or the judges. It is a duty, from which they may not shrink, to decide cases properly brought before them; and it is no fault of theirs, if others seek to turn their decisions to political purposes.

One section of our country believes slavery is right, and ought to be extended, while the other believes it is wrong, and ought not to be extended. This is the only substantial dispute. The fugitive slave clause of the Constitution, and the law for the suppression of the foreign slave trade, are each as well enforced, perhaps, as any law can ever be in a community where the moral sense of the people imperfectly supports the law itself. The great body of the people abide by the dry legal obligation in both cases, and a few break over in each. This, I think, cannot be perfectly cured; and it would be worse in both cases after the separation of the sections, than before. The foreign slave trade, now imperfectly suppressed, would be ultimately revived without restriction, in one section; while fugitive slaves, now only partially surrendered, would not be surrendered at all, by the other.

Physically speaking, we cannot separate. We cannot, remove our respective sections from each other, nor build an impassable wall between them. A husband and wife may be divorced, and go out of the presence, and beyond the reach of each other; but the different parts of our country cannot do this. They cannot but remain face to face; and intercourse, either amicable or hostile, must continue between them, Is it possible then to make that intercourse more advantageous or more satisfactory, after separation than before? Can aliens make treaties easier than friends can make laws? Can treaties be more faithfully enforced between aliens, than laws can among friends? Suppose you go to war, you cannot fight always; and when, after much loss on both sides, and no gain on either, you cease fighting, the identical old questions, as to terms of intercourse, are again upon you.

This country, with its institutions, belongs to the people who inhabit it. Whenever they shall grow weary of the existing government, they can exercise their constitutional right of amending it, or their revolutionary right to dismember, or overthrow it. I can not be ignorant of the fact that many worthy, and patriotic citizens are desirous of having the national constitution amended. While I make no recommendation of amendments, I fully recognize the rightful authority of the people over the whole subject, to be exercised in either of the modes prescribed in the instrument itself; and I should, under existing circumstances, favor, rather than oppose, a fair opportunity being afforded the people to act upon it.

I will venture to add that, to me, the convention mode seems preferable, in that it allows amendments to originate with the people themselves, instead of only permitting them to take or reject, propositions, originated by others, not especially chosen for the purpose, and which might not be precisely such, as they would wish to either accept or refuse. I understand a proposed amendment to the Constitution—which amendment, however, I have not seen, has passed Congress, to the effect that the federal government, shall never interfere with the domestic institutions of the States, including that of persons held to service. To avoid misconstruction of what I have said, I depart from my purpose not to speak of particular amendments, so far as to say that, holding such a provision to now be implied constitutional law, I have no objection to its being made express, and irrevocable.

The Chief Magistrate derives all his authority from the people, and they have conferred none upon him to fix terms for the separation of the States. The people themselves can do this also if they choose; but the executive, as such, has nothing to do with it. His duty is to administer the present government, as it came to his hands, and to transmit it, unimpaired by him, to his successor.

Why should there not be a patient confidence in the ultimate justice of the people? Is there any better, or equal hope, in the world? In our present differences, is either party without faith of being in the right? If the Almighty Ruler of nations, with his eternal truth and justice, be on your side of the North, or on yours of the South, that truth, and that justice, will surely prevail, by the judgment of this great tribunal, the American people.

By the frame of the government under which we live, this same people have wisely given their public servants but little power for mischief; and have, with equal wisdom, provided for the return of that little to their own hands at very short intervals.

While the people retain their virtue, and vigilance, no administration, by any extreme of wickedness or folly, can very seriously injure the government, in the short space of four years.

My countrymen, one and all, think calmly and well, upon this whole subject. Nothing valuable can be lost by taking time. If there be an object to hurry any of you, in hot haste, to a step which you would never take deliberately, that object will be frustrated by taking time; but no good object can be frustrated by it. Such of you as are now dissatisfied, still have the old Constitution unimpaired, and, on the sensitive point, the laws of your own framing under it; while the new administration will have no immediate power, if it would, to change either. If it were admitted that you who are dissatisfied, hold the right side in the dispute, there still is no single good reason for precipitate action. Intelligence, patriotism, Christianity, and a firm reliance on Him, who has never yet forsaken this favored land, are still competent to adjust, in the best way, all our present difficulty.

In your hands, my dissatisfied fellow countrymen, and not in mine, is the momentous issue of civil war. The government will not assail you. You can have no conflict, without being yourselves the aggressors. You have no oath registered in Heaven to destroy the government, while I shall have the most solemn one to "preserve, protect and defend" it.

I am loath to close. We are not enemies, but friends. We must not be enemies. Though passion may have strained, it must not break our bonds of affection. The mystic chords of memory, stretching from every battle-field, and patriot grave, to every living heart and hearthstone, all over this broad land, will yet swell the chorus of the Union, when again touched, as surely they will be, by the better angels of our nature.

PROBLEM 16:
CONNECTION TO TODAY

1. Is it fair that some contemporary writers have classified Lincoln as a racist? Explain.

2. Today's politicians who change their minds on a particular issue are accused of flip-flopping. Are there any issues today in which our President might be accused of flip-flopping? Is this a fair and accurate assessment, or are there other things to take into account?

3. There are still respected scholars today who write and speak about differences between races and ethnic groups in our country and in the world. Why are they not given the same open reception that Lincoln was given when he spoke about the Negroes? What has changed?

4. Does slavery still exist in the world today? If so, who, if anyone, is defending or attacking it?

PROBLEM 17:
SHOULD PRESIDENT ANDREW JOHNSON HAVE BEEN IMPEACHED AND REMOVED FROM OFFICE?

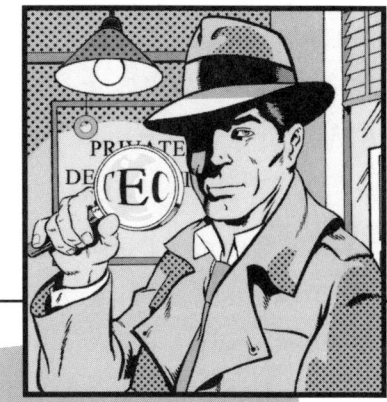

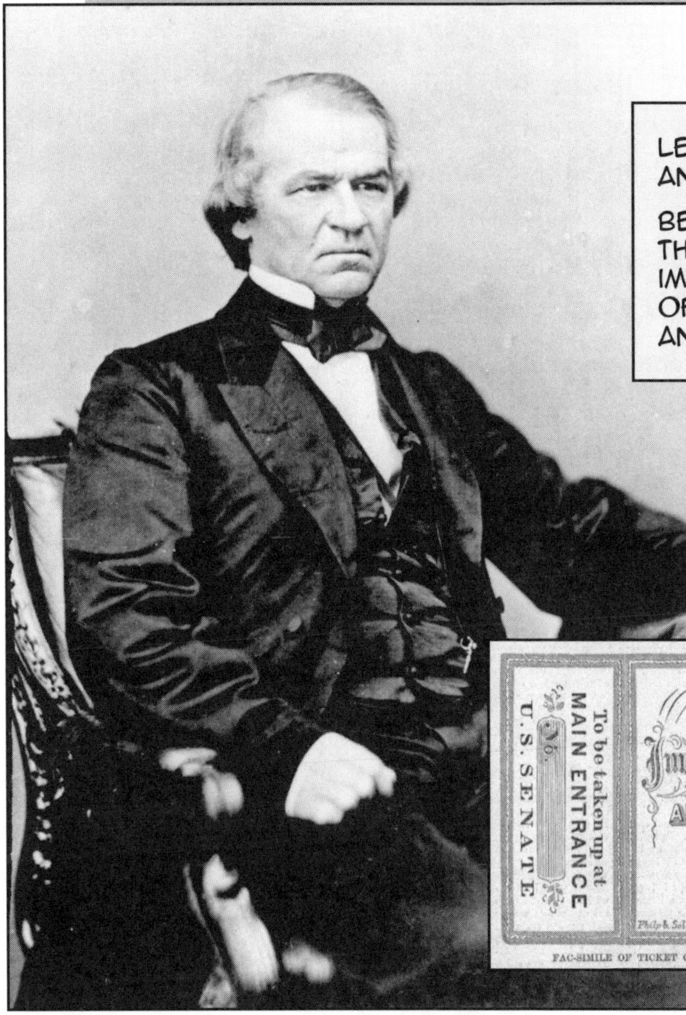

LEFT: PRESIDENT ANDREW JOHNSON

BELOW: TICKET TO THE U.S. SENATE IMPEACHMENT TRIAL OF PRESIDENT ANDREW JOHNSON

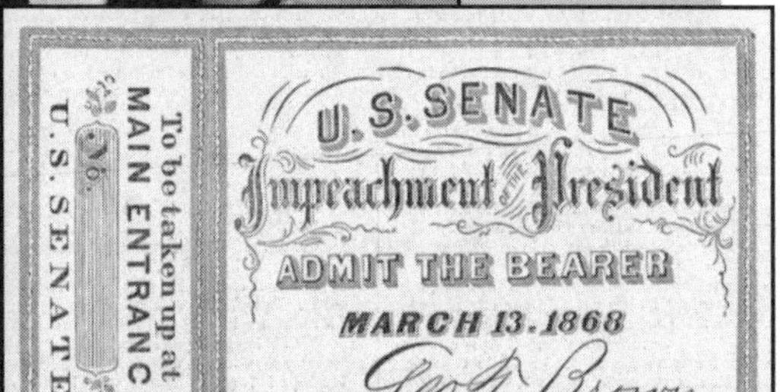

FAC-SIMILE OF TICKET OF ADMISSION TO THE IMPEACHMENT TRIAL.

PROBLEM 17: SHOULD PRESIDENT ANDREW JOHNSON HAVE BEEN IMPEACHED AND REMOVED FROM OFFICE?

Only two presidents in our history, Andrew Johnson and Bill Clinton, have been impeached. To be impeached means that the U.S. House of Representatives brings formal charges against a president. The U.S. Constitution states that the president can be removed from office, if found guilty, for "treason, bribery, or other high crimes and misdemeanors." The Constitution gives to the House of Representatives the power to charge, or impeach, the president, but he or she cannot be removed from office until he or she is found guilty in a trial conducted by the United States Senate. The first test of these constitutional provisions occurred after the Civil War with the impeachment and trial of President Andrew Johnson.

Andrew Johnson had served as vice president during the second term of President Abraham Lincoln and assumed the presidency upon Lincoln's assassination. Johnson was a self-educated man who never attended school and who had earned his living as a tailor in his early years. Upon entering politics he successfully won elections for mayor, congressman, governor, and senator in the state of Tennessee. President Lincoln, a Republican looking to win votes from Democrats in the 1864 election, selected Johnson as his vice presidential running mate.

Immediately there was tension between the Republicans in Congress and the new Democratic president both over Reconstruction policies as well as on a personal level. The Republicans saw Johnson, who had been a slave holder, as overly sympathetic to Southern concerns, while Johnson saw the Republicans' approach to the South and Reconstruction as too radical. The conflict went beyond public policy. The Republicans labeled Johnson a "drunken imbecile," because he had been drunk in public during his inauguration as vice president, while Johnson called the Republican radicals "factious, domineering, tyrannical" men.

The situation that led to Johnson's impeachment resulted from three acts of Congress that were vetoed by President Johnson and then overridden by Congress to become law. The Military Reconstruction Act divided the South into districts controlled by the federal government and put forth strict requirements for the defeated southern states to be readmitted to the Union. The second piece of legislation was the Command of the Army Act, which required the president to issue all military orders through the General of the Army rather than directly under his authority as Commander-in-Chief of the armed forces. The third Congressional act, the Tenure of Office Act, made it mandatory for the president to secure the consent of the Senate before he could remove from office any person whose appointment had been originally confirmed by the Senate.

The crisis came to a head when President Johnson moved to replace Secretary of War Edwin M. Stanton with his own selection, Lorenzo Thomas. Stanton refused to give up his position. Johnson also rejected the provisions of the Military Reconstruction Act and ordered the military governors in the South to report directly to him rather than to the General of the Army. On February 24, 1868, the House of Representatives voted for impeachment of Johnson, charging him with high crimes and misdemeanors and with instructions that more specific charges were to be drafted by a special committee. The committee wrote eleven articles of impeachment. The first eight articles charged President Johnson with violations of the Tenure of Office Act in illegally removing Stanton from office. Article 9 charged Johnson with violating the Command of the Army Act, and the final two articles charged Johnson with libeling the Congress through what they characterized as "inflammatory and scandalous harangues." The case then went to the United States Senate for trial.

Should Andrew Johnson have been impeached at all? Did his actions really represent high crimes and misdemeanors, and what does that Constitutional phrase really mean? Was Johnson merely defending what he believed were his powers and duties under the U.S. Constitution? Were the Articles of Impeachment real and serious accusations or merely trumped up charges to get rid of a president and individual so many Republicans just didn't like?

PROBLEM 17:
QUESTIONS FOR TEAM RESEARCH

1. Did the Tenure of Office Act really apply to Edwin Stanton or did the circumstances of his original appointment exempt him from the law?

2. Did Congress exercise its rightful authority in passing the three laws that Johnson vetoed or did it exceed its authority?

3. What provisions of the U.S. Constitution did President Johnson rely upon for a defense of his position?

4. What were the differences of position between Johnson and the Congress that brought the crisis to a head?

5. What were the arguments that saved Johnson from removal from office in the Senate trial?

6. Should Johnson have been impeached? Should he have been removed from office?

7. What precedents were at stake in this episode?

PROBLEM 17:
STARTING THE SEARCH FOR EVIDENCE

INTERNET: KEY WORDS AND PHRASES

Impeachment of Andrew Johnson

Andrew Johnson and the Articles of Impeachment

Andrew Johnson and the Radical Republicans

Reconstructions policies of Andrew Johnson

Newspaper opinion and the trial of Andrew Johnson

BOOKS

Beale, Howard K., *The Critical Year: A Study of Andrew Johnson and Reconstruction*, NY, F. Ungar Publishing Co., 1958

Benedict, Michael Les, *The Impeachment and Trial of Andrew Johnson*, NY, Norton, 1999

Hearn, Chester G., *The Impeachment of Andrew Johnson*, Jefferson, McFarland & Co., 2000

Mckitrick, Eric C., *Andrew Johnson and Reconstruction*, Chicago, University of Chicago Press, 1960

Trefousse, Hans Louis, *Impeachment of a President: Andrew Johnson, the Blacks and Reconstruction*, NY, Fordham University Press, 1999

CHARLES SUMNER'S OPINION OF THE IMPEACHMENT OF ANDREW JOHNSON

Battle with Slavery

This is one of the last great battles with slavery. Driven from these legislative Chambers; driven from the field of war, this monstrous power has found a refuge in the Executive Mansion, where, in utter disregard of the Constitution and laws, it seeks to exercise its ancient far-reaching sway. All this is very plain. Nobody can question it. Andrew Johnson is the impersonation of the tyrannical Slave Power. In him it lives again. He is the lineal ancestor of John C. Calhoun and Jefferson Davis. And he gathers about him the same supporters. Original partisans of slavery North and South; habitual compromisers of great principles; maligners of the Declaration of Independence politicians without heart; lawyers, for whom a technicality is everything, and a promiscuous company who at every stage of the battle have set their faces against Equal Rights; —these are his allies. It is the old troop of slavery, with a few recruits, ready as of old for violence— cunning in device and heartless in quibble. With the President at their head, they are now entrenched in the Executive Mansion.

Not to dislodge them is to leave this country a prey to one of the most hateful tyrannies of history. Especially is it to surrender the Unionists of the rebel States to violence and bloodshed. Not a month, not a week, not a day should be lost. *The safety of the Republic requires action at once.* The lives of innocent men must be rescued from sacrifice.

I would not in this judgment depart from that moderation which belongs to the occasion; but God forbid that, when called to deal with so great an offender, I should affect a coldness which I cannot feel. Slavery has been our worst enemy, murdering our children, filling our homes with mourning, and darkening the land with tragedy; and now it rears its crest anew with Andrew Johnson as its representative. Through him it assumes once more to rule the Republic and to impose its cruel law. The enormity of his conduct is aggravated by his barefaced treachery. He once declared himself the Moses of the colored race. Behold him now the Pharaoh. With such treachery in such a cause there can be no parley. Every sentiment, every conviction, every vow against slavery must now be directed against him. Pharaoh is at the bar of the Senate for judgment.

The formal accusation is founded on certain recent transgressions, enumerated in articles of impeachment, but it is wrong to suppose that this is the whole case. It is very wrong to try this impeachment merely on these articles. It is unpardonable to higgle over words and phrases when for more than two years the tyrannical pretensions of this offender, now in evidence before the Senate, as I shall show, have been manifest in their terrible, heartrending consequences.

Harper's Weekly Editorial on the Impeachment of Andrew Johnson

The Evidence Against the President

The case of the Managers of the House against the President, as we have elsewhere stated, has been conducted with great skill. The chain of evidence is continuous; nor has it been broken, or in any degree weakened, by the onsets in cross-examination of the President's counsel. Those gentlemen, or most of them, are very eminent lawyers. The ability of Mr. Stanbery has been manifested to the country while he was Attorney-General. Judge Curtis is acknowledged to be one of the most accomplished jurists in the United States. Mr. Evarts is also a very distinguished lawyer—man of remarkably clear, alert, and incisive mind. The other gentlemen of the President's counsel, Mr. Nelson and Mr. Groesbeck, have taken no part in the trial during the presentation of the case by the Managers.

There can be little question that upon all points susceptible of proof by evidence the Managers have justified their articles; and it was illustrative of the peculiar tact of General Butler that he reserved to the last one of his strongest points, and somewhat surprised and annoyed his antagonists when he produced it. This was the testimony of Mr. Creecy, Appointment-Clerk of the Treasury Department, and the autograph letter of the President to Secretary M'Culloch last August, notifying him that he had suspended Mr. Stanton in pursuance of the Tenure-of-Office Act, thereby shaming his own assertion that he had acted "Under the Constitution," and without recognizing the law in question. Indeed, General Butler has unquestionably had the best of the week's work. Only one serious effort of his has been baffled by the President's counsel; and Mr. Evarts's occasional caustic manner has not in the least disturbed the vast imperturbability of the practical advocate.

The case for the Managers, notwithstanding the array of articles, was really very simple. The most of it is of course already familiar, for all the transactions have been public. That there is a Tenure-of-Office law prescribing the conditions under which certain officers, including the Secretary of War, are to be removed, is not denied. That Mr. Stanton was peremptorily removed by the President during the session of the Senate is in evidence. That General Thomas, having been previously reinstated by the President as Adjutant-General, was appointed by him Secretary of War *ad interim* is proved. That General Thomas signed himself as such, and attempted to exercise the duties of the office; that he declared his intention to obtain possession by force if resisted, and that he stated his failure to do so was in consequence of the legal action of Mr. Stanton, is also proved. It is established further that the President officially acknowledged the validity of the law by confessedly acting under its authority, while he declared that he did not recognize it as binding; that in September, after the suspension of Mr. Stanton last summer, the President called General Emory to the command of the Department of the District, and upon his arrival to assume command had a detailed conversation in regard to the available military force there; that upon the day of the attempted removal of Mr. Stanton the President sent for General Emory and asked him again about the troops and what changes had been made; that when the General proceeded to explain the movements of regiments the President said he referred to other changes made within a day or two, to which the General replied that he knew of none, and that as all orders must by law pass through the hands of General Grant, if any new ones had been issued, he should of course be aware of them; that the President seemed surprised, and when the General showed him the order directing all orders for the army to pass through General Grant, the President said it was in derogation of his constitutional rights as Commander-in-Chief, to which General Emory replied that the officers of the army were of opinion that it was their duty to obey the order, which was in obedience to the law of Congress. It is further proved that the expressions ascribed to the President in the speeches during his Western trip were actually used by him.

The attempt of the Managers to show, in further proof of conspiracy, by the testimony of Mr. Chandler, that Mr. Edmund Cooper, late Private Secretary of the President, was made by him Assistant Secretary of the Treasury in order that the money of the Government might be obtained by the President for his purposes, was overruled by the Senate; the ground of its action being understood to be that the evidence would open too wide and irrelevant a range of inquiry. This was the only apparently important point not made by the Managers, and this was not essential. They closed the case promptly at the end of the first week, and the Senate then adjourned until the following Thursday to give the President's counsel an opportunity to prepare themselves fully, with the understanding that they will not call a great many witnesses.

The case is thus brought to the exact point which we have before indicated as the one upon which the force of the President's counsel was most likely to be concentrated. Conceding the facts claimed and substantially proved, that the law was regularly enacted, and that it forbade the removal during the session of the Senate of certain officers appointed by the President without the approval of the Senate; conceding that Mr. Stanton was Secretary of War, and was removed by the President without the consent of the Senate—then the question arises, was Mr. Stanton appointed Secretary of War by President Johnson? If he were, the law has been violated. If he were not, the law does not touch the case. The position taken by the Managers is revealed by a little remark of Mr. Wilson when he offered the first evidence for the prosecution. After putting in the commission of Mr. Stanton, signed by President Lincoln, Mr. Wilson said that it was the only commission the Managers proposed to prove, and that commission, in the judgment of the Managers, made Mr. Stanton Secretary of War. The battle will be joined just at this point. We will not anticipate the arguments, but the rule of common sense is plainly with the Managers. If a man holds an appointed office and the appointing power is changed, but the new power directs him to remain, it seems to be tolerably clear that he is reappointed. This is a subject, however, upon which there may be the utmost refinement of legal subtlety, of which we shall doubtless have a notable exhibition.

Should the appointment of Mr. Stanton as Secretary be maintained by the Managers, and he be judged to stand within the operation of the law, it is possible that the

President's counsel may try to show that there was no improper intention in its violation by the President. We doubt if the utmost skill can do this, for it is impossible to destroy the evidence that he had already recognized its validity. And even could it be done—even were it conceded that he had always refused to acknowledge the constitutionality of the law, yet the violation by the Executive of a law regularly enacted and not declared invalid by any court, is the substitution of the President's will for the law of the land, and the intention must be inferred from the fact. The President is not charged with what is generally called a crime, but with a high misdemeanor in the discharge of political functions. Should he be removed, he will not subsequently be pursued with a criminal prosecution, as the Constitution authorizes when a crime otherwise punishable has been committed. Indeed the case is very simple, and addresses itself to the common-sense of the whole country. Mr. Seward had already asked the people of the United States whether they would have Mr. Johnson for king; and we presume that the Senate will answer in their name—"Decidedly not."

PROBLEM 17:
CONNECTION TO TODAY

1. Why do you think the Founding Fathers made the reasons for impeachment so general and so vague?

2. Should there be more specific and detailed reasons for impeaching a president? What could those be?

3. Is there any problem with a president getting a fair deal when the charges against him are done in the House and the trial in the Senate? What might a different or more fair procedure be?

4. Did Andrew Johnson's impeachment and trial have any impact on the impeachment and trial of Bill Clinton? If so, what was that impact?

PROBLEM 18: DOES THE PERIOD FROM 1865 TO 1917 PROVE THE SUCCESS OR FAILURE OF CAPITALISM AS AN ECONOMIC SYSTEM?

LEFT:
ANDREW CARNEGIE

RIGHT:
JOHN D. ROCKEFELLER

PROBLEM 18: DOES THE PERIOD FROM 1865 TO 1917 PROVE THE SUCCESS OR FAILURE OF CAPITALISM AS AN ECONOMIC SYSTEM?

The years immediately following the end of the American Civil War witnessed an unprecedented period of economic growth and expansion. While the population of the country grew dramatically, the number of workers in manufacturing increased five and one-half times, and the value created by manufacturing increased almost twelve times. By 1890 the value of goods manufactured surpassed those of agriculture for the first time in our history. This economic boom had profound effects on the nation and its people.

A new class of entrepreneurs used their imaginations, hard work, creativity, and ambition to create a modern capitalist economy. Men such as John D. Rockefeller, Andrew Carnegie, Cornelius Vanderbilt, and J.P. Morgan built huge new businesses, gave employment to millions of people, and amassed previously unheard of amounts of personal wealth. They became so powerful that they far surpassed the impact and importance of most of the American presidents in the late 19th century. The distribution of wealth in the country became increasingly unbalanced, with a small percentage of individuals holding the majority of the nation's wealth. History has given some of these business giants the name "robber barons" because of the way they disregarded rules, regulations, laws, and ethical behavior. Others have seen this period and these businessmen in a different light.

These entrepreneurs represent what makes America unique and great. They represented a true living of the American Dream—starting small, working hard, and building great enterprises that brought them the enormous wealth that they had earned. They may have become fabulously rich, but they also provided huge opportunities both for Americans to make a living and for themselves to acquire social mobility. But what price did America pay for this rapid and huge movement to an industrialized country? Some clearly prospered, but the majority worked long hours in environments that were often unsafe and unsanitary and that offered no guarantee of ongoing employment.

Labor unions developed to counter these conditions, and strife between workers and owners became commonplace. Is this what capitalism was all about? Increasingly it became clear that capitalism was posing a new problem for society—how could we balance efficiency and maximum production against protection and benefits for the worker and consumer? Or was this a problem with no satisfactory solution? The period from 1865 to 1917 made Americans confront a fundamental question: How could society weigh the benefits and problems of modern capitalism? Did the Americans experience in those years prove that industrial capitalism was a success or a failure?

PROBLEM 18:
QUESTIONS FOR TEAM RESEARCH

1. What were the reasons that industrial capitalism suddenly "took off" in the years following the Civil War? Why had this not happened before the war?

2. Were the entrepreneurs who led the way really "robber barons" or just smart businessmen who deserved the wealth they received from their business?

3. What role, if any, did government play during this period in helping or hindering the growth of big business?

4. What were the reasons this period witnessed a movement toward "bigness" and "consolidation" of business enterprises?

5. What was the condition of the average American working in one of these new business enterprises? What were the employment options for these people at the time?

6. By what criteria should we judge whether industrial capitalism was a success or failure in the years 1865 to 1917?

PROBLEM 18:
STARTING THE SEARCH FOR EVIDENCE

INTERNET: KEY WORDS AND PHRASES

Civil War and industrialization

Andrew Carnegie

John D. Rockefeller

U.S. Supreme Court and big business in the 19th century

Robber barons

BOOKS

Carnegie, Andrew, *The "Gospel of Wealth" and Other Writings*, NY. Penguin Press, 2006

Coffey, Ellen Greenman, *John D. Rockefeller, Empire Builder*, Englewood Cliffs, NJ, Silver Burdett, 1989

Jones, Peter D'Alroy, *The Robber Barons Revisited*, Boston, Heath, 1968

Josephson, Matthew, *The Robber Barons: The Great American Capitalists, 1861–1901*, NY, Harcourt Brace, 1934

Latham, Earl, *John D. Rockefeller: Robber Baron or Industrial Statesman*, Boston, Heath, 1949

Andrew Carnegie's Statement Entitled "The Gospel of Wealth" (1889)

The problem of our age is the administration of wealth, so that the ties of brotherhood may still bind together the rich and poor in harmonious relationship. The conditions of human life have not only been changed, but revolutionized, within the past few hundred years. In former days there was little difference between the dwelling, dress, food, and environment of the chief and those of his retainers…The contrast between the palace of the millionaire and the cottage of the laborer with us today measures the change which has come with civilization.

This change, however, is not to be deplored, but welcomed as highly beneficial. It is well, nay, essential for the progress of the race, that the houses of some should be homes for all that is highest and best in literature and the arts, and for all the refinements of civilization, rather than that none should be so. Much better this great irregularity than universal squalor. Without wealth there can be no Maecenas [*Note: a rich Roman patron of the arts*]. The "good old times" were not good old times . Neither master nor servant was as well situated then as to day. A relapse to old conditions would be disastrous to both—not the least so to him who serves—and would sweep away civilization with it….

We start, then, with a condition of affairs under which the best interests of the race are promoted, but which inevitably gives wealth to the few. Thus far, accepting conditions as they exist, the situation can be surveyed and pronounced good. The question then arises—and, if the foregoing be correct, it is the only question with which we have to deal—What is the proper mode of administering wealth after the laws upon which civilization is founded have thrown it into the hands of the few? And it is of this great question that I believe I offer the true solution. It will be understood that fortunes are here spoken of, not moderate sums saved by many years of effort, the returns from which are required for the comfortable maintenance and education of families. This is not wealth, but only competence, which it should be the aim of all to acquire.

There are but three modes in which surplus wealth can be disposed of. It can be left to the families of the decedents; or it can be bequeathed for public purposes; or, finally, it can be administered during their lives by its possessors. Under the first and second modes most of the wealth of the world that has reached the few has hitherto been applied. Let us in turn consider each of these modes. The first is the most injudicious. In monarchial countries, the estates and the greatest portion of the wealth are left to the first son, that the vanity of the parent may be gratified by the thought that his name and title are to descend to succeeding generations unimpaired. The condition of this class in Europe today teaches the futility of such hopes or ambitions. The successors have become impoverished through their follies or from the fall in the value of land… Why should men leave great fortunes to their children? If this is done from affection, is it not misguided affection? Observation teaches that, generally speaking, it is not well for the children that they should be so burdened. Neither is it well for the state. Beyond providing for the wife and daughters moderate sources of income, and very moderate allowances indeed, if any, for the sons, men may well hesitate, for it is no longer questionable that great sums bequeathed oftener work more for the injury than for the good of the recipients. Wise men will soon conclude that, for the best interests of the members of their families and of the state, such bequests are an improper use of their means….

As to the second mode, that of leaving wealth at death for public uses, it may be said that this is only a means for the disposal of wealth, provided a man is content to wait until he is dead before it becomes of much good in the world…The cases are not few in which the real object sought by the testator is not attained, nor are they few in which his real wishes are thwarted….

The growing disposition to tax more and more heavily large estates left at death is a cheering indication of the growth of a salutary change in public opinion…Of all forms of taxation, this seems the wisest. Men who continue hoarding great sums all their lives, the proper use of which for public ends would work good to the community, should be made to feel that the community, in the form of the state, cannot thus be deprived of its proper share. By taxing estates heavily at death, the state marks its condemnation of the selfish millionaire's unworthy life.

…This policy would work powerfully to induce the rich man to attend to the administration of wealth during his life, which is the end that society should always have in view, as being that by far most fruitful for the people….

There remains, then, only one mode of using great fortunes: but in this way we have the true antidote for the temporary unequal distribution of wealth, the reconciliation of the rich and the poor—a reign of harmony—another ideal, differing, indeed from that of the Communist in requiring only the further evolution of existing conditions, not the total overthrow of our civilization. It is founded upon the present most intense individualism, and the race is prepared to put it in practice by degrees whenever it pleases. Under its sway we shall have an ideal state, in which the surplus wealth of the few will become, in the best sense, the property of the many, because administered for the common good, and this wealth, passing through the hands of the few, can be made a much more potent force for the elevation of our race than if it had been distributed in small sums to the people themselves. Even the poorest can be made to see this, and to agree that great sums gathered by some of their fellow citizens and spent for public purposes, from which the masses reap the principal benefit, are more valuable to them than if scattered among them through the course of many years in trifling amounts....

This, then, is held to be the duty of the man of Wealth: First, to set an example of modest, unostentatious living, shunning display or extravagance; to provide moderately for the legitimate wants of those dependent upon him; and after doing so to consider all surplus revenues which come to him simply as trust funds, which he is called upon to administer, and strictly bound as a matter of duty to administer in the manner which, in his judgment, is best calculated to produce the most beneficial result for the community—the man of wealth thus becoming the sole agent and trustee for his poorer brethren, bringing to their service his superior wisdom, experience, and ability to administer—doing for them better than they would or could do for themselves.

AUTHOR JOHN SPARGO DESCRIBES THE PLIGHT OF CHILD LABOR AT THE BEGINNING OF THE TWENTIETH CENTURY

Work in the coal breakers is exceedingly hard and dangerous. Crouched over the chutes, the boys sit hour after hour, picking out the pieces of slate and other refuse from the coal as it rushes past to the washers. From the cramped position they have to assume, most of them become more or less deformed and bent-backed like old men. When a boy has been working for some time and begins to get round-shouldered, his fellows say that "He's got his boy to carry around whenever he goes."

The coal is hard, and accidents to the hands, such as cut, broken, or crushed fingers, are common among the boys. Sometimes there is a worse accident: a terrified shriek is heard, and a boy is mangled and torn in the machinery, or disappears in the chute to be picked out later smothered and dead. Clouds of dust fill the breakers and are inhaled by the boys, laying the foundations for asthma and miners' consumption.

I once stood in a breaker for half an hour and tried to do the work a twelve-year-old boy was doing day after day, for ten hours at a stretch, for sixty cents a day. The gloom of the breaker appalled me. Outside the sun shone brightly, the air was pellucid, and the birds sang in chorus with the trees and the rivers. Within the breaker there was blackness, clouds of deadly dust enfolded everything, the harsh, grinding roar of the machinery and the ceaseless rushing of coal through the chutes filled the ears. I tried to pick out the pieces of slate from the hurrying stream of coal, often missing them; my hands were bruised and cut in a few minutes; I was covered from head to foot with coal dust, and for many hours afterwards I was expectorating some of the small particles of anthracite I had swallowed.

I could not do that work and live, but there were boys of ten and twelve years of age doing it for fifty and sixty cents a day. Some of them had never been inside of a school....

In the bituminous mines of West Virginia, boys of nine or ten are frequently employed. I met one little fellow ten years old in Mt. Carbon, W. Va., last year, who was employed as a "trap boy." Think of what it means to be a trap boy at ten years of age. It means to sit alone in a dark mine passage hour after hour, with no human soul near; to see no living creature except the mules as they pass with their loads, or a rat or two seeking to share one's meal; to stand in water or mud that covers the ankles, chilled to the marrow by the cold draughts that rush in when you open the trap door for the mules to pass through; to work for fourteen hours—waiting—opening and shutting a door—then waiting again—for sixty cents; to reach the surface when all is wrapped in the mantle of night, and to fall to the earth exhausted and have to be carried away to the nearest "shack" to be revived before it is possible to walk to the farther shack called "home."

Boys twelve years of age may be legally employed in the mines of West Virginia, by day or by night, and for as many hours as the employers care to make them toil or their bodies will stand the strain. Where the disregard of child life is such that this may be done openly and with legal sanction, it is easy to believe what miners have again and again told me—that there are hundreds of little boys of nine and ten years of age employed in the coal mines of this state.

PROBLEM 18:
CONNECTION TO TODAY

1. Are there parallels between the period 1865 to 1917 and our own time? If so, what are they?

2. What lessons should we have learned from the period 1865 to 1917 that we should apply today?

3. Are contemporary business leaders today better, worse, or just different from those of the historical period we are considering?

4. If business people like Rockefeller and Carnegie and today's Bill Gates of Microsoft give huge amounts of money back to society in charities and projects, does this justify the large, unbalanced income gaps in the country today? Explain.

5. What is the best way to maintain the dynamism that capitalism unleashes, while checking its excesses?

6. Given the great disparities in income distribution both in the period 1865 to 1917 and in our own time, why has socialism never succeeded in America?

PROBLEM 19: WHY HAS AMERICA, KNOWN AS A "NATION OF IMMIGRANTS," OFTEN SHOWN ORGANIZED HOSTILITY TO IMMIGRANTS?

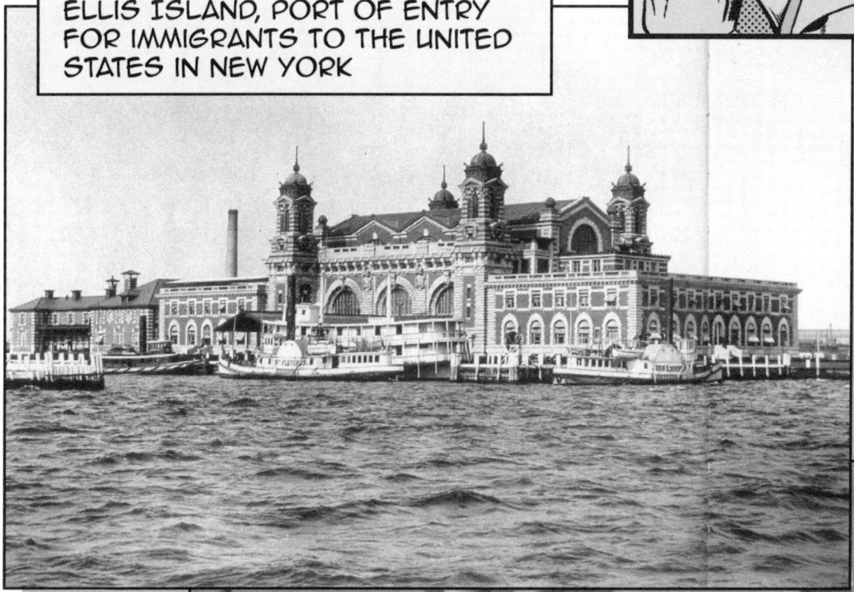

ELLIS ISLAND, PORT OF ENTRY FOR IMMIGRANTS TO THE UNITED STATES IN NEW YORK

IMMIGRANT FAMILIES COMING TO AMERICA

PROBLEM 19: WHY HAS AMERICA, KNOWN AS A "NATION OF IMMIGRANTS," OFTEN SHOWN ORGANIZED HOSTILITY TO IMMIGRANTS?

The words found on the United States Statue of Liberty, which have become famous throughout the land, offered a promise of welcoming, open arms to the nation. Inscribed on the monument are the words,

"Give me your tired, your poor,
Your huddled masses yearning to breathe free,
The wretched refuse of your teeming shore…"

Indeed, the history of the United States has been a history of immigration from the Old Worlds of Europe, Asia, and Africa to the New Worlds of America. Politicians often remind their various ethnic constituencies that we are a nation of immigrants and that today America has become a true "world" nation, with inhabitants whose origins are from every part of the globe.

But there are seeming contradictions in our words and in our deeds regarding immigrants coming to our shores. There have been three major periods of negative reactions of Americans toward large numbers of immigrants coming to the country: those taking place in 1830 to 1860, 1880 to 1917, and in our own time from the 1980s until the present. The first anti-immigrant movement centered on Irish immigrants and others from Europe who were mostly Roman Catholic in their religious affiliation. The Know-nothing Party arose as a force opposing this wave of immigration. The period after 1880 brought forth a new wave of anti-immigration sentiment and action. The huge numbers of immigrants arriving in the United States doubled the number of people in the country from 1870 to 1900. In the 1880s alone, a record-breaking 5,000,000 immigrants arrived in the country. These new immigrants came from southern and eastern Europe. In the 1880s immigrants from these areas constituted 19 percent of the immigrant population; by the first decade of the 20th century they represented 66 percent of the total newcomers.

The American response was to organize to stop the flow. The American Protection Association, formed in 1887 and claiming a million members, joined organized labor in an effort to restrict immigration. In 1882 an immigration restriction law was passed to bar what were classified as "undesirable" groups from every nationality and completely stopped immigration of Chinese to the country.

Why had this happened? What were the underlying reasons for this anti-immigrant feeling when everyone in the country, except Native Americans, had immigrant ancestors? What is the basis for anti-immigrant feeling in our own time and is it related to our past history?

PROBLEM 19:
QUESTIONS FOR TEAM RESEARCH

1. Was there any difference between the anti-immigration sentiment of the 1830–1860 period and that of the 1880–1917 period? If so, what was it?

2. Was the anti-immigration sentiment based on ignorance? Fear? Religious bigotry? Racism? Class? Explain.

3. Did Americans have any legitimate and understandable reasons for wanting to restrict immigration? If so, what were they?

4. What was the connection between pro- or anti-immigration policies and politics in the country?

5. Were there any differences in the attitude of Americans toward specific ethnic group immigrants? If so, what were they and what were they based on?

PROBLEM 19:
STARTING THE SEARCH FOR EVIDENCE

INTERNET: KEY WORDS AND PHRASES

Know-Nothing Party

Prejudice and immigration

American immigrants and intelligence

Legislation to restrict immigration to America

BOOKS

Beals, Carleton, *Brass Knuckle Crusade: the Great Know-Nothing Conspiracy, 1820– 1860,* NY, Hastings House Publishers, 1960

Higham, John, *Strangers in the Land: Patterns of American Nativism*, 1860–1925, New Brunswick, Rutgers University Press, 1988

Mandelbaum, Seymour J., *The Social Setting of Intolerance: The Know Nothings, the Red Scare, and McCarthyism*, Chicago, Scott Foresman, 1964

McKee, Delber, *Chinese Exclusion Versus the Open Door Policy, 1900–1906; Clashes Over China Policy in the Roosevelt Era*, Detroit, Wayne State University, 1977

Muller, Thomas, *Immigrants and the American City*, NY, New York University Press, 1994

Francis A. Walker's Statement About Restriction of Immigration

Let us now inquire what are the changes in our general conditions which seem to demand a revision of the opinion and policy heretofore held regarding immigration. Three of these are subjective, affecting our capability of easily and safely taking care of a large and tumultuous access of foreigners; the fourth is objective, and concerns the character of the immigration now directed upon our shores. Time will serve for only a rapid characterization.

First, we have the important fact of the complete exhaustion of the free public lands of the United States. Fifty years ago, thirty years ago, vast tracts of arable laud were open to every person arriving on our shores, under the Preemption Act, or later, the Homestead Act. A good farm of one hundred and sixty acres could be had at the minimum price of $1.25 an acre, or for merely the fees of registration. Under these circumstances it was a very simple matter to dispose of a large immigration. To-day there is not a good farm within the limits of the United States which is to be had under either of these acts. The wild and tumultuous scenes which attended the opening to settlement of the Territory of Oklahoma, a few years ago, and, a little later, of the so-called Cherokee Strip, testify eloquently to the vast change in our national conditions in this respect. This is not to say that more people cannot and will not, sooner or later, with more or less of care and pains and effort, be placed upon the land of the United States; but it does of itself alone show how vastly the difficulty of providing for immigration has increased. The immigrant must now buy his farm from a second hand, and he must pay the price which the value of the land for agricultural purposes determines. In the case of ninety-five out of a hundred immigrants, this necessity puts an immediate occupation of the soil out of the question.

A second change in our national condition, which importantly affects our capability of taking care of large numbers of ignorant and unskilled foreigners, is the fall of agricultural prices which has gone on steadily since 1873. It is not of the slightest consequence to inquire into the causes of this fall, whether we refer it to the competition of Argentina and of India or the appreciation of gold. We are interested only in the fact. There has been a great reduction in the cost of producing crops in some favored regions where steam-ploughs and steam-reaping, steam-threshing, and steam-sacking machines can be employed; but there has been no reduction in the cost of producing crops upon the ordinary American farm at all corresponding to the reduction in the price of the produce. It is a necessary consequence of this that the ability to employ a large number of uneducated and unskilled hands in agriculture has greatly diminished.

Still a third cause which may be indicated, perhaps more important than either of those thus far mentioned, is found in the fact that we have now a labor problem. We in the United States have been wont to pride ourselves greatly upon our so easily maintaining peace and keeping the social order unimpaired. We have, partly from a reasonable patriotic pride, partly also from something like Phariseeism, been much given to pointing at our European cousins, and boasting superiority over them in this respect. Our self-gratulation has been largely due to overlooking social differences between us and them. That boasted superiority has been owing mainly, not to our institutions, but to our more favorable conditions. There is no country of Europe which has not for a long time had a labor problem; that is, which has not so largely exploited its own natural resources, and which has not a labor supply so nearly meeting the demands of the market at their fullest, that hard times and periods of industrial depression have brought a serious strain through extensive non-employment of labor. From this evil condition we have, until recently, happily been free. During the last few years, however, we have ourselves come under the shadow of this evil, in spite of our magnificent natural resources. We know what it is to have even intelligent and skilled labor unemployed through considerable periods of time. This change of conditions is likely to bring some abatement to our national pride. No longer is it a matter of course that every industrious and temperate man can find work in the United States. And it is to be remembered that, of all nations, we are the one which is least qualified to deal with a labor problem. We have not the machinery, we have not the army, we have not the police, we have not the traditions and instincts, for dealing with such a matter, as the great railroad and other strikes of the last few years have shown.

I have spoken of three changes in the national condition, all subjective, which greatly affect our capability of dealing with a large and tumultuous immigration. There is a fourth, which is objective. It concerns the character of the foreigners now resorting to our shores. Fifty, even thirty years ago, there was a rightful presumption regarding the average immigrant that he was among the most enterprising, thrifty, alert, adventurous, and courageous of the community from which he came. It required no small energy, prudence, forethought, and pains to conduct the inquiries relating to his migration, to accumulate the necessary means, and to find his way across the Atlantic. To-day the presumption is completely reversed. So thoroughly has the continent of Europe been crossed by railways, so effectively has the business of emigration there been exploited, so much have the rates of railroad fares and ocean passage been reduced, that it is now among the least thrifty and prosperous members of any European community that the emigration agent finds his best recruiting-ground. The care and pains required have been reduced to a minimum; while the agent of the Red Star Line or the White Star Line is everywhere at hand, to suggest migration to those who are not getting on well at home. The intending emigrants are looked after from the moment they are locked into the cars in their native villages until they stretch themselves upon the floors of the buildings on Ellis Island, in New York. Illustrations of the ease and facility with which this Pipe Line Immigration is now carried on might be given in profusion. So broad and smooth is the channel, there is no reason why every foul and stagnant pool of population in Europe, which no breath of intellectual or industrial life has stirred for ages, should not be decanted upon our soil. Hard times here may momentarily check the flow; but it will not be permanently stopped so long as any difference of economic level exists between our population and that of the most degraded communities abroad.

But it is not alone that the presumption regarding the immigrant of today is so widely different from that which existed regarding the immigrant of thirty or fifty years ago. The immigrant of the former time came almost exclusively from western and northern Europe. We have now tapped great reservoirs of population then almost unknown to the passenger lists of our arriving vessels. Only a short time ago, the immigrants from southern Italy, Hungary, Austria, and Russia together made up hardly more than one per cent of our immigration. To-day the proportion has risen to something like forty per cent, and threatens soon to become fifty or sixty per cent, or even more. The entrance into our political, social, and industrial life of such vast masses of peasantry, degraded below our utmost conceptions, is a matter which no intelligent patriot can look upon without the gravest apprehension and alarm. These people have no history behind them which is of a nature to give encouragement. They have none of the inherited instincts and tendencies which made it comparatively easy to deal with the immigration of the olden time. They are beaten men from beaten races; representing the worst failures in the struggle for existence. Centuries are against them, as centuries were on the side of those who formerly came to us. They have none of the ideas and aptitudes which fit men to take up readily and easily the problem of self-care and self-government, such as belong to those who are descended from the tribes that met under the oak-trees of old Germany to make laws and choose chieftains.

Their habits of life, again, are of the most revolting kind. Read the description given by Mr. Riis of the police driving from the garbage dumps the miserable beings who try to burrow in those depths of unutterable filth and slime in order that they may eat and sleep there! Was it in cement like this that the foundations of our republic were laid? What effects must be produced upon our social standards, and upon the ambitions and aspirations of our people, by a contact so foul and loathsome? The influence upon the American rate of wages of a competition like this cannot fail to be injurious and even disastrous. Already it has been seriously felt in the tobacco manufacture, in the clothing trade, and in many forms of mining industry; and unless this access of vast numbers of unskilled workmen of the lowest type, in a market already fully supplied with labor, shall be checked, it cannot fail to go on from bad to worse, in breaking down the standard which has been maintained with so much care and at so much cost. The competition of paupers is far more telling and more killing than the competition of pauper-made goods. Degraded labor in the slums of foreign cities may be prejudicial to intelligent, ambitious, self-respecting labor here; but it does not threaten half so much evil as does degraded labor in the garrets of our native cities.

Finally, the present situation is most menacing to our peace and political, safety. In all the social and industrial disorders of this country since 1877, the foreign elements have proved themselves the ready tools of demagogues in defying the law, in destroying property, and in working violence. A learned clergyman who mingled with the socialistic mob which, two years ago, threatened the State House and the governor of

Massachusetts, told me that during the entire disturbance he heard no word spoken in any language which he knew,—either in English, in German, or in French. There may be those who can contemplate the addition to our population of vast numbers of persons having no inherited instincts of self-government and respect for law; knowing no restraint upon their own passions but the club of the policeman or the bayonet of the soldier; forming communities, by the tens of thousands, in which only foreign tongues are spoken, and into which can steal no influence from our free institutions and from popular discussion. But I confess to being far less optimistic. I have conversed with one of the highest officers of the United States army and with one of the highest officers of the civil government regarding the state of affairs which existed during the summer of 1894; and the revelations they made of facts not generally known, going to show how the ship of state grazed along its whole side upon the rocks, were enough to appall the most sanguine American, the most hearty believer in free government. Have we the right to expose the republic to any increase of the dangers from this source which now so manifestly threaten our peace and safety?

For it is never to be forgotten that self-defense is the first law of nature and of nations. If that man who careth not for his own household is worse than an infidel, the nation which permits its institutions to be endangered by any cause which can fairly be removed is guilty not less in Christian than in natural law. Charity begins at home; and while the people of the United States have gladly offered an asylum to millions upon millions of the distressed and unfortunate of other lands and climes, they have no right to carry their hospitality one step beyond the line where American institutions, the American rate of wages, the American standard of living, are brought into serious peril. All the good the United States could do by offering indiscriminate hospitality to a few millions more of European peasants, whose places at home will, within another generation, be filled by others as miserable as themselves, would not compensate for any permanent injury done to our republic. Our highest duty to charity and to humanity is to make this great experiment, here, of free laws and educated labor, the most triumphant success that can possibly be attained. In this way we shall do far more for Europe than by allowing its city slums and its vast stagnant reservoirs of degraded peasantry to be drained off upon our soil. Within the decade between 1880 and 1890 five and a quarter millions of foreigners entered our ports! No nation in human history ever undertook to deal with such masses of alien population. That man must be a sentimentalist and an optimist beyond all bounds of reason who believes that we can take such a load upon the national stomach without a failure of assimilation, and without great danger to the health and life of the nation. For one, I believe it is time that we should take a rest, and give our social, political, and industrial system some chance to recuperate. The problems which so sternly confront us to-day are serious enough without being complicated and aggravated by the addition of some millions of Hungarians, Bohemians, Poles, south Italians, and Russian Jews.

THE CHINESE EXCLUSION ACT (1882)

Be it enacted…, That all laws now in force prohibiting and regulating the coming of Chinese persons, and persons of Chinese descent, into the United States, and the residence of such persons therein…be, and the same are hereby, reenacted, extended, and continued so far as the same are not inconsistent with treaty obligations, until otherwise provided by law, and said laws shall also apply to the island territory under the jurisdiction of the United States, and prohibit the immigration of Chinese laborers, not citizens of the United States, from such island territory to the mainland territory of the United States, whether in such island territory at the time of cession or not, and from one portion of the island territory of the United States to another portion of said island territory: Provided, however, That said laws shall not apply to the transit of Chinese laborers from one island to another island of the same group; and any islands within the jurisdiction of any State or the District of Alaska shall be considered a part of the mainland under this section.

SEC. 2. That the Secretary of the Treasury is hereby authorized and empowered to make and prescribe, and from time to time to change, such rules and regulations not inconsistent with the laws of the land as he may deem necessary and proper to execute the provisions of this Act and of the Acts hereby extended and continued and of the treaty of…[December 8, 1894,]…between the United States and China, and with the approval of the President to appoint such agents as he may deem necessary for the efficient execution of said treaty and said Acts.

SEC. 3. That nothing in the provisions of this Act or any other Act shall be construed to prevent, hinder, or restrict any foreign exhibitor, representative, or citizen of any foreign nation, or the holder, who is a citizen of any foreign nation, of any concession or privilege from any fair or exposition authorized by Act of Congress from bringing into the United States, under contract, such mechanics, artisans, agents, or other employees, natives of their respective foreign countries, as they or any of them may deem necessary for the purpose of making preparation for installing or conducting their exhibits or of preparing for installing or conducting any business authorized or permitted under or by virtue of or pertaining to any concession or privilege which may have been or may be granted by any said fair or exposition in connection with such exposition, under such rules and regulations as the Secretary of the Treasury may prescribe, both as to the admission and return of such person or persons.

SEC. 4. That it shall be the duty of every Chinese laborer, other than a citizen, rightfully in, and entitled to remain in any of the insular territory of the United States (Hawaii excepted) at the time of the passage of this Act, to obtain within one year thereafter a certificate of residence in the insular territory wherein he resides, which certificate shall entitle him to residence therein, and upon failure to obtain such certificate as herein provided he shall be deported from such insular territory; and the Philippine Commission is authorized and required to make all regulations and provisions necessary for the enforcement of this section in the Philippine Islands, including the form and substance of the certificate of residence so that the same shall clearly and sufficiently identify the holder thereof and enable officials to prevent fraud in the transfer of the same…

APPROVED, APRIL 29, 1902.

PROBLEM 19:
CONNECTION TO TODAY

1. Is prejudice an innate human characteristic? Or is prejudice learned?

2. Why are individuals prejudiced against other races? Religions? Nationalities?

3. To what extent does prejudice against foreigners exist in our country today? If prejudice is present, against which group or groups is it directed?

4. Today the overwhelming immigration to the U.S. is non-European. How does this fact impact public attitudes toward immigration?

5. In the U.S. today there are approximately 12 to 14 million individuals who are here illegally. What should U.S. policy be regarding those people?

6. What should be current US. policy regarding immigrants? Should immigration be stopped? Restricted?

PROBLEM 20:
HOW DID AMERICA ATTEMPT TO BALANCE ECONOMIC GROWTH WITH AMERICAN VALUES IN THE NEW INDUSTRIAL AGE?

LEFT:
THEODORE ROOSEVELT CAMPAIGNING FOR PROGRESSIVE REFORM

BELOW: CHILD LABOR WORKING IN FACTORIES IN EARLY 20TH CENTURY AMERICA

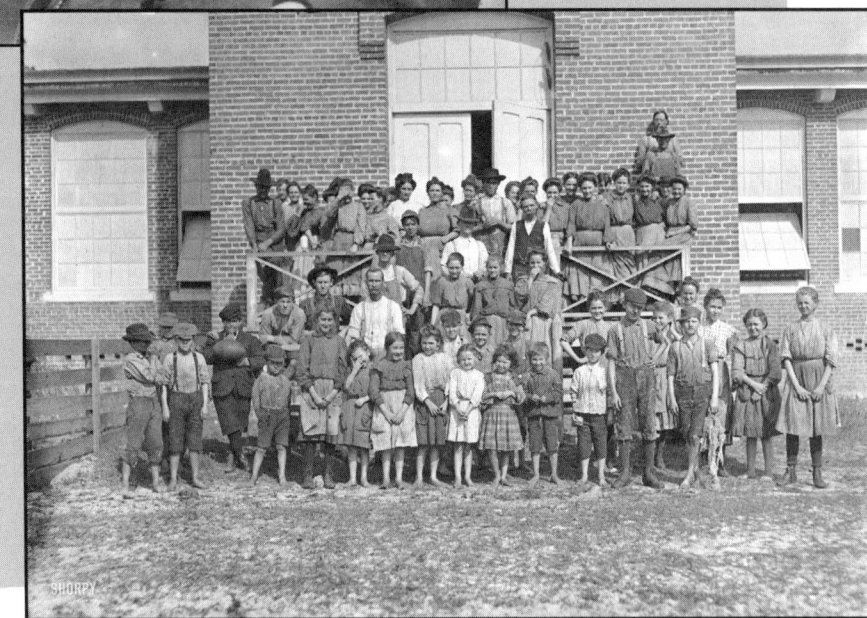

PROBLEM 20: HOW DID AMERICA ATTEMPT TO BALANCE ECONOMIC GROWTH WITH AMERICAN VALUES IN THE NEW INDUSTRIAL AGE?

By the beginning of the 20th century, three forces had merged to create an America far different from what had characterized the nation at the beginning of the Civil War. Industrialization had created a new economy with manufactured goods now surpassing agriculture as the major sector of the American economy. But it was not only the growth of business enterprise which was new; big business, which witnessed the consolidation of smaller firms into large national corporations, emerged and increasingly wielded both great economic and political power. A second force changing the country was the unprecedented influx of immigrants into the nation. These were men, women, and children primarily from southern and eastern Europe, who, for the most part, did not attempt to replicate the agrarian life they had left behind but, rather, crowded into American cities to work in various sectors of the industrial manufacturing factories that now had become the dominant element in the new economy. A third force in American life, the fast growing urbanization of the country, created issues and problems not seen in the nation on such a large scale in previous decades. Cities, some of which, like Chicago, doubled their populations within a short ten-year period, were confronted with problems of poverty, crime, slum housing, and dangerous sanitary conditions.

The convergence of these three forces—big monopolistic business, unprecedented levels of immigration, and the rapid urbanization of the country—forced the nation to ask new questions. The period following the Civil War had been characterized by a focus on material things, technology, new products, and economic growth, but little attention had been given to the question of what all this was doing to us as a nation. What impact was this having on people and their families? The concentration on material things had overpowered the issues of ethics and morality. Americans attempted to address these concerns in what became known as the Progressive Movement, which essentially tried to address the issue of how a society can strike a balance between efficiency and maximum production in the economic sector with protection for the laborer and the consumer. The nation searched for ways to find some accommodation between what was perceived as the innate greed of capitalism as an economic system and the rights of individuals and traditional American values.

How did they do it? Did they succeed?

PROBLEM 20:
QUESTIONS FOR TEAM RESEARCH

1. Is it true that capitalism as a system contains strong elements of greed? Explain.

2. What role did the "Muckrackers" play in the Progressive movement?

3. What was the philosophy behind Theodore Roosevelt's Square Deal and New Nationalism?

4. What was the philosophy behind Woodrow Wilson's New Freedom?

5. What was the problem with "The Trusts" in American society?

6. What were the goals of the Progressive Movement? Were they achieved? If they were achieved, how? If not, why not?

PROBLEM 20:
STARTING THE SEARCH FOR EVIDENCE

INTERNET: KEY WORDS AND PHRASES

William Jennings Bryan

The Muckrakers

Theodore Roosevelt and the Progressive Movement

Woodrow Wilson and the Progressive Movement

BOOKS

Buck, Solon J., *The Agrarian Crusade: A Chronicle of the Farmer in Politics*, New Haven, Yale University Press, 1920

Filler, Louis, *The Muckrakers*, University Park, Pennsylvania State University Press, 1976

Kazin, Michael, *A Godly Hero: The Life of William Jennings Bryan*, NY, Knopf, 2006

Link, Arthur S., *Woodrow Wilson and the Progressive Era, 1910–1917*, NY, Harper, 1954

Mowry, George Edwin, *The Era of Theodore Roosevelt, 1900–1912*, NY, Harper, 1958

President Theodore Roosevelt Speaks About the "New Nationalism" to Civil War Veterans (1910) (Selections)

At many stages in the advance of humanity, this conflict between the men who possess more than they have earned and the men who have earned more than they possess is the central condition of progress. In our day it appears as the struggle of freemen to gain and hold the right of self-government as against the special interests, who twist the methods of free government into machinery for defeating the popular will. At every stage, and under all circumstances, the essence of the struggle is to equalize opportunity, destroy privilege, and give to the life and citizenship of every individual the highest possible value both to himself and to the commonwealth. That is nothing new. All I ask in civil life is what you fought for in the Civil War. I ask that civil life be carried on according to the spirit in which the army was carried on. You never get perfect justice, but the effort in handling the army was to bring to the front the men who could do the job. Nobody grudged promotion to Grant, or Sherman, or Thomas, or Sheridan, because they earned it. The only complaint was when a man got promotion which he did not earn.

Practical equality of opportunity for all citizens, when we achieve it, will have two great results. First, every man will have a fair chance to make of himself all that in him lies; to reach the highest point to which his capacities, unassisted by special privilege of his own and unhampered by the special privilege of others, can carry him, and to get for himself and his family substantially what he has earned. Second, equality of opportunity means that the commonwealth will get from every citizen the highest service of which he is capable. No man who carries the burden of the special privileges of another can give to the commonwealth that service to which it is fairly entitled.

I stand for the square deal. But when I say that I am for the square deal, I mean not merely that I stand for fair play under the present rules of the game, but that I stand for having those rules changed so as to work for a more substantial equality of opportunity and of reward for equally good service. One word of warning, which, I think, is hardly necessary in Kansas. When I say I want a square deal for the poor man, I do not mean that I want a square deal for the man who remains poor because he has not got the energy to work for himself. If a man who has had a chance will not make good, then he has got to quit. And you men of the Grand Army, you want justice for the brave man who fought, and punishment for the coward who shirked his work. Is that not so?

Now, this means that our government, National and State, must be freed from the sinister influence or control of special interests. Exactly as the special interests of cotton and slavery threatened our political integrity before the Civil War, so now the great special business interests too often control and corrupt the men and methods of government for their own profit. We must drive the special interests out of politics. That is one of our tasks to-day. Every special interest is entitled to justice—full, fair, and complete—and, now, mind you, if there were any attempt by mob-violence to plunder and work harm to the special interest, whatever it may be, that I most dislike, and the wealthy man, whomsoever he may be, for whom I have the greatest contempt, I would fight for him, and you would if you were worth your salt. He should have justice. For every special interest is entitled to justice, but not one is entitled to a vote in Congress, to a voice on the bench, or to representation in any public office. The Constitution guarantees protection to property, and we must make that promise good. But it does not give the right of suffrage to any corporation.

The true friend of property, the true conservative, is he who insists that property shall be the servant and not the master of the commonwealth; who insists that the creature of man's making shall be the servant and not the master of the man who made it. The citizens of the United States must effectively control the mighty commercial forces which they have called into being.

There can be no effective control of corporations while their political activity remains. To put an end to it will be neither a short nor an easy task, but it can be done.

We must have complete and effective publicity of corporate affairs, so that the people may know beyond peradventure whether the corporations obey the law and whether their management entitles them to the confidence of the public. It is necessary that laws should be passed to prohibit the use of corporate funds directly or indirectly for political purposes; it is still more necessary that such laws should be thoroughly enforced. Corporate expenditures for political purposes, and especially such expenditures by public-service corporations, have supplied one of the principal sources of corruption in our political affairs.

It has become entirely clear that we must have government supervision of the capitalization, not only of public-service corporations, including, particularly, railways, but of all corporations doing an interstate business. I do not wish to see the nation forced into the ownership of the railways if it can possibly be avoided, and the only alternative is thoroughgoing and effective legislation, which shall be based on a full knowledge of all the facts, including a physical valuation of property. This physical valuation is not needed, or, at least, is very rarely needed, for fixing rates; but it is needed as the basis of honest capitalization.

We have come to recognize that franchises should never be granted except for a limited time, and never without proper provision for compensation to the public. It is my personal belief that the same kind and degree of control and supervision which should be exercised over public-service corporations should be extended also to combinations which control necessaries of life, such as meat, oil, or coal, or which deal in them on an important scale. I have no doubt that the ordinary man who has control of them is much like ourselves. I have no doubt he would like to do well, but I want to have enough supervision to help him realize that desire to do well.

I believe that the officers, and, especially, the directors, of corporations should be held personally responsible when any corporation breaks the law.

Combinations in industry are the result of an imperative economic law which cannot be repealed by political legislation. The effort at prohibiting all combination has substantially failed. The way out lies, not in attempting to prevent such combinations, but in completely controlling them in the interest of the public welfare. For that purpose the Federal Bureau of Corporations is an agency of first importance. Its powers, and, therefore, its efficiency, as well as that of the Interstate Commerce Commission, should be largely increased. We have a right to expect from the Bureau of Corporations and from the Interstate Commerce Commission a very high grade of public service. We should be as sure of the proper conduct of the interstate railways and the proper management of interstate business as we are now sure of the conduct and management of the national banks, and we should have as effective supervision in one case as in the other. The Hepburn Act, and the amendment to the act in the shape in which it finally passed Congress at the last session, represent a long step in advance, and we must go yet further.

President Woodrow Wilson Speaks About the "New Freedom": A Call for the Emancipation of the Generous Energies of a People (1912) (Selections)

…We have come upon a very different age from any that preceded us. We have come upon an age when we do not do business in the way in which we used to do business,—when we do not carry on any of the operations of manufacture, sale, transportation, or communication as men used to carry them on. There is a sense in which in our day the individual has been submerged. In most parts of our country men work, not for themselves, not as partners in the old way in which they used to work, but generally as employees,—in a higher or lower grade,—of great corporations. There was a time when corporations played a very minor part in our business affairs, but now they play the chief part, and most men are the servants of corporations.

You know what happens when you are the servant of a corporation. You have in no instance access to the men who are really determining the policy of the corporation. If the corporation is doing the things that it ought not to do, you really have no voice in the matter and must obey the orders, and you have oftentimes with deep mortification to co-operate in the doing of things which you know are against the public interest. Your individuality is swallowed up in the individuality and purpose of a great organization.

It is true that, while most men are thus submerged in the corporation, a few, a very few, are exalted to a power which as individuals they could never have wielded. Through the great organizations of which they are the heads, a few are enabled to play a part unprecedented by anything in history in the control of the business operations of the country and in the determination of the happiness of great numbers of people.

Yesterday, and ever since history began, men were related to one another as individuals. To be sure there were the family, the Church, and the State, institutions which associated men in certain wide circles of relationship. But in the ordinary concerns of life, in the ordinary work, in the daily round, men dealt freely and directly with one another. To-day, the everyday relationships of men are largely with great impersonal concerns, with organizations, not with other individual men.

Now this is nothing short of a new social age, a new era of human relationships, a new stage-setting for the drama of life....

We used to think in the old-fashioned days when life was very simple that all that government had to do was to put on a policeman's uniform, and say, "Now don't anybody hurt anybody else." We used to say that the ideal of government was for every man to be left alone and not interfered with, except when he interfered with somebody else; and that the best government was the government that did as little governing as possible. That was the idea that obtained in Jefferson's time. But we are coming now to realize that life is so complicated that we are not dealing with the old conditions, and that the law has to step in and create new conditions under which we may live, the conditions which will make it tolerable for us to live.

Let me illustrate what I mean: It used to be true in our cities that every family occupied a separate house of its own, that every family had its own little premises, that every family was separated in its life from every other family. That is no longer the case in our great cities. Families live in tenements, they live in flats, they live on floors; they are piled layer upon layer in the great tenement houses of our crowded districts, and not only are they piled layer upon layer, but they are associated room by room, so that there is in every room, sometimes, in our congested districts, a separate family. In some foreign countries they have made much more progress than we in handling these things. In the city of Glasgow, for example (Glasgow is one of the model cities of the world), they have made up their minds that the entries and the hallways of great tenements are public streets. Therefore, the policeman goes up the stairway, and patrols the corridors; the lighting department of the city sees to it that the halls are abundantly lighted. The city does not deceive itself into supposing that great building is a unit from which the police are to keep out and the civic authority to be excluded, but it says: "These are public highways, and light is needed in them, and control by the authority of the city."

I liken that to our great modern industrial enterprises. A corporation is very like a large tenement house; it isn't the premises of a single commercial family; it is just as much a public affair as a tenement house is a network of public highways....

The makers of our Federal Constitution read Montesquieu with true scientific enthusiasm. They were scientists in their way,—the best way of their age,—those fathers of the nation. Jefferson wrote of "the laws of Nature,"—and then by way of afterthought,—"and of Nature's God." And they constructed a government as they would have constructed an orrery,—to display the laws of nature. Politics in their thought was a variety of mechanics. The Constitution was founded on the law of gravitation. The government was to exist and move by virtue of the efficacy of "checks and balances."

The trouble with the theory is that government is not a machine, but a living thing. It falls, not under the theory of the universe, but under the theory of organic life. It is accountable to Darwin, not to Newton. It is modified by its environment, necessitated by its tasks, shaped to its functions by the sheer pressure of life. No living thing can have its organs offset against each other, as checks, and live. On the contrary, its life is dependent upon their quick co-operation, their ready response to the commands of instinct or intelligence, their amicable community of purpose. Government is not a body of blind forces; it is a body of men, with highly differentiated functions, no doubt, in our modern day, of specialization, with a common task and purpose. Their co-operation is indispensable, their warfare fatal. There can be no successful government without the intimate, instinctive co-ordination of the organs of life and action. This is not theory, but fact, and displays its force as fact, whatever theories may be thrown across its track. Living political constitutions must be Darwinian in structure and in practice. Society is a living organism and must obey the laws of life, not of mechanics; it must develop.

All that progressives ask or desire is permission—in an era when "development," "evolution," is the scientific word—to interpret the Constitution according to the Darwinian principle; all they ask is recognition of the fact that a nation is a living thing and not a machine.

Some citizens of this country have never got beyond the Declaration of Independence, signed in Philadelphia, July 4th, 1776. Their bosoms swell against George III, but they have no consciousness of the war for freedom that is going on to-day.

The Declaration of Independence did not mention the questions of our day. It is of no consequence to us unless we can translate its general terms into examples of the present day and substitute them in some vital way for the examples it itself gives, so concrete, so intimately involved in the circumstances of the day in which it was conceived and written. It is an eminently practical document, meant for the use of practical men; not a thesis for philosophers, but a whip for tyrants; not a theory of government, but a program of action. Unless we can translate it into the questions of our own day, we are not worthy of it, we are not the sons of the sires who acted in response to its challenge.

What form does the contest between tyranny and freedom take to-day? What is the special form of tyranny we now fight? How does it endanger the rights of the people, and what do we mean to do in order to make our contest against it effectual? What are to be the items of our new declaration of independence?

By tyranny, as we now fight it, we mean control of the law, of legislation and adjudication, by organizations which do not represent the people, by means which are private and selfish. We mean, specifically, the conduct of our affairs and the shaping of our legislation in the interest of special bodies of capital and those who organize their use. We mean the alliance, for this purpose, of political machines with selfish business. We mean the exploitation of the people by legal and political means. We have seen many of our governments under these influences cease to be representative governments, cease to be governments representative of the people, and become governments representative of special interests, controlled by machines, which in their turn are not controlled by the people.

Sometimes, when I think of the growth of our economic system, it seems to me as if, leaving our law just about where it was before any of the modern inventions or developments took place, we had simply at haphazard extended the family residence, added an office here and a workroom there, and a new set of sleeping rooms there, built up higher on our foundations, and put out little lean-tos on the side, until we have a structure that has no character whatever. Now, the problem is to continue to live in the house and yet change it.

Well, we are architects in our time, and our architects are also engineers. We don't have to stop using a railroad terminal because a new station is being built. We don't have to stop any of the processes of our lives because we are rearranging the structures in which we conduct those processes. What we have to undertake is to systematize the foundations of the house, then to thread all the old parts of the structure with the steel which will be laced together in modern fashion, accommodated to all the modern knowledge of structural strength and elasticity, and then slowly change the partitions, relay the walls, let in the light through new apertures, improve the ventilation; until finally, a generation or two from now, the scaffolding will be taken away, and there will be the family in a great building whose noble architecture will at last be disclosed, where men can live as a single community, co-operative as in a perfected, coordinated beehive, not afraid of any storm of nature, not afraid of any artificial storm, any imitation of thunder and lightning, knowing that the foundations go down to the bedrock of principle, and knowing that whenever they please they can change that plan again and accommodate it as they please to the altering necessities of their lives.

But there are a great many men who don't like the idea. Some wit recently said, in view of the fact that most of our American architects are trained in a certain *École* in Paris, that all American architecture in recent years was either bizarre or "Beaux Arts." I think that our economic architecture is decidedly bizarre; and I am afraid that there is a good deal to learn about matters other than architecture from the same source from which our architects have learned a great many things. I don't mean the School of Fine Arts at Paris, but the experience of France; for from the other side of the water men can now hold up against us the reproach that we have not adjusted our lives to modern conditions to the same extent that they have adjusted theirs. I was very much interested in some of the reasons given by our friends across the Canadian border for being very shy about the reciprocity arrangements. They said: "We are not sure whither these arrangements will lead, and we don't care to associate too closely with the economic conditions of the United States until those conditions are as modern as ours." And when I resented it, and asked for particulars, I had, in regard to many matters, to retire from the debate. Because I found that they had adjusted their regulations of economic development to conditions we had not yet found a way to meet in the United States.

Well, we have started now at all events. The procession is under way. The stand-patter doesn't know there is a procession. He is asleep in the back part of his house. He doesn't know that the road is resounding with the tramp of men going to the front. And when he wakes up, the country will be empty. He will be deserted, and he will wonder what has happened. Nothing has happened. The world has been going on. The world has a habit of going on. The world has a habit of leaving those behind who won't go with it. The world has always neglected stand-patters. And, therefore, the stand-patter does not excite my indignation; he excites my sympathy. He is going to be so lonely before it is all over. And we are good fellows, we are good company; why doesn't he come along? We are not going to do him any harm. We are going to show him a good time. We are going to climb the slow road until it reaches some upland where the air is fresher, where the whole talk of mere politicians is stilled, where men can look in each other's faces and see that there is nothing to conceal, that all they have to talk about they are willing to talk about in the open and talk about with each other; and whence, looking back over the road, we shall see at last that we have fulfilled our promise to mankind. We had said to all the world, "America was created to break every kind of monopoly, and to set men free, upon a footing of equality, upon a footing of opportunity, to match their brains and their energies," and now we have proved that we meant it....

PROBLEM 20:
CONNECTION TO TODAY

1. What parallels and/or differences are there between the government's attempt to break up John D. Rockefeller's Standard Oil Company and today's Microsoft Corporation headed by Bill Gates?

2. Are there similarities between the period 1865–1914 and today in regard to economic growth? If so what are they and what are the similarities and differences in how we responded in each era?

3. What do Americans believe is the proper role of government in regard to the economy?

4. Given the continuing problems of business getting out of control, people losing jobs, and the inability of the nation to eradicate poverty, why has Communism never been a major force in the United States as it has been in Europe and elsewhere?

PROBLEM 21: WHY DID THE UNITED STATES NOT JOIN THE LEAGUE OF NATIONS AFTER WORLD WAR I WHEN PRESIDENT WOODROW WILSON WAS THE KEY PERSON ADVOCATING THE CREATION OF SUCH A NEW INTERNATIONAL ORGANIZATION?

LEFT: PRESIDENT WOODROW WILSON

RIGHT: SENATOR HENRY CABOT LODGE OF MASSACHUSSETTS

PRESIDENT WOODROW WILSON AND WORLD LEADERS AT THE PARIS PEACE CONFERENCE

PROBLEM 21: WHY DID THE UNITED STATES NOT JOIN THE LEAGUE OF NATIONS AFTER WORLD WAR I WHEN PRESIDENT WOODROW WILSON WAS THE KEY PERSON ADVOCATING THE CREATION OF SUCH A NEW INTERNATIONAL ORGANIZATION?

As war broke out in Europe in 1914, it seemed to be an event far from American interest or involvement. President Woodrow Wilson, who had won the election of 1912, declared that the United States would not take sides or be involved in the conflict and would follow an official policy of neutrality. Events, however, made it increasingly impossible to maintain that position both in American public opinion and in official government policy. In January 1917 Germany decided to pursue a policy of unrestricted submarine warfare that included action even against shipping that was neutral. American intelligence also revealed that Germany was attempting to form an alliance with Mexico for war against the United States. Although Wilson had won reelection in 1916 on the slogan "He kept us out of war," in March 1917 United States ships were attacked by Germany, and the President went to the Congress on April 2, 1917, to ask for a formal declaration of war against Germany.

Throughout the involvement of the United States, which lasted until the war ended in 1918, President Wilson was thinking of those steps necessary to end the war in such a way that no country would be defeated, and no country would be the victor who would impose harsh terms on the loser, which would plant the seeds for resentment and potential future conflict. Wilson said in a speech to Congress that what he envisioned was a "peace without victory." He said the United States was willing to use its authority and power to maintain peace in the world through a new organization, a League for Peace. Others before had spoken of some kind of international body that could act to prevent conflict between nations. Theodore Roosevelt, who had earlier won the Nobel Peace Prize, advocated a League for Peace in a speech he delivered to the Nobel Prize Committee in 1910. And the powerful United States senator, Henry Cabot Lodge of Massachusetts, had said in 1916 that the United States should consider joining other nations in working to find ways to stop war and to develop some way "in which the united forces of the nations could be put behind the cause of peace and law."

President Wilson personally went to the peace conference in France, which was ending the war by drafting the Treaty of Versailles. The president was greeted as a world hero by tumultuous crowds wherever he went, and he vigorously and eloquently made the case for the establishment of a new international body to be known as the League of Nations. He personally worked with others on the structure of the organization and its charter which incorporated many of his 14 points for a lasting peace, which he had outlined in a speech to the U.S. Congress in January 1918. At home the president traveled the country, making his case for the new organization which he said would bring a lasting peace. Yet for all his dedication and personal involvement, the United States never ratified the Versailles Treaty and never became a member of the League of Nations. Why did the United States, which had lost so many young men in WWI, not participate in an organization created to stop all future wars? And why did they reject their own president, when throughout Europe, he was regarded as a savior who was trying to stop the horror of war from ever happening again?

PROBLEM 21:
QUESTIONS FOR TEAM RESEARCH

1. Was Wilson's policy of neutrality one that could work in 1917?

2. Why did the Germans decide to provoke the United States into war?

3. Why did Wilson decide to personally attend the Paris Peach Conference? Was this the right decision? Why?

4. What had caused Senator Lodge to change his position regarding the Treaty of Versailles and the League of Nations?

5. Was Wilson to blame for the failure of the Treaty in the U.S. or were other persons or factors to blame?

PROBLEM 21:
STARTING THE SEARCH FOR EVIDENCE

INTERNET: KEY WORDS AND PHRASES

Woodrow Wilson and the 14 Points

Woodrow Wilson and the League of Nations

Henry Cabot Lodge and the League of Nations

American public opinion and the League of Nations

BOOKS

Auchincloss, Louis, *Woodrow Wilson*, NY, Viking, 2000

Bailey, Thomas A., *Woodrow Wilson and the Great Betrayal*, NY. Macmillan, 1945

Marguiles, Herbert F., *The Mild Reservationists and the League of Nations Controversy in the Senate*, Columbia, University of Missouri Press, 1989

Ostrower, Gary B., *The League of Nations from 1919 to 1929*, Garden City Park, Avery Publishing Group. 1996

Scott, George, *The Rise and Fall of the League of Nations*, NY, Macmillan, 1974

President Woodrow Wilson's 14 Points, January 8, 1918

What we demand in this war, therefore, is nothing peculiar to ourselves. It is that the world be made fit and safe to live in; and particularly that it be made safe for every peace-loving nation which, like our own, wishes to live its own life, determine its own institutions, be assured of justice and fair dealing by the other peoples of the world as against force and selfish aggression.

All the peoples of the world are in effect partners in this interest, and for our own part we see very clearly that unless justice be done to others it will not be done to us. The program of the world's peace, therefore, is our program; and that program the only possible program, as we see it, is this:

1. Open covenants of peace, openly arrived at, after which there shall be no private international understandings of any kind but diplomacy shall proceed always frankly and in the public view.

2. Absolute freedom of navigation upon the seas, outside territorial waters, alike in peace and in war, except as the seas may be closed in whole or in part by international action for the enforcement of international covenants.

3. The removal, so far as possible, of all economic barriers and the establishment of an equality of trade conditions among all the nations consenting to the peace and associating themselves for its maintenance.

4. Adequate guarantees given and taken that national armaments will be reduced to the lowest points consistent with domestic safety.

5. A free, open-minded, and absolutely impartial adjustment of all colonial claims, based upon a strict observance of the principle that in determining all such questions of sovereignty the interests of the populations concerned must have equal weight with the equitable claims of the government whose title is to be determined.

6. The evacuation of all Russian territory and such a settlement of all questions affecting Russia as will secure the best and freest cooperation of the other nations of the world in obtaining for her an unhampered and unembarrassed opportunity for the independent determination of her own political development and national policy and assure her of a sincere welcome into the society of free nations under institutions of her own choosing; and, more than a welcome, assistance also of every kind that she may need and may herself desire. The treatment accorded Russia by her sister nations in the months to come will be the acid test of their good will, of their comprehension of her needs as distinguished from their own interests, and of their intelligent and unselfish sympathy.

7. Belgium, the whole world will agree, must be evacuated and restored, without any attempt to limit the sovereignty which she enjoys in common with all other free nations. No other single act will serve as this will serve to restore confidence among the nations in the laws which they have themselves set and determined for the government of their relations with one another. Without this healing act the whole structure and validity of international law is forever impaired.

8. All French territory should be freed and the invaded portions restored, and the wrong done to France by Prussia in 1871 in the matter of Alsace-Lorraine, which has unsettled the peace of the world for nearly fifty years, should be righted, in order that peace may once more be made secure in the interest of all.

9. A readjustment of the frontiers of Italy should be effected along dearly recognizable lines of nationality.

10. The peoples of Austria-Hungary, whose place among the nations we wish to see safeguarded and assured, should be accorded the freest opportunity of autonomous development.

11. Rumania, Serbia, and Montenegro should be evacuated; occupied territories restored; Serbia accorded free and secure access to the sea; and the relations of the several Balkan states to one another determined by friendly counsel along

historically established lines of allegiance and nationality; and international guarantees of the political and economic independence and territorial integrity of the several Balkan states should he entered into.

12. The Turkish portions of the present Ottoman Empire should be assured a secure sovereignty but the other nationalities which are now under Turkish rule should be assured an undoubted security of life and an absolutely unmolested opportunity of autonomous development, and the Dardanelles should be permanently opened as a free passage to the ships and commerce of all nations under international guarantees.

13. An independent Polish state should be erected which should include the territories inhabited by indisputably Polish populations, which should be assured a free and secure access to the sea, and whose political and economic independence and territorial integrity should be guaranteed by international covenant.

14. A general association of nations must be formed under specific covenants for the purpose of affording mutual guarantees of political independence and territorial integrity to great and small states alike.

President Woodrow Wilson's Address To Congress, 1919

Now, as to the character of the document, while it has consumed some time to read this document, I think you will see at once that it is very simple, and in nothing so simple as in the structure which it suggests for a league of nations, a body of delegates, an executive council, and a permanent secretariat.

When it came to the question of determining the character of the representation in the body of delegates we were all aware of a feeling which is current throughout the world.

Inasmuch as I am stating it in the presence of the official representatives of the various governments here present, including myself, I may say that there is a universal feeling that the world can not rest satisfied with merely official guidance. There has reached us through many channels the feeling that if the deliberating body of the league of nations was merely to be a body of officials representing the various governments, the peoples of the world would not be sure that some of the mistakes which preoccupied officials had admittedly made might, not be repeated.

It was impossible to conceive a method or an assembly so large and various as to be really representative of the great body of the peoples of the world, because, as I roughly reckon it, we represent as we sit around this table more than twelve hundred million people.

You can not have a representative assembly of twelve hundred million people, but if you leave it to each Government to have, if it pleases, one or two or three representatives, though only with a single vote, it may vary its representation from time to time, not only, but it may [originate] the choice of its several representatives....

Therefore we thought that this was a proper and a very prudent concession to the practically universal opinion of plain men everywhere that they wanted the door left open to a variety of representation, instead of being confined to a single official body with which they could or might not find themselves in sympathy.

And you will notice that this body has unlimited rights of discussion. I mean of discussion of anything that falls within the field of international relations—and that it is especially agreed that war or international misunderstandings or anything that may lead to friction or trouble is everybody's business, because it may affect the peace of the world.

And in order to safeguard the popular power so far as we could of this representative body it is provided, you will notice, that when a subject is submitted it is not to arbitration but to discussion by the executive council; it can, upon the initiative of either of the parties to the dispute, be drawn out of the executive council on the larger form of the general body of delegates, because through this instrument we are depending primarily and chiefly upon one great force, and this is the moral force of the public opinion of the world—the pleasing and clarifying and compelling influences of publicity—so that intrigues can no longer have their coverts, so that designs that are sinister can at any time be drawn into the open so that those things that are destroyed by the light may be promptly destroyed by the overwhelming light of the universal expression of the condemnation of the world.

Armed force is in the background in this program but it is in the background, and if the moral force of the world will not suffice the physical force of the world shall. But that is the last resort, because this is intended as a constitution of peace, not as a league of war.

The simplicity of the document seems to me to be one of its chief virtues, because, speaking for myself, I was unable to see the variety of circumstances with which this league would have to deal. I was unable, therefore, to plan all the machinery that might be necessary to meet the differing and unexpected contingencies. Therefore I should say of this document that it is not a straitjacket but a vehicle of life.

A living thing is born, and we must see to it what clothes we put on it. It is not a vehicle of power, but a vehicle in which power may be varied at the discretion of those who exercise it and in accordance with the changing circumstances of the time. And yet, while it is elastic, while it is general in its terms, it is definite in the one thing that we were called upon to make definite.

It is a definite guaranty of peace. It is a definite guaranty by word against aggression. It is a definite guaranty against the things which have just come near bringing the whole structure of civilization into ruin.

Its purposes do not for a moment lie vague. Its purposes are declared, and its powers are unmistakable. It is not in contemplation that this should be merely a league to secure the peace of the world. It is a league which can be used for cooperation in any international matter.

That is the significance of the provision introduced concerning labor. There are many ameliorations of labor conditions which can be effected by conference and discussion. I anticipate that there will be a very great usefulness in the bureau of labor which it is contemplated shall be set up by the league.

Men and women and children who work have been in the background through long ages and sometimes I seemed to be forgotten, while governments have had their watchful and suspicious eyes upon the maneuvers of one another, while the thought of statesmen has been about structural action and the larger transactions of commerce and of finance.

Now, if I may believe the picture which I see there, comes into the foreground the great body of the laboring people of the world, the men and women and children upon whom the great burden of sustaining the world must from day to day fall, whether we wish it to do so or not; people who go to bed tired and wake up without the stimulation of lively hope. These people will be drawn into the field of international consultation and help, and will be among the wards of the combined governments of the world. This is, I take leave to say, a very great step in advance in the mere conception of that.

Then, as you will notice, there is an imperative article concerning the publicity of all international agreements. Henceforth no member of the league can call any agreement valid which it has not registered with the secretary general, in whose office, of course, it will be subject to the examination of any body representing a member of the league. And the duty is laid upon the secretary general to earliest possible time....

There has been no greater advance than this, gentlemen. If you look back upon the history of the world you will see how helpless peoples have too often been a prey to powers that had no conscience in the matter. It has been one of the many distressing revelations of recent years that the great power which has just been, happily, defeated put intolerable burdens and injustices upon the helpless people of some of the colonies which it annexed to itself, that its interest was rather their extermination than their development; that the desire was to possess their land for European purposes, and not to enjoy their confidence in order that mankind might be lifted in these places to the next higher level.

Now, the world, expressing its conscience in law, says there is an end of that, that our consciences shall be settled to this thing. States will be picked out which have already shown that they can exercise conscience in this matter, and under their tutelage the helpless peoples of the world will come into a new light and into a new hope.

PROBLEM 21:
CONNECTION TO TODAY

1. What was the consequence for the United States in not joining the League of Nations?

2. Could World War II have been prevented if the U.S. had been an active force in the League of Nations?

3. After World War II the United Nations organization was created. Did the new organization learn anything from the failure of The League? If not, why not? If they did learn things, what were they?

4. Has the League's successor, the United Nations, been a successful organization? If so, how? If not, why not?

5. Both the League and the United Nations have had to deal with the issue of national "sovereignty." What does "sovereignty" mean and why has it caused problems? Is there some way to resolve this issue?

PROBLEM 22:
COULD PRESIDENT HERBERT HOOVER HAVE STOPPED THE ECONOMIC DOWNTURN OF 1929 FROM TURNING INTO THE GREAT DEPRESSION?

UNEMPLOYED AMERICANS IN LINE FOR FREE COFFEE AND DOUGHNUTS

LEFT:
A DEPRESSION-ERA FAMILY IN OKLAHOMA, 1936

RIGHT:
PRESIDENT HERBERT HOOVER

PROBLEM 22: COULD PRESIDENT HERBERT HOOVER HAVE STOPPED THE ECONOMIC DOWNTURN OF 1929 FROM TURNING INTO THE GREAT DEPRESSION?

*I*n October 1928 President Herbert Hoover delivered a speech in which he said, "…Our American experiment in human welfare has yielded a degree of well-being unparalleled in all the world. It has come nearer to the abolition of poverty, to the abolition of fear of want than humanity has ever reached before." Yet a year later, in 1929, on October 29—Black Tuesday—the U.S. stock market collapsed. More than 16 million shares were sold off as people panicked about what would happen to their investments. Because there were so few regulations of the market at that time, people had been able to buy stocks by putting down only 10 percent to 20 percent in cash to buy the stock, the remainder to be paid for by credit. Then, when the market crashed, brokers called investors to pay off the amounts owed on money they had borrowed, which made these investors sell off their stock to raise the needed cash. As stock prices fell, brokers called on customers to put up more cash, which resulted in more panic selling, and a downward spiral began. The entire economy was quickly in crisis. In one year 1,300 banks failed, and since there was no government program to insure people's savings, many lost everything. Unemployment reached unprecedented numbers, with 25 percent or more of the work force unemployed.

President Hoover looked to American history and saw that depressions had occurred before and were simply part of a recurring business cycle that would eventually work its way back to normalcy and even prosperity. In his mind, it had happened before, and it would happen again. The president was a firm believer in the ability of the market to correct itself, and he genuinely believed that America's hard work and individualism would once again end the crisis. He also believed that much of the economic situation was psychological and that people's emotions and fears triggered them to do irrational and hasty things that made the crisis worse. Thus, Hoover continually tried to assure the nation that "the corner had been turned" and that, as he said in January 1930, "We have now passed the worst." Conditions continued to deteriorate, however, as the president was assuring the nation that things were getting better.

What could Hoover have done? What could he have done to prevent the economic downturn from worsening into the Great Depression? And is it fair to blame President Hoover for the Great Depression?

PROBLEM 22:
QUESTIONS FOR TEAM RESEARCH

1. Doesn't American history bear out Hoover's assertion that there are business cycles in the economy which go from prosperity to recession to depression to recovery to prosperity again? Was anything different about 1929? What was it?

2. Was Hoover's attempt to attack the psychology of fear among people appropriate? Isn't that the same strategy used by President Franklin D. Roosevelt when he said in his inaugural address that "the only thing we have to fear, is fear itself?"

3. What concrete governmental steps did Hoover take as president to address the economic crisis? Did they work? If so, how? If not, why not?

4. Was Hoover wrong to be consistent in his deeply held beliefs about American individualism and the proper role of government in the economy?

PROBLEM 22:
STARTING THE SEARCH FOR EVIDENCE

INTERNET: KEY WORDS AND PHRASES

Herbert Hoover and free enterprise

Causes of the Great Depression

Societal consequences of the Great Depression

Hoover's response to the Great Depression

BOOKS

Hoover, Herbert, American *Individualism: The Challenge to Liberty*, West Branch, IA, Herbert Hoover Presidential Library Association, 1989

Leuchtenberg, William E., *Herbert Hoover*, NY, Times Books, 1993

McEvaine, Robert S., *The Great Depression 1929–1941*, NY, Times Books, 1993

Nardo, Don, ed, *The Great Depression*, San Diego, Greenhaven Press, 1993

Smith, Gene, *The Shattered Dream: Herbert Hoover and the Great Depression*, NY, Morrow, 1970

Senator Robert Wagner Supports Unemployment Relief

What is our problem? I know of no shorter way to describe it than to call it the vicious spiral of depression. When men lost their jobs they stopped buying. As buying was curtailed prices fell, profits disappeared, and factories reduced production. Reduced production meant that more men were laid off, deprived of their wages, and in turn more families curtailed their buying. So the vicious cycle continued. As it spread a great apprehension began to sweep through the country. A man who was at work was uncertain how long his job would continue and he, too, reduced his purchases. That quickened the decline. Then home owners out of work found that they could not meet interest and amortization on their mortgages; business houses unable to sell their merchandise could not pay their debts; and foreclosure and bankruptcy joined the forces of destruction....

This is not the first time that I speak of this problem. Long before the Nation was aware of any sign of approaching depression I publicly advocated adequate preparedness to meet this very situation which has brought untold agony to our people. Since then I have repeatedly urged action along the lines now proposed in the bill I shall describe. I am convinced that now, at last, all elements of responsible public opinion in this country have come to recognize the irresistible necessity of taking such action.

What do we propose to do? First, we propose to help relieve the desperate and irrepressible needs of the destitute so that no one in the United States shall have cause to go cold or hungry. Second, we propose to launch and finance a gigantic program of construction, both public and private. And, third, we propose to help finance agricultural, industrial, and commercial undertakings, where credit for proper enterprises can not be obtained through normal banking channels. Our ultimate object is to initiate a program which will create a demand for commodities and labor. We hope thereby to help check the decline of prices. When prices stop falling private business will resume its normal activity without government insurance....

Whatever theories we may personally entertain as to where responsibility lies for the relief of distress, it can no longer be denied that many communities throughout this country and many States are no longer able to carry unaided the crushing burden which the unprecedented demands for relief has placed upon them. These are days of emergency and it is, therefore, the sacred duty of the Federal Government to help meet that emergency and to mitigate the human misery which has been the unmerited lot of many of our citizens....

We shall resume employment to check and counteract the spiral of depression. For employment breeds more employment. There is no greater force for recovery than a job for the man who is eager to work.

The American people have never yet admitted defeat or succumbed to despair. We have the resources, the means, and the energy not only to check the depression but to lift our people to a higher level of prosperity than we have ever known. Our immediate task is to deal with the present emergency. The relief and construction bill is in my judgment a well-designed lever to give American industry a lift and a start until its own great native strength can be brought into vigorous action again. I repeat the hope that before the week is over the country may hear the encouraging news that the relief and construction bill has become a law and that this program of rehabilitation is under way.

PRESIDENT HERBERT HOOVER VETOES THE EMERGENCY RELIEF BILL, JULY 11, 1932

I have expressed myself at various times on the extreme undesirability of increasing expenditure on nonproductive public works beyond the $500,000,000 of construction already in the Budget. It is an ultimate burden upon the taxpayer. It unbalances the Budget after all our efforts to attain that object. It does not accomplish the purpose in creating employment for which it is designed, as is shown by the reports of the technical heads of the bureaus concerned that the total annual direct employment under this program would be less than 100,000 out of the 8,000,000 unemployed....

[This bill represents a] major extension of the authority of the Reconstruction Finance Corporation. The creation of the Reconstruction Finance Corporation itself was warranted only as a temporary measure to safely pass a grave national emergency which would otherwise have plunged us into destructive panic in consequence of the financial collapse in Europe. Its purpose was to preserve the credit structure of the Nation and thereby protect every individual in his employment, his farm, his bank deposits, his insurance policy, and his other savings, all of which are directly or indirectly in the safe-keeping of the great fiduciary institutions. Its authority was limited practically to loans to institutions which are under Federal or State control or regulation and affected with public interest. These functions were and are in the interest of the whole people....

This expansion of authority of the Reconstruction Corporation would mean loans against security for any conceivable purpose on any conceivable security to anybody who wants money. It would place the Government in private business in such fashion as to violate the very principle of public relations upon which we have builded [sic] our Nation, and render insecure its very foundations. Such action would make the Reconstruction Corporation the greatest banking and money-lending institution of all history. It would constitute a gigantic centralization of banking and finance to which the American people have been properly opposed for the past 100 years....

One of the most serious objections is that under the provisions of this bill those amongst 16,000 municipalities and the different States that have failed courageously to meet their responsibilities and to balance their own budgets would dump their financial liabilities and problems upon the Federal Government. All proper and insuperable difficulties they may confront in providing relief for distress are fully and carefully met under other provisions in the bill.

This proposal violates every sound principle of public finance and of government. Never before has so dangerous a suggestion been seriously made to our country. Never before has so much power for evil been placed at the unlimited discretion of seven individuals (i.e., the board of directors of the RFC).

With the utmost seriousness I urge the Congress to enact a relief measure, but I can not approve the measure before me, fraught as it is with possibilities of misfeasance and special privileges, so impracticable of administration, so dangerous to public credit, and so damaging to our whole conception of governmental relations to the people as to bring far more distress than it will cure.

PROBLEM 22:
CONNECTION TO TODAY

1. What government protections have been put in place since Hoover's time to lessen the impact of an economic downturn?

2. If these government actions have worked, why have we continued to have economic crisis periods? Do these justify Hoover's statement about business cycles?

3. What should be the role of government when our nation faces the possibility of economic depression?

4. What are the strengths and weaknesses of those who argue that the free market will adjust itself rather than having some kind of outside intervention?

PROBLEM 23:
DID FRANKLIN DELANO ROOSEVELT'S "NEW DEAL" SOLVE THE PROBLEM OF THE GREAT DEPRESSION?

PUTTING PEOPLE TO WORK UNDER THE PROGRAMS OF THE NEW DEAL

FRANKLIN DELANO ROOSEVELT'S INAUGURATION AS PRESIDENT

PROBLEM 23: DID FRANKLIN DELANO ROOSEVELT'S "NEW DEAL" SOLVE THE PROBLEM OF THE GREAT DEPRESSION?

The economic crisis that became known to history as the Great Depression had many causes. The lack of regulation of the stock market had encouraged risky investments by many who did not have the cash on hand to pay in full for the stock purchased. The country was also producing goods faster than consumers could buy them. When the stock market crashed, banks began to fail, people dramatically reduced purchases of all kinds, the nation enacted a protective tariff that diminished foreign markets for American products, and several drought conditions impacted American agriculture severely. The combination and interaction of these forces plunged the nation into financial turmoil, and on the date of Franklin Delano Roosevelt's inauguration as President of the United States, 13,000,000 people were unemployed.

In Roosevelt's speech when he accepted the nomination of the Democratic Party for president he had said; "I pledge to you, I pledge myself, to a new deal for the American people," but no one really knew what this New Deal was about. In his inaugural address, the new president attempted to convey a sense of confidence and optimism to the American people when he said, "Let me assert my firm belief that the only thing we have to fear is fear itself—needless, unreasoning, unjustified terror which paralyzes needed efforts to convert retreat into advance."

Despite these words of hope, the American people were afraid. Their banks were closing, their crops were failing, their jobs were disappearing, and they looked to Roosevelt to translate his words into action. Roosevelt's goals were summarized as "relief, recovery, and reform." In the first 100 days of his administration and in the years following his first and second terms as president, an unprecedented amount of legislation came from Washington focused on those three goals: agencies such as the Tennessee Valley Authority, the Emergency Banking Act, the Federal Emergency Relief Act, the Agricultural Adjustment Act, the Civilian Conservation Corps Act, the National Recovery Administration, the Works Progress Administration, and many, many more.

Did this flurry of legislation and activity actually bring relief, faster recovery, and reform of the economic system? Did the New Deal end the economic crisis and solve the problems brought on by the Great Depression?

PROBLEM 23:
QUESTIONS FOR TEAM RESEARCH

1. How much of the Great Depression was "psychological"? And how important was Roosevelt's personality in calming the nation?

2. What fundamental change occurred from the government philosophy of Herbert Hoover to that of FDR?

3. How did the U.S. Government pay for the huge number of new programs, agencies, and initiatives?

4. Did Roosevelt's New Deal save capitalism in America or initiate state socialism?

5. By what criteria can you judge whether or not the New Deal ended the Great Depression?

PROBLEM 23:
STARTING THE SEARCH FOR EVIDENCE

INTERNET: KEY WORDS AND PHRASES

The presidential campaign of 1932

Franklin D. Roosevelt's Inaugural Address

Elements of the New Deal

Statistics of U. S. unemployment 1932–1941

BOOKS

Badger, Anthony J., *The New Deal: The Depression Years, 1930–1940*, Chicago, Ivan R. Dee, 2002

Davis, Kenneth S., *Franklin D. Roosevelt, The New Deal Years, 1933–1937: A History*, NY, Random House, 1986

Leuchentenberg, William E., *Franklin D. Roosevelt and the New Deal, 1932–40*, NY, Harper & Row, 1963

Schlesinger, Arthur M., *The Coming of the New Deal, 1933–1935*, Boston, Houghton Mifflin, 2003

Stein, R. Conrad, *The New Deal: Pulling America Out of the Great Depression*, Berkeley Heights, Enslow Publishers, 2006

Senator Robert A. Taft Evaluates the New Deal, March 18, 1939

The New Deal tide is rapidly receding, and...the people are again looking to the Republican Party for leadership. It is most important that the Republicans, even though they are still in the opposition, formulate their program on which to appeal to the people for a change of administration.

After six years of New Deal rule, after every kind of experiment, and the addition of $20,000,000,000 to the national debt the fundamental problems are still unresolved. More than 10,000,000 people are unemployed in the United States today, about 3,000,000 of them receiving a bare subsistence from the W.P.A. Twenty million people are looking to the Government for food. Millions more are receiving inadequate wages and fall in that underprivileged class for whom the New Dealers have shed tears in every speech, and to whom they have repeatedly promised prosperity and security. And yet there are more people underprivileged today, more people who have barely enough to live on, than there have been at any time except at the very bottom of the depression.

[The New Deal has] relied on three types of Government activity. The first type consists of direct relief, in different forms, to the lower-income groups. The attempt to administer from Washington a great work-relief program throughout the entire United States has resulted in inefficiency, politics, and a vast expense which threatens a complete bankruptcy of the Federal Government.

The second type of New Deal activity included the Government regulatory measures, which attempt to raise the income of this group or that group by controlling prices, wages, hours, and practices throughout the United States. Such were the N.R.A. and the A.A.A. Such are the laws regulating agriculture today, the Guffey Coal Act, the wage-hour law. This type of law has completely failed in its purpose.

This type of law is one of the most discouraging to private enterprise. No man can tell when the Government may step into his business and nullify all of the effort and energy and ingenuity he may have shown in developing that business. He is hounded by inspectors, excessive regulation, reports, and red tape. Many have gone out of business and many have stayed out of business because they could not feel certain that with all this Government regulation they might be utterly wasting their time and their money.

The other type of New Deal experiment is direct Government-business activity in fields where the Government thinks that private enterprise has fallen down on its job. Of this character are the T.V.A., the Rural Electrification Administration, the lending agencies extending Government credit to home owners, the building of canals and other self-liquidating public works. Unquestionably some of this activity is justified, though usually the reason that private capital has failed the entire field is because the enterprise is unprofitable in spite of the glowing prospectus of some Government departments.

But there are some unprofitable things which a government should start, and governments always have done something of this kind. It is a question of degree. It is very doubtful in my mind whether the T.V.A. ever was justified in view of the development of public utilities in the Tennessee Valley, but now we have it and have to operate it to the best advantage.

I have pointed out that the New Deal seemed to be inspired with a hostility to the entire preexisting American economic system. The result is that these three types of measures which I have described have not been administered with any special care to preserve the best features of private industry and encourage it to bring about recovery. The relief measures have been inefficient and expensive. They have resulted in a tremendous burden of taxation which beats down on the man who is trying to make his own living. There has been no effort to preserve conditions under which a man, striving for a private job and doing his job well, shall be encouraged and preferred to the man on W.P.A. The other two types of measures, Government regulation and Government competition, have directly discouraged private activity of every kind. More men have gone out of business in the last five years than have gone into business because of the complete uncertainty whether they can survive a constant Government interference.

What then should be the Republican program? It must combine a policy of encouragement to private industry, which can put millions of men to work, with sincere and effective administration of relief measures to assist directly the lower-income groups. It must recognize the absolute necessity of relief measures in this country for many years to come…We must assist the lower-income groups by direct relief, by work relief, by old age pensions, by unemployment insurance and by some form of housing subsidy.

But the administration of this relief must be carried on with the greatest care that it may not destroy our entire American system and put the whole population on relief. It must be carried on with economy because the cost of supporting those who do not work is undoubtedly borne by those who are working.

[And] we must take every possible measure to cure the unemployment problem. It can only be cured by more jobs in private industry. We must, therefore, take every possible measure to encourage people to put their time and money again into the development of private industry…. The people must feel again that the making of a deserved profit is not a crime, but a merit. They must feel again that the Government is interested in the prosperity of the businessman. They must feel again that the Government does not regard every businessman as a potential crook.

But there must be more than mental reassurance. There must be an abandonment as far as possible of Government fixing of prices, wages, and business practices. Americans must be assured that they will not be met by Government competition in their field of business activity. They must feel that Government activity will be confined to keeping their markets open, free, and competitive, so that they will have an equal chance with their little neighbor or their big neighbor. They must feel that Government expenses will be held down as far as possible, so that the tax burdens may not deprive them of the fruits of their most successful efforts. They would like to know that the currency is stable, the Government's fiscal policy sound, and all danger of inflation of the currency removed.

Prosperity can only be brought about by increased production. This country was built up by millions of men, starting new enterprises…Employment increased steadily for 150 years, not by arbitrary building up of consumers' purchasing power, but by encouraging production and putting men to work. The theory that relief payments stimulate production is disproved by our own experience.

If we can stop spending money now, if we can stop the tremendous expansion of Government activity, regulation and taxation, it is not too late to resume the progress which made this country the envy of the world; but if we continue for six years more, the course which we have pursued, he is a bold man who will say that we can then restore prosperity under a democratic form of government.

PROBLEM 23:
CONNECTION TO TODAY

1. Has the basic approach to government's role in society changed since FDR's time or remained essentially the same? What examples from today can you cite to back up your argument?

2. Could we have another "Great Depression" today? Explain your answer.

3. What should be the relationship between minimal government regulation of business and maximum regulation? What are the problems and positives of both extremes?

4. What is the relationship of war to the American economy?

PROBLEM 24: WAS IT NECESSARY FOR THE UNITED STATES TO USE THE ATOMIC BOMB AGAINST JAPAN IN WORLD WAR II?

THE EXPLOSION OF THE ATOMIC BOMB

PRESIDENT HARRY S TRUMAN

PROBLEM 24: WAS IT NECESSARY FOR THE UNITED STATES TO USE THE ATOMIC BOMB AGAINST JAPAN IN WORLD WAR II?

On August 6, 1945, the American war plane, *Enola Gay*, dropped the first atomic bomb ever used in warfare on the Japanese city of Hiroshima. The bombing resulted in between 70,000 and 80,000 people being killed and more than another 70,000 seriously injured. More than 90 percent of the doctors and nurses working in Hiroshima were also killed. Because of the aftereffects of radiation, it is estimated that approximately 200,000 people had died by 1950. After the bombing the United States once again asked Japan to surrender or expect another similar attack. The Japanese refused, and on August 9, 1945, the United States dropped a second atomic bomb on the Japanese city of Nagasaki. It was estimated that this second bombing resulted in 80,000 more deaths. On August 12, 1945, the emperor of Japan made the decision to surrender and thus end World War II. The war had ended but at the price of a huge number of lives being lost. The aftereffects of this bombing continued for decades, as individuals suffered from terrible skin burns, leukemia, and cancer. Since that time some historians have asked the question Was it necessary to use this weapon to end this war? Why weren't other plans put in place?

President Harry S Truman was the person who had the final decision as to whether or not to use the bomb. The President's goal was to end the war and minimize American casualties. The American public's attitude toward the Japanese was intensely negative. The Japanese had launched a surprise attack on America at Pearl Harbor in 1941, and they had been especially cruel to American servicemen whom they captured and held as prisoners of war. But did these things justify such an intense revenge? President Truman's decision was based on history and intelligence estimates. Past experience had shown that the Japanese were prepared to fight to the death and not surrender. At the battle of Iwo Jima, 25,000 Americans had been killed and 21,000 Japanese troops had fought to the death. At the battle of Okinawa, 50,000 Americans were killed or wounded, and the Japanese lost 70,000 men. During the fighting on the island of

Saipan, nearly 900 Japanese soldiers killed themselves rather than be taken prisoner by the Americans. The president was told that a direct invasion of the Japanese mainland would encounter extremely fierce resistance and that between 500,000 to perhaps a million American soldiers would die. It was on the basis of these facts that Truman decided to use the bomb against Japan.

Could there have been another plan? The U.S. had been fire-bombing Japanese targets and could have continued to do so. Russia, America's ally in World War II, was preparing to enter the fight against Japan since Germany had already surrendered, and the Russians could now use all their armed forces against the Japanese. What did the United States gain by using the bomb? Was it worth the deaths of thousands of innocent civilians?

PROBLEM 24:
QUESTIONS FOR TEAM RESEARCH

1. To what extent was the U.S. use of the atomic bomb a part of "psychological" warfare?

2. Should President Truman have relied on estimates of American casualties that would happen in the event of a land invasion of Japan? Why or why not?

3. Did the United States give Japan adequate warning signals about what the consequences of refusing to surrender would be?

4. Some critics of the U.S. have said that since the Americans actually had this bomb and had spent millions to research and develop it, they had to use it or face criticism from those who wanted the war to end. Do you agree or disagree with this interpretation? Explain.

PROBLEM 24:
STARTING THE SEARCH FOR EVIDENCE

INTERNET: KEY WORDS AND PHRASES

U. S. casualties in the war against Japan, 1941–1945

The Manhattan Project

Truman's decision to use the atomic bomb

Americans' opinion after the use of the atomic bomb

BOOKS

Alperovitz, Gar, *The Decision to Use the Atomic Bomb*, NY, Vintage Books, 1996

McCullough, David G., *Truman*, NY, Simon and Schuster, 1992

McKain, Mark, *Making and Using the Atomic Bomb*, San Diego, Greenhaven Press, 2003

Purcell, John F., *The Best Kept Secret: The Story of the Atomic Bomb*, NY, Vanguard Press, 1963

Truman, Harry S, *Memoirs of Harry Truman*, Garden City, Doubleday, 1955–56

President Harry S Truman Announces the Atomic Bombing of Japan

Sixteen hours ago an American airplane dropped one bomb on Hiroshima and destroyed its usefulness to the enemy. That bomb had more power than 20,000 tons of T.N.T. It had more than two thousand times the blast power of the British "Grand Slam" which is the largest bomb ever yet used in the history of warfare.

The Japanese began the war from the air at Pearl Harbor. They have been repaid many fold. And the end is not yet. With this bomb we have now added a new and revolutionary increase in destruction to supplement the growing power of our armed forces. In their present form these bombs are now in production and even more powerful forms are in development.

It is an atomic bomb. It is a harnessing of the basic power of the universe. The force from which the sun draws its power has been loosed against those who brought war to the Far East.

Before 1939, it was the accepted belief of scientists that it was theoretically possible to release atomic energy. But no one knew any practical method for doing it. By 1942, however, we knew that the Germans were working feverishly to find a way to add atomic energy to the other engines of war with which they hoped to enslave the world. But they failed....

The battle of the laboratories held fateful risks for us as well as the battles of the air, land and sea, and we have now won the battle of the laboratories as we have won the other battles....

We now have two great plants and many lesser works devoted to the production of atomic power. Employment during peak construction numbered 125,000 and over 65,000 individuals are even now engaged in operating the plants. Many have worked there for two and a half years. Few know what they have been producing. They see great quantities of material going in and they see nothing coming out of these plants, for the physical size of the explosive charge is exceedingly small. We have spent two billion dollars on the greatest scientific gamble in history—and won.

But the greatest marvel is not the size of the enterprise, its secrecy, nor its cost, but the achievement of scientific brains in putting together infinitely complex pieces of knowledge held by many men in different fields of science into a workable plan. And hardly less marvelous has been the capacity of industry to design, and of labor to operate, the machines and methods to do things never done before so that the brain child of many minds came forth in physical shape and performed as it was supposed to do. Both science and industry worked under the direction of the United States Army, which achieved a unique success in managing so diverse a problem in the advancement of knowledge in an amazingly short time. It is doubtful if such another combination could be got together in the world. What has been done is the greatest achievement of organized science in history. It was done under high pressure and without failure.

We are now prepared to obliterate more rapidly and completely every productive enterprise the Japanese have above ground in any city. We shall destroy their docks, their factories, and their communications. Let there be no mistake; we shall completely destroy Japan's power to make war.

It was to spare the Japanese people from utter destruction that the ultimatum of July 26 was issued at Potsdam. Their leaders promptly rejected that ultimatum. If they do not now accept our terms they may expect a rain of ruin from the air, the like of which has never been seen on this earth. Behind this air attack will follow sea and land forces in such numbers and power as they have not yet seen and with the fighting skill of which they are already well aware….

The fact that we can release atomic energy ushers in a new era in man's understanding of nature's forces. Atomic energy may in the future supplement the power that now comes from coal, oil, and falling water, but at present it cannot be produced on a basis to compete with them commercially. Before that comes there must be a long period of intensive research.

It has never been the habit of the scientists of this country or the policy of this Government to withhold from the world scientific knowledge. Normally, therefore, everything about the work with atomic energy would be made public.

But under present circumstances it is not intended to divulge the technical processes of production or all the military applications, pending further examination of possible methods of protecting us and the rest of the world from the danger of sudden destruction.

I shall recommend that the United States consider promptly the establishment of an appropriate commission to control the production and use of atomic power within the United States. I shall give further consideration and make further recommendations to the Congress as to how atomic power can become a powerful and forceful influence towards the maintenance of world peace.

JOURNALIST FELIX MORLEY OPPOSES THE DROPPING OF THE ATOMIC BOMB

According to Japanese experts, accepted in Washington as probably truthful, some 30,000 human beings were blasted into eternity by the first atomic bomb, exploded over the city of Hiroshima on August 6.

Of the 160,000 who were injured by this act of annihilation, directed at a community of a quarter of a million persons, additional thousands are said to have died in subsequent agony from the delayed cremation of the neutron rays. The same report on after-effects comes from Nagasaki, where on August 9 the second atomic bomb caused a somewhat smaller number of casualties.

If December 7, 1941, is "a day that will live in infamy," what will impartial history say of August 6, 1945?

At Pearl Harbor the target was an isolated naval base; the material destruction was virtually limited to warships and military installations; the relatively small loss of life was for the most part confined to men who had voluntarily enlisted in the armed services.

At Hiroshima the target was the heart of a teeming city. The great majority of those obliterated were civilians, including thousands of children trapped in the thirty-three schools that were destroyed. It was pure accident if a single person slain at Hiroshima had any personal responsibility for the Pearl Harbor outrage. These victims, like ourselves, were merely the helpless instruments of the ruthless Moloch of Totalitarian Government.

Pearl Harbor was an indefensible and infamous act of aggression. But Hiroshima was an equally infamous act of atrocious revenge. Because perpetrated by a nation that calls itself Christian, on a people with less lofty spiritual pretensions, eventual judgment may call our action ethically the more shameful, morally the more degrading, of the two.

Undoubtedly Hiroshima shortened the war. The atomic bomb may well have saved more lives than it has destroyed to date. But to say that is to excuse rather than to explain.

The price we have paid for victory is terribly high. And perhaps the cost of this last installment, at Hiroshima, is even heavier for us than for the Japanese. For its measurement is the loss of ideals which, far more than our material strength, have made America great and distinctive in the long human story. The measurement of our loss may be seen, for instance, in the miserable farce put on by those who try to reconcile mass murder of "enemy children" with lip service to the doctrine that God created all men in his image.

We tend to forget, also, that under our system of government each of us must carry individual responsibility for the decisions of our rulers, civilian or military. The brilliant scientists who designed, the intrepid flyers who released, the atomic bomb are actually less responsible than the rest of us for its effects. They were our servants, paid by us to do what we wanted done.

The German people, we have decreed, have corporate responsibility for the acts of the National Socialist State. So, at Nazi concentration camps, we have paraded horrified German civilians before the piled bodies of tortured Nazi victims. We have drafted German women to bury these pitiful dead. We have forced German prisoners in this country to witness pictures of these abominable deeds.

It would be equally salutary to send groups of representative Americans to blasted Hiroshima. There, as at Buchenwald, are many unburied dead. There are many towards whose bereavement we can scarcely feel vindictive. There is a spiritual desolation for which we cannot dodge responsibility.

Great effort has been made to picture the atomic bomb as an eminently laudable achievement of American inventiveness, ingenuity and scientific skill. On the day of the destruction of Hiroshima the floodgates of official publicity were swung wide. Rivers of racy material prepared in our various agencies of Public Enlightenment poured out to the press and radio commentators whose well-understood duty it is to "condition" public opinion. Puddles of ink confusedly outlined the techniques whereby we have successfully broken the laws of God.

Never has any totalitarian propaganda effort fallen more flat. Instead of the anticipated wave of nationalistic enthusiasm, the general reaction was one of unconcealed horror. Even the immediate Japanese surrender, even the joy of "going places" on unrationed gas, even the universal sense of relief over the ending of the war, has not concealed an apprehension which reflection does less than nothing to diminish. Many who cannot voice their thoughts are none the less conscious of the withdrawal of the Governing Hand, are well aware that at the crossroads we have chosen the turning which leads back to Nothingness.

So a country dedicated by its founders to individual enlightenment now controls a secret which makes the individual look as does the insect in response to D.D.T. Quite naturally our new scale of values loses its moral grandeur and shifts to insect values—"full employment" or "security" within the meticulously organized anthill of the expanding State.

We have won the war. Now what is our purpose for the Power we control?

PROBLEM 24: CONNECTION TO TODAY

1. Is the fact that today not only the U.S. but other countries have nuclear weapons an actual deterrent to war? Explain.

2. Does the United States have the right to insist that nations such as North Korea and Iraq not have nuclear weapons? Explain.

3. Other than in retaliation for an attack on the United States, is there any situation you can imagine where the United States would today use nuclear weapons?

4. How effective are nuclear weapons against terrorists?

5. Should any president consider moral and ethical issues today when retaliating against an attack on our country?

PROBLEM 25:
DID THE 1960S REPRESENT AN AMERICAN CULTURAL REVOLUTION?

ANTI-WAR
DEMONSTRATION

AN ASPECT
OF 1960S YOUTH
CULTURE

PROBLEM 25: DID THE 1960S REPRESENT AN AMERICAN CULTURAL REVOLUTION?

The history of the decade of the 1960s is one of upheaval and changes. While it is true that every decade brings changes, few can equal those that occurred in the years 1960 through 1969. A number of forces converged during that time that, interacting together, brought about much change.

The first of these forces was simply the sheer number of people who were coming of age during that decade. The so-called Baby Boomer generation was one of the largest cohorts of individuals moving through the life cycle in all of our history, and a huge number were in their twenties during the 1960s. The second force was the expansion of individual rights that manifested itself through the black and Hispanic civil rights movement and the feminist initiative known as the Women's Liberation Movement. The third major force in society was the long continuation of an increasingly unpopular war Americans were fighting in Vietnam. The results of the interaction of these forces were unrest, upheaval, and political and social turmoil.

The decade was marked with sit-ins, civil rights marches, and violent confrontations with authorities who resisted change. Riots occurred in major American cities, and the assassinations of President John F. Kennedy, Dr. Martin Luther King, Jr., and Senator Robert F. Kennedy created a climate of fear and unrest. The opposition to the war in Vietnam led to violent eruptions on college campuses as students rebelled against the war and the Selective Service System, which drafted young men into the armed forces. Thousands of young people burned their draft cards, led protests on campuses, and even left to live in Canada.

The decade was also characterized by radical changes in clothing and hair styles; rampant drug use; and open attitudes toward sex and language. So-called proper behavior was challenged and dramatically changed. To some, the cumulative effect of all these developments was a sign the society was becoming liberated from the conservative 1950s. For others what was happening was a negative breakdown of all those things that kept a civil society functioning. Some believed these would result in the creation of a new society with new values. Others believed these events were a unique combination of things particular to this time period and would eventually subside as things became more normal.

How much of the 1960s upheaval is still with us today? Was it truly a unique special time, fostered by unique circumstances, which did not sustain themselves in subsequent years? Did the 1960s usher in a cultural revolution, or were those years and events that have had no real lasting impact on the nation?

PROBLEM 25:
QUESTIONS FOR TEAM RESEARCH

1. How did the three forces described in the previous essay interact to cause social upheaval?

2. What criteria would you use to assess whether or not there was a cultural revolution in the 1960s?

3. Have there been other comparable decades in American history? If so, when were they and what were their underlying causes? If not, why not?

4. Would there have been cultural upheaval had there not been an unpopular war? Explain.

5. What aspects of the 1960s are still with us today?

PROBLEM 25:
STARTING THE SEARCH FOR EVIDENCE

INTERNET: KEY WORDS AND PHRASES

Campus sit ins in the 1960s

Youth rebellion in the 1960s

American public opinion and the Vietnam War

Drug use and sexual attitudes in the 1960s

BOOKS

Betsworth, Roger G., *The Radical Movement of the 1960's*, Metuchen, NJ, Scarecrow Press, 1980

Bloch, Avital H.; Umansky, Lavri, *Impossible to Hold: Women and Culture in the 1960's*, NY, New York University Press, 2005

Havighurst, Robert J., *American Higher Education in the 1960's*, Columbus, Ohio State University, 1960

Isserman, Mauice, *America Divided: The Civil War of the 1960's*, NY, Oxford University Press, 1999

O'Neill, William L., *Coming Apart: An Informal History of America in the 1960's*, Chicago, Quadrangle Books, 1971

Tom Hayden's Port Huron Statement, June 15, 1962

Introduction: Agenda for a Generation

We are people of this generation, bred in at least modest comfort, housed now in universities, looking uncomfortably to the world we inherit.

When we were kids the United States was the wealthiest and strongest country in the world; the only one with the atom bomb, the least scarred by modern war, an initiator of the United Nations that we thought would distribute Western influence throughout the world. Freedom and equality for each individual, government of, by, and for the people—these American values we found good, principles by which we could live as men. Many of us began maturing in complacency.

As we grew, however, our comfort was penetrated by events too troubling to dismiss. First, the permeating and victimizing fact of human degradation, symbolized by the Southern struggle against racial bigotry, compelled most of us from silence to activism. Second, the enclosing fact of the Cold War, symbolized by the presence of the Bomb, brought awareness that we ourselves, and our friends, and millions of abstract "others" we knew more directly because of our common peril, might die at any time. We might deliberately ignore, or avoid, or fail to feel all other human problems, but not these two, for these were too immediate and crushing in their impact, too challenging in the demand that we as individuals take the responsibility for encounter and resolution.

While these and other problems either directly oppressed us or rankled our consciences and became our own subjective concerns, we began to see complicated and disturbing paradoxes in our surrounding America. The declaration "all men are created equal…" rang hollow before the facts of Negro life in the South and the big cities of the North. The proclaimed peaceful intentions of the United States contradicted its economic and military investments in the Cold War status quo.

We witnessed, and continue to witness, other paradoxes. With nuclear energy whole cities can easily be powered, yet the dominant nation-states seem more likely to unleash destruction greater than that incurred in all wars of human history. Although our own technology is destroying old and creating new forms of social organization, men still tolerate meaningless work and idleness. While two-thirds of mankind suffers under nourishment, our own upper classes revel amidst superfluous abundance. Although world population is expected to double in forty years, the nations still tolerate anarchy as a major principle of international conduct and uncontrolled exploitation governs the sapping of the earth's physical resources. Although mankind desperately needs revolutionary leadership, America rests in national stalemate, its goals ambiguous and tradition-bound instead of informed and clear, its democratic system apathetic and manipulated rather than "of, by, and for the people."

Not only did tarnish appear on our image of American virtue, not only did disillusion occur when the hypocrisy of American ideals was discovered, but we began to sense that what we had originally seen as the American Golden Age was actually the decline of an era. The worldwide outbreak of revolution against colonialism and imperialism, the entrenchment of totalitarian states, the menace of war, overpopulation, international disorder, supertechnology—these trends were testing the tenacity of our own commitment to democracy and freedom and our abilities to visualize their application to a world in upheaval.

Our work is guided by the sense that we may be the last generation in the experiment with living. But we are a minority—the vast majority of our people regard the temporary equilibriums of our society and world as eternally functional parts. In this is perhaps the outstanding paradox; we ourselves are imbued with urgency, yet the message of our society is that there is no viable alternative to the present. Beneath the reassuring tones of the politicians, beneath the common opinion that America will "muddle through," beneath the stagnation of those who have closed their minds to the future, is the pervading feeling that there simply are no alternatives, that our times have witnessed the exhaustion not only of Utopias, but of any new departures as well. Feeling the press of complexity upon the emptiness of life, people are fearful of the thought that at any moment things might be thrust out of control. They fear change itself, since change might smash whatever invisible framework seems to hold back chaos for them now. For most Americans, all crusades are suspect, threatening. The fact that each individual sees apathy in his fellows perpetuates the common reluctance to organize for change. The dominant institutions are complex enough to blunt the minds of their potential critics, and entrenched enough to swiftly dissipate or entirely repel the energies of protest and reform, thus limiting human expectancies. Then, too, we are a materially improved society, and by our own improvements we seem to have weakened the case for further change.

Some would have us believe that Americans feel contentment amidst prosperity—but might it not better be called a glaze above deeply felt anxieties about their role in the new world? And if these anxieties produce a developed indifference to human affairs, do they not as well produce a yearning to believe that there *is* an alternative to the present, that something *can* be done to change circumstances in the school, the workplaces, the bureaucracies, the government? It is to this latter yearning, at once the spark and engine of change, that we direct our present appeal. The search for truly democratic alternatives to the present, and a commitment to social experimentation with them, is a worthy and fulfilling human enterprise, one which moves us and, we hope, others today. On such a basis do we offer this document of our convictions and analysis: as an effort in understanding and changing the conditions of humanity in the late twentieth century, an effort rooted in the ancient, still unfulfilled conception of man attaining determining influence over his circumstances of life.

GOVERNOR RONALD REAGAN'S SPEECH "FREEDOM VS ANARCHY ON CAMPUS," 1968

The people of California founded and generously support what has become the finest system of public higher education in the land.

Within this system there are now nine university campuses, nineteen State-college campuses and 81 community colleges, plus many fine independent colleges and universities which are also supported, for the most part, by the people of California.

The system has worked well.

Yes, on these campuses, generations of Californians have pursued knowledge within the widest range of disciplines. They have sampled widely of man's knowledge of man, of the history of his ideas and what he knows of the world around him.

This is the role of higher education in California. At least this has been the case up until recently.

Within the past five or six years, something new has been added—a violent strident something that has disturbed all of us, a something whose admitted purpose is to destroy or to capture and use society's institutions for its own purpose. I say "whose admitted purpose" because the leadership minces no words. It is boastful, arrogant and threatening.

Consider these words from a campus teacher: "I think we agree that the revolution is necessary and that you don't conduct a revolution by attacking the strongest enemy first. You take care of your business at home first, then you move abroad. Thus we must make the university the home of the revolution."

From the capture of a police car and negotiations conducted in an atmosphere of intimidation, threats and fear; we went from free speech to filthy speech.

The movement spread to other campuses. There has been general incitement against properly constituted law enforcement authorities and general trampling of the will, the rights and freedom of movement of the majority by the organized, militant, and highly vocal minority.

Though the causes were cloaked in the dignity of academic and other freedoms, they are—in fact—a lusting for power. Some protesters even marched under banners that ranged from the black flag of anarchy, the red flag of revolution, to the flags of enemies engaged in killing young Americans—the North Vietnamese and the Viet Cong.

Academic freedom is one of the important freedoms to go in the new order envisioned by the New Left. There was no academic freedom in Hitler's Germany. There is no academic freedom in Mao's China or Castro's Cuba. And there is no academic freedom in the philosophies or the actions of the George Murrays, the Eldridge Cleavers or the Jerry Rubins.

It is therefore most imperative that we—the great and thoughtful majority of citizens of all races—keep our perspective. We must recognize the manipulations being carried out to frustrate our common interest in living together with dignity in one American society. And we must also recognize that those who exercise violence must be held accountable for their actions—and held equally accountable regardless of their color.

Nationwide, experience has shown that prompt dealing with disturbances leads to peace, that hesitation, vacillation and appeasement lead to greater disorder.

Isn't it logical, in view of past experience to ask that no campus official negotiate or hold conferences with any individual or group while such individual or group is disturbing or disrupting campus activities, violating any rule or regulation of the campus or its governing board, or committing any criminal offense? And, likewise, to insist that there shall be no consideration of the demands or requests of any such individual or group while their disruptive or disorderly conduct continues?

And finally, isn't it time to demand that when individuals have been arrested as a result of their participation in the disturbances and disorders, the chief campus officer—or such other person designated by him—shall sign a criminal complaint against such persons and shall co-operate in the prosecution of those individuals and shall immediately suspend them from the university?...

From which group will we—and, really, from which group will you young people now going to college—elect your future leaders? Will it be from the few, but militant, anarchists and others now trying to control and run our campuses? Or will we elect our future leaders from the majority of fine young men and women dedicated to justice, order and the full development of the true individual?

PROBLEM 25:
CONNECTION TO TODAY

1. What are the conditions in society which bring about social and political upheaval?

2. The 1960s generation of young men and women are said to be the most politically involved and active in our history. Why has that kind of activism and involvement not repeated itself since then?

3. What are the key forces today which you believe are fundamentally changing American society?

4. What role did the media play in the cultural upheaval of the 1960s? What similar or different role do the media play today?

PROBLEM 26: HOW DID THE UNITED STATES AVERT NUCLEAR WAR WITH THE SOVIET UNION IN THE MISSILE CRISIS OF 1962?

RIGHT: PRESIDENT KENNEDY MEETING WITH SOVIET PREMIER NIKITA KHRUSCHEV

BELOW: CARTOON DEPICTING THE CONFLICT BETWEEN THE SOVIET UNION AND THE UNITED STATES OVER THE MISSILE CRISIS

PROBLEM 26: HOW DID THE UNITED STATES AVERT NUCLEAR WAR WITH THE SOVIET UNION IN THE MISSILE CRISIS OF 1962?

American relations with Cuba had steadily deteriorated from the time Fidel Castro and his revolutionaries took control of that country. Castro turned out to be an advocate of Communism, and he forged stronger and stronger ties with the Communist Soviet Union. Soon after John F. Kennedy became president, he authorized activation of a plan that had been prepared during the Eisenhower administration. That plan called for invasion of Cuba in 1961. It was believed that would lead to a general uprising in that country and lead to the overthrow of the Castro government. The invasion was a gigantic failure that cost many lives, was perceived as a major United States failure, and made the new young president seem like an inexperienced, ineffectual leader. Former President Eisenhower warned Kennedy that the failure of the invasion "will embolden the Soviets to do something that they would otherwise not do."

Both Fidel Castro and the leader of the Soviet Union, Nikita Khruschev believed that the United States would not allow its failure in the invasion to simply be forgotten and do nothing. The two Communist leaders believed that another American invasion was inevitable. They also believed that Kennedy's handling of the failed invasion indicated that he was too young, too inexperienced, and weak. The decision they made was to place Soviet nuclear missiles in Cuba, a mere 90 miles away from the American mainland.

In October 1962, a United States spy plane photographed the missile sites that were being constructed by the Soviet Union in Cuba. The United States viewed this development as unacceptable because it would give the Soviet Union opportunity to launch missiles directly against American cities and also because it was a violation of America's Monroe Doctrine, which was a long-standing policy stating that European powers should stay out of issues that pertained to the Americas.

President Kennedy immediately issued a warning saying, "It shall be the policy of this nation to regard any nuclear missile launched from Cuba against any nation in the Western Hemisphere as an attack on the United States, requiring a full retaliatory response upon the Soviet Union." Thus, Kennedy made it clear that if the Soviets were to launch a missile, it would start a nuclear war; the United States demanded that the missile sites in Cuba be dismantled. The United States response in action was to call for a quarantine against Cuba, which meant that United States armed forces would intercept ships coming to Cuba that were carrying cargoes of offensive weapons and turn them back to their place of origin.

Khruschev called the United States position a "pirate action" that would lead to war, and he wrote to Kennedy, "If you coolly weigh the situation which has developed, not giving way to passions, you will understand that the Soviet Union cannot fail to reject the arbitrary demands of the United States." The Soviet leader said that his nation viewed the quarantine as a blockade that was "an act of aggression" and that the Soviet ships would be instructed to ignore it. Now the leaders of both world powers seemed to have put themselves into positions from which they could not back down without looking as if they had been defeated. They could not back down, but the alternative was war—the first nuclear war—that was sure to destroy millions of lives and destroy major population centers of both countries. As all the world followed these events with fear and apprehension, nuclear war did not come. The world had come closer to nuclear disaster than ever before or since.

How did this happen? How was disaster averted, and how did these two leaders avoid what seemed to be a no-win situation for both men?

PROBLEM 26:
QUESTIONS FOR TEAM RESEARCH

1. How justified was the feeling of Khruschev and Castro that the United States was planning a second invasion of Cuba?

2. What were the possible options or responses that President Kennedy considered in dealing with this crisis? What were the pros and cons of each choice?

3. Was the Monroe Doctrine a legitimate and still relevant policy for the United States to follow in 1962?

4. How did Kennedy and Khruschev "save face" in their respective countries and in the eyes of the world in this crisis?

5. Was the solution to the crisis a good one? Explain.

PROBLEM 26:
STARTING THE SEARCH FOR EVIDENCE

INTERNET: KEY WORDS AND PHRASES

The origins of the Cold War

Soviet-American relations after World War II

Nikita Khrushchev and the missile crisis

John F. Kennedy and the missile crisis

BOOKS

Frankel, Max, *High Noon and the Cold War: Kennedy, Khrushchev, and the Cuban Missile Crisis*, NY, Ballantine Books, 2004

Gavin, Francis J., *The Cold War*, Chicago, Fitzroy Dearborn Publishers, 2001

Gerdes, Louise I., *The Cold War*, San Diego, Greenhaven Press, 2004

Medina, Loretta, *The Cuban Missile Crisis*, San Diego, Greenhaven Press, 2002

White, Mark J., *Missiles in Cuba: Kennedy, Khrushchev, Castro and the 1962 Crisis*, Chicago, Ivan R. Dee, 1997

Soviet Premier Nikita S. Khrushchev's Comments Stating Communism Will "Bury" Capitalism, 1959

QUESTION: It is frequently attributed to you, Mr. Khrushchev, that at a diplomatic reception you said that you would bury us. If you didn't say it, you could deny it; and if you did say it, could you please explain what you meant?

KHRUSHCHEV: There is only a small section of the American people in this hall. My life would be too short to bury every one of you, if this were to occur to me. I did speak about it, but my statement has been deliberately misconstrued. It was not a question of any physical burial of anyone at any time but of how the social system changes in the course of the historical progress of society.

Every educated person knows that there is now more than one social system in the world. The various states, the various peoples, have different systems. The social system changes as society develops. There was the feudal system. It was superseded by capitalism. Capitalism was more progressive than feudalism. Capitalism created better conditions than feudalism for the development of the productive forces.

But capitalism engendered irreconcilable contradictions. As it outlives itself, every system gives birth to its successors. Capitalism, as Marx, Engles, and Lenin have proved, will be succeeded by Communism. We believe in that. Many of you do not. But among you, too, there are people who believe in that.

At the reception concerned, I said that in the course of historical progress, and in the historical sense, capitalism would be buried and Communism would come to replace capitalism. You will say that this is out of the question. But then the feudal lords burned at the stake those who fought against feudalism, and yet capitalism won out.

Capitalism fights against Communism. I am convinced that the winner will be Communism—a social system which creates better conditions for the development of a country's productive forces, enables every individual to prove his worth, and guarantees complete freedom for society, for every member of society.

You may disagree with me. I disagree with you. What are we to do, then? We must coexist. Live on under capitalism, and we will build Communism. The new and progressive will win; and the old and moribund will die.

You believe that the capitalist system is more productive, that it creates better conditions for social progress, that it will win. But the brief history of our Soviet state does not speak in favor of capitalism. What place did Russia hold for economic development before the Revolution? She was backward and illiterate. And now we have a powerful economy, our science and culture are highly developed. . . .We are seeing to it that there are more scientists in our country, that all our people are educated, because Communism cannot be built unless we do so. Communism is a science.

Thank you.

President John F. Kennedy's Address to the Nation on the Cuban Missile Crisis, October 22, 1962

Good evening my fellow citizens:

This Government, as promised, has maintained the closest surveillance of the Soviet Military buildup on the island of Cuba. Within the past week, unmistakable evidence has established the fact that a series of offensive missile sites is now in preparation on that imprisoned island. The purpose of these bases can be none other than to provide a nuclear strike capability against the Western Hemisphere.

Upon receiving the first preliminary hard information of this nature last Tuesday morning at 9 a.m., I directed that our surveillance be stepped up. And having now confirmed and completed our evaluation of the evidence and our decision on a course of action, this Government feels obliged to report this new crisis to you in fullest detail.

The characteristics of these new missile sites indicate two distinct types of installations. Several of them include medium range ballistic missiles capable of carrying a nuclear warhead for a distance of more than 1,000 nautical miles. Each of these missiles, in short, is capable of striking Washington, D.C., the Panama Canal, Cape Canaveral, Mexico City, or any other city in the southeastern part of the United States, in Central America, or in the Caribbean area.

Additional sites not yet completed appear to be designed for intermediate range ballistic missiles—capable of traveling more than twice as far—and thus capable of striking most of the major cities in the Western Hemisphere, ranging as far north as

Hudson Bay, Canada, and as far south as Lima, Peru. In addition, jet bombers, capable of carrying nuclear weapons, are now being uncrated and assembled in Cuba, while the necessary air bases are being prepared.

This urgent transformation of Cuba into an important strategic base—by the presence of these large, long range, and clearly offensive weapons of sudden mass destruction—constitutes an explicit threat to the peace and security of all the Americas, in flagrant and deliberate defiance of the Rio Pact of 1947, the traditions of this Nation and hemisphere, the joint resolution of the 87th Congress, the Charter of the United Nations, and my own public warnings to the Soviets on September 4 and 13. This action also contradicts the repeated assurances of Soviet spokesmen, both publicly and privately delivered, that the arms buildup in Cuba would retain its original defensive character, and that the Soviet Union had no need or desire to station strategic missiles on the territory of any other nation.

The size of this undertaking makes clear that it has been planned for some months. Yet only last month, after I had made clear the distinction between any introduction of ground-to-ground missiles and the existence of defensive antiaircraft missiles, the Soviet Government publicly stated on September 11, and I quote, "the armaments and military equipment sent to Cuba are designed exclusively for defensive purposes," that, and I quote the Soviet Government, "there is no need for the Soviet Government to shift its weapons…for a retaliatory blow to any other country, for instance Cuba," and that, and I quote their government, "the Soviet Union has so powerful rockets to carry these nuclear warheads that there is no need to search for sites for them beyond the boundaries of the Soviet Union." That statement was false.

Only last Thursday, as evidence of this rapid offensive buildup was already in my hand, Soviet Foreign Minister Gromyko told me in my office that he was instructed to make it clear once again, as he said his government had already done, that Soviet assistance to Cuba, and I quote, "pursued solely the purpose of contributing to the defense capabilities of Cuba," that, and I quote him, "training by Soviet specialists of Cuban nationals in handling defensive armaments was by no means offensive, and if it were otherwise," Mr. Gromyko went on, "the Soviet Government would never become involved in rendering such assistance." That statement also was false.

Neither the United States of America nor the world community of nations can tolerate deliberate deception and offensive threats on the part of any nation, large or small. We no longer live in a world where only the actual firing of weapons represents a sufficient challenge to a nation's security to constitute maximum peril. Nuclear weapons are so destructive and ballistic missiles are so swift, that any substantially increased possibility of their use or any sudden change in their deployment may well be regarded as a definite threat to peace.

For many years both the Soviet Union and the United States, recognizing this fact, have deployed strategic nuclear weapons with great care, never upsetting the precarious status quo which insured that these weapons would not be used in the absence of some vital challenge. Our own strategic missiles have never been transferred to the territory of any other nation under a cloak of secrecy and deception; and our history—unlike that of the Soviets since the end of World War II—demonstrates that we have no desire to dominate or conquer any other nation or impose our system upon its people. Nevertheless, American citizens have become adjusted to living daily on the Bull's-eye of Soviet missiles located inside the U.S.S.R. or in submarines.

In that sense, missiles in Cuba add to an already clear and present danger—although it should be noted the nations of Latin America have never previously been subjected to a potential nuclear threat.

But this secret, swift, and extraordinary buildup of Communist missiles—in an area well known to have a special and historical relationship to the United States and the nations of the Western Hemisphere, in violation of Soviet assurances, and in defiance of American and hemispheric policy—this sudden, clandestine decision to station strategic weapons for the first time outside of Soviet soil—is a deliberately provocative and unjustified change in the status quo which cannot be accepted by this country, if our courage and our commitments are ever to be trusted again by either friend or foe.

The 1930s taught us a clear lesson: aggressive conduct, if allowed to go unchecked and unchallenged ultimately leads to war. This nation is opposed to war. We are also true to our word. Our unswerving objective, therefore, must be to prevent the use of these missiles against this or any other country, and to secure their withdrawal or elimination from the Western Hemisphere.

Our policy has been one of patience and restraint, as befits a peaceful and powerful nation, which leads a worldwide alliance. We have been determined not to be diverted from our central concerns by mere irritants and fanatics. But now further action is required—and it is under way; and these actions may only be the beginning. We will not prematurely or unnecessarily risk the costs of worldwide nuclear war in which even the fruits of victory would be ashes in our mouth—but neither will we shrink from that risk at any time it must be faced.

Acting, therefore, in the defense of our own security and of the entire Western Hemisphere, and under the authority entrusted to me by the Constitution as endorsed by the resolution of the Congress, I have directed that the following initial steps be taken immediately:

First: To halt this offensive buildup, a strict quarantine on all offensive military equipment under shipment to Cuba is being initiated. All ships of any kind bound for Cuba from whatever nation or port will, if found to contain cargoes of offensive weapons, be turned back. This quarantine will be extended, if needed, to other types of cargo and carriers. We are not at this time, however, denying the necessities of life as the Soviets attempted to do in their Berlin blockade of 1948.

Second: I have directed the continued and increased close surveillance of Cuba and its military buildup. The foreign ministers of the OAS, in their communiqué of October 6, rejected secrecy in such matters in this hemisphere. Should these offensive military preparations continue, thus increasing the threat to the hemisphere, further action will be justified. I have directed the Armed Forces to prepare for any eventualities; and I trust that in the interest of both the Cuban people and the Soviet technicians at the sites, the hazards to all concerned in continuing this threat will be recognized.

Third: It shall be the policy of this Nation to regard any nuclear missile launched from Cuba against any nation in the Western Hemisphere as an attack by the Soviet Union on the United States, requiring a full retaliatory response upon the Soviet Union.

Fourth: As a necessary military precaution, I have reinforced our base at Guantanamo, evacuated today the dependents of our personnel there, and ordered additional military units to be on a standby alert basis.

Fifth: We are calling tonight for an immediate meeting of the Organ of Consultation under the Organization of American States, to consider this threat to hemispheric security and to invoke articles 6 and 8 of the Rio Treaty in support of all necessary action. The United Nations Charter allows for regional security arrangements—and the nations of this hemisphere decided long ago against the military presence of outside powers. Our other allies around the world have also been alerted.

Sixth: Under the Charter of the United Nations, we are asking tonight that an emergency meeting of the Security Council be convoked without delay to take action against this latest Soviet threat to world peace. Our resolution will call for the prompt dismantling and withdrawal of all offensive weapons in Cuba, under the supervision of U.N. observers, before the quarantine can be lifted.

Seventh and finally: I call upon Chairman Khrushchev to halt and eliminate this clandestine, reckless and provocative threat to world peace and to stable relations between our two nations. I call upon him further to abandon this course of world domination, and to join in an historic effort to end the perilous arms race and to transform the history of man. He has an opportunity now to move the world back from the abyss of destruction—by returning to his government's own words that it had no need to station missiles outside its own territory, and withdrawing these weapons from Cuba—by refraining from any action which will widen or deepen the present crisis—and then by participating in a search for peaceful and permanent solutions.

This Nation is prepared to present its case against the Soviet threat to peace, and our own proposals for a peaceful world, at any time and in any forum—in the OAS, in the United Nations, or in any other meeting that could be useful—without limiting our freedom of action. We have in the past made strenuous efforts to limit the spread of nuclear weapons. We have proposed the elimination of all arms and military bases in a fair and effective disarmament treaty. We are prepared to discuss new proposals for the removal of tensions on both sides—including the possibility of a genuinely independent Cuba, free to determine its own destiny. We have no wish to war with the Soviet Union—for we are a peaceful people who desire to live in peace with all other peoples.

But it is difficult to settle or even discuss these problems in an atmosphere of intimidation. That is why this latest Soviet threat—or any other threat which is made independently or in response to our actions this week—must and will be met with determination. Any hostile move anywhere in the world against the safety and freedom of peoples to whom we are committed—including in particular the brave people of West Berlin—will be met by whatever action is needed.

Finally, I want to say a few words to the captive people of Cuba, to whom this speech is being directly carried by special radio facilities. I speak to you as a friend, as one who knows of your deep attachment to your fatherland, as one who shares your aspirations for liberty and justice for all. And I have watched and the American people have watched with deep sorrow how your nationalist revolution was betrayed—and how your fatherland fell under foreign domination. Now your leaders are no longer Cuban leaders inspired by Cuban ideals. They are puppets and agents of an international conspiracy which has turned Cuba against your friends and neighbors in the Americas—and turned it into the first Latin American country to become a target for nuclear war—the first Latin American country to have these weapons on its soil.

These new weapons are not in your interest. They contribute nothing to your peace and well-being. They can only undermine it. But this country has no wish to cause you to suffer or to impose any system upon you. We know that your lives and land are being used as pawns by those who deny your freedom.

Many times in the past, the Cuban people have risen to throw out tyrants who destroyed their liberty. And I have no doubt that most Cubans today look forward to the time when they will be truly free—free from foreign domination, free to choose their own leaders, free to select their own system, free to own their own land, free to speak and write and worship without fear or degradation. And then shall Cuba be welcomed back to the society of free nations and to the associations of this hemisphere.

My fellow citizens: let no one doubt that this is a difficult and dangerous effort on which we have set out. No one can see precisely what course it will take or what costs or casualties will be incurred. Many months of sacrifice and self-discipline lie ahead— months in which our patience and our will be tested—months in which many threats and denunciations will keep us aware of our dangers. But the greatest danger of all would be to do nothing.

The path we have chosen for the present is full of hazards, as all paths are—but it is the one most consistent with our character and courage as a nation and our commitments around the world. The cost of freedom is always high—and Americans have always paid it. And one path we shall never choose, and that is the path of surrender or submission.

Our goal is not the victory of might, but the vindication of right—not peace at the expense of freedom, but both peace and freedom, here in this hemisphere, and, we hope, around the world. God willing, that goal will be achieved.

Thank you and good night.

PROBLEM 26:
CONNECTION TO TODAY

1. What lessons can we learn from the Cuban Missile Crisis that have relevance today?

2. Are there any international situations today which could lead to nuclear war? What would those be?

3. Today's American presidents, like President Kennedy, are given many different opinions as to how to react to an international crisis. How should our president deal with those many, sometimes conflicting, ideas?

4. To what extent does the United States have the right to insist that a given country, like Cuba, Iran, or North Korea, not possess nuclear weapons or not control another nation?

PROBLEM 27:
WHAT WERE THE STRATEGY
DIFFERENCES BETWEEN
DR. MARTIN LUTHER KING,
JR., AND MALCOLM X
FOR ENDING RACIAL
DISCRIMINATION IN AMERICA?

MALCOLM X

DR. MARTIN LUTHER KING, JR.

PROBLEM 27: WHAT WERE THE STRATEGY DIFFERENCES BETWEEN DR. MARTIN LUTHER KING, JR., AND MALCOLM X FOR ENDING RACIAL DISCRIMINATION IN AMERICA?

From the beginning, the history of black people in America had been a major stain on the American experience. The institution of slavery had been the most visible contradiction to the American value that "all men are created equal." For more than 200 years slavery had placed Negroes in a category labeled "less than human," resulting in blacks being beaten, tortured, raped, and having their family units torn apart. The end of slavery in 1863 was an end to legalized bondage but not an end to physical harm, racism, poverty, and being relegated to the position of second-class citizens. Throughout the South, and even in the North, legalized slavery was replaced with legalized discrimination and segregation. Schools, housing, and public facilities were legally segregated, and physical torture and lynching continued well into the 20th century.

World War II, however, planted seeds of change in regard to the place of the Negro in American society. Segregation continued in the armed forces, although black men and women served the nation in the armed forces with courage and distinction, which once again brought to the forefront the contradiction between our values and our actions. As we fought to protect democracy and oppose the racism of Nazi Germany, how could this nation, at the same time, deny equality for and practice racism against black Americans? By the late 1950s black America was ready for fundamental change that could be ignited with the right hand of leadership.

That leadership came in the persons of Dr. Martin Luther King, Jr., and a man named Malcolm Little, who had changed his name to Malcolm X. These two men came from very different life experiences. King was born into a middle-class family in the South and was a well-educated person who had earned his Ph.D.; Malcolm X was born in the North, had a limited formal education, had lived the life of a ghetto hustler and drug dealer, and had served time in prison. Yet each of these men, as different as they were, articulated a vision and strategy to both black and white America to end discrimination and second-class citizenship. Each man was a powerful speaker who could hold and inspire an audience and move them to action.

How did their messages differ? What strategy did each man believe was his road that black America needed to take? And who, in our own time, has proven to be more correct?

PROBLEM 27:
QUESTIONS FOR TEAM RESEARCH

1. How did the background and life experience of each man shape their view of the world and of the Negro's quest for equality?

2. Which man's strategy was eventually the most successful? Why?

3. How did each man believe blacks had to deal with white America to achieve their goals?

4. Why were both men assassinated and who was responsible for their killings?

PROBLEM 27:
STARTING THE SEARCH FOR EVIDENCE

INTERNET: KEY WORDS AND PHRASES

Discrimination and segregation of Negro Americans in the 20th century

The origins of the Civil Rights Movement

The philosophy and strategy of Dr. Martin Luther King, Jr.

The philosophy and strategy of Malcolm X

BOOKS

Dyson, Michael Eric, *Making Malcolm: The Myth and Meaning of Malcolm X*, NY, Oxford University Press, 1995

Frady, Marshall, *Martin Luther King, Jr.*, NY, Lipper/Viking, 2002

Haley, Alex, *The Autobiography of Malcolm X*, NY, Ballantine Books, 1999

King, Martin Luther, Jr., *The Autobiography of Martin Luther King, Jr.*, NY, Warner Books, 1998

Phillips, Donald T., *Martin Luther King, Jr., On Leadership, Inspiration and Wisdom for Changing Times*, NY, Warner Audio Books, 1999

Malcolm X Speech on "The Ballot or the Bullet," April 3, 1964

Mr. Moderator, Brother Lomax, brothers and sisters, friends and enemies: I just can't believe everyone in here is a friend, and I don't want to leave anybody out. The question tonight, as I understand it, is "The Negro Revolt, and Where Do We Go From Here?" or "What Next?" In my little humble way of understanding it, it points toward either the ballot or the bullet...

Although I'm still a Muslim, I'm not here tonight to discuss my religion. I'm not here to try and change your religion. I'm not here to argue or discuss anything that we differ about, because it's time for us to submerge our differences and realize that it is best for us to first see that we have the same problem, a common problem, a problem that will make you catch hell whether you're a Baptist, or a Methodist, or a Muslim, or a nationalist. Whether you're educated or illiterate, whether you live on the boulevard or in the alley, you're going to catch hell just like I am. We're all in the same boat and we all are going to catch the same hell from the same man. He just happens to be a white man. All of us have suffered here, in this country, political oppression at the hands of the white man, economic exploitation at the hands of the white man, and social degradation at the hands of the white man.

Now in speaking like this, it doesn't mean that we're anti-white, but it does mean we're anti-exploitation, we're anti-degradation, we're anti-oppression. And if the white man doesn't want us to be anti-him, let him stop oppressing and exploiting and degrading us. Whether we are Christians or Muslims or nationalists or agnostics or atheists, we must first learn to forget our differences. If we have differences, let us differ in the closet; when we come out in front, let us not have anything to argue about until we get finished arguing with the man. If the late President Kennedy could get together with Khrushchev and exchange some wheat, we certainly have more in common with each other than Kennedy and Khrushchev had with each other.

If we don't do something real soon, I think you'll have to agree that we're going to be forced either to use the ballot or the bullet. It's one or the other in 1964. It isn't that time is running out—time has run out!...

I'm not a politician, not even a student of politics; in fact, I'm not a student of much of anything. I'm not a Democrat. I'm not a Republican, and I don't even consider myself an American. If you and I were Americans, there'd be no problem. Those Honkies that just got off the boat, they're already Americans; Polacks are already Americans; the Italian refugees are already Americans. Everything that came out of Europe, every blue-eyed thing, is already an American. And as long as you and I have been over here, we aren't Americans yet.

Well, I am one who doesn't believe in deluding myself. I'm not going to sit at your table and watch you eat, with nothing on my plate, and call myself a diner. Sitting at the table doesn't make you a diner, unless you eat some of what's on that plate. Being here in America doesn't make you an American. Being born here in America doesn't make you an American. Why, if birth made you American, you wouldn't need any legislation; you wouldn't need any amendments to the Constitution; you wouldn't be faced with civil-rights filibustering in Washington, D.C., right now. They don't have to pass civil-rights legislation to make a Polack an American.

No, I'm not an American. I'm one of the 22 million black people who are the victims of Americanism. One of the 22 million black people who are the victims of democracy, nothing but disguised hypocrisy. So, I'm not standing here speaking to you as an American, or a patriot, or a flag-saluter, or a flag-waver—no, not I. I'm speaking as a victim of this American system. And I see America through the eyes of the victim. I don't see any American dream; I see an American nightmare….

So, what I'm trying to impress upon you, in essence, is this: You and I in America are faced not with a segregationist conspiracy, we're faced with a government conspiracy. Everyone who's filibustering is a senator—that's the government. Everyone who's finagling in Washington, D.C., is a congressman—that's the government. You don't have anybody putting blocks in your path but people who are a part of the government. The same government that you go abroad to fight for and die for is the government that is in a conspiracy to deprive you of your voting rights, deprive you of your economic opportunities, deprive you of decent housing, deprive you of decent education. You don't need to go to the employer alone, it is the government itself, the government of America, that is responsible for the oppression and exploitation and degradation of black people in this country. And you should drop it in their lap. This government has failed the Negro. This so-called democracy has failed the Negro. And all these white liberals have definitely failed the Negro…

And now you're facing a situation where the young Negro's coming up. They don't want to hear that "turn the-other-cheek" stuff, no. In Jacksonville, those were teenagers, they were throwing Molotov cocktails. Negroes have never done that before. But it shows you there's a new deal coming in. There's new thinking coming in. There's new strategy coming in. It'll be Molotov cocktails this month, hand grenades next month, and something else next month. It'll be ballots, or it'll be bullets. It'll be liberty, or it will be death. The only difference about this kind of death—it'll be reciprocal. You know what is meant by "reciprocal"? That's one of Brother Lomax's words. I stole it from him. I don't usually deal with those big words because I don't usually deal with big people. I deal with small people. I find you can get a whole lot of small people and whip hell out of a whole lot of big people. They haven't got anything to lose, and they've got everything to gain. And they'll let you know in a minute: "It takes two to tango; when I go, you go."

The black nationalists, those whose philosophy is black nationalism, in bringing about this new interpretation of the entire meaning of civil rights, look upon it as meaning, as Brother Lomax has pointed out, equality of opportunity. Well, we're justified in seeking civil rights, if it means equality of opportunity, because all we're doing there is trying to collect for our investment. Our mothers and fathers invested sweat and blood. Three hundred and ten years we worked in this country without a dime in return—I mean without a dime in return. You let the white man walk around here talking about how rich this country is, but you never stop to think how it got rich so quick. It got rich because you made it rich.…

Right now, in this country, if you and I, 22 million African-Americans—that's what we are—Africans who are in America. You're nothing but Africans. Nothing but Africans. In fact, you'd get farther calling yourself African instead of Negro. Africans don't catch hell. You're the only one catching hell. They don't have to pass civil-rights bills for Africans. An African can go anywhere he wants right now. All you've got to do is tie your head up. That's right, go anywhere you want. Just stop being a Negro. Change your name to Hoogagagooba. That'll show you how silly the white man is. You're dealing with a silly man. A friend of mine who's very dark put a turban on his head and went into a restaurant in Atlanta before they called themselves desegregated. He went into a white restaurant, he sat down, they served him, and he said, "What would happen if a Negro came in here? And there he's sitting, black as night, but because he had his head wrapped up the waitress looked back at him and says, "Why, there wouldn't no nigger dare come in here."

So, you're dealing with a man whose bias and prejudice are making him lose his mind, his intelligence, every day. He's frightened. He looks around and sees what's taking place on this earth, and he sees that the pendulum of time is swinging in your direction. The dark people are waking up. They're losing their fear of the white man. No place where he's fighting right now is he winning. Everywhere he's fighting, he's fighting someone your and my complexion. And they're beating him. He can't win any more. He's won his last battle. He failed to win the Korean War. He couldn't win it. He had to sign a truce. That's a loss….

The political philosophy of black nationalism means that the black man should control the politics and the politicians in his own community; no more. The black man in the black community has to re-educated into the science of politics so he will know what politics is supposed to bring him in return. Don't be throwing out any ballots. A ballot is like a bullet. You don't throw your ballots until you see a target, and if that target is not within your reach, keep your ballot in your pocket.

The political philosophy of black nationalism is being taught in the Christian church. It's being taught in the NAACP. It's being taught in CORE meetings. It's being taught in SNCC Student Nonviolent Coordinating Committee meetings. It's being taught in Muslim meetings. It's being taught where nothing but atheists and agnostics come together. It's being taught everywhere. Black people are fed up with the dillydallying, pussyfooting, compromising approach that we've been using toward getting our freedom. We want freedom now, but we're not going to get it saying "We Shall Overcome." We've got to fight until we overcome.

The economic philosophy of black nationalism is pure and simple. It only means that we should control the economy of our community. Why should white people be running all the stores in our community? Why should white people be running the banks of our community? Why should the economy of our community be in the hands of the white man? Why? If a black man can't move his store into a white community, you tell me why a white man should move his store into a black community. The philosophy of black nationalism involves a re-education program in the black community in regards to economics. Our people have to be made to see that any time you take your dollar out of your community and spend it in a community where you don't live, the community where you live will get poorer and poorer, and the community where you spend your money will get richer and richer.

Then you wonder why where you live is always a ghetto or a slum area. And where you and I are concerned, not only do we lose it when we spend it out of the community, but the white man has got all our stores in the community tied up; so that though we spend it in the community, at sundown the man who runs the store takes it over across town somewhere. He's got us in a vise.

So the economic philosophy of black nationalism means in every church, in every civic organization, in every fraternal order, it's time now for our people to become conscious of the importance of controlling the economy of our community. If we own the stores, if we operate the businesses, if we try and establish some industry in our own community, then we're developing to the position where we are creating employment for our own kind. Once you gain control of the economy of your own community, then you don't have to picket and boycott and beg some cracker downtown for a job in his business.

The social philosophy of black nationalism only means that we have to get together and remove the evils, the vices, alcoholism, drug addiction, and other evils that are destroying the moral fiber of our community. We ourselves have to lift the level of our community, the standard of our community to a higher level, make our own society beautiful so that we will be satisfied in our own social circles and won't be running around here trying to knock our way into a social circle where we're not wanted. So I say, in spreading a gospel such as black nationalism, it is not designed to make the black man re-evaluate the white man—you know him already—but to make the black man re-evaluate himself. Don't change the white man's mind—you can't change his mind, and that whole thing about appealing to the moral conscience of America—America's conscience is bankrupt. She lost all conscience a long time ago. Uncle Sam has no conscience....

We will work with anybody, anywhere, at any time, who is genuinely interested in tackling the problem head-on, nonviolently as long as the enemy is nonviolent, but violent when the enemy gets violent. We'll work with you on the voter-registration drive, we'll work with you on rent strikes, we'll work with you on school boycotts; I don't believe in any kind of integration; I'm not even worried about it, because I know you're not going to get it anyway; you're not going to get it because you're afraid to die; you've got to be ready to die if you try and force yourself on the white man, because he'll get just as violent as those crackers in Mississippi, right here in Cleveland. But we will still work with you on the school boycotts because we're against a segregated school system. A segregated school system produces children who, when they graduate, graduate with crippled minds. But this does not mean that a school is segregated because it's all black. A segregated school means a school that is controlled by people who have no real interest in it whatsoever....

Last but not least, I must say this concerning the great controversy over rifles and shotguns. The only thing that I've ever said is that in areas where the government has proven itself either unwilling or unable to defend the lives and the property of Negroes, it's time for Negroes to defend themselves. Article number two of the constitutional amendments provides you and me the right to own a rifle or a shotgun. It is constitutionally legal to own a shotgun or a rifle. This doesn't mean you're going to get a rifle and form battalions and go out looking for white folks, although you'd be within your rights—I mean, you'd be justified; but that would be illegal and we don't do anything illegal. If the white man doesn't want the black man buying rifles and shotguns, then let the government do its job.

The Rev. Martin Luther King, Jr., Speech: "Where Do We Go From Here?" (1967)

Now, in order to answer the question, "Where do we go from here?" which is our theme, we must first honestly recognize where we are now. When the Constitution was written, a strange formula to determine taxes and representation declared that the Negro was sixty percent of a person. Today another curious formula seems to declare he is fifty percent of a person. Of the good things in life, the Negro has approximately one half those of whites. Of the bad things of life, he has twice those of whites. Thus, half of all Negroes live in substandard housing. And Negroes have half the income of whites. When we turn to the negative experiences of life, the Negro has a double share: There are twice as many unemployed; the rate of infant mortality among Negroes is double that of whites; and there are twice as many Negroes dying in Vietnam as whites in proportion to their size in the population.

In other spheres, the figures are equally alarming. In elementary schools, Negroes lag one to three years behind whites, and their segregated schools receive substantially less money per student than the white schools. One-twentieth as many Negroes as whites attend college. Of employed Negroes, seventy-five percent hold menial jobs. This is where we are.

Where do we go from here? First, we must massively assert our dignity and worth. We must stand up amid a system that still oppresses us and develop an unassailable and majestic sense of values. We must no longer be ashamed of being black. The job of arousing manhood within a people that have been taught for so many centuries that they are nobody is not easy.

Even semantics have conspired to make that which is black seem ugly and degrading. In Roget's *Thesaurus* there are some 120 synonyms for blackness and at least sixty of them are offensive, such words as blot, soot, grim, devil, and foul. And there are some 134 synonyms for whiteness and all are favorable, expressed in such words as purity, cleanliness, chastity, and innocence. A white lie is better than a black lie. The most degenerate member of a family is the "black sheep." Ossie Davis has suggested that maybe the English language should be reconstructed so that teachers will not be forced to teach the Negro child sixty ways to despise himself, and thereby perpetuate his false sense of inferiority, and the white child 134 ways to adore himself, and thereby perpetuate his false sense of superiority. The tendency to ignore the Negro's contribution to American life and strip him of his personhood is as old as the earliest history books and as contemporary as the morning's newspaper.

To offset this cultural homicide, the Negro must rise up with an affirmation of his own Olympian manhood. Any movement for the Negro's freedom that overlooks this necessity is only waiting to be buried. As long as the mind is enslaved, the body can never be free. Psychological freedom, a firm sense of self-esteem, is the most powerful weapon against the long night of physical slavery. No Lincolnian Emancipation Proclamation, no Johnsonian civil rights bill can totally bring this kind of freedom. The Negro will only be free when he reaches down to the inner depths of his own being and signs with the pen and ink of assertive manhood his own emancipation proclamation. And with a spirit straining toward true self-esteem, the Negro must boldly throw off the manacles of self-abnegation and say to himself and to the world, "I am somebody. I am a person. I am a man with dignity and honor. I have a rich and noble history, however painful and exploited that history has been. Yes, I was a slave through my foreparents, and now I'm not ashamed of that. I'm ashamed of the people who were so sinful to make me a slave." Yes, yes, we must stand up and say, "I'm black, but I'm black and beautiful." This, this self-affirmation is the black man's need, made compelling by the white man's crimes against him.

Now another basic challenge is to discover how to organize our strength into economic and political power. Now no one can deny that the Negro is in dire need of this kind of legitimate power. Indeed, one of the great problems that the Negro confronts is his lack of power. From the old plantations of the South to the newer ghettos of the North, the Negro has been confined to a life of voicelessness and powerlessness. Stripped of the right to make decisions concerning his life and destiny he has been subject to the authoritarian and sometimes whimsical decisions of the white power structure. The plantation and the ghetto were created by those who had power, both to confine those who had no power and to perpetuate their powerlessness. Now the problem of transforming the ghetto, therefore, is a problem of power, a confrontation between the forces of power demanding change and the forces of power dedicated to the preserving of the status quo. Now, power properly understood is nothing but the ability to achieve purpose. It is the strength required to bring about social, political, and economic change. Walter Reuther defined power one day. He said, "Power is the ability of a labor union like UAW to make the most powerful corporation in the world, General Motors, say 'Yes' when it wants to say 'No.' That's power…"

Now, let me rush on to say we must reaffirm our commitment to nonviolence. And I want to stress this. The futility of violence in the struggle for racial justice has been tragically etched in all the recent Negro riots. Now, yesterday, I tried to analyze the riots and deal with the causes for them. Today I want to give the other side. There is something painfully sad about a riot. One sees screaming youngsters and angry adults fighting hopelessly and aimlessly against impossible odds. And deep down within them, you perceive a desire for self-destruction, a kind of suicidal longing.

Occasionally, Negroes contend that the 1965 Watts riot and the other riots in various cities represented effective civil rights action. But those who express this view always end up with stumbling words when asked what concrete gains have been won as a result. At best, the riots have produced a little additional anti-poverty money allotted by frightened government officials and a few water sprinklers to cool the children of the ghettos. It is something like improving the food in the prison while the people remain securely incarcerated behind bars. Nowhere have the riots won any concrete improvement such as have the organized protest demonstrations.

And when one tries to pin down advocates of violence as to what acts would be effective, the answers are blatantly illogical. Sometimes they talk of overthrowing racist state and local governments and they talk about guerrilla warfare. They fail to see that no internal revolution has ever succeeded in overthrowing a government by violence unless the government had already lost the allegiance and effective control of its armed forces. Anyone in his right mind knows that this will not happen in the United States. In a violent racial situation, the power structure has the local police, the state troopers, the National Guard, and finally, the army to call on, all of which are predominantly white. Furthermore, few, if any, violent revolutions have been successful unless the violent minority had the sympathy and support of the non-resisting majority. Castro may have had only a few Cubans actually fighting with him and up in the hills, but he would have never overthrown the Batista regime unless he had had the sympathy of the vast majority of Cuban people. It is perfectly clear that a violent revolution on the part of American blacks would find no sympathy and support from the white population and very little from the majority of the Negroes themselves.

This is no time for romantic illusions and empty philosophical debates about freedom. This is a time for action. What is needed is a strategy for change, a tactical program that will bring the Negro into the mainstream of American life as quickly as possible. So far, this has only been offered by the nonviolent movement. Without recognizing this we will end up with solutions that don't solve, answers that don't answer, and explanations that don't explain.

And so I say to you today that I still stand by nonviolence. And I am still convinced, and I'm still convinced that it is the most potent weapon available to the Negro in his struggle for justice in this country.

And the other thing is, I'm concerned about a better world. I'm concerned about justice; I'm concerned about brotherhood; I'm concerned about truth. And when one is concerned about that, he can never advocate violence. For through violence you may murder a murderer, but you can't murder murder. Through violence you may murder a liar, but you can't establish truth. Through violence you may murder a hater, but you can't murder hate through violence. Darkness cannot put out darkness; only light can do that.

And I say to you, I have also decided to stick with love, for I know that love is ultimately the only answer to mankind's problems. And I'm going to talk about it everywhere I go. I know it isn't popular to talk about it in some circles today. And I'm not talking about emotional bosh when I talk about love; I'm talking about a strong, demanding love. For I have seen too much hate. I've seen too much hate on the faces of sheriffs in the South. I've seen hate on the faces of too many Klansmen and too many White Citizens Councilors in the South to want to hate, myself, because every time I see it, I know that it does something to their faces and their personalities, and I say to myself that hate is too great a burden to bear. I have decided to love. If you are seeking the highest good, I think you can find it through love. And the beautiful thing is that we aren't moving wrong when we do it, because John was right, God is love. He who hates does not know God, but he who loves has the key that unlocks the door to the meaning of ultimate reality....

I want to say to you as I move to my conclusion, as we talk about "Where do we go from here?" that we must honestly face the fact that the movement must address itself to the question of restructuring the whole of American society. There are forty million poor people here, and one day we must ask the question, "Why are there forty million poor people in America?" And when you begin to ask that question, you are raising a question about the economic system, about a broader distribution of wealth. When you ask that question, you begin to question the capitalistic economy. And I'm simply saying that more and more, we've got to begin to ask questions about the whole society. We are called upon to help the discouraged beggars in life's marketplace. But one day we must come to see that an edifice which produces beggars needs restructuring. It means that questions must be raised. And you see, my friends, when you deal with this you begin to ask the question, "Who owns the oil?" You begin to ask the question, "Who owns the iron ore?" You begin to ask the question, "Why is it that people have to pay water bills in a world that's two-thirds water?" These are words that must be said.

PROBLEM 27:
CONNECTION TO TODAY

1. What is the legacy of each man's strategy in America today?

2. Were either of these men "successful" in their strategy? Explain.

3. Is the civil rights movement alive today? If not, why not? If so, describe its characteristics and strategy.

4. Are there civil rights leaders today of a stature comparable to King and Malcolm X? If so, who are they? If not, why not?

5. What is necessary for an "idea," such as equality for blacks, to become a "movement" in which thousands of people are collectively engaged in trying to bring about some change?

PROBLEM 28:
SHOULD GERALD FORD HAVE PARDONED RICHARD M. NIXON?

THE WHITE HOUSE

WASHINGTON

August 9, 1974

Dear Mr. Secretary:

I hereby resign the Office of President of the United States.

Sincerely,

Richard Nixon

11.35 AM

HK

The Honorable Henry A. Kissinger
The Secretary of State
Washington, D.C. 20520

ABOVE: PRESIDENT GERALD FORD ANNOUNCING HIS PARDON OF RICHARD M. NIXON

LEFT: RICHARD M. NIXON'S LETTER RESIGNING FROM THE PRESIDENCY OF THE UNITED STATES

PROBLEM 28: SHOULD GERALD FORD HAVE PARDONED RICHARD M. NIXON?

On June 17, 1972, five men were arrested for breaking into the Democratic National Committee headquarters, which was located in the Watergate office complex in Washington, D.C. President Richard Nixon was running for reelection that year, and these men were connected to Nixon's campaign organization, called the Committee to Reelect the President. The men who broke into the Democratic headquarters were allegedly looking for information from the opposition party that they could use in helping to see that Nixon was reelected. When the break-in was discovered, Nixon's staff attempted to find ways to cover up the event and not implicate the president's office or campaign. The news media began digging deeper into this situation, and the U.S. Senate and House of Representatives conducted hearings to seek facts regarding the episode.

During these congressional hearings, it was revealed that President Nixon had a tape recording system in his office that recorded conversations that took place between the president and his staff. At first Nixon refused to allow the tapes to be heard, but eventually the United States Supreme Court ruled that Nixon had to release the tapes, and the president complied. When the tapes were heard, it was revealed that on June 23, 1972, Nixon and his top aide, Bob Haldeman, had planned ways to block any investigation of the break-in. Prior to the existence of this tape, known as the "smoking gun" tape, the president had denied that any senior campaign officials had been involved. The president also agreed to make blackmail payments so that key senior administration individuals would not be named and implicated in the scandal. These actions amount to what was perceived by many to be an obstruction of justice. The evidence against Nixon grew to such an extent that he faced certain impeachment by the House of Representatives and conviction by the Senate. A conviction would have removed Nixon from office and left him facing possible criminal charges and even prison. Seeing he had no way out, Nixon resigned the office of president on August 9, 1974, and his vice president, Gerald Ford, became president of the United States.

The nation's feelings about Nixon were strong and negative. He had lied to the American people, deliberately planned to thwart an investigation, and disgraced and dishonored the office of the presidency. No other president in American history had resigned the office in such disgrace, and some were calling for Nixon to be prosecuted and jailed.

This is the situation the new President Gerald Ford faced as he assumed his new office. He could choose to move on and let whatever legal consequences Nixon might face take their course. His other option was to give the former president an official presidential pardon, which would spare Nixon a possible trial, conviction, and jail. Many Americans stressed that we were a country of laws and that no person, even the president of the United States, was above the law. Nixon, they believed, had broken the law and should suffer the consequences. President Ford, however, chose another way, which was to issue a pardon to Richard Nixon and thus spare him the possibility of further legal action.

Should Ford had done that? Why did he do it? How could he answer those who demanded that no man could or should be above the law? What message and what precedent for the future might such a pardon set?

PROBLEM 28:
QUESTIONS FOR TEAM RESEARCH

1. How serious were Richard Nixon's actions? Why were they illegal?

2. Were Nixon's actions "impeachable offenses" in regard to what the Constitution of the United States states?

3. If Nixon had destroyed the tapes or simply admitted his actions and apologized to the American people, could he have kept his office as president?

4. How did Gerald Ford become vice president? Did the way he assumed that office have any impact on his decision to pardon Nixon?

5. How did the American people react to Ford's pardon?

6. Do you agree with Ford's reasons for issuing the pardon? Explain.

PROBLEM 28:
STARTING THE SEARCH FOR EVIDENCE

INTERNET: KEY WORDS AND PHRASES

Richard Nixon and the Watergate Crisis

Nixon's resignation of the presidency

Gerald Ford as vice president

Gerald Ford and the pardon of Richard Nixon

BOOKS

Cook, Fred J., *The Crimes of Watergate*, NY, F. Watts, 1981

Drew, Elizabeth, *Richard M. Nixon*, NY, Times Books, 2007

Ford, Gerald, *A Time to Heal: The Autobiography of Gerald R. Ford*, NY, Harper & Row, 1979

Hillstorm, Kevin, *Watergate*, Detroit, Omnigraphies, 2004

Mollenhoff, Clark R., *The Man Who Pardoned Nixon*, NY, St. Martins Press, 1976

President Richard M. Nixon's Speech Resigning the Presidency, August 8, 1974

Good evening.

This is the 37th time I have spoken to you from this office, where so many decisions have been made that shaped the history of this Nation. Each time I have done so to discuss with you some matter that I believe affected the national interest.

In all the decisions I have made in my public life, I have always tried to do what was best for the Nation. Throughout the long and difficult period of Watergate, I have felt it was my duty to persevere, to make every possible effort to complete the term of office to which you elected me.

In the past few days, however, it has become evident to me that I no longer have a strong enough political base in the Congress to justify continuing that effort. As long as there was such a base, I felt strongly that it was necessary to see the constitutional process through to its conclusion, that to do otherwise would be unfaithful to the spirit of that deliberately difficult process and a dangerously destabilizing precedent for the future.

But with the disappearance of that base, I now believe that the constitutional purpose has been served, and there is no longer a need for the process to be prolonged.

I would have preferred to carry through to the finish whatever the personal agony it would have involved, and my family unanimously urged me to do so. But the interests of the Nation must always come before any personal considerations.

From the discussions I have had with Congressional and other leaders, I have concluded that because of the Watergate matter I might not have the support of the Congress that I would consider necessary to back the very difficult decisions and carry out the duties of this office in the way the interests of the Nation would require.

I have never been a quitter. To leave office before my term is completed is abhorrent to every instinct in my body. But as President, I must put the interest of America first. America needs a full-time President and a full-time Congress, particularly at this time with problems we face at home and abroad.

To continue to fight through the months ahead for my personal vindication would almost totally absorb the time and attention of both the President and the Congress in a period when our entire focus should be on the great issues of peace abroad and prosperity without inflation at home.

Therefore, I shall resign the Presidency effective at noon tomorrow. Vice President Ford will be sworn in as President at that hour in this office.

As I recall the high hopes for America with which we began this second term, I feel a great sadness that I will not be here in this office working on your behalf to achieve those hopes in the next 2 1/2 years. But in turning over direction of the Government to Vice President Ford, I know, as I told the Nation when I nominated him for that office 10 months ago, that the leadership of America will be in good hands.

In passing this office to the Vice President, I also do so with the profound sense of the weight of responsibility that will fall on his shoulders tomorrow and, therefore, of the understanding, the patience, the cooperation he will need from all Americans.

As he assumes that responsibility, he will deserve the help and the support of all of us. As we look to the future, the first essential is to begin healing the wounds of this Nation, to put the bitterness and divisions of the recent past behind us, and to rediscover those shared ideals that lie at the heart of our strength and unity as a great and as a free people.

By taking this action, I hope that I will have hastened the start of that process of healing which is so desperately needed in America.

I regret deeply any injuries that may have been done in the course of the events that led to this decision. I would say only that if some of my judgments were wrong, and some were wrong, they were made in what I believed at the time to be the best interest of the Nation.

To those who have stood with me during these past difficult months, to my family, my friends, to many others who joined in supporting my cause because they believed it was right, I will be eternally grateful for your support.

And to those who have not felt able to give me your support, let me say I leave with no bitterness toward those who have opposed me, because all of us, in the final analysis, have been concerned with the good of the country, however our judgments might differ.

So, let us all now join together in affirming that common commitment and in helping our new President succeed for the benefit of all Americans.

I shall leave this office with regret at not completing my term, but with gratitude for the privilege of serving as your President for the past 5 1/2 years. These years have been a momentous time in the history of our Nation and the world. They have been a time of achievement in which we can all be proud, achievements that represent the shared efforts of the Administration, the Congress, and the people.

But the challenges ahead are equally great, and they, too, will require the support and the efforts of the Congress and the people working in cooperation with the new Administration.

We have ended America's longest war, but in the work of securing a lasting peace in the world, the goals ahead are even more far-reaching and more difficult. We must complete a structure of peace so that it will be said of this generation, our generation of Americans, by the people of all nations, not only that we ended one war but that we prevented future wars.

We have unlocked the doors that for a quarter of a century stood between the United States and the People's Republic of China.

We must now ensure that the one quarter of the world's people who live in the People's Republic of China will be and remain not our enemies but our friends.

In the Middle East, 100 million people in the Arab countries, many of whom have considered us their enemy for nearly 20 years, now look on us as their friends. We must continue to build on that friendship so that peace can settle at last over the Middle East and so that the cradle of civilization will not become its grave.

Together with the Soviet Union we have made the crucial breakthroughs that have begun the process of limiting nuclear arms. But we must set as our goal not just limiting but reducing and finally destroying these terrible weapons so that they cannot destroy civilization and so that the threat of nuclear war will no longer hang over the world and the people.

We have opened the new relation with the Soviet Union. We must continue to develop and expand that new relationship so that the two strongest nations of the world will live together in cooperation rather than confrontation.

Around the world, in Asia, in Africa, in Latin America, in the Middle East, there are millions of people who live in terrible poverty, even starvation. We must keep as our goal turning away from production for war and expanding production for peace so that people everywhere on this earth can at last look forward in their children's time, if not in our own time, to having the necessities for a decent life.

Here in America, we are fortunate that most of our people have not only the blessings of liberty but also the means to live full and good and, by the world's standards, even abundant lives. We must press on, however, toward a goal of not only more and better jobs but of full opportunity for every American and of what we are striving so hard right now to achieve, prosperity without inflation.

For more than a quarter of a century in public life I have shared in the turbulent history of this era. I have fought for what I believed in. I have tried to the best of my ability to discharge those duties and meet those responsibilities that were entrusted to me.

Sometimes I have succeeded and sometimes I have failed, but always I have taken heart from what Theodore Roosevelt once said about the man in the arena, "whose face is marred by dust and sweat and blood, who strives valiantly, who errs and comes short again and again because there is not effort without error and shortcoming, but who does actually strive to do the deed, who knows the great enthusiasms, the great devotions, who spends himself in a worthy cause, who at the best knows in the end the triumphs of high achievements and who at the worst, if he fails, at least fails while daring greatly."

I pledge to you tonight that as long as I have a breath of life in my body, I shall continue in that spirit. I shall continue to work for the great causes to which I have been dedicated throughout my years as a Congressman, a Senator, a Vice President, and President, the cause of peace not just for America but among all nations, prosperity, justice, and opportunity for all of our people.

There is one cause above all to which I have been devoted and to which I shall always be devoted for as long as I live.

When I first took the oath of office as President 5 1/2 years ago, I made this sacred commitment, to "consecrate my office, my energies, and all the wisdom I can summon to the cause of peace among nations."

I have done my very best in all the days since to be true to that pledge. As a result of these efforts, I am confident that the world is a safer place today, not only for the people of America but for the people of all nations, and that all of our children have a better chance than before of living in peace rather than dying in war.

This, more than anything, is what I hoped to achieve when I sought the Presidency. This, more than anything, is what I hope will be my legacy to you, to our country, as I leave the Presidency.

To have served in this office is to have felt a very personal sense of kinship with each and every American. In leaving it, I do so with this prayer: May God's grace be with you in all the days ahead.

President Gerald R. Ford's Speech Pardoning President Richard M. Nixon, September 8, 1974

Ladies and gentlemen:

I have come to a decision which I felt I should tell you and all of my fellow American citizens, as soon as I was certain in my own mind and in my own conscience that it is the right thing to do.

I have learned already in this office that the difficult decisions always come to this desk. I must admit that many of them do not look at all the same as the hypothetical questions that I have answered freely and perhaps too fast on previous occasions.

My customary policy is to try and get all the facts and to consider the opinions of my countrymen and to take counsel with my most valued friends. But these seldom agree, and in the end, the decision is mine. To procrastinate, to agonize, and to wait for a more favorable turn of events that may never come or more compelling external pressures that may as well be wrong as right, is itself a decision of sorts and a weak and potentially dangerous course for a President to follow.

I have promised to uphold the Constitution, to do what is right as God gives me to see the right, and to do the very best that I can for America.

I have asked your help and your prayers, not only when I became President but many times since. The Constitution is the supreme law of our land and it governs our actions as citizens. Only the laws of God, which govern our consciences, are superior to it.

As we are a nation under God, so I am sworn to uphold our laws with the help of God. And I have sought such guidance and searched my own conscience with special diligence to determine the right thing for me to do with respect to my predecessor in this place, Richard Nixon, and his loyal wife and family.

Theirs is an American tragedy in which we all have played a part. It could go on and on and on, or someone must write the end to it. I have concluded that only I can do that, and if I can, I must.

There are no historic or legal precedents to which I can turn in this matter, none that precisely fit the circumstances of a private citizen who has resigned the Presidency of the United States. But it is common knowledge that serious allegations and accusations hang like a sword over our former President's head, threatening his health as he tries to reshape his life, a great part of which was spent in the service of this country and by the mandate of its people.

After years of bitter controversy and divisive national debate, I have been advised, and I am compelled to conclude that many months and perhaps more years will have to pass before Richard Nixon could obtain a fair trial by jury in any jurisdiction of the United States under governing decisions of the Supreme Court.

I deeply believe in equal justice for all Americans, whatever their station or former station. The law, whether human or divine, is no respecter of persons; but the law is a respecter of reality.

The facts, as I see them, are that a former President of the United States, instead of enjoying equal treatment with any other citizen accused of violating the law, would be cruelly and excessively penalized either in preserving the presumption of his innocence or in obtaining a speedy determination of his guilt in order to repay a legal debt to society.

During this long period of delay and potential litigation, ugly passions would again be aroused. And our people would again be polarized in their opinions. And the credibility of our free institutions of government would again be challenged at home and abroad.

In the end, the courts might well hold that Richard Nixon had been denied due process, and the verdict of history would even be more inconclusive with respect to those charges arising out of the period of his Presidency, of which I am presently aware.

But it is not the ultimate fate of Richard Nixon that most concerns me, though surely it deeply troubles every decent and every compassionate person. My concern is the immediate future of this great country.

In this, I dare not depend upon my personal sympathy as a longtime friend of the former President, nor my professional judgment as a lawyer, and I do not.

As President, my primary concern must always be the greatest good of all the people of the United States whose servant I am. As a man, my first consideration is to be true to my own convictions and my own conscience.

My conscience tells me clearly and certainly that I cannot prolong the bad dreams that continue to reopen a chapter that is closed. My conscience tells me that only I, as President, have the constitutional power to firmly shut and seal this book. My conscience tells me it is my duty, not merely to proclaim domestic tranquility but to use every means that I have to insure it. I do believe that the buck stops here, that I cannot rely upon public opinion polls to tell me what is right. I do believe that right makes might and that if I am wrong, ten angels swearing I was right would make no difference. I do believe, with all my heart and mind and spirit, that I, not as President but as a humble servant of God, will receive justice without mercy if I fail to show mercy.

Finally, I feel that Richard Nixon and his loved ones have suffered enough and will continue to suffer, no matter what I do, no matter what we, as a great and good nation, can do together to make his goal of peace come true.

Now, therefore, I, Gerald R. Ford, President of the United States, pursuant to the pardon power conferred upon me by Article II, Section 2, of the Constitution, have granted and by these presents do grant a full, free, and absolute pardon unto Richard Nixon for all offenses against the United States which he, Richard Nixon, has committed or may have committed or taken part in during the period from July (January) 20, 1969, through August 9, 1974.

In witness whereof, I have hereunto set my hand this eighth day of September, in the year of our Lord nineteen hundred and seventy-four, and of the Independence of the United States of America the one hundred and ninety-ninth.

PROBLEM 28:
CONNECTION TO TODAY

1. How could we change the U.S. Constitution to make more clear what offenses would be impeachable? Why should or should not we make those changes?

2. What was the difference in outcome between Nixon's problem and that faced by President Clinton? Why did Nixon have to resign, but Clinton stayed on as president?

3. Have other presidents received criticism for the pardons they issued? Explain.

4. Are there times when the cost in terms of money, time, disruption, and energy are not worth forcing any president from office? Explain.

PROBLEM 29: WAS PRESIDENT RONALD REAGAN RESPONSIBLE FOR ENDING THE COLD WAR?

LEFT: PRESIDENT RONALD REAGAN MEETING WITH SOVIET GENERAL SECRETARY MIKHAIL GORBACHEV

BELOW: GERMAN CITIZENS AND SOLDIERS TEAR DOWN THE BERLIN WALL

PROBLEM 29: WAS PRESIDENT RONALD REAGAN RESPONSIBLE FOR ENDING THE COLD WAR?

Even though the United States and the Soviet Union were allies in the fight against Nazi Germany during World War II, the two countries soon became suspicious antagonists after the war. The United States viewed the Soviet Union as a nation that sought to spread its ideology of Communism across the globe, and the Soviet Union saw the United States as its major obstacle to the spread of world Communism. Both nations had developed nuclear weapons, and any armed conflict between them promised to bring mass death and destruction to both countries. Thus, the conflict between the nations was labeled the Cold War. The official policy of the United States was not to engage in military conflict with the Soviets. Instead, the United States tried to restrict Soviet expansionist ideas by aiding countries that might otherwise fall under Soviet domination and by threatening the use of military force; either action could lead to a third World War. This policy came to be known as containment, and from 1945 to the final collapse of the Soviet Union in 1989, it was essentially successful. Only once, in the Cuban Missile crisis of 1962, had there been a real possibility that the two nations might go to war and use the nuclear weapons they both possessed.

Ronald Reagan was elected president in 1980, and verbally attacked the Soviet Union as an "evil empire." In this same period a younger more progressive individual, Mikhail Gorbachev, became premier of the Soviet Union. President Reagan, in a famous speech he delivered in Germany, challenged the Soviet leader to end the division the Communists had created in Germany by building a wall that separated east and west Germany, by saying, "Mr. Gorbachev, tear down this wall!" By the end of Reagan's term as president, the Soviet Union was suffering from economic and political instability, and a year after President Reagan left office, the Berlin Wall was dismantled. Soon after that the Soviet Union and its satellite countries had disintegrated, and the evil empire had fallen.

President Reagan has been widely praised and given credit for actions leading to the collapse of the Soviet Union and for ending and winning the Cold War. Is that true? What did Reagan actually do that led to the collapse of Soviet Communism? Or did the Soviet Union fall and the Cold War end for other reasons? Should Mikhail Gorbachev really be given the credit for leading the Soviet Union to a non-Communist direction? What role did President Reagan really play?

PROBLEM 29:
QUESTIONS FOR TEAM RESEARCH

1. Did President Reagan change his attitude and approach to the Soviet Union from his first to second term as president? If so, how and why?

2. To what extent was the Soviet Union falling apart before Reagan became president? What would be the things to look for to support or reject such an idea?

3. How and why was Mikhail Gorbachev such a different Soviet leader from those who had preceded him?

4. How do you think the fact that both the United States and the Soviet Union had nuclear weapons kept the peace in the world?

PROBLEM 29:
STARTING THE SEARCH FOR EVIDENCE

INTERNET: KEY WORDS AND PHRASES

The election of 1980

The government philosophy of Ronald Reagan

Mikhail Gorbachev and the Soviet Union

Ronald Reagan and the Cold War

BOOKS

Busch, Andrew, *Reagan's Victory: The Presidential Election of 1980 and the Rise of the Right*, Lawrence, University Press of Kansas, 2005

Drew, Elizabeth, *Portrait of an Election: The 1980 Presidential Campaign*, NY, Simon and Schuster, 1981

Mann, Jim, *The Rebellion of Ronald Reagan: A History of the End of the Cold War*, NY, Viking, 2009

Matlock, Jack F., *Reagan and Gorbachev: How the Cold War Ended*, NY, Random House, 2004

Schweizer, Peter, *Reagan's War: The Epic Story of his Forty Year Struggle and Final Triumph Over Communism*, NY, Doubleday, 2002

President Ronald Reagan's Speech on the Communist "Evil Empire," 1982

If history teaches anything, it teaches self-delusion in the face of unpleasant facts is folly. We see around us today the marks of our terrible dilemma—predictions of doomsday, antinuclear demonstrations, an arms race in which the West must, for its own protection, be an unwilling participant. At the same time we see totalitarian forces in the world who seek subversion and conflict around the globe to further their barbarous assault on the human spirit. What, then, is our course? Must civilization perish in a hail of fiery atoms? Must freedom wither in a quiet, deadening accommodation with totalitarian evil?...

We cannot ignore the fact that even without our encouragement there has been and will continue to be repeated explosion against repression and dictatorships. The Soviet Union itself is not immune to this reality. Any system is inherently unstable that has no peaceful means to legitimize its leaders. In such cases, the very repressiveness of the state ultimately drives people to resist it, if necessary, by force.

While we must be cautious about forcing the pace of change, we must not hesitate to declare our ultimate objectives and to take concrete actions to move toward them. We must be staunch in our conviction that freedom is not the sole prerogative of a lucky few but the inalienable and universal right of all human beings. So states the United Nations Universal Declaration of Human Rights, which, among other things, guarantees free elections.

The objective I propose is quite simple to state: to foster the infrastructure of democracy, the system of a free press, unions, political parties, universities, which allows a people to choose their own way to develop their own culture, to reconcile their own differences through peaceful means.

This is not cultural imperialism; it is providing the means for genuine self-determination and protection for diversity. Democracy already flourishes in countries with very different cultures and historical experiences. It would be cultural condescension, or worse, to say that any people prefer dictatorship to democracy. Who would voluntarily choose not to have the right to vote, decide to purchase government propaganda handouts instead of independent newspapers, prefer government to worker-controlled unions, opt for land to be owned by the state instead of those who till it, want government repression of religious liberty, a single political party instead of a free choice, a rigid cultural orthodoxy instead of democratic tolerance and diversity…

What I am describing now is a plan and a hope for the long term—the march of freedom and democracy which will leave Marxism-Leninism on the ash heap of history as it has left other tyrannies which stifle the freedom and muzzle the self-expression of the people. And that's why we must continue our efforts to strengthen NATO even as we move forward with our zero-option initiative in the negotiations on intermediate-range forces and our proposal for a one-third reduction in strategic ballistic missile warheads.

Our military strength is a prerequisite to peace, but let it be clear we maintain this strength in the hope it will never be used, for the ultimate determinant in the struggle that's now going on in the world will not be bombs and rockets but a test of wills and ideas, a trial of spiritual resolve, the values we hold, the beliefs we cherish, the ideals to which we are dedicated….

Well, the task I've set forth will long outlive our own generation. But together, we too have come through the worst. Let us now begin a major effort to secure the best—a crusade for freedom that will engage the faith and fortitude of the next generation. For the sake of peace and justice, let us move toward a world in which all people are at last free to determine their own destiny.

PRESIDENT RONALD REAGAN'S SPEECH AT GERMANY'S BRANDENBURG GATE, 1987

In the 1950s, Khrushchev predicted: "We will bury you." But in the West today, we see a free world that has achieved a level of prosperity and well-being unprecedented in all human history. In the Communist world, we see failure, technological backwardness, declining standards of health, even want of the most basic kind—too little food. Even today, the Soviet Union still cannot feed itself. After these four decades, then, there stands before the entire world one great and inescapable conclusion: Freedom leads to prosperity. Freedom replaces the ancient hatreds among the nations with comity and peace. Freedom is the victor.

And now the Soviets themselves may, in a limited way, be coming to understand the importance of freedom. We hear much from Moscow about a new policy of reform and openness. Some political prisoners have been released. Certain foreign news broadcasts are no longer being jammed. Some economic enterprises have been permitted to operate with greater freedom from state control.

Are these the beginnings of profound changes in the Soviet state? Or are they token gestures, intended to raise false hopes in the West, or to strengthen the Soviet system without changing it? We welcome change and openness; for we believe that freedom and security go together, that the advance of human liberty can only strengthen the cause of world peace. There is one sign the Soviets can make that would be unmistakable, that would advance dramatically the cause of freedom and peace.

General Secretary Gorbachev, if you seek peace, if you seek prosperity for the Soviet Union and Eastern Europe, if you seek liberalization: Come here to this gate! Mr. Gorbachev, open this gate! Mr. Gorbachev, tear down this wall!...

In Europe, only one nation and those it controls refuse to join the community of freedom. Yet in this age of redoubled economic growth, of information and innovation, the Soviet Union faces a choice: It must make fundamental changes, or it will become obsolete.

Today thus represents a moment of hope. We in the West stand ready to cooperate with the East to promote true openness, to break down barriers that separate people, to create a safe, freer world. And surely there is no better place than Berlin, the meeting place of East and West, to make a start. Free people of Berlin: Today, as in the past, the United States stands for the strict observance and full implementation of all parts of the Four Power Agreement of 1971. Let us use this occasion, the 750th anniversary of this city, to usher in a new era, to seek a still fuller, richer life for the Berlin of the future. Together, let us maintain and develop the ties between the Federal Republic and the Western sectors of Berlin, which is permitted by the 1971 agreement.

And I invite Mr. Gorbachev: Let us work to bring the Eastern and Western parts of the city closer together, so that all the inhabitants of all Berlin can enjoy the benefits that come with life in one of the great cities of the world.

To open Berlin still further to all Europe, East and West, let us expand the vital air access to this city, finding ways of making commercial air service to Berlin more convenient, more comfortable, and more economical. We look to the day when West Berlin can become one of the chief aviation hubs in all central Europe.

With our French and British partners, the United States is prepared to help bring international meetings to Berlin. It would be only fitting for Berlin to serve as the site of United Nations meetings, or world conferences on human rights and arms control or other issues that call for international cooperation.

There is no better way to establish hope for the future than to enlighten young minds, and we would be honored to sponsor summer youth exchanges, cultural events, and other programs for young Berliners from the East. Our French and British friends, I'm certain, will do the same. And it's my hope that an authority can be found in East Berlin to sponsor visits from young people of the Western sectors…

As I looked out a moment ago from the Reichstag, that embodiment of German unity, I noticed words crudely spray-painted upon the wall, perhaps by a young Berliner: "This wall will fall. Beliefs become reality." Yes, across Europe, this wall will fall. For it cannot withstand faith; it cannot withstand truth. The wall cannot withstand freedom.

PROBLEM 29:
CONNECTION TO TODAY

1. What is different about the world today which makes the policy of "mutually inflicted destruction" by nuclear powers outdated?

2. What role did the media play in the collapse of the Soviet Union, and what role do the media play today in foreign policy?

3. Can some policy of "containment" work today in the war against terrorism? Explain.

4. Explain how Ronald Reagan's personal meetings with Gorbachev might have made a difference in how the two men viewed each other's position? How important is it today for an American president to meet face to face with real or potential "enemies"? Explain.

PROBLEM 30:

WAS THE UNITED STATES JUSTIFIED IN GOING TO WAR WITH IRAQ IN 2003?

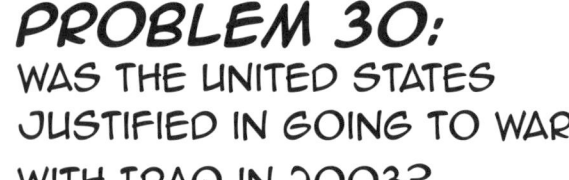

TOP: PRESIDENT GEORGE W. BUSH DECLARING VICTORY REGARDING IRAQ CONFLICT

LEFT: SENATOR TED KENNEDY

BELOW: AMERICAN SOLDIERS ON PATROL IN IRAQ

PROBLEM 30: WAS THE UNITED STATES JUSTIFIED IN GOING TO WAR WITH IRAQ IN 2003?

On March 20, 2003, armed forces of the United States and other cooperating nations began an invasion of the country of Iraq. The alleged purpose of the invasion was to stop the country's ruler, Saddam Hussein, from having weapons of mass destruction (WMD) and to remove him as head of the nation. The invasion was unique for the United States because it represented a major shift in historic American policy. As a policy, the United States had not taken the initiative to invade another country unless that country had first attacked the United States. Iraq had not attacked the United States, but many surrounding President George W. Bush believed that unless the United States acted first, Iraq would be in a position to threaten the stability of the entire Middle East by developing weapons as well as threatening the interests of the United States in the region. This policy, to take the initiative and strike first, was called preemptive war.

While the actual invasion of Iraq went smoothly and quickly for the United States, the subsequent attempt to occupy the country and build a democracy soon began to fall apart as various groups within Iraq used terrorist techniques to kill Americans as well as their own people. It was also subsequently discovered that, in fact, there were no weapons of mass destruction in Iraq, and American public opinion was divided between those who felt that the invasion was still the right action and those who felt the president had been given faulty information or that he had deliberately lied to the nation to justify an American invasion.

Thus, the real reasons to invade Iraq are not clear. In his 2002 State of the Union address, President Bush said Iraq was part of an "axis of evil" that was allied with terrorists and posed "a grave and growing danger" to the United States because of its possession of weapons of mass destruction. A variety of reasons were discussed in the country offering explanations for the war. Such reasons were that Iraq had violated United Nations resolutions; they had human rights violations; there had been ties between Iraq and the September 11, 2001, attack on the United States; we needed to establish a democratic nation in the Middle East; or simply that we had to protect and control our oil interests in the region.

But which, or any, of these reasons was a justification to launch a preemptive attack on Iraq? Did the invasion mean that the United States could, would, or should invade any nation that was involved in activities that were against American interests? Did the United States have a legitimate reason to invade this Middle East nation?

PROBLEM 30:
QUESTIONS FOR TEAM RESEARCH

1. What is the evidence that the United States had real information that Iraq had weapons of mass destruction?

2. If the administration misled the American people about the existence of weapons of mass destruction, what would be its reason for doing so?

3. What was the role of oil in this episode? Would we have invaded Iraq if that nation had not been a major oil producer and supplier?

4. What mistakes, if any, did the United States make in occupying Iraq after the successful military action?

5. What are the criteria you would use to determine whether or not the U.S. was justified in going to war with Iraq?

PROBLEM 30:
STARTING THE SEARCH FOR EVIDENCE

INTERNET: KEY WORDS AND PHRASES

The September 11 attack on the World Trade Center

George W. Bush's decision to invade Iraq

The doctrine of "Pre-emptive" War

American public opinion and the war in Iraq

BOOKS

Daadler, Ivo H., *America Unbound: The Bush Revolution in Foreign Policy*, Washington D.C., Brookings Institution, 2003

Isikoff, Michael, *Hubris: The Inside Story of Spin, Scandal, and the Selling of the Iraq War*, NY, Three Rivers Press, 2007

Lando, Barry, *Web of Deceit: The History of Western Complicity in Iraq, From Churchill to Kennedy to George Bush*, NY, Other Press, 2007

McClellan, Scott, *What Happened: Inside the Bush White House and Washington's Culture of Deception*, NY, Public Affairs, 2008

Woodward, Bob, *Plan of Attack*, Waterville, ME, Wheeler Publishing, 2004

President George W. Bush's Address to the Nation Announcing the Invasion of Iraq, March 19, 2003

My fellow citizens, at this hour American and coalition forces are in the early stages of military operations to disarm Iraq, to free its people and to defend the world from grave danger.

On my orders, coalition forces have begun striking selected targets of military importance to undermine Saddam Hussein's ability to wage war. These are opening stages of what will be a broad and concerted campaign.

More than 35 countries are giving crucial support, from the use of naval and air bases, to help with intelligence and logistics, to the deployment of combat units. Every nation in this coalition has chosen to bear the duty and share the honor of serving in our common defense.

To all of the men and women of the United States armed forces now in the Middle East, the peace of a troubled world and the hopes of an oppressed people now depend on you.

That trust is well placed.

The enemies you confront will come to know your skill and bravery. The people you liberate will witness the honorable and decent spirit of the American military.

In this conflict, America faces an enemy who has no regard for conventions of war or rules of morality. Saddam Hussein has placed Iraqi troops and equipment in civilian areas, attempting to use innocent men, women and children as shields for his own military; a final atrocity against his people.

I want Americans and all the world to know that coalition forces will make every effort to spare innocent civilians from harm. A campaign on the harsh terrain of a nation as large as California could be longer and more difficult than some predict. And helping Iraqis achieve a united, stable and free country will require our sustained commitment.

We come to Iraq with respect for its citizens, for their great civilization and for the religious faiths they practice. We have no ambition in Iraq, except to remove a threat and restore control of that country to its own people.

I know that the families of our military are praying that all those who serve will return safely and soon.

Millions of Americans are praying with you for the safety of your loved ones and for the protection of the innocent.

For your sacrifice, you have the gratitude and respect of the American people and you can know that our forces will be coming home as soon as their work is done.

Our nation enters this conflict reluctantly, yet our purpose is sure. The people of the United States and our friends and allies will not live at the mercy of an outlaw regime that threatens the peace with weapons of mass murder.

We will meet that threat now with our Army, Air Force, Navy, Coast Guard and Marines, so that we do not have to meet it later with armies of firefighters and police and doctors on the streets of our cities.

Now that conflict has come, the only way to limit its duration is to apply decisive force. And I assure you, this will not be a campaign of half measures and we will accept no outcome but victory.

My fellow citizens, the dangers to our country and the world will be overcome. We will pass through this time of peril and carry on the work of peace. We will defend our freedom. We will bring freedom to others. And we will prevail.

May God bless our country and all who defend her.

Senator Edward M. Kennedy of Massachusetts Opposes Military Action in Iraq, September 27, 2002

I have come here today to express my view that America should not go to war against Iraq unless and until other reasonable alternatives are exhausted. But I begin with the strongest possible affirmation that good and decent people on all sides of this debate, who may in the end stand on opposing sides of this decision, are equally committed to our national security....

Just a year ago, the American people and the Congress rallied behind the President and our Armed Forces as we went to war in Afghanistan. Al Qaeda and the Taliban protectors who gave them sanctuary in Afghanistan posed a clear, present and continuing danger. The need to destroy Al Qaeda was urgent and undeniable.

In the months that followed September 11, the Bush Administration marshalled an international coalition. Today, 90 countries are enlisted in the effort, from providing troops to providing law enforcement, intelligence, and other critical support.

But I am concerned that using force against Iraq before other means are tried will sorely test both the integrity and effectiveness of the coalition. Just one year into the campaign against Al Qaeda, the Administration is shifting focus, resources, and energy to Iraq. The change in priority is coming before we have fully eliminated the threat from Al Qaeda, before we know whether Osama Bin Laden is dead or alive, and before we can be assured that the fragile post-Taliban government in Afghanistan will consolidate its authority...

There is clearly a threat from Iraq, and there is clearly a danger, but the Administration has not made a convincing case that we face such an imminent threat to our national security that a unilateral, pre-emptive American strike and an immediate war are necessary...

The President's challenge to the United Nations requires a renewed effort to enforce the will of the international community to disarm Saddam. Resorting to war is not America's only or best course at this juncture. There are realistic alternatives between doing nothing and declaring unilateral or immediate war. War should be a last resort, not the first response. Let us follow that course, and the world will be with us—even if, in the end, we have to move to the ultimate sanction of armed conflict...

We know all this—and we also know that it is an open secret in Washington that the nation's uniformed military leadership is skeptical about the wisdom of war with Iraq. They share the concern that it may adversely affect the ongoing war against Al Qaeda and the continuing effort in Afghanistan by draining resources and armed forces already stretched so thin that many Reservists have been called for a second year of duty, and record numbers of service members have been kept on active duty beyond their obligated service...

A largely unilateral American war that is widely perceived in the Muslim world as untimely or unjust could worsen not lessen the threat of terrorism. War with Iraq before a genuine attempt at inspection and disarmament—or without genuine international support—could swell the ranks of Al Qaeda sympathizers and trigger an escalation in terrorist acts. As General Clark told the Senate Armed Services Committee, it would "super-charge recruiting for Al Qaeda."

General Hoar advised the Committee on September 23 that America's first and primary effort should be to defeat Al Qaeda. In a September 10th article, General Clark wrote: "Unilateral U.S. action today would disrupt the war against Al Qaeda." We ignore such wisdom and advice from many of the best of our military at our own peril.

We have known for many years that Saddam Hussein is seeking and developing weapons of mass destruction. Our intelligence community is also deeply concerned about the acquisition of such weapons by Iran, North Korea, Libya, Syria and other nations. But information from the intelligence community over the past six months does not point to Iraq as an imminent threat to the United States or a major proliferator of weapons of mass destruction…

I do not accept the idea that trying other alternatives is either futile or perilous—that the risks of waiting are greater than the risks of war. Indeed, in launching a war against Iraq now, the United States may precipitate the very threat that we are intent on preventing—weapons of mass destruction in the hands of terrorists. If Saddam's regime and his very survival are threatened, then his view of his interests may be profoundly altered: He may decide he has nothing to lose by using weapons of mass destruction himself or by sharing them with terrorists.

Some who advocate military action against Iraq, however, assert that air strikes will do the job quickly and decisively, and that the operation will be complete in 72 hours. But there is again no persuasive evidence that air strikes alone over the course of several days will incapacitate Saddam and destroy his weapons of mass destruction. Experts have informed us that we do not have sufficient intelligence about military targets in Iraq. Saddam may well hide his most lethal weapons in mosques, schools and hospitals. If our forces attempt to strike such targets, untold numbers of Iraqi civilians could be killed…

This escalation, spiraling out of control, could draw the Arab world into a regional war in which our Arab allies side with Iraq, against the United States and against Israel.

And that would represent a fundamental threat to Israel, to the region, to the world economy and international order....

Before we go to war, we should give the international community the chance to meet the President's challenge—to renew its resolve to disarm Saddam Hussein completely and effectively. This makes the resumption of inspections more imperative and perhaps more likely than at any time since they ended in 1998.

PROBLEM 30:
CONNECTION TO TODAY

1. Should the United States use the policy of "preemptive war"? Explain.

2. If the President of the United States cannot trust the accuracy of his intelligence reports, what can he do to ensure a correct decision is made?

3. If and when the United States ever becomes independent of foreign oil, how will this change America's foreign policy?

4. Does the United States have a right and a legitimate role to play in determining which nations should and should not have weapons of mass destruction?

5. Where else does the United States attempt to engage in "nation building"? Is that a legitimate role for America?

PROBLEM 31:
DID THE ELECTION OF BARACK OBAMA TO THE PRESIDENCY OF THE UNITED STATES SIGNAL THE END OF DISCRIMINATION IN AMERICA?

LEFT: SIGN DISPLAYED DURING THE OBAMA CAMPAIGN

BELOW: BARACK OBAMA CAMPAIGNING FOR PRESIDENT

PROBLEM 31:
DID THE ELECTION OF BARACK OBAMA TO THE PRESIDENCY OF THE UNITED STATES SIGNAL THE END OF DISCRIMINATION IN AMERICA?

*I*n November 2008 Barack Obama was elected president of the United States. The election was hailed as a new milestone for the nation because he was the first African-American elected to that office. In fact, however, while the new president identified himself as an African-American, he was of mixed racial origin, his father being a black man from Africa and his mother a white woman from the United States. To many observers the election signaled the beginning of a new era, one of post-racism, in which issues of race, gender, age, and religion would now become secondary to the character and policies of individuals running for the nation's highest political office.

The election of 2008 was unique in that there were candidates who possessed traits not seen in previous contests. Obama was African-American, Hillary Clinton a female, Mitt Romney a Mormon, and Rudy Giuliano an Italian-American who was thrice married. Candidates with these traits had never been elected to the presidency in the entire history of the United States.

It is true that John F. Kennedy had been elected as the first Roman Catholic president, but a Gallup poll in 2008 found that only one in five Americans was "completely comfortable" with the special traits of these candidates, and about a third of those polled had reservations about them. A Gallup poll taken 50 years earlier had revealed that Americans would not vote for a well qualified individual if the candidate were Catholic, Jewish, female, black, or atheist. The 2008 Gallup poll showed change but not the elimination of prejudice. In that poll one in ten persons reported they would not vote for a woman or Hispanic, and one in 20 said they would not vote for a black, Jew, or Catholic. More than 40 percent said they would not vote for a gay candidate, one who was in his seventies, or an atheist. So while the nation's prejudices had diminished in some areas and shifted in others, prejudice still existed.

Yet Barack Obama was able to overcome these attitudes and be elected. How did this happen? Did it now mean that we had entered a post-racial era? Did his election mean that we would now see a continuing decline in discrimination?

The new president's slowness in attacking both the problems he inherited and the new ones he had identified quickly brought forth widespread and personal criticism and attacks from those who opposed him. Their stated reasons were that they strongly opposed the direction in which he was leading the nation; others suspected the real reason for such strong and vicious opposition was because the opponents simply could not accept the fact that an African-American had become president. Former president Jimmy Carter was one of the few who publicly declared that the kind of opposition being mounted against Obama was based on racism. The Secret Service revealed that threats against the life of the president had increased by 400 percent over the last holder of the office.

How can we sort through these complicated facts? What evidence can we find that the opposition to Obama was based on his agenda and not his race? What evidence can we find that his election did signal, if not the end, the beginning of an end to discrimination of all kinds in America?

PROBLEM 31:
QUESTIONS FOR TEAM RESEARCH

1. What role does the fact that Barack Obama was of mixed race have on his election? Would it have made any difference if both his mother and father had been black? Explain.

2. Does an analysis of the votes in the presidential election of 2008 reveal information regarding the existence or non-existence of prejudice among the voters?

3. Was Obama fortunate that his two major opponents, Hillary Clinton and John McCain, were also in categories that worried voters? Explain.

4. Is there a way to discover if the opposition to Obama after his election was based on race or policies? What would that analysis be?

PROBLEM 31:
STARTING THE SEARCH FOR EVIDENCE

INTERNET: KEY WORDS AND PHRASES

The election of 2008

American opinion of a black candidate for president from 1950 to 2008

Barack Obama's campaign speech on race in America

Racism and opposition to President Obama and his policies

BOOKS

Balz, Daniel; Johnson, Haynes, *The Battle for America, 2008, The Extraordinary Election of 2008*, NY, Viking, 2009

Entman, Robert M., *The Black Image in the White Mind: Media and Race in America*, Chicago, University of Chicago Press, 2000

Sears, David O., ed, *Racialized Politics: The Debate About Racism in America*, Chicago, University of Chiago Press, 2000

Steele, Shelby, *A Bound Man: Why We Are Excited about Barack Obama and Why He Can't Win*, NY, Free Press, 2008

Thomas, Evan, *A Long Time Coming: The Inspiring, Combative 2008 Campaign and the Historic Election of Barack Obama*, NY, Public Affairs, 2009

SENATOR BARACK OBAMA ADDRESSES THE ISSUE OF RACE IN THE 2008 PRESIDENTIAL CAMPAIGN

Throughout the first year of this campaign, against all predictions to the contrary, we saw how hungry the American people were for this message of unity. Despite the temptation to view my candidacy through a purely racial lens, we won commanding victories in states with some of the whitest populations in the country. In South Carolina, where the Confederate Flag still flies, we built a powerful coalition of African Americans and white Americans.

This is not to say that race has not been an issue in the campaign. At various stages in the campaign, some commentators have deemed me either "too black" or "not black enough." We saw racial tensions bubble to the surface during the week before the South Carolina primary. The press has scoured every exit poll for the latest evidence of racial polarization, not just in terms of white and black, but black and brown as well....

Segregated schools were, and are, inferior schools; we still haven't fixed them, fifty years after Brown v. Board of Education, and the inferior education they provided, then and now, helps explain the pervasive achievement gap between today's black and white students.

Legalized discrimination—where blacks were prevented, often through violence, from owning property, or loans were not granted to African-American business owners, or black homeowners could not access FHA mortgages, or blacks were excluded from unions, or the police force, or fire departments—meant that black families could not amass any meaningful wealth to bequeath to future generations. That history helps explain the wealth and income gap between black and white, and the concentrated pockets of poverty that persists in so many of today's urban and rural communities.

A lack of economic opportunity among black men, and the shame and frustration that came from not being able to provide for one's family, contributed to the erosion of black families – a problem that welfare policies for many years may have worsened. And the lack of basic services in so many urban black neighborhoods—parks for kids to play in, police walking the beat, regular garbage pick-up and building code enforcement—all helped create a cycle of violence, blight and neglect that continue to haunt us....

And occasionally it finds voice in the church on Sunday morning, in the pulpit and in the pews. The fact that so many people are surprised to hear that anger in some of Reverend Wright's sermons simply reminds us of the old truism that the most segregated hour in American life occurs on Sunday morning. That anger is not always productive; indeed, all too often it distracts attention from solving real problems; it keeps us from squarely facing our own complicity in our condition, and prevents the African-American community from forging the alliances it needs to bring about real change. But the anger is real; it is powerful; and to simply wish it away, to condemn it without understanding its roots, only serves to widen the chasm of misunderstanding that exists between the races.

In fact, a similar anger exists within segments of the white community. Most working- and middle-class white Americans don't feel that they have been particularly privileged by their race. Their experience is the immigrant experience—as far as they're concerned, no one's handed them anything, they've built it from scratch. They've worked hard all their lives, many times only to see their jobs shipped overseas or their pension dumped after a lifetime of labor. They are anxious about their futures, and feel their dreams slipping away; in an era of stagnant wages and global competition, opportunity comes to be seen as a zero sum game, in which your dreams come at my expense. So when they are told to bus their children to a school across town; when they hear that an African American is getting an advantage in landing a good job or a spot in a good college because of an injustice that they themselves never committed; when they're told that their fears about crime in urban neighborhoods are somehow prejudiced, resentment builds over time. Like the anger within the black community, these resentments aren't always expressed in polite company. But they have helped shape the political landscape for at least a generation. Anger over welfare and affirmative action helped forge the Reagan Coalition. Politicians routinely exploited fears of crime for their own electoral ends. Talk show hosts and conservative commentators built entire careers unmasking bogus claims of racism while dismissing legitimate discussions of racial injustice and inequality as mere political correctness or reverse racism.

Just as black anger often proved counterproductive, so have these white resentments distracted attention from the real culprits of the middle class squeeze—a corporate culture rife with inside dealing, questionable accounting practices, and short-term greed; a Washington dominated by lobbyists and special interests; economic policies that favor the few over the many. And yet, to wish away the resentments of white Americans, to label them as misguided or even racist, without recognizing they are grounded in legitimate concerns—this too widens the racial divide, and blocks the path to understanding.

This is where we are right now. It's a racial stalemate we've been stuck in for years. Contrary to the claims of some of my critics, black and white, I have never been so naïve as to believe that we can get beyond our racial divisions in a single election cycle, or with a single candidacy—particularly a candidacy as imperfect as my own.

But I have asserted a firm conviction—a conviction rooted in my faith in God and my faith in the American people—that working together we can move beyond some of our old racial wounds, and that in fact we have no choice if we are to continue on the path of a more perfect union. For the African-American community, that path means embracing the burdens of our past without becoming victims of our past. It means continuing to insist on a full measure of justice in every aspect of American life. But it also means binding our particular grievances—for better health care, and better schools, and better jobs—to the larger aspirations of all Americans—the white woman struggling to break the glass ceiling, the white man who has been laid off, the immigrant trying to feed his family. And it means taking full responsibility for own lives—by demanding more from our fathers, and spending more time with our children, and reading to them, and teaching them that while they may face challenges and discrimination in their own lives, they must never succumb to despair or cynicism; they must always believe that they can write their own destiny....

In the white community, the path to a more perfect union means acknowledging that what ails the African-American community does not just exist in the minds of black people; that the legacy of discrimination—and current incidents of discrimination, while less overt than in the past—are real and must be addressed. Not just with words, but with deeds—by investing in our schools and our communities; by enforcing our civil rights laws and ensuring fairness in our criminal justice system; by providing this generation with ladders of opportunity that were unavailable for previous generations. It requires all Americans to realize that your dreams do not have to come at the expense of my dreams; that investing in the health, welfare, and education of black and brown and white children will ultimately help all of America prosper.

In the end, then, what is called for is nothing more, and nothing less, than what all the world's great religions demand—that we do unto others as we would have them do unto us. Let us be our brother's keeper, Scripture tells us. Let us be our sister's keeper. Let us find that common stake we all have in one another, and let our politics reflect that spirit as well....

There is a young, twenty-three year old white woman named Ashley Baia who organized for our campaign in Florence, South Carolina. She had been working to organize a mostly African-American community since the beginning of this campaign, and one day she was at a roundtable discussion where everyone went around telling their story and why they were there.

And Ashley said that when she was nine years old, her mother got cancer. And because she had to miss days of work, she was let go and lost her health care. They had to file for bankruptcy, and that's when Ashley decided that she had to do something to help her mom.

She knew that food was one of their most expensive costs, and so Ashley convinced her mother that what she really liked and really wanted to eat more than anything else was mustard and relish sandwiches. Because that was the cheapest way to eat.

She did this for a year until her mom got better, and she told everyone at the round-table that the reason she joined our campaign was so that she could help the millions of other children in the country who want and need to help their parents, too.

Now Ashley might have made a different choice. Perhaps somebody told her along the way that the source of her mother's problems were blacks who were on welfare and too lazy to work, or Hispanics who were coming into the country illegally. But she didn't. She sought out allies in her fight against injustice.

Anyway, Ashley finishes her story and then goes around the room and asks everyone else why they're supporting the campaign. They all have different stories and reasons. Many bring up a specific issue. And finally they come to this elderly black man who's been sitting there quietly the entire time. And Ashley asks him why he's there. And he does not bring up a specific issue. He does not say health care or the economy. He does not say education or the war. He does not say that he was there because of Barack Obama. He simply says to everyone in the room, "I am here because of Ashley."

"I'm here because of Ashley." By itself, that single moment of recognition between that young white girl and that old black man is not enough. It is not enough to give health care to the sick, or jobs to the jobless, or education to our children.

But it is where we start. It is where our union grows stronger. And as so many generations have come to realize over the course of the two-hundred and twenty one years since a band of patriots signed that document in Philadelphia, that is where the perfection begins.

PROBLEM 31:
CONNECTION TO TODAY

1. Are Americans willing to vote for a minority, racial, female, or older candidate for one office but not another? Explain.

2. By today's standards and events, has America entered a "post-racial" area? Give some examples of the position you take.

3. Which of the following candidates would today have the most likely chance of being elected president of the United States:

    a. A well-qualified woman

    b. A full-blooded qualified black candidate

    c. A qualified Mormon candidate

    d. A qualified openly gay man or woman candidate?

    Explain your choice.

4. Explain how you believe people think a person's race, gender, religion, or sexual orientation would affect their ability to function as a successful president of the United States.

ABOUT THE AUTHOR

Michael J. Bakalis is president and CEO of American Quality Schools, a not-for-profit educational management organization. He was formerly Illinois State Superintendent of Education and Deputy Undersecretary in the United States Department of Education. He has taught history at every educational level and has served on the faculty of Northern Illinois University, Loyola University of Chicago, and Northwestern University. He received his Ph.D in American history from Northwestern University.